TG
30/11/24

TG Trouper lives with his wife in Essex, England. He has one son who currently resides in America.

TG worked in live music production for many years, dealing with the technical requirements of some of the biggest artists in the world. Only after retiring to look after ailing parents did he find the time to take up writing, something he regrets not taking up sooner. He is also a singer and guitarist in a couple of bands.

With thanks to my wife, my good friend Gary, Louise and Lucy.

T G Trouper

Astrid-Book 1: War Changes People

Austin Macauley Publishers™
London • Cambridge • New York • Sharjah

A CIP catalogue record for this title is available from the British Library.

ISBN 9781398470729 (Paperback)
ISBN 9781398470736 (ePub e-book)

www.austinmacauley.com

First Published 2023
Austin Macauley Publishers Ltd®
1 Canada Square
Canary Wharf
London
E14 5AA

I thank Austin Macauley for having faith in my work.

Prologue

My name is Astrid Peterman, and I am a citizen of Arralan.

When I was a kid, I had a very clear idea of what I wanted to do when I grew up. I didn't have a plan as such, but just sort of knew all the steps I'd take and where I'd end up. But then one day, there was a ripple in the ether, so yeah, my life didn't turn out how I expected.

This is my story.

The Audition

"Where were you last night?" Karina snapped.

"What?" said Damien, surprised at the sharpness of the question.

"I said, where were you? Were you with her again, that girl?" Karina sneered as she spoke.

"I don't know what you're talking about; what girl?"

"Don't lie to me, Damien!" she shouted. "You said you'd never see her again, but you just can't keep away, can you?"

Damien was stunned by Karina's anger and speechless for a few moments. "I don't know what to say."

"Well, you'd better think of something, and it better not be one of your lame excuses this time."

"I don't bloody well know what to say, because I'm not bloody well acting," Damien shouted, then turned to face the couple sitting three rows back in the auditorium. "How the bloody hell am I supposed to know what to say if there isn't a script. Why haven't you given me a script?"

Bernie Krovitz, the theatre artistic director, waved up at the lighting crew; the stage lights dimmed, and the house lights came up. "Thomas, Thomas, Thomas, this is an audition for an improvisational play. You were told that your character, Damien, is newly married to Karina and she suspects you of seeing an old girlfriend. The two of you are supposed to improvise an argument. It's pivotal to the play. You did read the brief, didn't you?"

Thomas shuffled uncomfortably for a couple of seconds, making it obvious that he hadn't read the brief. He pouted then poked himself on the chest a couple of times. "I studied at the central school of drama for three years." He poked himself in the chest again. "I learned how to read and memorise a script, I learned how to memorise the cues, I learned how to remember the stage positions." He puffed out his chest. "I don't improvise," he said pretentiously.

Astrid Peterman stayed put, waiting for the inevitable. Thomas pointed at her. "I don't know where you got her from, sixth form amateur dramatics maybe?

I mean, can she even understand a script? Is that why you've got her to 'improvise'?" he said disdainfully.

"Thomas, there is no need to be rude!" snapped Bernie, irritated at Thomas's discourteous comments.

Thomas put his hands on his hips. "I'll have you know that I find this totally unacceptable."

"Get off the stage, Thomas," said Bernie.

Thomas pouted. "Don't you tell me to get off the stage like that." Someone in the lighting booth stifled a laugh. Thomas glowered up at them.

"Get off the stage, Thomas," said Bernie, firmly.

Thomas huffed again. "You do know who my uncle is, don't you? He's going to hear about this and then we'll see who's getting off the stage."

"Get…off…the…stage, Thomas."

Thomas fidgeted for a couple of seconds, making fists with his hands. Someone else in the lighting booth stifled a laugh. His face turned red and his bottom lip started to quiver; he turned and stomped off stage, slamming doors behind him. They could hear him slamming doors all the way down the corridor as he stormed out of the building.

Bernie turned to the woman sitting beside him. "Sorry about that, old girl. Twice now his agent had told me that Thomas is a gifted improviser."

"Well, his agent is clearly being economical with the truth." She nodded towards Astrid, who was still on stage. "But she's good."

"Yes, she is, natural talent; not seen anything like it for years," said Bernie, swelling with pride. "I spotted her a couple of years back and I wanted you to see her, I think she's going to be big."

"I think you're right."

Bernie looked up at Astrid. "That's all for today, love, I'll come and see you in your dressing room shortly. I just have a couple of things I want to discuss with my friend here."

Bernie had indeed found Astrid in a sixth form play. It was an Avant Garde improvised play and he had been astonished at just how quick she had been to respond to the other players, most of whom struggled to keep up with her. He made inquiries and went to see her in another couple of plays, one scripted and the other improvised, just to make sure that her previous performance hadn't been a one-off. He contacted her and gave her a job in the theatre sorting out his paperwork, which was a real job, because his paperwork was in dire need of organisation, but more importantly, to give her acting opportunities.

For the past couple of years, he had been not so much a father figure, more of a mentor to Astrid; he had given her small parts in plays and had watched her grow. At first these were just walk-on parts, but it soon became clear that she was out-acting all the other cast members and needed to move into more challenging roles. During one scripted play, an actor had made a mistake which would have made her dialogue nonsensical. She had immediately disregarded her lines and improvised so fluently that the audience never noticed.

Bernie knocked on Astrid's door, waited for her to answer, then strode into the room, beaming from ear to ear, then sat down beside her. "I'm not going to give you the part of Karina."

"What!" Astrid sighed, disappointed. "Oh Bernie, is it because of Thomas's uncle?"

"No, most certainly not. Thomas's uncle is an alcoholic nobody with delusions of grandeur. He had one hit play donkey's years ago and has drunk away all the royalties. Everyone who know him, hates him, so no-one takes any notice of anything he says."

He sat back in the chair and folded his arms. "Now, do you think I'd be smiling if it was bad news, eh?" Astrid noticed the twinkle in his eye. "The woman who was sitting next to me is an old friend, well actually an old girlfriend from before I, well, you know. Her name is Davida Yeoh; she is an established television producer and she's now moving into film. I brought her here to see you and as a result, she wants to put you in a drama."

Astrid was stunned but composed herself quickly. "So, this was never an audition for the part of Karina. You tricked me."

Bernie stood up, put the back of his hand to his forehead and wandered around the room in an overly dramatic way. "Oh Astrid, I am wounded, how could you think that I would deceive you in such away. I of all people, why don't you plunge a dagger into my heart?" He sat back down in the chair. "Yes, you're right, darling, it was a ruse. I thought it best that you didn't know."

"I can't leave the theatre."

"Yes, you can, and you must, this is a big deal for you, chances like this don't come along very often."

"When I said I couldn't leave 'the theatre', I meant I can't leave you. You've done so much for me."

He thought for a moment while stroking his goatee beard. "Yes, come to think of it, it is all down to me, isn't it?"

Astrid smiled, because she knew how he liked to mock some of the other actors who always took themselves far too seriously. She also was well aware that he used frivolous asides like this to cover his emotions; she found it endearing.

"I felt a bit sorry for Thomas, he was quite upset," she said, genuinely concerned about him, despite his rudeness to her.

"Oh he'll get over it, he'll go home and have a little cry on his boyfriend's shoulder. He'll call me tomorrow with a grovelling apology, I guarantee it."

"Are you going to give him a part in the play?"

"Oh yes, I'll eventually give him a part… a small part… not a speaking part—obviously… he'll be at the back… of a crowd," Bernie said with a mischievous smile.

"Oh, don't be mean to him." Astrid slapped Bernie lightly with the back of her hand.

Bernie frowned a little. "Well, he has to learn. He needs to understand, and quickly, that the whole 'do you know who dot, dot, dot is' routine will get him fired. And for a nineteen-year-old, he really is a bit too pompous. Incidentally, my friend did not believe me when I said you are only eighteen, she thought you were in your late twenties."

"That's because, darling…" Astrid frowned, then put her hand on her chest, looked up into the distance and with a dramatic wave of her other hand, said in a haughty voice "…I was acting, darling, acting," mocking the pomposity of some of the old theatre lags that propped up the bar every evening. Then she felt a little embarrassed for being disrespectful.

Bernie roared with laughter. "See what I mean. That's why you have to take the part, use your talent. I want to see you raise the standard of film and television acting, goodness knows, the standards need raising and you are the one to do it." He turned serious. "You don't know who Davida is do you, she's not some also-ran doing frivolous daytime stuff, she does serious work, and produces TV drama under the name Mitchel Noah."

Astrid's jaw dropped, "Mitchel Noah!" she gasped.

"The very same."

"Wow, I can't believe it, Mitchel Noah. And he—I mean she, wants to put me in one of her films. Thank you so much Bernie." She put her arms around him and hugged him.

"Davida was very good to me, we were still together when I came out, and she was so understanding. A wonderful woman, the kindest, sweetest, person I know." Astrid noticed Bernie's eyes going a bit watery. He smiled and turned playful again. "Except for you, that is." She knew that this was to stop himself from getting emotional.

"You're not with anyone at the moment are you. Having a partner is so important." Bernie put his finger on his forehead in an exaggerated gesture of concentration. "Now let me think, do I know any girls that I can fix you up with."

"Thanks, but no thanks, and anyway, it's boys for me please Bernie."

"Nonsense, you don't know what it's like. After all, girls know what girls like, just as boys know what boys like."

"Erm, I think I know what boys like," she said, glancing down at her chest.

"Oh yes that's what all boys want. I know, I was just the same back then. Ooh I can still remember the thrill of being with a girl for the first time, undoing the buttons of her blouse, then opening it and there they were in all their magnificence. Boobs don't interest me nowadays, of course, but I have fond memories, or is it fondled memories." He stopped short. "How did we get from your chance of a lifetime, to my former obsession with boobs?"

"I don't know, Bernie," she laughed, "I just don't know with you."

The Drama of War

Astrid and Bernie waited in the reception of Davida's production company while Davida finished what sounded like a very important phone call. Bernie seemed a little nervous and fiddled with a piece of paper, whereas Astrid was excited but tried hard to not let it show.

On the walls were large screenshots of some of Davida's productions, below each one was a small plaque. Astrid got up and read each one.

Mitchel Noah, best director for 'The Times of Our Lives'.

Mitchel Noah, best drama documentary for 'This Land of Ours'.

Mitchel Noah, best factual documentary for 'The Lost Children'.

Mitchel Noah, Golden Lens award for best cinematic photography for 'The Foreign Land'.

"I've seen all of these," she said to the receptionist, who smiled knowingly.

"There are plenty more, but Davida doesn't like to have them all on show, she finds it a bit too boastful when you see walls plastered with awards and accolades," said the receptionist.

Next was a framed sheet of plain paper, signed by some of the biggest names in film and television. Astrid pointed to some of them. "Are all these people who have worked with Davida?"

"Oh yes, all of them. That was a birthday present."

Astrid turned to Bernie. "Why doesn't Davida work under her own name, why use a man's name?"

"Oh Astrid, you are so wonderfully young. You've grown up with total equality, but it wasn't always like that, even here in Arralan. When she started it was damn near impossible for a woman to get any job in television other than a secretary. She could have stuck to her own name, but then her programs would never have been made and she had so many new ideas and so much energy, she just had to get it all out. So she made programs under a man's name and it stuck. Everyone in the business knows who she is, but the public doesn't know, which means that she doesn't get anyone coming up and bothering her when she's out and about."

Just then, Davida opened the door and beckoned them in. She was slightly taller than average, with long grey hair that flowed down onto her shoulders. The set of her eyebrows gave her a serious look, but her hazel eyes had a warmth to them. Her complexion was clear, and her skin was slightly dark, and an aspect that Astrid did not expect to see was a small stud in her nose; it sparkled and looked expensive. On any other woman her age, this would have looked tacky, but it suited her. The dress was stylish and immaculate with a slender necklace and brooch that set it off perfectly. Her shoes were shiny, black and had just enough of a heel to give her calves and elegant shape. She was a beautiful woman.

Davida shook Astrid's hand and hugged Bernie for maybe a little bit longer than necessary. Astrid noticed but didn't pay too much attention, after all, they were old friends. Davida gestured for them to sit then got straight down to business, put on some reading glasses and addressed Astrid directly.

"The production I am making has the working title of 'The Drama of War', though that will probably change. Your character is Tatiana Reece and is a civilian reporter who gets sent to a war zone and gets caught up in the fighting. This is a new departure for me as there is no script, just scene outlines and all the acting and dialogue is to be improvised within those guidelines. There'll be no rehearsals, just plot points which you will be given immediately before filming. So for this to work, the improv' has to be top quality. Now, Astrid, I saw you the other day at the theatre and I must say, I was very impressed."

"Thank you," said Astrid and blushed slightly at the praise from such a high-powered individual.

"Now I'd like to see a bit more. Imagine yourself entering a bombed-out village and doing a report to your cameraman. Improvise that for me now, please."

Astrid immediately jumped out of her chair and scuttled, crouching, to the other side of the room and bopped down with her back to the wall. She held her fist in front of her as if she was holding a microphone. She eased herself up a faction, glanced over her shoulder and quickly ducked down, putting her other hand on her head.

"I'm here in what remains of Halina," she said in a firm but slightly breathless voice. "The government forces are pushing the rebels out, but they are not leaving..." she flinched and crouched down a little lower. "... that was a close one. They are not leaving without a sending a message, you can probably hear the machine guns, they are not very far away."

She looked to her right as if someone had just sat beside her. She pretended to be talking to someone, nodding her head a few times. "Uh-huh, yeah, okay." She glanced back nervously over her shoulder again. "I've just been told that the rebels are leaving, and this small arms fire is their way of saying that it's not over and that they'll be back in force sometime. This is Tatiana Reece reporting from Halina for ATV News." She pretended to hand back a microphone, then looked worried. "This is dangerous, we've got to get out of here."

Davida started to clap. "Well done, that was very good."

Astrid sat back on the chair next to Bernie, he reached over, put his hand on her knee, squeezed it gently and beamed like proud father.

"You don't have an agent or manager do you," said Davida.

"No I don't."

"Well then, in order to comply with the Arralan Actors' Guild rules, you have to have one or the other or both, so I will put Bernie down as your nominal agent. Your part in the shoot is scheduled to take about three weeks, but realistically these things always over-run, so I'd like to book you for six weeks, is that okay?"

"I will check with my client to see if she is available," said Bernie, mocking all the bombastic agents he had dealt with over the years. Davida looked over the top of her glasses at Bernie, sighed, then looked at Astrid.

"Yes, I am available," said Astrid smirking at Bernie's flippancy.

"Okay, good." Davida wrote a figure on a piece of paper and handed it to Astrid. "That's your fee." Astrid's eyes opened wide as she saw the amount. Bernie looked over and read it.

"Ooh, do I get twenty percent of that?"

"No Bernie, you don't, you are just down as her agent for paperwork purposes." He huffed, pouted, and turned his face away, again mocking the theatrical agents who always seemed to be far more over-dramatic than their clients.

"Filming starts up in Brandon in two weeks' time. I've done a deal with the local authority. There's an abandoned village just outside the town which is due for redevelopment. We'll make it look like a war zone, and after we've finished, we'll pay half of the demolition costs. I'll send you all the details of accommodation etc. Any questions?"

Astrid frowned slightly. "Brandon, that's near the border, the Correlan army is quite near there, and I read that there's a lot of tension."

"Oh no need to worry about that," said Davida with a disarming smile. "I've got a friend in the department of defence; an agreement has been made with the Correlans. They're pulling back their troops. It's being kept out of the papers for the time being though; because, you know—politics. Besides, they're on the other bank of the river; it's got to be three kilometres wide at that point, and Brandon is fifteen kilometres inland, well out of range of their machine guns. And there's a temporary Arralan army base there—lots of young soldiers all too willing to protect a damsel if she may be in distress."

The Café

Astrid and Bernie stopped for a coffee and something to eat on the way back from Davida's office. It was mid-afternoon, and the café was all but deserted. Both of them were buzzing with excitement, they had always been close, but now felt even closer.

Astrid was hungry and ate her pastry quickly, washing it down with a glass of orange juice. She wiped her hands with a paper napkin and brushed the crumbs off the table. "I've been thinking about what you said the other day, and it's a load of old rot," she said, playfully.

A confused Bernie looked at her. "What's a load of old rot?"

"You referred to your 'former' obsession with boobs. There's nothing 'former' about it, you're still are obsessed with boobs."

"No I'm not, I'm a gay man, and gay men aren't interested in boobs," he said unconvincingly.

"I've watched you; when you see a woman, it's like this." She put a finger up to each eye, then moved them down onto Bernie's chest.

"Oh, do I do that?"

"Yep, every time."

Bernie suddenly looked anxious. "I don't look at your boobs, honestly I don't."

"I know you don't, it's only women of a certain age or older."

"Is it?"

"Oh yes, and when there's more than one woman present, it's like a radar, beep, beep, beep, beep, multiple targets detected, locking on now."

"Oh dear, I didn't realise it was so bad. I'll have to change my ways, won't I?"

"You can't change who you really are Bernie, you know that."

Bernie sighed. "Yes, you're quite right, you can only kid yourself for so long." He suddenly became serious and started to fiddle with his napkin, avoiding eye contact with her. "Nick was the one I left Davida for."

"But you still love her, don't you."

Bernie looked sad and sighed again. "Is that really obvious as well?"

"Let's just say that you might as well wear a T shirt with 'I love Davida Yeoh' printed on it."

"I hurt her so much when I met Nick. I never meant to, she was so understanding, so kind. There were a lot of tears, and I've felt terrible about that ever since." He put the napkin to one side and absentmindedly arranged the sachets of mustard, tartare sauce, vinegar, tomato ketchup, salt and pepper into alphabetical order.

Astrid sensed that he wanted to talk more. She reached over and held his hand. "You can talk to me I'm a good listener and you know I won't tell anyone else."

Bernie sighed again and shook his head slightly. "Nick and I have been together for over twenty years, in the beginning he was so exiting, it felt so good to be with him, but in the last few years we've argued an awful lot. He's always wanted to get married, but I've always thought, what's the point? Since we met, society has changed and now we have all the same rights as a married couple. I think that deep down he wants to own me so he can show me off to his business friends. *'Look what I've got, Bernie Krovitz, he's the artistic director at the metropolitan theatre, don't you know. What have you got?'*. I'll be just another possession, like that vintage sports car that he never drives or the eighty-year-old bottle of wine that he's never going to open. Maybe that's why we row so much."

He looked out of the window lost in thought. "The past couple of months have been horrible. Nick says that I'm not a 'real' gay man." He paused and breathed deeply for a few seconds. "Nick can be very cruel sometimes."

"I'm so sorry Bernie, I had no idea, you're always so perky, so, well, you."

"I've always thought that you don't bring your home problems to work, it's not fair on everyone else. Anyway, I've stayed in contact with Davida off and on over the years, and lately after Nick and I have had a tiff, I've called her." He paused and smiled weakly. "I've called her at stupid times of the night, and she's always made time for me, always listened to me, and after all that I put her through."

"Only a very good friend would do that."

"Yes, she is a very good friend." He stopped, and she could see him searching for the right words. "About three weeks ago Nick and I had a humongous row, a real humdinger. I think the whole street heard it. He said some really hurtful things, he was…" Bernie looked away, unwilling to let her see his distress. "…he was nasty, horrible. He said he was going away for a week and for me to have a good long think about our relationship. He said that when he came back, he wanted a one hundred percent commitment from me. He packed a bag and stormed out; I called Davida, she said she had just opened a bottle of red wine so why not come over." He stopped and smiled, his face lighting up at the thought of her. "You know, within five minutes of getting there she had me laughing, I have no idea what she said though. Long story short, it was late, one bottle of wine became two bottles of wine and I was too drunk to drive. I wasn't hammered, just a bit too far over the limit. I said I'd have to get a taxi, she said why not sleep on the couch. To which I said yes straight away."

"Because you wanted to be in her presence for a few more hours."

"Yes, you're right. I just wanted to know that she was in the next room, I wanted to make her coffee and toast for breakfast, tidy her house, do the washing up for her. I wanted to just see her in the morning." He smiled. "She said that she was going for a shower; and I remembered that she always liked to shower before bed. I was sitting on the couch, just about to get in when she walked back in wearing a bath robe. She didn't say anything, but just let it drop off her. She stood there in front of me, naked, and oh my God, she is perfect. And erm, I, erm, well I, erm."

He smirked and looked at Astrid with a twinkle in his eye. "Oh, let's just say I didn't sleep on the couch."

Astrid's eyes opened wide, and her jaw dropped a fraction. "Did you have sex with her?"

"Yes, it was…" Bernie blushed and smiled awkwardly "…good." He regained his composure and started to fiddle with the condiments again, rearranging them unnecessarily. "So, I guess Nick is right, I'm not a 'real' gay man after all. And bang goes my one hundred percent commitment."

Astrid smirked, and he realised why. "Yes, that was a poor choice of words wasn't it."

He finished moving the salt and pepper and went back to folding and unfolding the napkin. "He came back after a week and was all sweetness and light, saying that he never meant the things he said, he said he'd do anything I wanted. But you can't ever un-hear things, can you? particularly when they hurt so much."

"It sounds to me that he was the one who had been doing the thinking."

"I couldn't see him the same way again, I couldn't 'be' with him, if you know what I mean. Since he's been back I've made a lot of excuses to avoid intimacy; pressure of work, headaches, you know the sort of thing, I've had a lot of headaches—apparently. But Nick will find out, he'll either work it out, that shouldn't take long with the lack of you know what, or I'll say something during our next row, and he'll leave me. Then what do I do?"

"Isn't it obvious?"

"Isn't what obvious?"

"You go back to Davida."

Bernie gasped and put his hand to his mouth in shock. "What if she won't have me back?"

"She will, she loves you. I saw how when we left her office, she held on to your hand for as long as possible. She's been divorced for ten years and her children have all grown up and moved out. She's waiting for you."

"Do you really think so?"

"Yes, and I suspect that she wants to be Mrs Davida Krovitz."

Bernie bit his bottom lip and turned away; he didn't want Astrid to see his tears. He wiped his eyes and turned back to her. "You, young lady, have an old head on young shoulders." He smiled broadly and took a swig of his drink and grimaced. "Ah, this coffee's like an old dog."

"How do you mean?"

"It's a bit RUFF."

"Oh dear, let's go," said Astrid. Throughout the time Bernie had spent pouring out his heart to her she had been waiting for his emotional defence mechanism to kick in and for him to make a terrible joke.

As she went to stand up, he grabbed her arm; he looked worried. "I don't look at your boobs, honestly I don't. You're like a daughter to me, and that would be sick. You've got to believe me."

"I believe you Bernie, I really do, now don't worry about it."

"Yes, but I will."

After two weeks it was time to go to Brandon to start filming. Two weeks for Astrid to deal with the slight anxiety that was building in her and two weeks of Bernie reassuring her.

"You'll be fine," he would say as he put his arm around her. "Just remember everything I've taught you and channel that wonderful talent you have." His smile and his confidence in her always made her fears go away.

Bernie turned onto highway four and headed towards Manchia. Once there, they'd take the ring road before hitting the B eighty-eight road. It had already been a long drive; they had started out early and there were many more hours to go. The small talk had fizzled out and Astrid had dozed until Bernie pulled into a service station. He fuelled the car and went to pay, emerging with a couple of cartons of drink and some snack bars.

"You didn't have to drive me to filming, so let me pay you for the fuel," said Astrid as she reached for her purse.

"Absolutely not," said Bernie firmly.

"Oh come on, I saw how much you put in."

"When you are a stinking rich TV and film mega-star—which you will be, of that I am certain—then maybe you can pay me back. But not now." He started the car and pulled onto the road. "Besides, I wanted to come up."

"So you could see Davida again?"

"Well, yes… Duh."

"That'll be nice for you."

Bernie pulled out of the service station and headed North. Astrid placed her bag against the glass and rested her head on it. She began to daydream about her future; what If Bernie was right? What if she did become rich and famous? It would change her, no doubt about that, but would it be for the better or worse? Would she stay level-headed or would she become aloof and arrogant but not be able to see that in herself. It was not difficult for her to imagine being successful and have all the trappings that went with that, so she had to keep reminding herself to take one step at a time; this was the first step of many, and she could trip and fall at any one of them.

The vista slowly changed from urban to countryside; towns and villages giving way to fields and rolling hills. She looked out at the landscape as it passed by, fascinated as she always was with the hedgerows that flashed past but the trees in the distance seeming to be moving with the car. Ahead in the road, some magpies were pecking at a piece of roadkill and waiting until the very last moment before flying away. She turned to look out of the rear screen to see them return to the flattened carcass as soon as they had passed. Off to one side a bird of prey was hovering five or so meters above the ground, gently moving its wings to stay motionless in the air while it scanned the ground below for its next meal. Suddenly it dropped down, then took off again with a rodent in its beak.

They passed a farm where cows were being loaded into a truck, and she just managed to catch the word 'Abattoir' on the side of the vehicle. Sheep were grazing in a nearby field unaware that the truck would soon come for them. She thought about all the wild creatures, all living their lives oblivious to the human world and precious few of them having the luxury of dying of old age peacefully in their sleep. Everything dying so that something else can live, from flies caught in spider's webs, mice being pounced on by cats, young deer being taken by larger predators, all the way up through the food chain.

"Everything gets killed," she said quietly to herself.

"What?" said Bernie.

She snapped out of her daydream. "I was just thinking about the animals, big or small, cute or ugly, young or old, they all get killed and become food for something else. We are so lucky; nothing eats us and when our time comes we get medical aid to make the passing as comfortable as possible."

"That's a bit deep for this time in the morning," chuckled Bernie.

"Well it just made me realise that we only get one shot at life, so we have to make the most of it."

"That is so very true, our lives can change so quickly, one minute you are just getting on with the minutia of your life and all the things that seem so important but are not really, then it's all gone in the twinkling of an eye," he said, frowning slightly.

"Now who's being deep," she laughed.

There was a long silence as both got lost in their own thoughts. Bernie suddenly spoke. "There's been some developments," he said, smiling and not able to hide his joy.

"Oh, okay."

"Nick's been away on a business trip for the past two weeks and is not due to get back for at least a week from now." There was a long pause. "I've been staying with Davida, we've done a lot of talking and I mean an awful lot of talking."

"I knew there was something going on, you've been different, happier. Maybe nobody else spotted it, but I did."

"There was a lot of re-discovery as well, and…" He smirked and blushed "… and a huge amount of intimacy," he said triumphantly. "I'm surprised we can still walk," he muttered under his breath, but just loud enough for Astrid to hear.

"This is leading up to something isn't it."

"You were right, she does want to be Mrs Davida Krovitz, and I want her to be, I want it so much now."

"Oh Bernie, that's wonderful."

He wiped a little tear from his eye. "Why did I ever walk away from her in the first place? I was so stupid. What was I thinking?"

"What about Nick? Does he know?"

"No, I know he suspects something, but not this. When he gets back, I'm going to tell him that we are over, then I'll move in with Davida. She's already making the wedding arrangements."

"That is brilliant news; can I be a maid of honour?" Astrid suddenly felt embarrassed for presuming to ask, and blushed.

"Don't worry, you are, it's already sorted, Davida wants it and so do I."

Brandon

Late in the afternoon, and after six and a half hours of solid driving they finally arrived on the film set just outside Brandon; a security guard at the side of the road checked their identities against a list of expected visitors and waved him through. Davida ran to meet them as they pulled up and got out. She hugged Bernie and kissed him on the cheek. Eventually she let go but kept her arm around him while she shook Astrid's hand.

Davida gestured to a portacabin. "Let's go to my office."

As they walked, Astrid looked at all the paraphernalia of film production; lights, cameras, generators and all manner of things that she only had a vague idea of what they were. Technicians were running cables, checking equipment, and moving flight cases. It looked chaotic, but she quickly saw that there was an order to the activity.

"I need to get used to this," she said to herself.

There were equipment racks; she recognised the radio receivers in one of them, at least she knew how they worked as she had used radio mics in theatre productions when she had, on occasion, been part of the backstage technical crew. Bernie had insisted that she should know every aspect of production.

Some distance away, she saw the portacabins of the military base that was scheduled to be moving out a couple of months after filming has finished. Most of the soldiers had already gone, but there were still quite a few around, and she became aware that they had seen her and were staring at her. She didn't feel intimidated though, she felt their presence somehow reassuring.

The army had assisted the production by demolishing some of the buildings in the village and blowing craters in the ground with explosives. It was already a convincing war zone, but she noticed that film technicians were throwing liquid on the walls of a wrecked building.

"What are they doing there?" she asked.

"Stage blood," said Davida. "One of the storylines is that a bomb hit the house, and a family who had ignored an evacuation order was in there. They'll put the corpse dummies in tomorrow, and it's one of the places you'll be going in. I should warn you though; the blast injuries to the dummies are very realistic and unpleasant to look at. This is going to be a very graphic film; so I hope you've got a strong stomach." Then she turned serious.

"I'm so tired of seeing the prettied-up war films, you know the sort of thing: a guy gets shot, puts his hand on his stomach and says 'I've been shot, I'm a goner, tell my wife I love her' then falls to the ground and ends up laying in what is so obviously a comfortable position. I've seen the newsreel footage from real war zones, all the stuff they don't put on the news in case it offends someone." She frowned deeply. "But I tell you, it's fucking disgusting what bombs do to a human body and all the dummies are direct copies of what I've seen. My hope is that if enough people see the film, then they might not be quite so keen to let their sons and daughters go to war."

She checked herself. "Oh, I'm sorry, I was getting a bit intense then, wasn't I?"

Bernie turned to Astrid and nodded his head towards Davida. "She is a very passionate woman…" he put his arm around her and hugged her as they walked. "…fortunately." Davida smiled and rested her head on his shoulder.

On one wall of Davida's portacabin was a storyboard, a collection of rough drawn cartoons of the scenes to be shot the next day. There was very little detail, just stick figures. Davida pointed to a few of them.

"These are your scenes. Normally my storyboards are pretty much exactly what I want the actors to do, but I don't want to influence you too much in this film."

Astrid's heart fluttered, it was really happening, and she hoped that she wouldn't get red-light fever as the camera turned on and the nerves got to her. One of the first things Bernie had taught her was how to channel nervous energy into performance. She scanned through the drawing and noticed that her part required a lot of running around, so channelling her nerves should be relatively easy. But all the same, she owed all of this to Bernie and didn't want to let him down.

Davida opened up a weather page on her computer. "Ah good, weather is set to be fine for the next week, so all being well we can start filming around midday tomorrow." She closed her laptop and rubbed her hands together. "Now, who's hungry?" She looked at Bernie and Astrid. "Silly question, I know you both are, it's too late to do anything else today so let's go to the hotel. I've booked you both in there and it has a great restaurant. I'll drive you there now."

<<<◇>>>

Bernie collected the suitcases and put them in Davida's car. "So, where are you staying?" Bernie asked innocently.

Davida rolled her eyes and sighed. "I'm…staying…with…you," she said, then raised her eyebrows and looked at Astrid who covered her mouth and sniggered.

"Oh," said Bernie, then the penny dropped. "Oh…ooooh…good," he said grinning.

"Just get in the car you silly old fool." Davida looked at Astrid and shook her head slightly. "Men, they really are a bit thick sometimes."

The meal was excellent, Astrid was hungry but resisted the urge to bolt her food or have too much. She declined the wine stating that she didn't want a fuzzy head the next day.

"Very wise," said Davida, increasingly impressed with the young woman sitting opposite her. Astrid wiped her mouth. "Thank you for the meal it was lovely, now if you don't mind, I want to get an early night."

"Good idea," said Davida. "I need you to be ready to go to site at seven thirty tomorrow morning." She pushed a key card over to Astrid. "You're in room three-o-one." Then she reached out and took Bernie's hand. "We're in room three-hundred." She looked at Bernie and squeezed his hand, he smiled, and Astrid noticed his eyes getting a bit watery. "I guess Bernie's told you about us?"

"Yes, he has and it's very, very sweet."

Bernie turned to Davida. "Astrid knows how much I love you, and what a fool I was," his voice faded as emotion caught his throat.

Astrid excused herself and went to her room, prepared herself then got in bed. She had been asleep for about ten minutes when a noise woke her. It was the rhythmic squeaking of a bed. It was coming from room three hundred.

"Young love," she said to herself and pulled a pillow over her ears.

War Zone

A noise woke Astrid during the night, it was the squeaking bed in room three-hundred and the sound of a couple of voices panting. She looked at the clock, it was three in the morning. She glared at the wall then turned over and pulled a pillow tight over her head. She didn't need an alarm clock to wake her in the morning, as the rhythmic squeaking started again at six.

"Bernie, really?" she said as she resigned herself to not getting the extra half hour in bed that she had allowed herself. She showered, got dressed and was just about to go down to the restaurant when the squeaking stopped and was replaced with the sound of a man and woman climaxing. Astrid frowned at the wall.

"You do know I've got to eat my breakfast now," she muttered to herself as she left her room.

Bernie and Davida walked in for breakfast at around seven twenty. Davida was immaculately dressed but her hair and makeup were a little less perfect than usual. Both Davida and Bernie looked a little coy and they both looked tired. Bernie sat next to Astrid while Davida got coffee and toast. He leant over and whispered in her ear. "You didn't, erm, hear anything last night, did you?" he said, a bit embarrassed.

"Bernie!" she whispered back, quietly, but firmly. "Your bed was squeaking, and the walls are quite thin. I heard everything, every squeak, every grunt and every groan, and the end bit! Twice in the night and again this morning! What are you like?"

He cringed. "We haven't seen each other for a few days, and I did say that she is a very passionate woman." He tried to sound apologetic but failed.

"As I recall, it does take two," she said, buttering her last piece of bread. "I was going to have soft-boiled eggs for breakfast, but for some reason I didn't fancy dipping my toast in them." Bernie blushed, and she laughed at his embarrassment.

Bernie grinned proudly. "We're just catching up on lost time."

Davida sat down and handed Bernie a coffee, there was an awkward silence for a couple of seconds as they looked at each other. He smirked and Davida put her hand over her mouth to stifle a laugh. He got up to get a pot of jam for his toast; Davida leant over and whispered to Astrid.

"I hope we didn't keep you awake, the walls are quite thin, and Bernie is a very passionate man."

"It wasn't a problem."

"Oh dear, that means you heard everything doesn't it! Oh, how embarrassing."

"It's all good, you love each other, and I'm pleased for you."

They arrived on set at eight and went straight to the cast portacabin. There were three men already there: one with a slight frame to his body, one tall and the other tall and thick set. After shaking hands and performing the usual pleasantries they sat while Davida pointed at a storyboard pinned to the wall.

"Orin will play the part of your camera man." The skinny man looked at Astrid and nodded. "Tariq is playing the part of your local fixer and Faraz is playing your bodyguard, they are escorting you to into a dangerous part of a village."

Faraz scowled and grunted. Astrid looked confused.

"Faraz is in a method actor; I've asked him to get in character," Davida explained. Faraz's frown deepened, and he grunted again.

She tapped one of the storyboard images. "This is what we will be filming this morning, and in this scene, Faraz and Tariq get shot; Faraz gets hit in the head and is killed straight away, Tariq gets hit in the leg and yells at you to get to cover he then gets hit in the chest and dies." Davida pointed to another part of the storyboard. "A camera crew will track you with a hand-held as you run to this bombed out house. We're not using a Steadicam in this sequence; I want it to be jerky. Pyro guys have put charges in the ground to simulate gunshots landing. You won't know where they are, but as you four are slowly walking the pyro chief will detonate them when you get to the right spot. They puff up dirt quite effectively but sound a bit puny, don't worry about that, they're just for your cues. We'll add the gunshot sounds in post-production."

A military man knocked and entered the room and shook hands with Davida.

"This is Captain Tavares, army media relations officer. He's going to talk you through some technical points."

“Thank you,” he said and removed his cap. Aware that these were civilians he was addressing, he adopted an informal style and sat on the edge of a desk.

“Good morning everyone. Davida has told me that in this part of the story a village comes under artillery fire. She has asked me to explain the different types of munitions that are commonly used in this situation, and she has also asked me not to hold back on the details of the unpleasant things that my profession does.”

He cleared his throat. “In an artillery bombardment of a built-up area two types of shell would be used. High explosives detonate either on, or immediately after impact and use this blast to do the damage. These would be used to demolish buildings or other hard targets. For use against soft targets, fragmentation munitions are used. They explode in the air at a pre-set altitude, around fifteen to twenty metres; they have a forward-facing charge and blast out shrapnel in cone that would cover and area about twenty metres across.”

“By ‘soft targets’ you mean people,” said Astrid.

“Mostly, yes,” he said unapologetically. “Anyone underneath when it goes off will have their day spoiled by things like these.” He opened a bag and tipped out some jagged pieces of twisted metal.

Orin frowned. “Disgusting,” he muttered. Astrid reached forward and picked up a piece. She studied it, turning it over and running her finger along the edges. She did not feel judgmental, as this was the reality of war and she knew that the Arralan army was a volunteer army and that these men had sworn to put themselves in harm’s way to keep civilians like her safe. They all knew that one day they might face weapons such as these and she doubted that she could ever have the same courage.

“Often, artillery crews will alternate between high explosive and fragmentation shells, the high explosive destroys the buildings, forcing the people out who are then killed by the fragmentation shells. Oh, I should add, these metal pieces become red hot once the charge detonates.” He looked at everybody, gauging their responses. “This is what happens in war.”

There was silence in the room, Davida had heard this before and hid her feelings, Faraz didn’t show anything, Tariq was shocked, but Astrid was attentive. Orin grunted quietly, just loud enough to be heard; Tavares ignored him.

“The shells make a whooshing sound that lasts about a second just before they hit, an experienced news crew would know that and duck for cover as soon as they heard it. The other thing that a crew would know is that depending on where a high explosive round hits, debris can be thrown out or up at very high speed. If it gets thrown up, masonry can take several seconds to come back down, so stay crouched down."

He sensed that Astrid was interested and continued. "Regular Army artillery units use heavy cannons, but rebel forces and infantry units across the world like to use mortars, they are lightweight and easy to set up. The sixty millimetre is common but it's range is limited to about three kilometres."

"How effective are they," said Astrid, genuinely curious.

"Not as effective as the heavy artillery, obviously, as the warhead is much smaller, but they can be fired much more rapidly which increases their effectiveness."

"With 'effectiveness' being a military euphemism for killing people," said Orin, with a contemptuous tone to his voice.

"Yes, that is right. And you don't hear them coming."

Orin put his head down and mumbled "sick."

Tavares ignored him, he encountered many anti-war, anti-military people in his role as a liaison officer and was quite used to their distain. It was not his job to apologise or get into arguments. Astrid put her hand up. "Just as a matter of interest, what is the range of the heavy artillery?"

"A one-hundred-and-twenty-millimetre shell can easily travel 35 kilometres."

"Thank you, Captain," said Davida. Tavares shook her hand, nodded to them all and left.

"Going on from what Captain Tavares has said, there are small charges placed around the set to simulate artillery shells landing. These will go off at random intervals; use these as cues to your acting, hesitate for a few seconds and technicians behind walls will throw debris on to you. It looks like bricks and gravel, but it's painted cork. This is the only direction that I am giving you, dialogue is all up to you, except for you, Astrid. I liked the name 'Halina' that you used the other day, keep that."

She rubbed her hands together, signalling that the briefing was coming to an end. "We're not going to be using clapper boards, this is total freestyle." She handed them all a sheet of paper. "These are your scene outlines for today's shoot. Now, Tariq and Faraz, go and get your blood packs fitted, Orin, go to makeup and props. Astrid, I'll introduce you to the camera crew, then go to makeup and props. Be back here in an hour."

As they went to leave the portacabin, Faraz pushed in front of Astrid and held his hand up to stop her. He carefully looked out of the door, stepped outside and scanned the area. "All clear," he said, then waved Astrid on. She looked at Davida.

"Method acting," Davida said.

Jacqui was the camera girl and Kim the sound recordist. Jacqui was an amazon, and tall, way above average height; she was lean but muscular with broad shoulders and well-defined biceps. She was dressed all in black; Dr Martin boots, black combat pants with camera battery packs stuffed into the thigh pockets and a tight black vest, which did nothing to hide the fact that she had pierced nipples and was not wearing a bra, even though she really should. Her head was shaved to a number one on the right side and cut into that was the shape of a spider's web.

The hair on her left side was long, dyed matte black and pulled into a ponytail with a black cloth. She had a spike that went from the top of her right ear down to her earlobe, and a couple of rings in both eyebrows. Deep, dark, almost black hazel eyes sparkled as she smiled. She had a stud across the bridge of her nose, rings through her nostrils, both lips, and studs in her chin. An elaborate dragon tattoo covered the length of her left arm; a tattoo of a cobweb ran from her right shoulder down to her elbow with a fine line leading down to a spider tattoo on the back of her right hand that was new and looked very real. Astrid guessed that she was in her mid to late thirties.

She smiled warmly, exposing a gold tooth as she shook Astrid's hand. "I'm Jacqui, call me Jacqui, Jax, Jacko, I don't mind." She laughed. "I've been called worse. This is Kimberly. I call her poppet, don't I poppet." Jacqui roughed up Kim's mop of ginger hair.

Kim beamed and shook Astrid's hand enthusiastically. "Hi," she squeaked. "Pleased to meet you." Kim was the opposite of Jacqui, she was short, almost half Jacqui's height. She had a freckly face and light blue eyes, but no visible tattoos or piercings. She had the svelte physique of an adolescent boy and looked to be about half Jacqui's age.

Jacqui noticed Astrid looking at her tattoos. "We like spiders, don't we poppet."

"Yeah, spiders are cool."

“And I know what you’re thinking,” said Jacqui, grinning, “…you’re thinking ‘Jacqui’s got a lot of metal in her face’. Well, they’re just the ones you can see.” She looked down at herself, winked and laughed. “We have a lot of fun going through airport scanners, don’t we poppet?”

“Yeah, a lot of fun.”

“This is going to be a good shoot. We like doing freestyle work, don’t we poppet,” said Jacqui.

“Yeah, freestyle’s good.” said Kim, excited.

“We don’t like doing scripted stuff, we do it, we have to, it pays the bills, but we don’t really like a director telling us ‘get this shot, I want this angle, use this lens, record this sound, use this microphone’. It gets us all pissed off, doesn’t it poppet?”

“Yeah, all pissed off.”

“In a way, this is more like what we normally film. Isn’t it poppet?”

“Yeah.”

“What do you normally film?” said Astrid, bemused by this odd but completely charming couple.

“Porn, we film porn,” said Jacqui. She nodded thoughtfully. “You know, there’s a lot of creative freedom in porn, much more than you’d think. I can have my camera as close up as I want. Make no mistake, what we do is full on, but we like to think that our porn is high quality. We like doing porn don’t we poppet?”

“Yeah, we like it a lot,” said Kim wide-eyed. Astrid wondered if Kim ever blinked.

“We could do you if you want,” said Jacqui. “A nice and tasteful glamour shoot, a present for your boyfriend.” She checked herself. “Or girlfriend, naughty Jacqui,” she slapped the back of her own hand. “We mustn’t assume people’s preferences, must we poppet?”

“No, we mustn’t.”

“No thank you,” said Astrid politely, she knew that ‘Glamour’ was a code word for nudity, and she felt slightly awkward at the thought of being filmed naked. “I don’t have a boyfriend and I’m straight.”

“That’s a shame, isn’t it poppet?”

“Yeah, shame.”

“Still, the offer’s open if you ever change your mind, isn’t it poppet?”

“Yeah, any time.”

Astrid smiled to herself as she walked to props and makeup. She couldn't decide what they meant when they said 'Shame'; was it because she declined Jacqui's offer, or was it because she didn't have a boyfriend or more probably, a girlfriend.

Jacqui and Kim were a peculiar mix, and Jacqui could so easily be dominating, but there was an endearing style about their relationship. Something else Astrid couldn't quite decide was whether Jacqui and Kim were a couple, or just had a very close working relationship.

She realised that all actresses get asked to do nude scenes at some point in their careers, and a lot of them do them. And she had no doubt that at some point she would be asked to do a nude scene and that would be a decision to be made then, but first, she needed to actually start her career.

Bernie ran up behind her and walked alongside. "I see you've met Jacqui and Kim. They're interesting aren't they."

"Oh yeah."

"Davida says that Jacqui is the best camera op' she's ever worked with. Kim's lovely and Jacqui has a heart of gold, well they both have hearts of gold, and they'll both do anything for you. You'll meet a lot of people like them; film is actually quite a small business and you'll be surprised at just how quickly you get to know absolutely everybody. It's like a family, pretty much everyone looks out for each other."

He paused, and Astrid knew he wanted to say something else. "Look, I'm sorry that we kept you awake last night, it's just that, well, we can't help ourselves."

"It's all good, Bernie, it's all good. You love each other and that's all that matters."

"If you need me, I'll…"

"You'll be in Davida's portacabin, won't you?"

Bernie grinned.

Props And Makeup

"These are much lighter than I expected." Astrid held the blue 'PRESS' body armour and helmet weighing them up and down.

Sal, the girl in charge of props handed a set to Orin. "Oh, they're not real, they look exactly like the real thing, but just have foam inside instead of the armour and the helmet is just thin plastic with a cloth covering." She took the helmet and chucked it in the air and caught it with one hand. "See, very light."

Orin put his on and shrugged. "This is okay."

Astrid frowned. "Why can't we have the real thing?"

"For one, they're expensive, and in film land when you don't need to spend money you don't spend money. These are cheap so if they get lost or damaged it's not a big deal. The other thing is that the real ones are heavy. The Kevlar's pretty light, but there's ceramic and metal plates front and back for the body protection. The helmet's heavy too, we tried them once, never again."

"So?"

"Well, do you want to be running around all day wearing all that weight? you'll get really tired, really quickly."

"Just like real reporters."

"And really sweaty."

"Just like real reporters."

"I'm happy with props," said Orin, fiddling with the straps. "If they look the same, what difference will it make? I can make it look like it's heavy." He'd already had his hair and make-up done and left to get a coffee.

Davida entered the room and heard the conversation. Astrid turned to her. "I want the real thing. If that's what they wear, then that's what I want."

Davida thought for a moment, then turned to the prop's girl.

"Sal, be a love, pop over to the Army stores, I know they've got some press jackets and helmets there, but we're not supposed to have them, they're for the real press. So just flutter your eyelashes at that corporal that you fancy."

Sal blushed and left the room. Davida turned to Astrid. "How are you going to have your hair?"

Astrid ran her hand along the length of her hair, it was long, past her elbow. She pulled it back into a ponytail. “I think that hair this long would be a hinderance to a war reporter.” She held it just above her collar. “I’ll get it cut off here.”

Davida was startled. “Your hair is beautiful, you don’t have to sacrifice it, we can fit you with a wig.”

“No, it’s okay, it’s only hair, it’ll grow back.”

Astrid sat in a chair while a makeup artist got to work. After a few minutes Sal returned with the body armour and dumped it on a table.

“Well, did you see your ‘friend’,” said Davida, raising one eyebrow.

“No,” said Sal grumpily. “He wasn’t there, I saw this old duffer instead. I had to flutter my eyelashes at a bloke old enough to be my granddad.”

The make-up girl sniggered.

“It’s not funny,” Sal protested. “He looked at me all pervy like.” She shuddered and grimaced. “He kept staring at my boobs.”

“Well they’re big enough,” muttered the make-up girl quietly. “Doesn’t matter where he looked. Can’t really miss them.”

“Oh, shut up you, you’re only jealous and you know it. I’ve seen fried eggs bigger than yours.”

There was a snipping sound and the hairdresser held up a lock of light brunette hair, half a metre long. “I’ll just neaten it up for you.”

“No, leave it like that please, I want it to look like Tatiana has cut it off herself.”

Davida smiled and nodded approvingly at Astrid’s commitment. ‘Oh she is going to be good’ she thought to herself.

First Day of Shooting

Astrid, Orin, Tariq and Faraz gathered in the track that led to the village. Astrid had the real body armour and helmet and was already feeling the weight. Orin had the props and looked a little bit smug. Fifty metres in front of them was a bombed-out building, just one corner remained. Jacqui and Kim stood a little way off from the group and gone was the light-hearted attitude, both had their professional heads on. They were walking the fifty or so metres to the building, checking the route they would take and clearing away anything that may trip them up. They returned, and Jacqui showed Orin the correct way to hold a camera as Kim was checking the sound levels.

"Can you say something please Astrid?" said Kim as she angled a shotgun microphone towards the group. "Use the same voice that you will use when we start filming."

"This is Tatiana Reece reporting from Halina. We are about to enter a village on the outskirts of town and…"

"That's great, I don't need any more. Thanks," Kim interrupted.

Jacqui stood next to Astrid and held up a light meter, made a mental note of the reading, then moved away from the group and adjusted her camera. Kim moved next to her and they talked for a moment. Jacqui looked beyond the group for anything that might be wrong in the background. "I'm not going to tell you when we start recording," she said. "Whenever you're ready, just start walking and talking."

The group started to walk towards the village, Faraz looked around nervously. "Miss Tatiana" said Tariq. "This is not a good idea."

"I thought you had spoken to your contact," said Astrid.

"I did, but…"

"You told me that he said we would have safe passage into Halina."

"Yes, but miss Tatiana, there are other groups that have broken away from the rebels. My friend cannot speak for the…"

The blood pack on Faraz's head popped and he dropped to the ground. A split second later a blood pack on Tariq's thigh popped, he screamed and fell to the ground holding his leg. A line of tiny charges in the ground detonated one after the other, simulating machine gun hits.

"Run! Get to that building." screamed Tariq. Two blood packs popped on his chest and he fell on his back.

Astrid and Orin ran, Jacqui and Kim ran alongside them, sticking to the track that they had cleared, then started to run faster until they were some distance ahead. Even though they were behind her now, Jacqui kept the camera on them. Orin stumbled but quickly got to his feet as more charges popped in the ground. Jacqui and Kim reached the house first. Kim positioned herself, and Jacqui laid down so that Astrid and Orin would have to jump over her. A few seconds later she got the shot of Astrid above her, 'slo-mo' she thought, 'this will look good in slo-mo'. She quickly rolled to her feet and positioned herself next to Kim in the far corner of the room.

Astrid landed and immediately recoiled in horror. At her feet was a corpse dummy, blue and bloated with its legs missing below the knee, white shattered bones smeared with dried blood poked out through muscle tissue. She knew it was a dummy, but it looked so real, and she felt herself gag.

"Good reaction," whispered Jacqui.

"Film that." Astrid shouted to Orin, pointing at the dummy.

"Tariq and Faraz have just been killed, we've got to get out of here," cried Orin.

Charges popped along the top of the wall. They both ducked.

"You've got to film this, these people are civilians, the world has to know what's happened here. We are the only people who can tell them. Give me the microphone."

"Okay, okay. But then we get out of here," said Orin. With shaking hands, he plugged in the mic and gave it to Astrid then pointed the camera at the dummy.

"No, on me first," she said, "Then pan around to the body."

"Oh this is good," whispered Jacqui as she watched through the viewfinder. She pulled the zoom slowly back to get both of them and the dummy in the shot. Astrid looked directly into Orin's prop camera and spoke breathlessly.

"This is Tatiana Reece in Halina. A rebel faction has not left the area and the cease-fire is not holding, I repeat, the cease-fire is not holding. Our fixer and bodyguard have been killed…" another load of charges popped along the wall, she ducked down. "…and we are trapped and being shot at. Civilians have died here." Orin slowly panned his camera around and onto the dummy.

“Good,” whispered Jacqui. “Keep going.”

“On me again,” said Astrid.

Orin panned hack to her. There was a louder bang from the other side of the wall that made them all jump; Jacqui wobbled the camera a little to add drama to the shot. A few seconds later, Astrid was showered with bits of painted cork from the technician the other side of the wall.

“We are under mortar attack now and I don’t know how long we have got.” Astrid was suddenly aware of loud bangs in the distance. Jacqui pulled focus to a close-up of Astrid’s face, and captured the fear in her eyes. She looked at Jacqui and dropped her mic. “There’s a problem, I’m not acting, something’s wrong.”

Suddenly there was a much louder bang and a stone the size of a golf ball smashed into the side of Jacqui’s camera, shattering the lens.

“What the fuck,” said Jacqui. There was another deafening bang close by and a chunk of rock the size of a man’s fist struck her in the back, bursting out through the middle of her chest. She crashed forward, spraying blood over Kim.

“JACQUI!” Kim screamed.

Captain Tavares ran up to them. “We’re under attack from the Correlans. Stay here, stay close to that wall, and get as low as possible. We’ll get you out of here just as soon as we can. Find something to cover yourselves with. It’s creeping barrage so it should miss you.”

“SHOULD MISS US!” screamed Kim. “I’m not fucking staying here.”

“Please, you must not go out in the open.” He turned and ran back towards the base.

Orin pulled at the remains of a table-top that Jacqui had landed on. Kim screamed hysterically as Jacqui’s body flopped over, exposing the massive hole in her chest. Another shell landed close by, there was a scream from the other side of the wall that cut short. A fraction of a second later a brick slammed down onto Orin’s head, shattering his thin plastic helmet and splitting his skull open, killing him. He slumped forward over Jacqui’s body.

Kim screamed again. Astrid reached out to her. “Come closer, get behind me I’ve got body armour on, you’ll be safe.”

“No I won’t be fucking safe. I’m not staying here.” Kim screamed.

“Please Kim, you must stay here.”

“Fuck off, I’m not staying here to end up like Jacqui. Oh Jacqui,” she cried as she looked at the wrecked bodies. Before Astrid could stop her, she got up and ran towards the portacabins.

“No Kim, come back, it’s not safe.” Astrid screamed. But it was too late. She heard the whoosh of an incoming shell. Instinctively, she grabbed the table-top, pulled it up and crouched behind it.

The fuse in the anti-personnel shell detected the pre-set distance from the ground and detonated the charge. Kim was underneath. A piece of shrapnel punched through the table-top and hit Astrid in the chest, throwing her backwards hard up against the wall. She felt the ceramic plate shatter and absorb the impact. The jacket felt uncomfortable now as the steel plate behind the ceramic was bent and pushing on her sternum. She looked down and saw the shard; a large section of the shell casing as big as her hand was tangled in the Kevlar. She could feel the heat it was giving off and smelled the acrid aroma of explosive.

A high explosive shell landed next to the fuel bowser that fed the generators, blasting thousands of litres of burning diesel into the air. Some of the technicians were running for cover and were blind to the danger. They ran into the path of the fuel as it landed. She could hear the screams and looked out at the scene and saw a body, engulfed in flames, walk out of the inferno, drop to its knees and slump to the ground. Another body crawled out, then rolled onto its back. She watched, unable to turn away from the horror as the arms and legs pulled up, the heat forcing the muscles to contract.

The shells were landing away from her now, and she watched in terror as she saw the portacabins being hit, their walls and roofs blasting away. She couldn’t watch any more, she pushed herself as tight into the corner as she could, pulled the table-top over herself again and sat sobbing, waiting for it to somehow end.

Aftermath

Five minutes had passed since the last big explosion, the last few had been in the distance, and she guessed that these were in the army camp. She could hear smaller explosions, though nothing as powerful and the artillery barrage, she thought that these might be small army explosives, burning and detonating.

Gingerly, she moved the wood away and stood up; she pulled at the shell fragment that was snagged in her body armour and tossed it away. She removed her helmet and was shocked to see two rips in the blue cloth covering. She pulled the fabric apart and saw two deep gouges in the helmet from shrapnel. Instinctively, she felt her head, there were no injuries, but she hadn't even known that she'd been hit.

She looked down at the bodies of Jacqui and Orin, she sighed and shook her head. There was some cloth nearby, old curtains. Tears ran down her cheeks as she placed it over their faces, she didn't quite know why she did it; it just seemed the right thing to do. Then she started to walk slowly back towards what remained of the film company base.

She looked around the wall to where the technician had been. His shattered body lay in a pool of blood, she hadn't met him, didn't know his name and even though that was irrelevant, it bothered her. She carried on walking and saw a body; Kim had been wearing the same sort of clothes. She froze, then slowly approached. It was Kim, shrapnel had ripped her body apart; all that was recognisable was a clump of ginger hair matted with blood. Astrid turned away and vomited.

The smoke from the diesel fire was subsiding and a gust of wind revealed Davida's portacabin, it had taken a direct hit.

"Oh, no," she gasped. "Bernie, Davida," she screamed as she ran towards the wreck. She saw Bernie's body; he was laying on his side with his back to her.

"Please be alive, please be alive, please be alive," she cried as she ran to him. Without thinking, she grabbed his shoulder and rolled him onto his back. She shrieked in horror, something in the blast had torn off his lower jaw and ripped open his throat. She staggered backwards and fell to the ground and sat screaming his name. Then she suddenly remembered, he would have been with Davida, where was she? She wasn't near the cabin, Astrid stood up and started to frantically search for her. She forced herself to look at some burned bodies, gagging at the smell of burned flesh and diesel oil. Some of the bodies were just recognisable as female, but their shoes, though burned were not like the ones Davida had been wearing.

A high explosive shell had landed close to a group of people. There were bodies without arms or legs; there were bodies with heads missing and eviscerated bodies with their internal organs torn out and laying on the ground beside them. There were lumps of meat all around her, unrecognisable as to what body part they once were, but there was nothing that could identify Davida. Then she saw a body in a skirt laying a little way off.

"Oh God, no," she gasped as she approached. It was Davida, she had been caught in the blast of an antipersonnel round. She was moving.

Davida was still alive, but had horrifying injuries, her eyes had gone, they were just bloody holes in her face. Blood dribbled out of both of her ears. She had multiple deep lacerations across her face, throat and chest, her abdomen was ripped open, and she was trying to hold in her intestines. Blood was pooling all around her.

"Davida, it's me, Astrid, I'm here, you're going to be alright." She got no response.

"Medic!" yelled Astrid as loud as she could.

A soldier with a red cross arm band ran up to her. He stopped short when he saw Davida. He knelt down opposite Astrid, shook his head, and mouthed 'she's not going to make it'. Blood spluttered from Davida's mouth as she tried to breathe.

"Can't you do something?" Astrid cried in desperation, knowing in her heart of hearts that nothing could be done to save Davida.

"There's nothing I can do to save her. I'm sorry. She's blind, deaf…" he looked at the horrific wounds to her body. "… And even if we could get her to hospital, they'd not be able to save her either." He pulled a syringe from his bag. Davida's head rolled from side to side; she writhed, her body moving as she tried to ease the pain. He studied what was left of her face. "She's in a lot of pain, and I can at least give her something for that."

He took a bottle from his bag. "This is a very powerful anaesthetic…" He spoke with a deliberate emphasis "…and you can wait with her while she dies, it could be five minutes, ten minutes, maybe even longer before she passes." He looked Astrid straight in the eye. "You and I are the only people who aren't injured." He pushed the syringe needle up into the bottle, as he did so he turned the bottle so she could read the label. It stated in large letters:

'It is dangerous to exceed the stated dose, ensure that the antidote is ready before administering'.

He started to draw the plunger back, filling the syringe to the first graduation. "This much will stop the pain completely." Again, he looked directly into her eyes. "There are other people who need us, other people we can save, and I need your help."

Astrid realised what he meant. She swallowed hard. "What happens if you give her too much?"

"Her breathing and heart will stop almost immediately."

"It will kill her?" she cried.

"Yes."

"Will it hurt her?" she said as she wiped tears from her face.

"No, she'll feel no pain; she'll get a feeling of intense euphoria for a few seconds. She's your friend and I know you love her, and this is the kindest thing to do for her."

Astrid said nothing, and just nodded, then looked away as he drew liquid up to the tenth graduation. He found a vein in her arm, inserted the needle then abruptly took his hands away.

"Why aren't you giving it to her?" she gasped.

"I can't, I swore the hypocritic oath, I can't knowingly do anything the causes harm."

Astrid cried out; she knew what he wanted her to do. "No, no, I can't do it." she screamed in anguish.

He reached over and held her head. "You must be strong; you must do this for your friend."

She reached down, and with trembling hands, took the syringe.

"It will be quick," he said.

Shaking, and crying uncontrollably, she put her hand on the plunger and pressed it all the way in.

Within a couple of seconds, the pained expression on Davida's face disappeared and a faint smile appeared. A couple of seconds later her head rolled to one side. He put his hand on Davida's neck and felt for a pulse, there was none.

"She's gone," he said.

Astrid collapsed onto her, sobbing. He removed the syringe and placed it in a sharp-safe box, then took her arm and pulled her away.

"Stow your feelings and grieve for her later, we have people to save, they need me, and I need you. Do it for your friend. Honour your friend."

His last three words stuck home, she stood up straight and wiped the tears from her eyes. She turned and was about to go to the film set. He grabbed her arm.

"I've just come from there; they were hit hard during the first salvo. I'm sorry, but there are no survivors."

"What do you want me to do?" she said firmly as her grief evaporated.

"We need to get to the camp, now." They started running. "Triage 101. If they're walking, ignore them, it they're screaming, ignore them, it means they can breathe. If they're not breathing, check for a pulse. Do you know how to check for a pulse?" He tapped his wrist.

"Yes."

"Good, if you can't find a pulse or if it's slow, call me. Check people who are bleeding from the arms or legs. Do you know what a tourniquet is?"

"Yes."

"Do you know how to put one on?"

"I think so, use any piece of cloth or rope, put it around the arm or leg above the injury and tighten it until the blood stops."

"Good, very good. Ignore their cries as you do it, you are saving their lives, but it hurts them." He pulled out a bag of bandages and gave them to her then produced a packet of tampons. "If there are holes in them that are bleeding, poke one of these in, but if you drop one and it gets dirty, don't use it, throw it away."

They got to the camp, he stopped and held her by the shoulders. "Now for the hard part. If it's obvious that they are about to die, leave them. I know that will be a very difficult thing for you to do, but we can't make others wait."

Though shocked at the thought of doing this, Astrid understood his reasoning and nodded.

"Now go. You're going to do great, just remember what I said."

The first person she saw was Captain Tavares. He was sitting on the ground but appeared to be breathing normally. His uniform was scorched, the skin on the side of his face was burnt and his hair singed down to the scalp on one side. He was cradling an obviously broken arm. 'Low priority' she thought to herself and ran past him. She rounded the corner of a destroyed hut to a scene of carnage. Body parts were everywhere; she couldn't avoid stepping on some of them. A large crater bore witness to the force of the blast. It was eerily quiet, then she heard someone moan. She looked around and saw a soldier laying on the ground with his foot blown off.

The sense of horror dissipated as she worked her way through the dead and injured. She tended to their wounds quickly and methodically, patching up those that she could before moving on to the next casualty. Other than asking their names, she didn't engage in conversation, she knew that this would just waste time.

Two hours later, Astrid and the medic dragged the last of the corpses into the line of the dead. Army ambulances arrived, and medics poured out.

"Forty-two army personnel dead. Eight moribund, one hundred and eighty-three wounded, fifteen of them seriously. Most of those won't make it," said the medic, rubbing his forehead and trying hard to stay professional. "And we haven't started on the civilians."

"I'll see to the bodies," she said wearily. She had gone beyond grief and was just doing what needed to be done; she knew she would hurt later.

"I'll help you."

"No, I need to do this, they were my people, you tend to yours."

She turned and started to walk back to the film set. He called a female medic over and pointed to Astrid. "Get some body bags and go with her."

He watched her walk away for a few moments then got some groundsheets from what was left of a store and spread them out over the bodies of the soldiers.

She saw Captain Tavares again. "Why did they do this? I thought the Correlans were pulling back."

"They're saying, fuck you, we'll be back." He gasped as the burnt skin on his cheek split open and pink tinged fluid seeped out. "The bastards waited until all of our artillery was gone and we couldn't return fire." He winced and tried to move his arm to a less painful position. "They're not going to give up, and when they do come back, we better have a strategy to deal with them, or we're fucked."

Astrid's blood ran cold, it was exactly as she had improvised in Davida's office.

Astrid and the female medic worked in silence as they put bodies in bags and gathered up body parts from the film set. There were no words to be said. The horror of it all had numbed her and there was nothing now to shock her, everything was either red, brown or black. Bodies were just pieces of meat and she couldn't even see them as human anymore. She knew this would pass, and that she would remember their faces, but right now, there was still work to be done.

She had decided to leave Davida and Bernie's bodies until last, she didn't quite know why, it just seemed appropriate, but the shock returned when it came to put their bodies in the bags. She dropped to her knees, unable to bring herself to touch them. She slowly sank down, then collapsed onto the ground, curled up in the foetal position and cried uncontrollably.

The medic called over a colleague and they did what was necessary.

Deep inside Correla, Lieutenant Brigit Malaya sat in her quarters reading the first report of the attack on Brandon by the third heavy artillery regiment less than three hours ago. She was pleased that the army council had finally given the go-ahead for the attack.

"At last," she muttered and nodded with approval as she read the damage assessment of the Arralan military base. "And you thought we were pulling back, well this is just the start," she said menacingly, as she poured herself a glass of brandy.

Correlan artillery spotters had infiltrated across the border and taken up position on a hill a few kilometres outside of Brandon. They had orders to direct fire onto the Arralan army base, and with the usual Correlan ambiguity, to direct fire on any buildings or potential targets in the surrounding vicinity.

In addition to their report on the military target, the spotters also included a section on the potential for civilian deaths at the film set.

"Civilian deaths?" Malaya scoffed. "Get used to it," she said as she downed her drink.

It was getting dark before a transport truck arrived to take the walking wounded to hospital. The medic insisted that she had to go and be checked, and she was just too tired to argue. Wounded soldiers climbed aboard and sat in silence waiting for the last person. Astrid sat at the back staring out at the scene; more ambulances had arrived, and their crews were out putting the dead into body bags and tending to those more seriously hurt. Everything seemed to be going in slow motion, occasionally it seemed to freezeframe and everything would stand still. She knew those images would stay with her for the rest of her life.

It was late in the evening and getting cold, a medic gave her a blanket. She took it but put it over a soldier next to her who had lost a lot of blood and was shivering.

She thought about her life and her dreams of becoming an actress and how as a child she would re-enact programs she had seen on television. Then there were the acting classes at school where she'd been told that she was a natural and that a career in TV or film was right for her. She had tried not to let it go to her head but couldn't help dreaming of a life of fame and fortune. She looked at the body bags and thought of the dead soldiers in them; her dreams of stardom seemed so shallow now, so selfish.

The last person got on; a couple of medics helped him. He was dressed in a Colonel's uniform and had a bandage around his head that covered his eyes. They sat him opposite her, and she noticed wet blood seeping through the gauze.

"I am Colonel Collard. I was the senior ranking officer at this base." He held his right hand out, waving it vaguely in her direction. "You are the young lady that helped my men, are you not?" He paused, imagining her looking at him and wondering how he knew she was there. She reached over and shook his hand.

"Soldiers have their own particular smell, how can I put it politely, it's an earthy smell, and you do not have that particular odour. I am going to have to rely much more on my sense of smell from now on. Now, they tell me that you saved a lot of lives and I thank you for that most sincerely."

"I did what I could sir," and even though she was a civilian, it seemed right to call him 'sir'. "I'm sorry that I couldn't save more; I have no medical training."

"You did what you could and that was enough, you couldn't have done more."

"Thank you," she said weakly.

"You are young, eighteen maybe?"

She nodded, then cringed "Yes," she said, quickly.

"You nodded, didn't you?"

"Yes, I'm sorry."

"No need for apologies, it's a natural reaction." He paused, then sighed. "I have a fifteen-year-old daughter, I'll never see her again, so for the rest of my life she will be fifteen."

He turned to face outside, to where sounds were coming from. "I don't want to leave my men. I may be blind, but I'm still their commanding officer. However, the medics outrank me in matters of health, and they have insisted that I go to hospital." He heard her gasp slightly. "You are wondering why I am so calm, yes?"

"Yes, how can you be?"

"Well, I'm not in pain, the medics have seen to that, and anyone that joins the military and expects not to get hurt is a fool. If you sign-up, you have to have the mindset that at some random time, you could easily get serious, life-changing injuries or even be killed. This was my mindset, and this was my time."

The truck's engine started, and the diver pulled out of the camp.

A nurse finished examining Astrid. "You're fine, just wait here, someone wants to talk to you," she said, then left for another patient. A female officer wearing the uniform of military intelligence shook Astrid's hand.

"My name is Captain Meyer; I need to know what you experienced."

Meyer took notes while Astrid described the start of the film shoot. She choked on her words and struggled as she described the Correlan bombardment and the deaths of Jacqui, Orin and Kim. She was about to describe the situation with Davida when Meyer put her hand up.

"Stop there, I have already spoken to the medic, I don't need to know about that part."

"But I was the one who pressed the plunger, I killed her," said Astrid, and started crying uncontrollably.

Meyer put her hand on Astrid's shoulder to comfort her a little. "There are provisions in the law, both civil and military, that cover situations such as the one you found yourself in," she said softly. "Your action was the correct thing to do."

"She was my friend."

Meyer handed her a box of tissues. "She was your friend, and you did the only thing you could for her, don't feel bad about it, given what the medic has told me it was an act of kindness."

The nurse reappeared. "The doctor will see you now."

"Why? you said I was okay."

"It's just routine," said the nurse and led Astrid into a side room.

A doctor smiled at her. "Please lay down and relax, we're just going to insert a canular in the back of your hand."

"What for? I'm not injured."

"Not physically, but mentally you'll be a wreck in a couple of days' time."

He held up a large syringe and went to put it into the canular that she hadn't even felt being inserted.

"This will help you forget everything."

She put her hand over the canular to stop him. "No, I don't want to forget."

He looked her in the eye and smiled benignly. "You are not a soldier; soldiers are trained to witness the things you have seen and not let it affect them. You haven't had that training."

"NO." she said firmly.

"I strongly advise you to let me administer this," he said, equally firmly.

"NO."

"As you wish, I cannot force you, but I do now have a legal duty to tell you what will happen if you don't have this medication. You will get flashbacks, and they will be more vivid, more realistic than any of the scenes that you witnessed. I've been told what happened, and you will see you friend's face over and over again. You will see yourself pressing the plunger over and over again, and you will have nightmares."

"I will deal with it," she said angrily as she pulled the canular out. Blood flowed out onto her hand. The nurse quickly put cotton wool on the hole that was left and taped it down.

"Don't take this off for twenty-four hours." she said.

"Okay." The doctor was cross as he scribbled a note. "I have to respect your wishes, but if you do change your mind, there's medication that can help. Just give this note to your doctor. You are free to go."

As she left the treatment room and entered the atrium of the hospital, she saw some of the injured soldiers waiting to be treated. She screwed up the note and chucked it in a bin, then and an odd feeling suddenly gripped her. All her dreams of fame had left her, she felt disgusted at the thought now. She had to do something, she had to be part of something bigger than herself. She saw Meyer and told her how she felt.

"I want to do something; I want to help."

"Become a nurse then. Because if there's a war, what you saw today will be canapes compared to the ten-course meal that the Correlans will dish up." Mayer said in the odd style of black military humour.

Astrid went straight to the reception desk, picked up an application form for a nursing post and filled it out. The events of today had dramatically changed her life. Little did she know that a significant event in two years' time would change her life even more drastically.

Davida's funeral was hard for her to bear; it was supposed to be just family, but hundreds turned up. News had spread through the production industry and stars of film and TV were present. Luckily, few people outside of the industry knew who Davida was, and the news media was not present; covering her funeral would not be interesting enough to the public to warrant any time on the news that night.

Davida's divorce had been amicable; her ex-husband stood looking drawn as he comforted their children and stared down at the coffin. Nobody present knew who Astrid was, and no-one spoke to her; something she was grateful for, as she couldn't bear the thought of making small talk with any of Davida's friends, knowing what she had done.

Bernie's funeral was a small affair, he had no family, so it was just friends from the theatre, and Nick. Nick was distraught, and Astrid comforted him. "Why was he up there with you?" Nick sobbed.

"He was looking after me." She choked back the grief as the images of that day flooded back.

"Things were not good between us, I loved him so much, but something was wrong. Was he seeing another man? You'd know, you knew him so well. Please, I need to know."

She held him tight. "No, Nick, Bernie wasn't seeing another man." She closed her eyes and cried. She hadn't lied, and she could have told him the truth, but why make his suffering worse.

<<<◇>>>

Bernie rolled over and sat up. He slowly got to his feet. In his hand was his lower jaw, he lifted it up and attached it to his face.

"What are you doing to Davida?" he said, his voice aggressive and demanding in a way that Astrid had never heard from him before.

"I'm trying to help her," Astrid cried.

"But you're not helping her, are you," he said. "You're going to kill her. She can be saved you know."

Astrid looked down at the syringe, it was huge; glowing green liquid swirled inside it. Davida's head turned towards her. "You know I can be saved, so why are you doing this? I thought you were my friend."

"She can be saved, but you are going to kill her, aren't you," said Bernie. His jaw was now missing, and the words came out of a hole in his throat.

"I can be saved," said Davida, lifting her head. The empty eye sockets in her face growing ever larger. Astrid looked down, her arm was now the plunger, and was slowly pushing the liquid into Davida's arm. Davida screamed.

"You are hurting her, why are you doing this? And after all she has done for you," shouted Bernie.

"Why are you doing this, why do you hate me?" Davida started thrashing around shrieking. Bernie grabbed Astrid and tried to pull her away, his arms blending into her shoulders. Astrid looked at Davida, she had no injuries.

"Stop hurting her. I thought you loved her, but you're killing her, she's in pain because of you."

"You're killing me," Davida screamed.

"You're killing her," yelled Bernie.

Astrid sat bolt upright in bed, her heart was pounding, she was drenched in sweat and shaking. It was four-twenty in the morning; it was the same nightmare at the same time that she had dreamt every night for the past three weeks since the attack. She looked at the phone number of her doctor. "No," she said. "No, I don't want to forget."

Riedel

Five years later.

She laid down in bed and tried to go to sleep, knowing what thoughts would soon fill her head; the thoughts she had every night when not on a mission. The thoughts that would keep her awake. She thought of Riedel. She didn't think of him when she was on a mission, or in training, or planning for a mission, but once that was done it all came back to her. It was as if her sub-conscious was saying to her 'the important stuff is over, now you can torment yourself over a love lost forever'.

She closed her eyes and tried to think of anything but him, but it never worked. In the past she had tried to empty her mind, but that only created space for him to fill. She didn't quite know why it was that she had loved him so much. They had never made love, he had never kissed her, he had never held her in his arms, he had never even held her hand. And she didn't even know his real name, she only knew him as Riedel.

All they had done was talk. He had been an emergency admission to the hospital where she had worked; he had been shot. She was his nurse and they talked throughout the long months of his recovery. He was articulate, intelligent, and funny, and had a powerful sense of loyalty to his country. He spoke of the rights of the individual; of how people should be given the tools to make their own future without interference from the state, and how education was the key to the country's future. He spoke with eloquence and conviction, and at first she just listened, but the more she listened, the more she realised that she was falling in love with him. He didn't tell her what he did, or how it came for him to get shot. It was only much later that Captain DeSalva confirmed that he was an agent working for military intelligence; she had guessed as much.

Nine months after he was discharged from hospital, he was back with another gunshot wound, and she braced herself for the feelings that she would get, this part was always the same and she held her eyes as tightly closed as she could to try to stop the tears, but this always failed. His wound was bad, and he was put in a medically induced coma, but not before he had told her that he had never stopped thinking of her. DeSalva told her later that Riedel had vital information and somehow the Correlans had worked out where he was.

She could still hear the sound of his heart monitor flatlining, she could still see the blood on his chest and could still see the face of his assassin and the knife in his hand. That was three years ago, and on the day Riedel died, she changed forever. She was now no longer a nurse, dedicated to saving lives, but a skilled killer, dedicated to taking lives; part of DeSalva's team of assassins.

She took a tissue and wiped her eyes, she might get some sleep now, but she knew it would happen all over again tomorrow night. She hoped that she wouldn't have the dream tonight, she hadn't had the nightmare for months now, but at five thirty it came to her.

She was with Bernie and Davida, they were walking across a meadow. She stopped to pick a flower while they walked on. They stopped and embraced, kissing passionately, but the sky behind them had turned black and the ground was crumbling away. She tried to call out to warn them, but she had no mouth. She tried to run to them, but her legs had grown roots that were working their way into the ground. She frantically waved her arms, finally they saw her and waved back, smiling, unaware of the danger. They couldn't see the ground crumbling away, getting closer to them. The roots suddenly disappeared, and she ran to them, she reached out to grab them, but the ground beneath them gave way and they fell into an abyss.

She sat bolt upright in bed, her heart thumping in her chest. She checked the time, she knew she wouldn't sleep anymore and wearily, she got out of bed.

Major Pell

Astrid stood in the office of Captain DeSalva, he gestured for her to sit.

"This is Major Pell," said DeSalva, taking a folder from a filing cabinet. He sat at his desk, opposite her. "He is your next assignment."

Astrid was puzzled. "A Major is a pretty low-status target, sir. We've never hit anybody that low ranking before."

"It's not who he is now, but who he will eventually become."

"I'm not sure I understand sir."

"Pell is clever, he is unlike any other Correlan officer, he thinks differently. We suspect that this is because he went to university here in Arralan and was taught critical thinking, rather than learning by rote as they do in Correlan universities—if you can call them that."

He opened Pell's file and read some bullet points from it. "Fluent Arralan speaker, could easily pass for a native. A scholar of Arralan military history, with a keen interest in our technology."

He slid the file to Astrid. "You must read this and thoroughly digest its contents, then present me with a plan."

She went to stand, but he waved her down. "At first, because of his language skills and his knowledge of the country, we thought he would be a deep cover spy, a sleeper maybe. But he joined the Correlan Army as a volunteer, and this is unheard of, usually only kids with no prospects volunteer, and then it's because they have a fixed four-year term. And because he was university educated, he went straight into officer training. He is intelligent and has a huge ego.

"He is arrogant, conceited even, and he made himself very unpopular with the Army Council by writing to them, criticising their tactics and strategy. He suggested better training and investment in modern technology. He advocated smaller elite units based on the Arralan model. This did not go down well and has definitely held up his promotions."

Astrid thought for a moment. "The Correlans rely on weight of numbers and crude weapons that are inaccurate; but are effective if fired in a great enough volume. Retraining the entire Correlan army with new tactics would require a paradigm shift. Could they do it, sir?" she mused.

"No, at least, not yet. The army council members are ultra-conservative, highly resistant to change, and they are all very old. They suffer from the same malaise that all old soldiers have, in that they think the way to win a war is to fight the same way as they won the last war. And as you correctly say, they will rely on weight of numbers. But we can easily hold them, our tactics will see to that."

"So why take Pell out now, sir?"

"As the army council members die off, younger men, well, relatively younger men, will take their place and we think that some of his ideas might then gain traction. And if he gets promoted any higher, then they might start to take a bit more notice of him. We can't wait for that, and with him out of the way there'll be no-one with the nerve to challenge the Army council and effect any changes."

Astrid flicked through the file as she listened to DeSalva.

"How soon do you want it done sir?"

"Obviously, the sooner the better, but there is no desperate urgency, he has only just been promoted to Major and no senior officers are going to give him the time of day—for the time being." DeSalva noticed that she was looking at his address.

"As you can see, he lives off-base. He's just been posted and hasn't moved his family down yet. One thing that will work in your favour is that his arrogance means that he sticks rigidly to the same routines in his personal life. It should be a relatively low-risk mission for you, and you have a week to come up with a plan. It's up to you how you carry out the mission, but the usual caveat applies; it must look like an accident. Dismissed."

Astrid stood, saluted, and left the office.

‹‹‹○›››

Astrid sat in her quarters with the file open and documents spread out on her desk. She pinned some pictures of Pell on a cork board that hung on the wall and studied them. Surveillance teams took most, and these were the usual, grainy, long distance shots of him leaving his house, getting in his car, shopping with his wife and family etc… but one image was different and stood out. It was a posed picture of Pell in Correlan uniform with some Arralan officers, all smiling while standing outside the gates of an Arralan army base.

Before Godin Hallenberg had come to power in Correla; declared himself the Grand Field Marshal and imposed his dictatorship, there had been some co-operation between the Arralan and Correlan military and the occasional exchange visits of officers. A report from the time of the photo showed that Pell had made several visits and was well liked by the Arralan officers, but that military intelligence was concerned, particularly as two of the visits occurred after tensions between the two countries began to rise. There was no doubt in the mind of the report's author of Pell's fanatical commitment to Correla.

Astrid sat studying the pictures of Pell, she was deep in concentration and absentmindedly picking at the laminate on the edge of her desk. A small piece broke off and stuck under her fingernail. It hurt; she flinched and flicked her hand to dislodge it, then looked at the damage to the corner.

Annoyed that she had distracted herself, she muttered, "Gotta stop doing that," as she looked at the splintered wood. She went back to the picture, unaware that her hand was back on the corner with her fingernails scraping the edge again.

She read his personal file; he was married with three children, all still at school in the north. She presumed that he would move his family down once the school year had finished. That gave her a couple of months grace before the presence of a family could interfere with her mission. He was renting a large, detached house a few kilometres outside the base. It was at the end of a long no-through road and was fairly remote, with few neighbours and not overlooked. At the time of writing, it was being reported that he went back to his family every weekend; leaving late Friday night and getting home late Sunday evening, and that no-one else ever visited the property.

The Arralan asset in the Correlan Army headquarters had obtained a letter that Pell had written to a three-star General who was in line for a seat on the Army council. The letter was hand-written and had been intercepted before it reached its intended recipient. It made for uncomfortable reading. It outlined the Arralan tactics, the use of technology and the superior training. It proposed matching and surpassing these, and had detailed, lengthy descriptions of how this could be achieved.

His hubris was enormous, and his letter was unlikely to be taken seriously at the moment, but if his letter had reached the general and his plans had been adopted, they would have negated any advantage that Arralan had. It was considered doubtful that the General was aware of Pell's ideas, and the hand-written nature meant that the possibility of any copies of the letter was remote.

The Pell Mission

A light came on in the bedroom, a few seconds later, the light came on in the bathroom. Five-thirty a.m. the same time as yesterday and the day before. Astrid started a stopwatch and raised her field glasses. Four minutes and thirty-seven seconds later, the window started to steam up; six seconds earlier than yesterday and five seconds later than the day before that, she guessed that he had been having a shave before a shower. She kept the stopwatch running. Twelve minutes after the light came on, the window opened, thirty seconds after that, the bathroom light went out. Five minutes and fifteen seconds later, the bedroom light went out and the bathroom light came back on, a minute later it went out. Then, at precisely six o'clock, the front door opened, and Major Pell left the house and got into his car.

It was Thursday, she would watch him tomorrow and implement the next part of her plan when he leaves to visit his family. She put down the field glasses and settled down into her hide in the ditch. She opened a packet of food rations, took out an energy bar then settled down and continued the waiting game. The compressed cereal bar was packed with carbs, vitamins and minerals; all the nutrition her body would need, though the flavour was deliberately bland. This was to ensure than they were only eaten when they were needed and not as a quick snack.

To occupy her time, she thought through all the strategies that she could use. Gradually they coalesced into one. For three days now she had been living in a ditch with a cover over her, and a slit just big enough for her field glasses to see through. She was cold, tired, and wanted some hot food. But these creature comforts would have to wait for another night. After he left to visit his family tomorrow night, she would break in and work out the next part of the plan.

She watched as Pell put a suitcase on the back seat of his car, get in and drive away. She waited an hour, then grabbed her bag and ran to the house. Squatting down by the door, she took a set of lock picks, selected a couple, inserted them in the keyhole and a few seconds later she opened the door. She took a cloth from her bag, placed it on the floor, removed her boots and placed them on it so as to not leave any dirt. Moving slowly through the house, she memorised the positions of everything and touched nothing. She would stay here tonight and tomorrow night, then wait for his return.

She went upstairs, noting that steps three, five and eight squeaked. She checked the bedrooms, only one had been used. It was late summer, and though the weather was cooler now, the days spent laying in a ditch had given her a particularly strong body odour. She needed to make sure this didn't linger in the air, so she went into the bathroom, got undressed and had a shower, using a small amount of his shower gel, so as not to leave a different aroma in the house, and made sure to put the bottle back in exactly the same position. She dried herself with another cloth from her bag, put on clean underwear and some light clothes, then an all-in-one cotton overall of the type that forensic teams use so as to not leave any contamination. She placed all her other clothes in a zip-top bag then went downstairs. She needed to eat but could not risk using any of the food in the kitchen as he might notice this when he returned. Instead she got out a ration pack and ate that, then moved some cushions off a sofa, laid down and went to sleep.

She woke early the next morning; ration packs were starting to get bland now, and she would have to put up with many more days of them before she could have some proper food. She left all glasses and mugs where they were and drank water directly from the tap to wash down the dry biscuits and energy bars. She put the cushions back in position, and now there was only one more facility that she had to use, a proper toilet, but even then, she used tissue that she had brought with her.

A good sleep had cleared her head, and it was time to plan. She had the idea of taking him in the bathroom, where he would be easier to surprise, but how to make it look like an accident was eluding her. She went to the bathroom and looked around, eventually she zeroed in on the mixer tap. It was a substantial design with a solid outlet spout which was rounded to an almost perfect hemisphere at the end. This also controlled the shower. She realised what she had to do.

There were concrete slabs in the back garden that formed a path that led to a wooden workshop, she found a bunch of keys in the kitchen then went to the shed. It looked like it hadn't been opened for some time. Inside was a workbench covered in tools, amongst them was a heavy ball pein hammer with a loop of leather through the handle. As she picked it up, she noticed that it left a perfect outline in the dust. She went back to the bathroom and compared the size of the hammer's ball to the end of the water outlet; they were almost exactly the same.

If she could find a way to have the doors and windows locked from the inside, it would serve to reinforce in the mind of any investigator that Pell's death really was an accident. Though just how to achieve this also eluded her. She sat and thought, channelling her creativity, and slowly an idea came to her. She looked around the house, all the doors and windows had locks and bolts. She went to the front door and studied the lock. Then she went into the kitchen and looked through the drawers. She found what she hoped was there and took it. Removing an item was slightly risky, but she doubted very much that Pell would need this particular item when he got home on Sunday night.

Now to play the waiting game again.

At three o'clock on Sunday afternoon, she took off her outer clothes, put them in her bag, donned her camo overall, then, after checking that everything was exactly as she found it, picked up the hammer and went outside. She locked the door with a pick and went to the ditch. More waiting.

At eleven thirty that evening, a car pulled up outside the house and Major Pell got out. He grabbed his bags and went inside, within a couple of minutes, the light went on in the bathroom, then off and the light came on in the bedroom. Ten minutes later that went out. Astrid set her alarm and settled down to sleep.

At four-thirty, Monday morning, the alarm beeped; she immediately woke up and stopped it. She ran through her plan in her mind half a dozen times. She would not have much time, she needed to be entering the house no earlier than five-thirty-five, she would then have only ten minutes to find him and carry out her mission. At five-fifteen, she ran to the front door of the house, she removed her boots and camo overalls and put on the forensic suit. At five-thirty, she saw the bathroom light come on. She checked her watch and counted down the minutes. At exactly five-thirty-six, she slipped the lock picks into the keyhole and opened the door. She picked up the hammer and went inside. She went upstairs, being careful to not tread on steps three, five and eight.

She reached the bathroom door, it was open a fraction, she could see his silhouette through the shower curtain and waited for him to turn so that his back would be towards her. She slipped the leather loop of the hammer over her hand to stop it from falling if she lost her grip. He turned so his back was to her and she made her move. She moved quickly into the room and yanked back the curtain. Startled, he turned around and she swung the hammer at him. He ducked away in a reflex move, but he was not quick enough; she hit him hard just above his right temple. She heard the crunch of his skull as it shattered from the blow. He collapsed unconscious. She put the plug into the bath, then pressed the button to switch off the shower and redirected the water which now flowed through the tap's spout, then took a bath flannel and wiped blood from his wound and smeared it on the water outlet. She put the flannel on the back of his head and pressed down with the palm of her hand so as to not leave any finger marks. In seconds, the water level was above his mouth and nose. She held his head under the water for five minutes, then felt his neck for a pulse. There wasn't one.

She wiped down some small flecks of blood from the wall then wiped the blood off the hammer and dropped the flannel into the water along with a bar of soap, then pulled down the shower curtain. Leaving the water running, she picked up the hammer, went downstairs to the shed and put it back in the dust outline, but it was now clean. She found a sack on the floor and shook it above the bench, a large cloud of dust billowed out and immediately settled on all the tools. Satisfied that there was no way of telling that she had been there, she grabbed her bag, went outside, changed back into her camo overalls and after a few attempts, managed to lock the door the way she had planned. It was five-fifty.

At ten-thirty on Monday morning, Major Pell was officially recorded as absent without leave. Less than an hour later, three squads of armed military police arrived at his house. A police Captain got out of his car, he looked up at the bathroom light that was still on; he dialled Pell's number and waited. No reply. He nodded to the sergeant in charge of the squads, who in turn, gestured for his men to encircle the building.

The Captain banged on the door. "Come out Pell," he shouted. "We know you're in there; you're surrounded, so don't try anything stupid."

No reply.

He called out again to Pell. Again, no reply.

The Captain turned to the sergeant. "Use the knocker."

The sergeant called a team up to the door, one man had a sledgehammer, the others wore body armour and helmets with visors that covered their faces; they had their weapons drawn and cocked, and with their safety catches off. Two hammer blows broke the lock; the man wielding the hammer stood back as his colleagues burst in through the door, shouting and yelling at the tops of their voices. They fanned out into the downstairs rooms but stopped short when they saw the water flowing down the stairs and the collapsed ceiling in the back room.

The Captain entered and immediately realised the danger they were all in. "Find the mains power supply and turn it off. Find the water stop cock and turn that off."

That done, he sent teams upstairs. Within seconds a voice called out from the bathroom. "Sir, up here."

The Captain and sergeant entered the room to see Pell's body floating face-down in the overflowing bath. "Stand your men down and call an ambulance."

Two days later, the Captain handed his preliminary report to Pell's commanding officer. He sat while the commander read the conclusion.

All indications are that Major Pell was about to take a bath, when he slipped on a bar of soap and fell, banging his head of the outlet spout of the mixer tap. It appears that he tried to grasp the shower curtain, but this broke away, turning his body as he fell, leading to the impact with the side of his head. The injury to his head matches the shape of the tap's spout. The medical examiner has ascertained that this rendered him unconscious, and he drowned as the water level rose.

The door was locked from the inside with a key. The key was still in the lock, but the bolts top and bottom were still drawn back. A check for forced entry elsewhere in the building was made and nothing was found. All the other doors and windows were locked with a key and further secured with bolts.

Given all of the evidence, I therefore deduce that this can be nothing more than a tragic accident.

“Thank you Captain. This is very sad; he was a good officer and would have gone far.” The commander handed the report back. “You are going to see his family now?”

“Yes sir.”

“Please give my condolences to his wife.”

The Captain felt a twinge of emotion. Under Correlan law, families of military personnel whose deaths occurred outside of combat are not informed until the reason for their death is established. It had been two days and there was never an easy way to tell somebody that a loved-one had died. He remembered the look of realisation and horror that he always got when relatives answered the door to him.

<<<◇>>>

“But he was not on combat duties,” she cried. He then had the onerous task of telling her about the accident. After her crying had stopped, she looked up at him. “I was prepared for his death in combat, but not this, what do I tell my children…” she stopped short and put her hand to her mouth and shut her eyes. “…his children, our children.”

The Captain felt a lump in his throat, he had children and wondered how he would cope if his wife died in an accident. A six-year-old boy entered the room, he was carrying a plastic model of a tank painted with the colours of Pell’s regiment.

“Is daddy going to be away for a long time, this time mummy?”

She swallowed hard and held the child tight. “Yes, daddy is going to be away for a very long time.”

“When will he be back?”

“I don’t know.”

“Can I play outside now?”

“Yes but be careful.”

The boy ran outside, dropped to the ground, and made engine noises as he pushed the toy through the grass.

The Captain could deal with the emotions of adults, he’d seen far too much in his time, but the innocence of children always got to him. Watching this child’s bliss-filled ignorance, coupled with the knowledge that the child would slowly realise that he would never see his father again, was hard to witness.

“How am I going to cope? I have three children and no job. What am I going to do? We have debts, bills to pay, we had no insurance. What am I going to do for money?” Desperation rose in her as the realisation fully sunk in.

The Correlan state provided precious little for the families of servicemen who died in combat, as it was considered that this was just an occupational hazard. The army would continue to pay half the wages to families of servicemen that died accidentally, but there were a couple of good charities that offered help. He placed their cards in her hand, said goodbye and left her to her grief. As he left, she looked up at him.

“Why was he having a bath? he never had baths, he hated them, he couldn’t understand why people would want to sit in their own dirt. He only ever showered.”

“We will never know that. I’m sorry.”

He added a note of her comment in the preliminary report but left it out of the final draft, he considered it irrelevant.

Dantu

The war had not penetrated far into Correla and people were relatively free to move around the country. Only near the south-west border with Arralan were there restrictions. Astrid made her way back to the abandoned industrial buildings that she had prepared before the Pell mission. The weather had turned over the past couple of days and was much cooler. She took some fresh clothes from a bag she had hidden there, changed into them then dropped all her old clothes and boots through the access hatch of a disused underground oil storage tank.

She was now wearing a thick check shirt and body warmer, tough trousers and stout walking boots. She pulled on the backpack, put on a bobble-hat, extended a walking pole, and strode out of the building looking every bit the committed walker.

Solo hiking through the countryside was a popular pastime for Correlan women her age; it was a good way to keep fit and was preferable to going to a gym and suffering the tedium of the constant male gaze and judgement. Long walks were common, and some women took all their holiday entitlement in one, spending as much time as they could in the beautiful Correlan countryside.

She headed out south east towards the hinterland, it would be a long hike that could take her over two weeks. She had enough Correlan Dhat to allow her to stay in the hostels that dotted the route, and when these were not available, she could sleep in the one-man tent that she was carrying in her backpack. It was not too cold at night and she'd done it many times before. She had money and excellently forged Correlan identity papers. These, coupled with her fluent use of the language and her command of regional dialects, should be all she needed when encountering people.

The first four days were easy, she managed to get good rest at the hostels along the way and she made good progress as a result, averaging fifty kilometres a day. She bought some food at a farm shop and noticed that there wasn't an over-abundance on offer. The shop was run by the farmer's wife, who complained that there were no young people going into farming any more. She grumbled that they were either being drafted into the Army or moving to the cities to work. She doubted that her farm would still be around in ten years' from now.

Astrid met a few people along the way, mainly women like her on a walking holiday. She chatted with them for a while until their paths diverged and she waved goodbye to her erstwhile friends.

Day five. At midday it grew cold and started to rain; torrential rain that saturated her clothes. The storm-proof jacket that she had bought in a hiking shop was not very good; it kept the rain out, but all it seemed to do was keep her sweat in and she ended up just as wet. She checked her map and saw that the next hostel was almost thirty kilometres away and the rain was making her progress slow; she would have to pick up the pace if she was to make it before darkness. The wind was blowing hard now, driving the rain at her, but it was from behind and helped just a little.

The ground started to undulate; she was in the rise of the range of hills that reached down to the border. The road was now just a track, and she knew that it would end at the hostel. Tomorrow she would be in rough stony ground with rocks covered in slippery moss. It would be hard going from then on.

She reached the hostel just as the light started to fade. She was exhausted, hungry, and soaked through. The manager of the hostel, a petite woman in her late fifties, offered to take her clothes, wash them and put them in a drier overnight; it was an offer that Astrid gladly accepted. The manager found her a bath robe and took her clothes. Astrid had a shower and washed her hair for the first time in just under two weeks, making her feel a little bit more human again.

Food was self-catering, but the hostel fee covered basic meals and a cupboard had various tins of meat and vegetables along with some bread. She took a small saucepan and opened a can of vegetable soup; the bread roll was a little bit stale, but it didn't matter as the warm food only made her realise just how tired she was. It was late in the season and she was the only person in the hostel apart from the manager. Nothing was going to stop her getting a good night's sleep.

Next morning she awoke early and refreshed, her legs ached from the forced march that she had made herself do, but she had to move on. The manager asked her why she was heading south-east, as there was nothing much to see. Astrid said she was going to visit the village at Dantu, which had been abandoned just ten years ago. And that her intention then was to then head north and back home.

She lied; she would head for Dantu but keep going south-east. Dantu was just on the way.

Astrid thanked the manager for drying the clothes so well, then said goodbye and started out again. The ground here was still wet from the previous day's storm, but the stony nature of the soil meant that it was draining quickly, reducing the risk of her getting bogged down, though she had to pick her way carefully as some of the larger rocks were still slippery. The terrain was rising and falling, gradually at first then steeper as she approached the first hill.

Four hours after she started out, she stopped for a rest and something to eat; there were ten sugar loaded energy bars left in her backpack, she doubted that she would be able to make these last and realised that she would have to find things in the wild to eat. She had a pack of water sterilisation tablets, but they made the water taste bad, and she was concerned as to their efficacy; she would save these for emergencies. A spring babbled out of a hole in a rock, it was quite fast flowing and crystal clear, and there was no evidence of mineral deposits building up around the outflow, so it was possibly safe to drink. She cupped some in her hand and tipped it in her mouth. She held it between her teeth and bottom lip and waited for a few minutes. There was no tingling, and no unpleasant taste; she swallowed and waited, after an hour she had no indications that the water was bad, so she drank some more, then filled up a canteen and set off again.

She had covered more ground that she expected over the two days since leaving the hostel and felt her stomach rumble as she pitched her tent in the lee of a large rock. She was completely alone, save for some small animals that she heard scrubbing about in the undergrowth. She took a loop of wire from her bag and set it across a small track in the grass a little way off. She made a circle of rocks and picked up dried leaves and twigs, placed them in the circle then found some larger branches, snapped them into shorter lengths and formed a pyramid out of them above the twigs. There was a rustling sound then the sound of an animal panicking. A rabbit was caught in her snare, she grabbed it and wrung its neck, killing it.

She took a wad of shredded wood from a plastic bag, then scraped her knife along a fire stick, shooting sparks onto the wood shavings. The wad caught fire quickly and she skinned and gutted the rabbit while the flames spread to the larger pieces of wood. Minutes later the rabbit was hanging from a stick close to the flames. She had picked some wild dandelions, the leaves would be bitter at this time of year, but still nutritious. The rabbit was okay, she didn't eat it all, and what she didn't eat, she cut into thin strips and laid them out on one of the hot rocks to dry. In no time at all she had rabbit jerky. She got into her sleeping bag, zipped up the front of her tent and slept.

She woke at first light; the sun's rays streaming in through the thin nylon of the tent, dazzling her. It had been an uncomfortable night's sleep and her legs were stiff. She checked her map, Dantu was about five kilometres away.

"Onwards," she said to herself and she chewed a piece of dried rabbit for breakfast and set off.

She crested a hill and could see Dantu in the distance, a tiny village with a farm and seven or eight houses; she stopped to survey the vista. The entire village had been a home to a sheep farming family along with their workers and had been abandoned a decade ago when the farmer died. It was far too remote for anyone to take up farming here; there was just one rough track leading to the farm, and now the costs of raising a flock of sheep was greater than they could fetch at market. She would need to pass through the village; she might even stay there overnight. She'd make that decision when she got there as she set off down the hill.

She was about five hundred metres outside of the village when she noticed a bad odour in the air, it was faint, but she recognised it. It was the smell of death. She had smelled it too many times before on the battlefield, it was Cadaverine, a smell you never forget. It triggered a disgust reflex in her, it was her body's defence mechanism telling her to stay away, and the smell was getting stronger as she got closer.

As she entered the village, she noticed tyre tracks, tracks from a double axle vehicle, they were almost weathered away, but still visible. There had been no rain here for a couple of weeks until the storm a couple of days back, so a vehicle had to have been here within the last two weeks. The tyre tracks stopped outside a barn, then it appeared that the vehicle had reversed out and driven away. The smell was overpowering and seemed to be coming from within the barn.

The grass leading up to the barn door was trampled flat, clearly by a lot of feet. She hoped they were animal feet, but a sinking feeling in her stomach told her otherwise. With uncharacteristic trepidation, she walked to the barn door and opened it. She recoiled at the overpowering stench that hit her and turned away unable to stop herself from vomiting.

Inside the barn there were the bloated bodies of dead humans, adults and children. She grabbed a cloth from her bag and held it over her mouth and nose. Retching, and fighting her revulsion, she forced herself to go in, the rag only taking away part of the smell. Swarms of flies filled the air and flew around her, some occasionally settling on her face. Despite every fibre in her body telling her to get out of this ghastly place, she felt compelled to examine the bodies. From the clothing she could see that the adults were all female, the children were male and female and from their height could have ranged from six to sixteen. One woman's hand was still clutching a piece of paper, it was a travel permit that was issued by the Correlans to those Arralan citizens that wanted to leave the country.

"They thought they were going home," she said, shaking her head in sorrow.

During her time as a nurse she had taken a course in pathology, that had taught her that bloated bodies with red skin meant they had all died eight to ten days ago. There were holes in the wall on the far side of the barn. They had been machine gunned. All had been shot in the chest; but some had not died immediately, and had made a futile effort to crawl away, only to die a slow death. She counted the bodies; there were forty-nine. As she turned to leave, she saw a mark on the back of the door that had been recently carved with a knife. It was a triangle with the letters S, O, G.

Astrid stepped outside to catch a breath of air that was only marginally less foul. She walked around the back of the barn and hidden from sight she found a large patch of soil with nothing growing in it and it was clear that the soil had been recently disturbed. On the far side of the plot was a digger, obviously old, but its track marks were clearly visible on the ground. She walked over to it and noticed that one of the hydraulic hoses was new. There was fresh dirt on the bulldozer blade. She closed her eyes as she realised the significance.

"There are more bodies, this is a mass grave," she whispered. "Who could do this?"

Going Home

Dark clouds were rolling in from the North and the wind grew chilly. Some of the houses near the farm would have provided shelter for the night, and she might even be able to start a fire. But staying in Dantu was out of the question now. There was nothing more she could do here and had to leave. Heading out south east again, she estimated that she could cover fifteen kilometres before needing to pitch her tent and maybe by then her appetite may have returned, she hadn't eaten anything since breakfast and could not face eating anything now.

She had seen dead bodies before, in or after combat on the battlefield. She had been to places where bodies had lain for days, weeks even, some of them her enemies, some of them her comrades. She had killed people with machine guns, explosives, and knives; death was no stranger to her, but that was war, where each side knew what awaited them. These people were civilians, duped into thinking they were travelling back to Arralan.

As she walked, her mind kept drifting back to the gradual realisation that the women must have felt as they grasped the fact that they were not heading to the border, then trying to reassure the children without their anxiety showing, and the sheer terror that they must have felt facing the machine guns in the barn.

Rain started, light at first, then heavier. The wind shifted and strengthened, blowing the rain into her face. She put her head down and struggled on, relying more and more on the walking pole for balance. But at least the wind was blowing the smell of rotting flesh away.

It was dark by the time she had pitched her tent, and although even the thought of eating was making her feel nauseous, she knew she was getting weak and must have something to eat. She could not bring herself to kill another rabbit and ate one of the energy bars instead. She got into her sleeping bag and zipped up the tent but after only a couple minutes the humid air inside brought out the stench of death that was still lingering in her clothes.

Her sleep was fitful and uncomfortable, she woke every half-hour, either from the uneven, rocky ground that made it impossible to lay flat, or from the rain that lashed against her tent, or from the images of the dead that haunted her dreams. She was awake to witness the first light breaking over the hills and tried to ignore the headache developing over her eyes. Wearily, she packed her sleeping bag and tent and trudged off into the desolate landscape.

Four arduous days and nights later; cold days and nights of torrential rain and gales, exhausted, hungry, and dehydrated, she crossed into Arralan territory. She had put up with four days of wearing wet clothes and four nights of getting into a damp sleeping bag. Four days of not eating enough and only drinking the water she could collect in the folds of her tent. The cough had started after two days and she was starting to shiver; she knew that this was not just from the cold.

She had been walking along a metaled road for about two hours when she saw a vehicle approach. It was an armoured Arralan army patrol car. It stopped, soldiers got out, and trained their weapons on her.

"Remove your back-pack very slowly, then place your hands on your head and kneel on the ground, or we will open fire," shouted a sergeant. She did as she was told, and he approached her, keeping his firearm aimed at her. "Who are you?" he demanded.

"Captain Astrid Peterman of the Arralan army under Major DeSalva." His posture relaxed very slightly. "Stand up and keep your hands where I can see them."

She stood, and he took a small camera from his pocket and took a picture of her face. "Wait there and don't move your hands."

He went back to the vehicle and plugged a cable into the camera. Five minutes later he received a confirmation of her identity and returned to her with his weapon holstered.

"Captain Peterman, welcome home. This way please." He picked up her backpack and led her to the vehicle. They continued their patrol before driving her back to the Arralan base. Though she was desperate for a shower and something wholesome to eat, she was pleased to just be sitting comfortably for the first time in weeks. She started coughing violently, hacking up phlegm, the sergeant handed her a cloth which she held over her mouth. One of the soldiers gave her a bottle of water, another gave her a chocolate bar, both of which she eagerly consumed, ignoring the pain in her throat.

"Sorry about all that back there, ma'am," said the sergeant, now fully aware that she was a senior officer. "We have had the odd incursion in the past couple of years, so we do have to check."

“I understand sergeant,” she wheezed, “anything less and I would have been suspicious.” She coughed a few times, then smiled. “And then I would have had to kill you all.” The soldiers all turned and looked at her doubtfully, she grinned and nodded.

“Yeah.” Within a few seconds she had fallen asleep.

DeSalva

"My report on the Pell mission sir, it contains a very disturbing part." Astrid coughed as she handed a file to DeSalva. He took it and scanned through the documents, noticing that she was trying to not let him see that she was rubbing her chest.

"Thank you, I shall read this later. You said that there is a disturbing element in the report, what is it?"

"There has been a war crime, sir." Her breath was short, and she looked drawn. Darkness under her eyes told of fatigue.

He sat up straight. "What!"

"A massacre of civilians, and recently, sir. Arralan civilians."

"How many and where?" he said with urgency in his voice.

Astrid swallowed hard and couldn't avoid wincing at the pain in her neck. "Forty-nine women and children…" The memory of the barn caught the words in her throat, and she struggled to keep from getting emotional "…at Dantu sir."

He gasped, then composed himself, and thought for a moment.

"They had travel papers sir; they must have thought they were being taken to the border."

"Dantu." He rubbed his forehead, trying not to let the shock affect his thoughts. "That makes a sort of sense. There nothing around for kilometres in any direction, the nearest conurbation must be at least twenty-five kilometres away. No-one to see anything; and even Correlan citizens would baulk at massacres." He started making some notes. "Forty-nine, you say."

"I counted forty-nine bodies, but sir, there is what appears to be a mass grave there as well." She was aware that she was shaking slightly and didn't know if this was emotion or illness. "It's all in the report sir, but there is one more thing. The bodies I counted were in a barn, and on the wall, there was a triangle with the letters S O G carved into it."

"That's the emblem of the special operations group. It's a small unit that was formed by General Nillzen just over a year ago, he's a two-star general and we don't know that much about him. The SOG were supposed to be trained to work in any of the Correlan army groups. So, if, say, an artillery unit was short on men they could go in and be familiar with procedures, and so on."

DeSalva looked worried. "Mass murder is…" He checked himself "…was, not their remit. I'll task the analysts to get more information on the SOG."

"What do you want me to do sir?"

"Well first, you are obviously ill, so I want you to get to the hospital and get yourself sorted out. The squad that picked you up said you were dehydrated and that you looked like you had 'flu."

"It is just a cough sir, it's nothing," her voice descended into a wheeze as she spoke.

"Peterman, you look dreadful, so get to the hospital—that's an order, and tell the doctors that I want a full medical report on you, plus I want a psychological report. Then I want you to have a week's leave for rest and recuperation and when you come back, I want you to have some more advanced training with special forces to get you back to peak fitness."

"Is there a mission for me sir?"

"We don't have a mission planned for you just yet, but I suspect that this SOG business will throw up something. Dismissed."

Astrid saluted and left. The doctors diagnosed acute bronchitis and ordered her to stay in her quarters until her cough subsided. Within hours of the hospital visit, her condition deteriorated. The week's rest and recuperation stretched into a month, the first week was spent in bed, too weak to do anything other than cough up grey-green mucus. She felt cold, and shivered constantly, but sweated so much that she had to get out of bed to change her clothes three or four times a day.

Analgesics helped regulate her temperature and ease some of the symptoms but did not bring her hunger back. She knew she had to eat to be strong enough to fight the infection, but eating made her feel sick, and tore at her throat which was already raw from the bronchitis and constant coughing. She forced herself to swallow some multivitamins and drank hot honey and lemon, and at least she could keep that down.

DeSalva visited her during the second week and was shocked by her appearance, the fever had passed but had taken a huge toll. She sat in a dressing gown; her hair, unwashed for days, was matted and unkempt from her sweat. Her skin was pale and her cheeks hollow; her eyes seemed to have sunk into their sockets with dark rings surrounding them. Occasionally she would breathe through an atomiser, wheezing with every breath. She struggled to concentrate when he spoke.

"The doctors say that you will get over this and make a full recovery, but it will take time."

"What about the missions, sir?" she asked breathlessly, unable to stop the weariness in her voice, and panting before taking another breath through the atomiser.

"We are gathering information on Nillzen and the SOG, but have no assignments planned. We have to be careful; you have hit a lot in the past two years, and as yet they have all been recorded as accidents, which is the objective. If we hit too many then the Correlans might start to get suspicious and do proper investigations."

"I want to get back out in the field sir, I can't stand being cooped up in here."

"Out of the question."

"Can't I at least do some paperwork sir?"

"Peterman," he said, in a friendly but firm way. "Even you must accept that you will be in no fit state for anything for quite some time. Fortunately, the doctors say that the risk of you developing pneumonia has passed."

"I will let you know when I'm ready for duty sir." Her voice trailed off into a coughing fit.

"No. I will check with the doctors and they will tell me when you are ready for active service again. Now, nurses will be coming in to check on you every day…"

"That's really not necessary sir."

"…nurses will be coming in to check on you every day. And it is necessary; you were a nurse, accept their help and let them do their job."

She looked at him with an air of resignation.

"Don't make me order you," he said, smiling.

She smiled back, weakly. "You are right sir."

"Just this small amount of interaction has exhausted you. Now, go back to bed. I will let myself out."

"Thank you, sir." She struggled to her feet and went to her bedroom as he left.

Five weeks after crossing the border, Astrid finally reported for duty. Her wheeze had not quite left her, so she was assigned office duties, liaising with communications corps and channelling information on Nillzen through to the intelligence analysts. Three weeks later she was finally clear and fit to start training with special forces.

Nillzen

"This is what we have on Salazar Nillzen so far." DeSalva opened a document file. "He's a two-star general, and overdue for promotion to three-star, and we think we know why his promotion has been held up. More on that later."

Astrid took the pictures of Nillzen and selected a close-up of his face, studied it for a few moments, then turned back to listen to DeSalva. He selected a photograph of a stately home. "Nillzen comes from an extremely wealthy family, this is his residence. His father was a billionaire and a fanatical supporter of Hallenberg, and pretty much financed his rise to power. Because of that he was allowed to keep the family home and all of his money after the deposition of the monarchy. All other large houses were seized by the central planning committee; assets were stripped, and family wealth subsumed into the Correlan central bank. Vast amounts of money became available to Hallenberg, and this enabled him to build up his military."

"What happened to the other families sir?"

"Most were reduced to poverty; all their income was from tenant farmers on land that they owned. With their land taken by the government they had no means of making money. Some even ended up working on the farms that they used to own!"

DeSalva opened a file and produced a picture of a young Nillzen in military uniform. "After his father's death, Salazar joined the military at the rank of Major."

"Joined at the rank of Major sir?" Astrid was puzzled.

"Yes. When the progeny of wealthy Correlan families join the military, it is assumed that because they are rich, they are automatically excellent soldiers with no need for any formal training. The resulting incompetence of the officers is one of the main reasons why the Correlan army is so poor. Salazar Nillzen is different though, he requested basic training and wrote to the army council, suggesting that everyone joining the military should go through the same basic training and that there should be no exceptions."

"That hasn't happened though, has it sir."

"No, not yet. The letter did not go down well with the army council and was only tolerated because of the connection to Hallenberg. There are still families that cling to the notion that because they were once rich they are still somehow superior, and their sons still join at the rank of Major. But the stock is dwindling."

"What about the daughters, there are females in the Correlan military, how many are from these families sir?"

"Not many, daughters are not supposed to join the military; it's seen as not the proper thing for them to do. Daughters are supposed to marry officers and have boys who will then join the military. For those females that do join, the rules are different—as you might expect in Correla. All females go through basic training, regardless of background, but few ever rise above the rank of Major. I think it would be incredible if a woman was ever to become a general in their army."

"You said once before sir, that the SOG was formed by Nillzen."

"I told you that when you were ill, you remembered it—remarkable."

"It's just about the only thing do I remember sir. But my question is: how a two-star general was allowed to form a unit, I thought only the army council could do that."

"It seems that it's to do with the family link to the grand field marshal, we think that the army council are indulging him to a certain extent because of that connection. The unit is very small at the moment, only around thirty men, and it seems that the army council does not consider this to be of any significance in their overall running of the army. After all, they lose more men than that with every engagement."

"Where is their base sir."

"They move around the country a lot, so they don't have a base as such, but they frequently stay at an outpost of the Balssen camp."

"I've been to Balssen sir, it's a rough town, the troopers cause a lot of trouble."

"I went there before the war, and yes, it is rough."

DeSalva pulled out a map. "This is Balssen, and here…" he pointed to an aerial photograph, "…is Nillzen's stately home. He has an office there and seems to run the unit remotely. It's about twenty kilometres outside of the town." He rubbed his chin thoughtfully. "Nillzen is a professional soldier and known to have a strong moral compass. From what we have discovered, it seems highly unlikely that he would have ordered a massacre."

"Sir, I don't understand why these people were killed, when so many others have been allowed to leave Correla."

"Perhaps they couldn't pay and had no assets."

"Pay, sir?"

"In order for an Arralan citizen to be allowed to leave, they have to buy an extremely expensive permit and sign over all their property and assets to the Correlan government. The Correlans have made untold millions that way."

"Sir, perhaps there were those who couldn't pay, and the government decided to deport them rather than set up internment camps, then someone else had the idea of eliminating them instead," mused Astrid, trying to remain professional and not let the implication of what she just said to cloud her thoughts.

"That's possible, but whoever did that would have had to have a lot of guts; as brutal as the Correlans are they've never killed civilians like this before, and the army hierarchy takes a very dim view of actions against civilians; the Army Council would have come down very hard on them. But whatever the reason, we need to find out. It's an escalation that is worrying."

DeSalva closed the file and handed it to Astrid. "Obviously Nillzen is your next target. It is no secret that the army council does not like the idea of small specialist units, they are still stuck in the mass attack theory of war, with huge regiments and centralised control. We have very strong indications that the SOG will be disbanded once Nillzen is removed. Study his file and come up with a plan. As ever, it needs to look like an accident."

She took the file. "How much time have I got sir?"

"The sooner the better, but this is not urgent he is still a two-star general and won't have the authority to expand and solidify the SOG into a regular unit until he is a three-star general. Promotion is being held up for all of the reasons I have stated. We estimate six to nine months before that happens."

"That is still plenty of time for the SOG to carry out atrocities against our people, sir."

"We believe that there are no more Arralan citizens left in Correla. So take your time to make your plans. As he is a two-star general, he will have extra security so this one will be a bit more of a challenge than previous missions."

Planning the Nillzen Mission

Astrid sat in her quarters surrounded by documents; it was all the information that she had been able to gather on Salazar Nillzen. Pinned to a large cork board on the wall were photographs and a print-out of the intelligence analysis. On another wall was the original plan of Nillzen's stately home, the grounds and all the buildings on the land. The layouts of every room on all floors were shown in great detail. Next to this plan was the architects' drawing of recent alterations to some of the rooms and out-buildings. Obtaining this had been an impressive piece of espionage, intelligence had discovered the name of the architect and had hacked his computer.

She studied the room on the first floor marked 'Nillzen Office'. The plans for this room were particularly detailed and annotated. One element caught her eye; it showed a box on the wall with the words 'Headquarters Hotline'. On another plan there was a drawing of the refurbished gatehouse, on that there was a box that said, 'Incoming telephone lines' there were five in all, and one was labelled 'Headquarters hotline incomer'. She focussed on this; it would be a critical part of the plan that was forming in her mind.

As Astrid sat examining the plans of Nillzen's stately home, she subconsciously rolled her fingers over the tape she had put on her desk to protect the exposed wood. As she ran her fingers back and forth, she twisted up the edge of one piece until it came off and fell on the floor. Small strands of glue clung to her fingertips. Deep in thought, she rubbed them together and only succeeded in spreading the glue instead of removing it. She wasn't aware that she was doing this until she picked up a cup and felt her fingers sticking to it. She examined the damage to the desk and pulled off some remaining bits of tape.

"Well that didn't work, did it?" she said to herself, a little cross that she was still not able to stop her habit of picking at the wood and damaging it while she was concentrating on something else.

She refocussed herself and went back to her planning. Beside Nillzen's office was a room marked, 'Aide / Secretary Office'. Comparing the original plan with the new plans she noticed that a connecting door had been installed between the two offices, meaning that there was free movement between the two without having to go out into the corridor. There was a grand central staircase leading from the imposing foyer to the first floor, but she wouldn't be able to use this as it was far too open. Instead she could use the service stairs that led from the kitchen. This had an unobtrusive door not far from Nillzen's office. She would need to get into the kitchen.

On a table were a few glossy lifestyle magazines from Correla. After Hallenberg came to power, he initiated his 'Equalisation program' under which, vast amounts of property and wealth were seized and absorbed into the government. Some of this money, as promised, was fed back to the working class but only a tiny fraction, just enough to lower taxes and keep the people in his power base quiet.

But despite this, there was still an obvious fascination in the public's imagination for information about the few upper-class families left in the country. As the Nillzen family was still viewed by many as the richest in the country, the magazines that she had purchased contained lengthy articles about Nillzen's annual family gatherings. There were many photographs, along with somewhat excessive details about the evening's proceedings. One article compared the events with family gatherings previous in previous years, and Astrid noticed that the cocktail waitresses in the photographs were similar in every year. Each girl looked the same and was dressed the same way year after year. So it was likely that a catering agency supplied the staff, the appearance of which was dictated by Nillzen or one of his staff. In this case it was most likely that the same agency would be used for all the engagements.

The staff needed to be skilled and used to working discretely, and they would be drawn on a job-by-job basis from various restaurants around Balssen, as there was not enough work to have permanent staff. A bit of research showed her that there was only one catering agency that provided this level of service in the area.

DeSalva looked up from the plan and frowned with incredulity. "You want to get a job at a restaurant in Balssen?"

"Yes sir. Once a year Nillzen has a family gathering and a catering agency uses waitresses from the surrounding area. I can use this to gain access to the property."

"How can you be sure of getting a job?"

"Sir, I have discovered that restaurants in Balssen all have a very high staff turnover rate, so I don't expect it to be a problem."

DeSalva flicked through her plan, and studied one page, frowning slightly. "The items you have requested are highly unusual."

"I will need to be in disguise for quite some time before the event sir, and afterwards."

He read some more, raising his eyebrows as he went. "Bold, even by your standards," said DeSalva as he finished reading Astrid's plan.

"I have studied his movements, sir, and this is the only way. The annual parties are family only events with no colleagues from the army present. His personal security guards are always given the night off, and there are no other military personnel other than the two guards at the gatehouse."

"And you want to stay in-country indefinitely? Are you sure you want to be in-country indefinitely? Why?"

"Yes sir I do. After the mission I will need time so I that can find out who gave the order to murder the civilians."

"That is not the mission," said DeSalva firmly.

"But we must find out sir, if they can order the massacre of civilians, then who knows what else they may do?"

"If you are caught, we would not be able to rescue you."

"I know sir."

"You are a valuable asset, it's too risky."

"Sir, with the plan I have chosen, I believe that the longer I stay, the less likely I am to be caught. Sir, with the Nillzen—Hallenberg connection, if they realise that it is not an accident, they will focus their efforts on finding someone trying to flee the country. Not someone staying put."

"You can't let your desire for revenge cloud your judgement, you could make mistakes," he said with a hint of concern.

"It's not for revenge sir. You read my report, they didn't die quickly, they suffered, and justice is required. We know that the SOG carried it out, but sir, we have to find out who gave the order. It's a dangerous escalation, you acknowledged that yourself sir."

DeSalva listened, heard the passion in her voice, and understood her desire. He pulled the psychiatric report that was carried out when she arrived back from the Pell mission. She had not been allowed to see the report and was unaware of its contents.

'Captain Peterman will seek to uncover the Dantu perpetrators' identities and eliminate them. But this will not be out of a desire for revenge. Peterman's sense of justice is strong, and this will be her driving force. Failure to discover the identities of the person or persons who ordered the killings may have a negative impact on her future performance'.

DeSalva closed the file and was unwilling to share its conclusion with her. He held up her plan. "Give me one really good reason why I should approve this."

"I can think of at least forty-nine really good reasons sir."

DeSalva thought for a moment, then signed his name in the 'Approved' box.

Optician

"Tell me the smallest print you can read," said the optician.

Astrid read the bottom line on the chart on the wall opposite. "The bottom row is: K J O Q I Z X B T."

"Very good," he said as he moved the opaque disc from her left eye to her right. "And now with the other eye."

"K J O Q I Z X B T"

"Very good." He removed the opaque disc and dropped lenses into the frame. "Now tell me the smallest print that can you read with both eyes."

Astrid concentrated hard on the chart. "I can only read the second line: A M."

"Good." The optician made a note of the lens, then picked up another set of lenses and added them into to frame. He changed the chart to stop her from just remembering the letters. "What can you read now?"

She concentrated hard, trying to cut through the fuzzy image. "The bottom line is Z something H P B something, M N something."

The optician rotated the new lenses a few degrees and the image snapped into sharp focus. "Now what can you read?"

"Z X H P B Q M N I"

"Excellent." He made a note of the second set of lenses. "What colour do you want the contact lenses?"

"Grey/Green, something dull."

"And what frame do you want for your glasses?"

Astrid held out an unstylish empty glasses frame, a cheap frame that was only available in Correla and had signs of wear. "Can you put a light tint on the top half of the lenses please, and a couple of scratches."

"Of course." The optician took the frame. "They'll be ready for you in three days' time."

"Thank you." Astrid shook the optician's hand and left.

Three days later Astrid collected the contact lenses and glasses. Back in her quarters, she put the contacts in her eyes and instantly her vision blurred. She had never worn contact lenses before, and her eyes started to stream within seconds. She dabbed them dry with a tissue then fumbled for her phone, flipped the camera to face towards her and took a picture of her eyes. Then she took the glasses from her pocket and put them on. Her eyesight returned to normal, and she took another picture.

Nobody wears contact lenses and glasses at the same time, so anyone noticing the apparent colour of her eyes would think that the dull Grey/Green was her natural colour and not the medium Hazel that they really were. The tint that graduated down from the top of the lenses served to obscure the fact that her pupils would not dilate in lower light conditions.

She quickly realised that in order for her vision to remain sharp, the glasses had to be in exactly the right position in respect to the contact lenses. She took them off and bent the arms to hold the frame tight and provided she didn't have any sudden movements of her head she should be able to maintain her visual acuity. Slow movements are what she had planned for her character and she didn't anticipate too many problems.

She removed the glasses and took out the contact lenses, placing them carefully in a sterile box, then put drops in her eyes and blinked heavily. She pressed playback on her phone and scrolled through to the pictures she had taken moments before. The contacts were very good and only the lack of pupil dilation and contraction would indicate that the irises were unnatural, though the image of the glasses showed that they did hide this to a certain extent, and as her character was to be a little shy no-one was likely to get close enough to see.

Satisfied that these would be adequate, she opened another container of contact lenses and took two out. They were clear and had no corrective form and where simply for her to get used to wearing contact lenses. Within seconds her eyes had started to stream again. She had been told to expect this, but that it would pass after a while, and she resigned herself to a few days of bloodshot eyes and constantly dabbing away tears.

Next was the footwear; she had selected a pair of old, well-worn, plain black lace up shoes, ones that she had always meant to throw out but found herself hanging on to because they were comfortable to wear for long periods. They were flat and had a shallow heel. She took a cork tile off the wall put the heel of the right down on it, marked the outline, then took some stout scissors and cut it out, cutting a few millimetres inside the line. She slipped it into the shoe and tried on both.

Standing up, she found that even though the cork added less than five millimetres under her right heel, it made her stance awkward. When she walked it affected her stride, making her wobble to the left slightly, and required her to consciously correct her gait with every step. She removed the cork and pared down the edge with a knife so as not to get a blister on her sole and replaced the cork.

She dressed herself; thick light brown tights, a grey knee length pleated skirt, a light blue blouse with a twee lace collar and finished off with a grey baggy cardigan that she had washed until it lost its shape. Now the wig. She had contacted a friend from her theatre days and described what she wanted. She didn't tell them why and they didn't ask. A couple of days later it had arrived, a plain, mousey blonde with an unstylish cut.

She put on her clothes, shoes, the wig, then put in the contact lenses and put on the glasses, set her phone on a stand, selected video then tapped the screen. She rounded her shoulders and stooped then stood back little while the recorder ran, stopping it after twenty seconds

She looked at the stack of milk chocolate bars, this was going to be hard. She had suffered with acne as a young teenager, and chocolate always seemed to make it worse. Binging on chocolate for the next couple of days should make it reappear. She had long since weaned herself off chocolate and reluctantly opened a bar and ate it all, feeling sick as she forced the last square down.

"Layered pixie cut please," Astrid said to the army hairdresser. "Like this." She held up a magazine showing a picture of a young woman with a short, stylish modern haircut, and can you bleach it afterwards."

"Okay, I'll do my best," said the young woman as she nervously tried to figure out how to get the look.

Astrid smiled at her in the mirror, aware that what she was asking for was difficult. "It doesn't matter if you can't get it exactly right, it would actually be better if you didn't."

A couple of hours later, Astrid was back in her quarters and tried on the wig. The short haircut made the wig a much better fit now. She removed the wig and ran her fingers through her hair, smoothing it easily back to its own style. The cut wasn't very good and was only an approximation of what she had asked for, but a cheap haircut was exactly what she wanted.

She looked at her face in a mirror, she had eaten four large bars of chocolate over the previous three days and the high fat content was doing its job. Her skin was greasy, and the first spots had started to appear. She picked a few of them and let them bleed; she dabbed them dry and put some cover-up makeup on after a scab had formed. She checked herself again in the mirror, her skin looked awful, and the spots were clearly visible under the makeup.

"Good," she said to herself. "No more chocolate now."

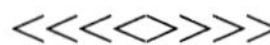

She opened the video on her mobile and handed the phone to DeSalva. He looked at it and raised his eyebrows. He frowned as he watched the awkward woman limping as she walked around the room. "Who is this?" he said as handed the phone back.

"Her name is Eva Munck sir."

DeSalva looked up at Astrid, puzzled. "Eva Munck? what's she got to do with anything?"

"It's me sir, it's my disguise," she said, feeling a tiny bit proud that DeSalva had not recognised her.

"Good grief, you look terrible."

"Thank you, sir."

He put his hands together under his chin and looked at her for a moment.

"Do you really think you can do this?"

She raised the pitch of her voice a few semitones

"I think I can pull it off sir," she answered in the slow, feeble, immature way that she would use when in character.

"Okay, you've convinced me. You go at the end of the week. I will have a flat booked in the name of Eva Munck. It will be in the eastern sector; it's a nondescript part of Balssen with a transient population so you shouldn't draw too much attention."

Back in her quarters, she packed a bag with the items she needed; forged Correlan identity papers, money, a few sets of clothes, makeup and cheap perfume. She went to her knife drawer and selected a Falchion. This was a combat knife like a Machete but shorter and a bit lighter. The principal difference being a Quillon, a crossbar where the handle meets the blade, the function of which serves to stop a bloodied hand from sliding down onto the blade and causing injury to the user during a thrust. It also added a little protection and could be used to block an attackers blade. A small pommel at the end of the grip helped stop the weapon from slipping out of her hand, and also helped her grip when drawing the weapon from its scabbard.

The Falchion blade was a similar shape to a Machete when viewed side on, but it was much thinner, though still had a good weight and was well balanced. She took a whetstone and honed the edge, occasionally checking the sharpness by drawing the edge across her thumbnail, when it was truly sharp it would drag and cut into her nail. Once the edge was sharpened to her satisfaction, she worked on the tip, easing the stone across it. Half an hour of honing took it to a needle-sharp point.

She tried on the scabbard, slipping the straps over her shoulders, and positioning it across her back with the locket just below her left shoulder. She inserted the Falchion and practiced drawing it a few times, and though she hadn't used this particular blade for some time, found she could still draw the weapon into an attack position in one swift move. She had also taken some leather and modified the locket on the scabbard to prevent the blade ringing as it was drawn.

She was ready.

The Mid-Town Grill

The Mid Town Grill was the sixth restaurant that Astrid had visited in the four days that she had been in Balssen, and she finally saw what she was looking for. One of the waitresses was exactly like the cocktail girls at Nillzen's annual party's. She would almost certainly be booked by the agency, and all Astrid had to do was to stop her and take her place. She noticed that there didn't seem to be enough staff on duty and some patrons were complaining that it was taking too long for their meals to be served.

She went to the till to pay for her meal. "Are there any jobs here?" she asked. The waitress looked at her bad glasses and frumpy clothes and sneered slightly. "I'll ask the boss."

A man in his late middle age walked over to her, raised his eyebrows and sighed with obvious disappointment. "You ever worked in a restaurant before?"

"Yes." she lied.

"Okay, you start tomorrow." He turned to the waitress. "Get her a uniform." He turned back to Astrid who beamed inanely. "The shift I'll put you on will be eight 'till four; there's not too much trade then and we'll see how you go. The pay is Two-Hund… err, One Eighty Dhat a week. And provided I don't lose any customers, you can stay."

"Thank you," she squeaked as she took the uniform from the waitress who watched her leave and looked at her as if she was a leper, then turned to the boss and pointed at Astrid. "Her, really?"

"I know I need the staff, but good grief, where do these girls come from? Simple town?" he muttered.

"Maybe if you paid a bit more boss, you never know, you might just get better staff, just a thought," said the waitress.

"Don't start on that again." he grumbled.

"You didn't ask her name."

"What the fuck do I want to know her name for?" he muttered, as he went to his office.

<<<◇>>>

The work was not at all challenging and keeping up the simpleton character was easy. All she really had to do was limp and say sorry all the time, even when there was nothing to say sorry for. She knew that the other girls were laughing at her, sometimes to her face; she just smiled as if their insults hadn't registered. This was exactly what she had planned for.

When the boss put her on an evening shift, the work got a bit harder, lots more customers, many of whom were either drunk when they arrived, or got drunk during the meal. These people would try to confuse her and trip her up with the orders, but she endeared herself to the boss by always remembering what had been ordered by pulling her fingers one by one as she told him, and always added a 'I think that's all' at the end. It had seemed childish to him at first, but he knew that some of the customers were playing with her and was pleased that they never succeeded. After a while he began to feel a little bit sorry for her and reduced the number of times he put her on the evening shift.

The waitress that Astrid kept an eye on was Dana Lubeck. She was tall, blonde, flat chested and pencil thin; Astrid had heard her talking to one of the other girls about being booked for the party soon. She had no doubt now that the catering agency would book Dana to work at Nillzen's party. Astrid had also found out that the booking was always in the form of a letter that would have to be shown to the gatehouse. The party was two weeks away and she needed to intercept that letter before it got to Dana.

She asked to be put on permanent early shifts and offered to take a bit of a pay cut and had been allowed to, as the boss thought some of the customers were being particularly unkind to her. He appreciated her offer of a pay cut but refused and kept her on the same pay.

She always made sure she arrived early for work, before the post was delivered, and tried to catch the mail and hand it to the boss. He assumed that she was either sucking up to him or didn't realise that this was how it looked. She was, in reality, checking the post, and eventually picked up a letter addressed to Dana Lubeck. She quickly opened it and saw what she expected, a booking for the Nillzen party. She dropped the letter into a food waste grinder in the sink.

The local football team had played a home game and the boss had asked her to stay on for an evening shift as he was expecting a lot more customers than usual. It was late when the shift had finished, the manager had told her to stay on and clear up. It had been a hard day at the restaurant, customers had been demanding, and rude to the point of making offensive sexual remarks to the waitresses. Some customers at one table had got very drunk and decided to start throwing food around. They got violent when the manager had asked them to leave. He called the police, but they left before the police arrived. Throughout the confrontation, Astrid had cowered in a corner of the kitchen, shaking and close to tears. The other waitresses had told her she was pathetic, whereupon she had cried. They had backed up the manager, ready to help deal with the rowdy customers, but she had not. Because of this, he was cross with her and had let the other girls go home but told her to stay and clean the mess that had been created.

The walk back to her flat would be uncomfortable. It was one thirty in the morning and her guise as an awkward, timid young woman would make her vulnerable. She would normally tag along behind the other girls and have a degree of safety in numbers, but now she was on her own and she had to go through a particularly risky part of town. She couldn't avoid one narrow road, and street lighting here was sparse with some parts completely dark.

She walked into a poorly lit area. Hands grabbed her from behind, one clamped over her mouth, the other grabbing her breast. "We're gonna fuck you little girl," snarled a voice as she got dragged into a side alley. "You make a sound, and we'll knife you," said another voice. The hand moved from her breast down between her legs and started pulling her skirt up. There was enough light for her to see a man in front of her. She guessed there were only two, one holding her and the one in front. Getting out of this would be easy for her, and killing them would also be easy, but that would draw too much attention. She decided to hurt their male pride to ensure their silence.

"Me first," said the man in front of her, stepping forward and undoing his belt. As he got close, she kicked him hard between the legs. Special forces had taught her that it didn't matter how hard she kicked, the pain would always be the same; excruciating and debilitating, and the harder the kick, the longer that pain would last. He dropped to the ground, curled up in the foetal position, gasping and unable to speak. She ran her heel down the shin of the man behind her and stamped on the arch of his foot, he cried out. She let her body go limp and slid down and out of his grasp. She turned to face him; they were in a cul de sac, and he was between her and the way out.

He pulled out a switchblade knife and pressed the button, the blade flicked out and locked in position. “I’m gonna gut you for that, you fuckin’ little bitch,” he snarled as he lunged forward, aiming for her abdomen. Instead of pulling away as he expected, she stepped forward, grabbed the hand that was holding the knife, pushing it away from her and slammed her fist into his stomach. As he doubled up, she brought her knee up sharply into his face, breaking his nose, then grabbed his head and smashed it sideways onto the wall. He dropped the knife and she kicked it away as he fell to the ground.

Both men were on the ground, one groaning in pain with his hands between his legs, the other panicking and gasping for breath. She grabbed them both by the hair and dragged them onto a pile of rubbish. She put her hands on their necks and felt for a pressure point. She located them on each man, then pressed hard with her thumbs. Neither could cry out as the pain shot through them; she maintained the pressure and spoke calmly.

“The next time you two arseholes decide you are going to rape a girl, just stop and think, ‘what if she fights back’, because you are lucky that I just can’t be bothered to kill you both. But if I ever see you again, I will.”

She released her grip, put her hands on the backs of their heads and banged them together. She stood up, and they looked up at her, their lust filled arrogance replaced by abject terror.

She looked down at the pathetic sight. “I doubt that you two would ever admit to a woman getting the better of you in a fight, particularly both at the same time, and no-one would believe you anyway. So what you are going to tell everyone is that you had a disagreement with each other, and it turned into a fight. Understood?”

They nodded fearfully. She turned and left; she found the knife, pushed the blade into a crack in the pavement, then kicked the handle, snapping the blade off. “You won’t be needing that again.”

She walked out of the alley to the sound of one of them crying.

Two days before the party, she heard Dana talking to the boss. “I ain’t going to need the time off this year, I ain’t been booked an’ I’m a bit pissed off about it.”

“I can’t say I’m disappointed, it a pain in the arse when you’re not here. But if you want to make up your money you can do a double shift that day instead.”

Dana grunted and walked away. “I’ll think about it,” she grumbled. The pay at Nillzen’s party would have been four times what the boss paid her, even after a double shift.

The Nillzen Mission

The last of the cars had arrived; the article about Nillzen's parties stated that all the guests would arrive by six thirty, and it was nearly seven now. The guards had relaxed, their job was over for the moment, and although they couldn't have anything to drink, they could spend the evening as they liked, provided they stayed near the guard house. On any other day, army vehicles would arrive at all times of the day and night, and they had to be on their best behaviour, but not tonight, tonight would be easy.

Astrid had already spotted the collection of cigarette butts around the back of the guard house and had positioned herself behind a tree near them. After a few minutes, one of the guards strolled out and lit a cigarette. She drew her Falchion and crept up behind him. In one quick move, she grabbed his head, yanked it back and drew the blade across his throat. She held the wide part of the blade across his open windpipe to stop any sounds as his lungs emptied of breath. She let the blood from his head drain away as she lowered him to the ground.

There was a noise from the front of the building, she glanced around the side to see the second guard with his back to her. He had white earphones in and was selecting some music from an MP3 player. He started to nod his head and tap his feet in time with the tinny sounds that she could hear from the obviously loud music. He was taller than her, and on a slight rise in the ground; she couldn't use the same move again, he also had a neck guard on the back of his helmet. This was a flexible, but tough flap of reinforced leather, designed to stop blows to the back of the neck, so a strike there would be difficult.

She holstered the Falchion and crept up behind him, the music in his head masking the sounds she made. She bopped down, then grabbed his ankles, pulling them back as she stood up throwing him face first onto the ground. She kicked him between the legs, he doubled up in pain, rolling onto his side and curling up. With his head down in his chest, the guard flap on the back of his helmet rose up leaving his neck exposed. In one swift move, she drew the Falchion and struck him between the first and second vertebra, killing him instantly.

She dragged the body around the back of the guardhouse and grabbed her bag. She entered the guard house and took out the box of electronics. Suddenly, another guard appeared from a rest room; there should have only been two on duty. She drew her blade and lunged at him; he jumped and did a scissor kick, hitting her right arm and knocking the Falchion out of her hand. It clattered to the floor behind her. He spun around and threw a kick at her; she expected this and stepped back. The kick missed her, but he immediately spun around again with another kick. Again, she ducked back, but be he anticipated this and corrected his move. His heel caught her on the chin, jerking her head to one side.

He was good; this was bad, she had not encountered a Correlan soldier with this level of skill before. Their usual tactic was to force their way forward, absorbing punishment and overpowering an opponent. She needed to think quickly; he was obviously stronger than her and every bit as agile. She aimed a kick between his legs, and as she had expected he grabbed her foot; she used this to assist her as she jumped and kicked him in the face. He fell back, releasing his grip, but instead of falling he turned and landed up against a wall. He braced himself with his hands, then pushed off and turned to her.

She had turned and was diving for her weapon, he dived as well and grabbed her ankle, pulling her back out of reach of the Falchion. She kicked out at his face with her other foot, but he grabbed it and twisted her ankle, forcing her onto her back, then jumped on top of her. He drew his combat knife and raised it ready to plunge it into her chest. And in the moment, he lost focus. He was exactly where she wanted him; in his triumphal state, he didn't see that she was lying next to a rock that they used to prop the door open during summer. She grabbed the rock and slammed it into the side of his head, then back into his face, knocking out his front teeth and tearing his lip open.

A third blow to the side of his face broke his cheek bone; he dropped his knife and fell off her. She scrambled away to get her weapon, snatching it up and rolling up into a combat stance. His soldier's fighting instinct kicked in and he grabbed his knife and stood up. The pressure on his eye from the broken bone below the socket doubled his vision and he staggered towards her thrashing his knife wildly as he tried to work out where she was. He lunged at her; she stepped aside and thrust her blade, it struck him between the third and fourth rib on the left side of his chest, ripping through his heart and emerging out of his back. Her thrust only stopping when the Quillon hit his body. There was a moment when their faces were only centimetres apart, then his eyes rolled back, and he fell to the ground, dead.

She had to work fast; she dragged the body back into the rest room then located the box with the incoming telephone lines. There were five lines in, and she noted that one was labelled as 'Headquarters hotline', she disconnected the two wires and attached the two cables from the electronics that she had brought. She then set the timer for 60 minutes.

She quickly washed the blood from her hands and removed her combat clothes, put on the waitress uniform, the wig, and the shoes. She put in the contact lenses, put on the glasses, and started to walk briskly to the house. As she walked, she was struck by an unwelcome sense of anxiety, if the information about the number of guards was wrong, what else could be wrong? But there was too much at stake to abort the mission now, and she carried on towards the house. She could use any sign of nerves to her advantage to enhance the timid persona that she had adopted.

Nillzen's senior aide gasped as Astrid entered the kitchen. "Who the fuck are you?"

"Sorry sir, I'm Eva Munck sir," she said feebly, looking down and fidgeting. "One of the girls couldn't make it sir, so the agency asked me to take her place, sorry sir."

"What's wrong with your chin?" he snapped, grabbing her head roughly for a better look at the wound caused when the guard kicked her.

"I was rushing to get here sir and I fell off my bicycle, sorry sir."

"Oh, for fuck's sake," he grunted contemptuously, then grabbed her by the arm and dragged her roughly to the door that lead into the reception room. "Look at the other girls."

Eight, tall, elegant girls glided effortlessly around the room, each one balancing a tray of champagne glasses on the tips of their fingers. Each girl was tall, had shoulder length straight blonde hair, pale skin and blood red lipstick. They wore white blouses with small black bow ties, black knee length pencil skirts and shiny black patent leather shoes with very high heels.

"Look at them, they are all beautiful and sophisticated—everything that you are not. I can't have you out there," he snapped.

“Sorry sir,” she said, looking at the floor and fiddling with the sides of her blouse.

“Well now you are here, you might as well do something. You can pull the corks on the champagne.” He pointed angrily at her. “Just don’t let any of the guests see you.”

“I won’t sir, sorry sir.”

“The agency is going to hear about this tomorrow,” he huffed, as he turned and walked away.

Fifty-five minutes after setting the timer, Astrid slipped out of the kitchen up the service stairs and into Nillzen’s office. She took a heavy brass statuette from a shelf and bopped down behind a chair. She checked her watch. “Any second now,” she whispered. A few moments later, the timer in the guard house clicked over and sent its signal.

An aide tapped Salazar Nillzen on the shoulder, interrupting the lively conversation that he and his wife, Tanja, were having with some of his female relatives. “Sorry to disturb you sir, but the phone in your office is ringing.”

“Headquarters? At this time of night? Oh well, please excuse me ladies, duty calls—literally.”

He smiled and nodded respectfully then made his way upstairs.

Astrid heard his footsteps in the corridor outside as he approached his office. Her heart was in her mouth, this was by far the riskiest mission she had ever undertaken. There were a lot of people around and a lot could go wrong. She heard him open the door and enter the room. She watched from behind the armchair as he stepped onto the rug. As she had guessed from the layout of the furniture, he had his back to her as he went to his desk.

She quickly moved out from behind the armchair, grabbed the rug and pulled it out from under his feet, throwing him onto the floor. He fell down hard and hit his head on the parquet floor. Stunned, he rolled onto his back, she grabbed the heavy metal statuette and fell onto him, bringing the flat base down onto his head and putting the whole weight of her body into the blow. She quickly stood up, and with a tissue in her hand so as to not leave any fingerprints, lifted the phone handset to silence the ring.

Nillzen was not dead, he groaned quietly and moved a fraction. Astrid dropped on him again, hitting him in the same place and heard the bones of his skull crack. He stopped moving and she rolled him over onto his front and positioned his head so the injuries she caused were in contact with the floor. Suddenly she heard a noise outside; staff knew that they could not enter the office if Nillzen was on the phone, but they could listen and realise that he was not talking and then enter.

There was no time to check for a pulse. She replaced the statuette and slipped through the connecting door and into his secretary's office, closing it as quietly as she could. She went to the door and listened for any sounds of activity in the corridor outside, there were none. She opened the door and stepped out of the room. She had only taken one step when Nillzen's aide appeared.

"What are you doing up here?" he demanded.

"Sorry sir," she replied in a feeble voice, stooping submissively and again fidgeting nervously with the side of her blouse. "I was looking for the toilet."

"The staff facilities are downstairs, you know that."

"I couldn't find them sir," she said bowing her head.

"Don't bullshit me," he snarled. "You were up here looking for something to steal, weren't you?"

"No sir, I wasn't sir."

"Come here you little thief, what have you got in your pockets?"

"Nothing sir."

He stepped closer to her, "You're coming with me you lit…"

A carotid punch to the side of his neck was all that Astrid needed to silence him. The overstimulated carotid sinus nerve sent a message to the heart to slow down, instantly dropping his blood pressure and knocking him out. She caught him as he fell and lowered him silently to the floor. She opened the office door and dragged him in. She found some parcel tape and bound his hands behind his back then put some over his mouth, taped his legs together and bound him to one of the iron radiators in the room.

He would not be out for long and the general hubbub from the floor below should muffle any sound that he would make, but she would not have much time now, soon someone would notice that the aide was missing and that Nillzen's call was be taking a long time. She put the roll of tape in her pocket then left the office and made her way down the back stairs.

Astrid's choice to play a simple girl meant that nobody took any notice of her as she moved in and out of the kitchen, and she entered without anyone paying any attention. She pulled corks on champagne bottles and nervously kept an eye on the passage that lead to the guest's toilet. After a few minutes her next target made her way along the passage. The woman was a similar body size and height, and Astrid was able to leave the kitchen as un-noticed as when she came back in a few minutes previously.

She followed the woman into the toilet; the woman looked at Astrid, sneered then turned to the mirror to check her make-up. A sharp punch to the side of the head dropped her unconscious. Astrid caught her as she collapsed and dragged her into a stall. She locked the door, quickly undressed the woman and taped her mouth shut, bound her hands and feet then bound her to the down pipe from the old-fashioned cistern.

She took off her uniform then put on the woman's dress; it was an okay fit, not good, just okay but it had to do. She left the woman's shoes; they were high heels, and she was not used to wearing high heels so they would be a hinderance. She emptied out the woman's bag, then took off her glasses, took out the contact lenses and removed her wig and stuffed them all in the bag along with the uniform. She picked up a set of car keys and saw that they were for a modern car with remote locking.

"Good," she said to herself.

There were no sounds from the other side of the stall door, so she took off the uneven shoes that she was wearing then jumped up and hauled herself over the top, landing lightly. She reached under the door, grabbed her shoes and the bag. She removed the cork insert from her right shoe then put them on; exited the toilet and bumped into a woman who was exceedingly drunk. It was Karan, Nillzen's sister. Astrid pushed past her and headed towards a fire exit.

"Wrong way love," slurred Karan. "The party's that way."

"I'm going out for a cigarette."

"Oh, okay," said Karan, staggering sideways and flopping up against the wall. "Do I know you?" she slurred.

"No, you don't."

"Oh okay… bye then," she said as she slid down the wall, ending up siting on the floor, giggling.

Astrid left the building and ran to the car park, pressing the 'unlock' button on the key fob as she closed on the vehicles. Side lights flashed on an expensive sports car. She got in and drove away carefully. In minutes she was at the gate house; she left the car running and went inside, she found the bag that she had left earlier, and quickly changed into a new set of casual clothes, and then removed the device from the telephone junction box and re-attached the incoming cables, leaving the box exactly as it was. Taking everything with her, she got back in the car and headed to back to Balssen along the back roads.

About a kilometre outside of the town was the remains of a gravel pit with a rusty warning sign on the gate said:

'DANGER. NO SWIMMING. VERY DEEP WATER.'

The gate was not locked, and she drove in right up to the edge of the water. A concrete ramp led down into the water and she left no tyre marks. She got out, leaving the woman's clothes and her Eva Munck disguise, then reached in and released the handbrake and watched as the car slowly rolled into the water, in seconds it had disappeared completely.

She took the Falchion and its scabbard and thought for a moment; she decided that she would not need them now and flung them far into the pit where they would sink into the fine silt at the bottom of the pit and would probably never be found. She started the walk back to her flat and contemplated her next move. Her primary mission was over, and DeSalva would hear about that via radio intercepts. Now for the part that he was not at all keen on: her staying in the enemy country while she attempted to find out who gave the order for the Dantu massacre.

"He's alive, but he's hit his head and there's a lot of damage." The family doctor tried hard to hide his fears about Salazar's injuries as he spoke to Tanja Nillzen. "We'll know more once he's at the hospital, there are scans and tests we can do. The chief neuro-consultant is a friend of mine and he's the best in the country." He paused, unable to hide the concerned look in his eyes. "But I do have to be honest with you Tanja, and you must prepare yourself. From what I've seen, I doubt that it will be good news." He handed her a tissue. "Do you want me to drive you to the medical centre?"

"No, no thank you," said Tanya, wiping her eyes and breathing deeply to calm herself. "I'll go with him in the ambulance, can you bring Jon and Milo please. I want my boys with me at the hospital."

The attention of a medic irritated the aide. "I'm fine you fool, go and find someone else to fuss over." He brushed the young woman away as he spoke to a military police officer. "She was obviously up here to steal something. I challenged her, and the little bitch attacked me."

“We’ve spoken to the other girls, no-one seems to know who she was,” said the officer.

“She said that one of the regular girls couldn’t make it and that the agency had sent her, why, God only knows,” he growled. “She didn’t exactly fit with the girls we always use, and the agency must have known that” said the aide as he absent-mindedly picked glue strands from his face.

“Do you think that she was in General Nillzen’s office and attacked him?”

“Attacked and overpowered General Nillzen?” the aide scoffed, “Are you mad? he’d have ripped her arms off. No, she was looking for something to take. Isn’t it obvious that this was the reason she was up there?”

In another area of the foyer, a worried medic was taking the blood pressure of the woman from the toilet. She had been hysterical when she had been found and had been given a strong tranquiliser. A member of house staff was wiping the glue from her wrists with surgical spirit as another medic prepared to take her to hospital.

On the other side of the foyer, Karan Nillzen was sitting on the floor, babbling incoherently. “I saw a woman coming out of the toilet… at least I think I saw a woman coming out of the toilet… She was wearing bad shoes… yes, that was it, bad shoes, they didn’t match her dress at all… but I can’t really say anything else about her…” she suddenly looked worried. “Oh no, I think I’ve wet myself. You see, I’ve had a lot of champagne and I’m a bit tipsy.”

Her head rolled from side to side, and she frowned heavily, trying to concentrate. She looked up at the people surrounding her. “I did see her coming out of the toilet. Yes, that was it, I did see her. I suppose a lot of women have to use the toilet, don’t they?” She belched loudly and looked anxious. “Oh dear, I think I’m going to be sick.”

“Why does aunty Karan always have to get so drunk, she’s such an embarrassment,” said Jon, the youngest of Nillzen’s sons. “She saw someone and now she can’t remember anything.”

The doctor approached the two teenage boys. “Come with me boys, we’ve got to go to the hospital now.”

Milo, the older of the two sneered down at Karan. “Thanks for nothing aunty Karan. We don’t want to see you ever again,” he said as they left with the doctor.

“What did he say?” Karan slurred as she tried to get up. “I didn’t hear what he said, what did he say?”

Soldiers in the Bar

Astrid noticed a group of four young men walking past her flat. She could tell that they were soldiers by the way they walked and their mannerisms. One of them was wearing a T-shirt with a large triangle with the letters SOG inside. The men were talking animatedly about going to their usual bar. She quickly changed into a set of racy clothes, got in character and became the sexy miss Nikka Feistel. She slipped out of the flat and followed them.

The bar was busy and she was able to place herself within earshot of the men without drawing attention to herself. She would let herself be noticed when she was ready. Another young man spotted them and went over.

"Here he is. Hello Zap, ain't seen you since Dantu," said a young man in the group sitting at a table.

"Hi Rezza, Baz, Stokie, Gal." He slapped a greeting on their arms as they shuffled around to make a space for him at the table.

Dodi Zappan sat down with them. "How long are you guys in town for?"

"Just tonight, got here this afternoon, moving up north tomorrow."

"What are we?" Zap said.

"The Dantu crew," they said in unison.

Zap snapped his fingers at a one of the barmaids who was gathering empty glasses, then made a circling gesture with his finger. "Beers for my mates, and fuckin' hurry up, I'm parched."

"Bad news about Nillzen, isn't it," said Baz.

"Yeah, real bad news. It's one thing to cop it in battle, but to trip over and bang your head and end up in a coma? That's just real bad shit," said Gal.

"I heard that he's never gonna wake up," said Baz.

The waitress appeared with the drinks and the interruption stopped the conversation.

"What have you been up to since Dantu?" said Zap.

"Berg took a group of us to sort something out. But we ain't seen him for a while." said Gal.

Baz took a large swig of his beer then belched loudly. "I hear Berg got promoted to Major."

"Yeah, that's right, someone was pleased with us and he got made up to Major. But since he's got promoted, he's become a bit bourgeois," said Zap.

"Bourgeois? that's a big word for you Zap," said Rezza.

"You been eating a dictionary since we last saw you, Zap?" laughed Gal.

"Okay then, he's become a bit of a stuck-up cunt. Too good to drink with the likes of us. Stays at home, I suppose he's got to keep his bitch of a wife happy." Zap took a swig of his drink. "He goes to a poncy restaurant now, 'The Silk River', takes his wife there once a week. Have you ever met her? I have, she's a right miserable cow."

The guys looked at each other and shrugged.

"And I know why." said Zap.

"Why's that then?"

"Coz he's got an eye for the ladies and his misses knows it."

"We've all got an eye for the ladies," said Rezza.

"Yeah, but you tossers only ever look. Guys like Berg and me, we follow through."

"I've been in a foxhole with you when you've followed through," said Gal. "Man, it fuckin' stunk."

"Shat himself, did he?" said Stokie

"Yeah, I told him not to eat the rations; they smelled really bad, but not as bad as his arse though," said Gal, laughing at Zap's embarrassment.

"Oh fuck off you two, I suppose you've never shit your pants."

"No I haven't, come to think of it. Have you Gal?" said Stokie, turning to Gal and pretending to be serious.

Gal frowned and stroked his chin. "Shit my pants? No, not me. Zap's obviously not got as much control as us."

The rest of the guys laughed at Zap, and he was keen to change the subject.

"I've seen Berg in action with the ladies; I don't know how he does it. He sees a bird, makes eye contact with her, gets this little twinkle in his eye and before you know it, he's outside, banging her up against a wall." He smiled, knowing that he'd got their attention. "He once told me that he only stays with his old lady for the sake of his daughter, he loves that kid. The old bag knows what goes on. He won't divorce her, coz she'd get custody, and she won't divorce him because she wants to stay with him as a sort of punishment. So he ain't getting it off her, that's for sure."

Zap downed a beer in one and banged the glass down, snapping his fingers at the barmaid again and pointing to the glasses. "Dantu was fun though, wasn't it?"

Gal looked a bit troubled. "For you maybe, but we ain't all psychopaths like you."

"You lot were a bunch of pussies; all you did was stop them from leaving. I did all the work."

"Yeah, but you sure looked like you were enjoying it," said Rezza, frowning slightly.

"Look, the way I see it, Berg gave the order, and I carried it out. So why not enjoy it?"

"That's fucking sick man," snapped Gal.

"I seem to remember that you enjoyed driving the digger, Gal," Zap reminded Galen, firmly.

Baz looked a bit concerned. "Yeah, but that last lot, we just left them, what if they get found."

Zap sneered at him. "Oh, fuck off you lot, what are you worried for. No one's going to that shit hole again. Now, you're not going all bleeding-heart on me, are you?"

"Nah, it ain't that. It's just that the rest got buried."

"Are you lot a bunch of fuckin' gay boys or what, have some balls."

Embarrassed, Baz raised his glass. They all raised their glasses and chinked them together, "Dantu crew." They said in unison.

Stokie leant forward, speaking to Zap. "What about that old woman, she tried to shield a kid, what did she think you would do."

Zap laughed. "Yep, got both of them with one shot, straight through the old bat and into the kid, two for the price of one," he said triumphantly. "And that was my good deed for the day, not wasting ammo and thereby…" He raised a finger to emphasise his point "…saving the Army money."

Astrid sat at the bar, dressed the way a lot of the girls were; with high heels, a short skirt and a low-cut top. She listened to the men and hid her disgust, she now knew them to be SOG soldiers, and even with the beer talking, they were beyond contempt. The loud-mouthed Zap noticed her looking at him; she smiled and with a slight sideways nod, beckoned him over.

“Oi, oi, Zap’s pulled,” said Baz as Zap strolled over to Astrid.

Zap leant casually on the bar and smiled at her. He looked her up and down, letting his gaze linger on her breasts before looking her in the eye. “’ello sweetheart.”

She saw he was wearing a ring with the SOG emblem and pointed it out. “Nice ring.”

“I bet you’ve got a nice ring too, darlin’.”

She giggled at the innuendo. “You a soldier boy then?” she said, running her finger around the top of her glass.

“Yeah.”

“Oh, cool, what do you do? Hope it ain’t no dull shit like logistics, or administration, or some other crap,” she asked, as she rolled her chewing gum from one side of her mouth to the other. She took a swig of her drink, not breaking eye contact with him.

He leered at her, looking her up and down.

“Let’s just say, we’re sort of pest control. We take care of … problems.”

“Have you ever killed anyone,” she said, excitedly.

“Oh yeah.”

“How many people have you killed then?” She uncrossed her legs, then leant back, allowing her skirt to ride up.

“Loads, fuckin’ loads.” He glanced down and saw the top of her inner thigh. He couldn’t stop the lustful look in his eyes.

She had hooked him, now to lead him on. She ran her finger and thumb up and down the sides of a tall drink tumbler, suggestively. “Oh, cool, I like tough guy soldiers, mainly because…” She leant forward and whispered in his ear “…they’ve got huge cocks.” She sat back. “You wanna fuck?”

“Yeah, but how much are you gonna charge me?”

“Oh, this one’s free.” She put her hand between his legs and stroked his penis; it was already erect. “It’ll be my pleasure,” she said, staring at his crotch.

He looked around at his mates and pumped the air with his fist, they cheered.

“Drink up then,” he ordered. She downed her drink then discretely put her hand in her bag and pressed a key on her phone, setting off a buzz. She took out her phone and looked at it. “Oh fuck, oh fuck, I’m gonna be late,” she said with a frightened look on her face. “Shit, shit, shit. Sorry babe, I’ve gotta go.”

“Are you dicking me around?” He grabbed her arm and turned nasty. “Are you playing a game or what?”

“No babe, you don’t understand. I can’t be late for this guy; you don’t know what he’s like. He’ll kill me if I don’t arrive on time.”

He let go of her arm.

“Why say you wanted to fuck me then?”

“I want to, but I’ve gotta go now.” She pulled up her top, exposing her breasts. “Just think of these later and knock one out.” She got off the stool and kissed him on the cheek. “We’ll catch up sometime eh?” she said as she hurried out of the bar.

She left the building and stayed in character until she was back at her flat. Of all the roles she would assume during a mission, the nasty girls in this town were the most distasteful, but the easiest to imitate. However, she had the information she required; confirmation that the special operations group carried out the massacre and the name of the officer in command; Major Berg, moreover, she now knew where to find him. He would not have done this without orders, and Astrid had to find out who gave the order. Given what she had heard about Berg’s sexual appetite, she had a pretty good idea of how she could get that information.

Dodi Zappan

Astrid had seen the loud-mouth soldier from the bar going into a shop a few times to buy cigarettes. It was late in the afternoon and this time he had some groceries, and she guessed that this meant that he would not be on any operations for a while. This was good. She tailed him as he went home and saw that he was staying in a basement flat. She waited until he had entered and walked calmly past. There was an iron picket fence with a gate at one end, through the gate was a flat area then a ninety degree turn to ten, deep stone steps down to the front door. The building was old, and there was no handrail.

Across the road from his flat was a green area, a small park with a few trees, flower beds and benches. She bought a trashy romantic novel and sat on one of the benches, shoulders hunched, pretending to read. He emerged from his flat at seven, dressed in the same casual clothes that he had worn when she had spoken to him in the bar. He walked directly across the road towards the park, passing close but taking no notice of her. She put away her book and tailed him; he went to the same bar.

For the next two evenings, she sat and watched him leave his flat and tailed him as he went to the bar again, his routine was the same.

"A creature of habit," she muttered to herself. "Good." She went back to her flat, straightened up and felt her back crack from the hours of her stooping posture. She had a shower, fixed herself something to eat then sat and refined her plan. She would make her move tomorrow night.

Astrid put on the second set of clothes she had brought and became sexy Nikka Feistel again, the good time bar girl. She left her flat and went to the street where she knew Dodi Zappan would be.

"Hello again, soldier boy," she said as Zap passed her.

"Oh it's you. Were you late for your 'meeting'," he grunted.

"Nah, got there in time. No bruises that time."

Zap looked genuinely concerned. “Does he hit you?”

“Only if I’m late.”

“Tell me next time and I’ll fuckin’ kill him.”

“Oh, let’s not worry about him. You gonna buy me a drink or what?”

“Okay, then what?”

“We’ll see… what comes up, shall we?” she laughed, looking down at his jeans.

She put her arm around him as they walked to his favourite bar. As they crossed the park, he pushed her against a tree, kissed her, fondled her breasts then put his hand between her legs.

“Oh, that’s feels good, but let’s get a drink first, eh? Then I’m gonna fuck you ‘till your balls shrivel up,” she said, easing him away from her.

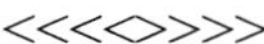

Astrid had a double Vodka and Zap had a litre glass of strong lager.

“Close your eyes and down it in one,” she said, grinning, rolling her chewing gum around her mouth.

He closed his eyes, took a deep breath, and started to drink. Astrid tipped her drink in to a flowerpot. He finished and opened his eyes to see her taking her glass away from her mouth.

“Phew,” she gasped. “That was strong. Another.” The barmaid produced a litre of lager and a double Vodka.

“I don’t wanna get too pissed,” said Zap. “I wanna perform later.”

She stood up and moved close to him, rubbing her breasts across his chest and slipping her hand between his legs. “Don’t worry babe,” she whispered in his ear as she stroked his penis. “I can give a corpse a hard-on. You’ll be fine once you’ve got your cock in my mouth.” She sat back and downed the Vodka in two hits. “The only thing about Vodka, is that it goes right through me and I’ve got to have a piss now.”

She went to the ladies, locked herself in a stall then put her fingers down her throat, throwing up the vodka she had just drunk. She took a bottle of water from her bag, drank most of it, then put her fingers down her throat again to bring up any alcohol that was left. She wiped her face, calmed herself while she straightened her clothes then tottered back to the bar and ordered another double Vodka and litre of lager.

“Just have these and we’ll go, yeah?” she said to Zap, giggling.

He took a couple of mouthfuls of his beer. "Yeah, okay, but I've got to have a piss now."

While he was away, she tipped her Vodka into his beer, then ordered another double, tipping most of it into the beer that was waiting for him.

"Down it in one," she said as he returned. He drank half the glass, shaking his head.

"Man, that's strong," he said.

"Oh come on, I've had six, you've only had two, you don't want to waste that third one. Down it and we'll go."

He finished the beer and wobbled on his feet as they left. Once outside he started to stagger from side to side. She let out a loud drunk laugh, and matched his stagger, holding on tight to his arm.

"Fuck me that beer was really strong." His voice was slurred; he blinked his eyes hard and shook his head to try to focus his vision.

She cackled out a pointless laugh. "I am gonna fuck you so hard," she shouted then staggered to one side and grabbed a railing for support. "You know what," she drawled out. "Why don't I just suck you off right now. Go on, get your cock out."

"Nah, not here," he gasped, trying to think straight. "We're nearly at my place,"

A couple walking on the other side of the road stopped and glared at her. "What are you fuckin' looking at. Piss off," she shouted at them, then burst out laughing.

A few minutes later they were at the gate to his basement flat, he fumbled with keys until it opened. She quickly glanced around to check that no-one was around, then as he stepped through, she grabbed his arm, turning him to face her, pretending that she was going to kiss him. He looked confused and didn't notice her slipping her foot behind his ankle. She put her hand on his chest and shoved him. He fell backwards, and with nothing to grab hold of, crashed down the steps, banging his head hard as he fell. He landed headfirst lying unconscious in a heap, Astrid ran down the steps, grabbed his head and slammed it down onto the concrete.

She checked for a pulse, there wasn't one. "That's for Dantu," she said and left.

As she walked back to her flat, she saw a girl that had been in the bar.

"Oh, that was a quick one, darlin'," the girl said.

"Nah, it wasn't anything, he was too pissed. He had to have a little sit down on a park bench, I left him there when he fell asleep. He ain't no use to me like that," said Astrid, looking a bit dejected.

"Go home and play with a battery powered friend, they don't get pissed and let you down," said the girl, as she laughed and winked.

The Seedy Side of Town

There was a street, a long straight street that led from the main shopping area. A road cut across this street, creating a barrier between the two areas of town. She crossed the road and was now in the seedy part of an already rough town; it was mid-afternoon, and drunks and hustlers were already out on the streets. Later there would be drunks fighting, drug deals being made, sex workers hassling passers-by. Men in cars would be crawling along the kerb assuming that every woman was a prostitute, winding their windows down and asking them what depraved things they would do and how much they would charge for them.

Astrid was here to find a particular shop. Some men in a beer garden, well on the way to getting drunk, called out to her, inviting her for a drink and group sex. She ignored them and headed to the shop that she knew would be there, somewhere. It wasn't hard to spot; no sign outside, blacked out windows and a solid door. There were two small CCTV cameras looking up and down the street. She popped some gum in her mouth and chewed it with her mouth open, then entered the sex shop.

Inside, the walls had racks full of DVD's and magazines, above each section was a banner describing the content style. There were glass cases full of sex toys of every conceivable size and shape, flavoured condoms, and pots of lubricant. In one corner there was what she had come for; the banner read 'Fem Dom Discipline'. She ignored the various whips, gags and handcuffs and picked up a DVD. It was called 'Fifty Lash Bash'. On the cover was a naked man spread-eagled on a cross and a dominatrix about to whip him.

She put it down and picked up another featuring a man in a tight latex suit that covered his whole body with just a small tube to breathe through. He was hanging by his feet from a beam, with two women in tight antique style corsets hauling him up with a rope. She put that down and went to the magazine section. There were so many to choose from; she picked up one called 'Heavy Bondage, Trampling Special' and flicked through the pages. Most featured pictures of naked muscled men tied to the floor with women wearing nothing except stiletto heels standing on their chests.

This was not what she wanted, but next to it was. The magazine was called 'Asphyxia Heaven' she opened it and saw a picture of a naked man tied in a chair with a naked woman holding a plastic bag over his head. She flicked through the pages and saw that all the pictures were variations on the same theme—naked men being suffocated by naked women.

"You into all that then," said the girl behind the counter.

"Nah, not yet, but I'm curious," said Astrid affecting a sleazy voice, rolling the chewing gum from one side of her mouth to the other as she spoke.

"You wanna see a guy suffer, eh," said the girl.

Astrid picked up a couple of magazines and went to the counter.

"Yeah, but how do I find a guy who wants it like that?"

"I dunno," said the girl unconvincingly, then she looked at the magazines Astrid had chosen. "Can't interest you in a couple of DVDs', can I? they're two for one. They'll give you some good ideas."

"Nah, these are enough for me to be going on with."

"Okay, that's fifteen Dhat."

Astrid paid, and the girl put the magazines in a plain brown paper bag. "Now you've paid, I know you ain't the law or the council. So, here's how you find these guys." She reached under the counter and pulled out a small, poorly printed magazine. "We're not supposed to have these, it's from working girls offering their services, and we're not supposed to take any advertising money from them. Now if you stick an ad in here, you'll have any number of guys who are just gagging to be whipped or humiliated or gagged even." She laughed at her own joke; Astrid laughed as well.

"They'll want you to do all the things that they can't ask their uptight wives to do, and they'll pay good money. You'll have a good time." The girl leant forward and lowered her voice, even though there was no-one else in the shop. "The thing is, they don't want any sex. They ask, you say no, and that's all part of it for them. They want you to say no. Is that weird or what?"

Astrid picked up the bag. "I'll think about an ad. See ya later." She went to the door and looked up at the TV screens, checked that the street was clear and left.

She walked down the path past the beer garden. The men were regulars there and recognised the paper bag. "Got a new dildo love?" one shouted. "Size of a horse's dick is it?" another man shouted.

She stopped and looked at them. “Why don’t you just fuck right off,” she snarled. The men looked at each other then laughed. “Yeah, it’s as big as a horse’s dick,” one of them said.

Astrid sneered and raised her middle finger at them, then walked away while they all burst out laughing.

As distasteful as this whole episode had been, she needed to be seen, she needed to interact with the locals. Above all, she needed to speak and act like the girls who lived here, she needed to blend in and become just like them and be invisible as a result.

Back in her flat, she opened the contact magazine and scanned through the hundreds of adverts from all over the country. One caught her eye.

Are you a pathetic, worthless worm? Well, are you? Mistress Zelda will take you to her dungeon and punish you with hard bondage, trampling, smothering, face sitting and breath play...

Astrid had read enough; she took a red pen and drew a large circle around the advert. She didn’t look at the magazines, she found them disgusting.

The Silk River

Five weeks after the Nillzen mission, and four weeks after killing Dodi Zappan, she finally saw a vacancy for a waitress at the Silk River. Five weeks of being in plain sight but invisible; five weeks of being seen but avoiding conversations. Five weeks of playing a transient, uninterested in forming acquaintances. She had her hair cut and dyed back to its natural colour, then changed into another set of clothes and became her third character.

She walked into the Silk River restaurant, a small restaurant with just eight tables and a quiet air of quality and exclusivity. A waitress approached her. "Table for one madam?" she said sweetly. Astrid decided on the accent that an educated north western woman would have. "Nothing to eat, I would like to apply for the waitress job."

"Oh, right," said the waitress. "Come with me, I'll show you to the manager's office." She entered the office and Astrid followed her in. "This is…" she turned to Astrid. "Sorry, I didn't ask for your name."

"Janie Fischer, pleased to meet you," said Astrid as she shook the manager's hand.

"You've come about the job advert, yes?"

"That's correct."

"What experience of fine dining do you have?"

"My parents ran a hotel, we had a very good restaurant, not quite fine dining, but we always got good reviews in the local papers." She smiled knowingly. "I grew up in hospitality."

"In the north-west from the sound of your voice," he smiled back at her. "Very good, but what brings you to this part of the country?"

"My parents retired and sold the hotel. I didn't want to work for the new owners, it didn't seem right."

He glanced at her hand and noticed the absence of a wedding ring. "Are you married? Husbands often complain when their wives are working late shifts, it puts a strain on relationships, and I like my staff to be happy."

"I'm divorced," she smiled. "He was one of those, he didn't like it when I worked the evening shifts, so we parted, and it was all a bit messy. I had some friends out here so after the hotel was sold, I decided to move and make a new beginning."

"Well good for you." He shuffled some papers and got a little serious. "Now Janie, can I call you Janie?"

"Of course."

"Okay Janie, I'll be perfectly honest with you, we have difficulty getting the right staff, this is an up-market restaurant and not many girls in this town have the right skill set. Do you have any references?"

"I'm afraid not; I've not worked anywhere else and a reference from my parents would be a little bit biased, wouldn't it," she said with a disarming smile.

"Yes, I can see that." The manager thought for a moment. "Okay, our Sea Bass is very popular, and our wine cellar is the best in the region, so if you were asked to recommend a wine to go with it, what would you suggest?"

"Well, white would obviously be best: Chablis, Schiava or Chenin Blanc, maybe a good Riesling."

"And if they didn't want white wine?"

"A crisp dry rosé, Grenache maybe, or Syrah, and if they wanted red, it would need to be something like a light Pinot Noir."

"Good." He looked up at the waitress. "Zita, can you get me a plate and a knife and fork please?"

She disappeared for a few seconds and returned with the items and placed them on the manager's desk. He placed the fork vertically on the plate then placed the knife at a right angle across it. "What does it mean when a diner does this?"

"It means that the diner is ready for the next dish."

"Correct. What does it mean if the knife is put through the tines of the fork?"

"The diner did not like the dish."

"And how would the diner indicate that they enjoyed the meal?"

"By placing the knife and fork horizontally across the plate, both pointing in the same direction; left to right."

"Good. In fact, very good, not many people know that last one." He gestured for Zita to take the items away. "So, as you've obviously got experience, I'll give you a job, but I'll have to put you on a probationary period of one month. Is that okay?"

“Thank you very much, when can I start?”

“When *can* you start?”

“Well I’ve got nothing else to do, so how about I start tomorrow?”

“That’s good, we’re always busy on Monday nights. Come in at three, I’ll introduce you to everyone and Zita will sort you out with a uniform. Service starts at five and we close at eleven. Pay is four hundred for a six-day week, with a rota for Sunday working; Zita will sort that out for you. See you tomorrow.” He smiled and shook her hand.

“Thank you very much.”

Zita led Astrid out of the office. “There are not many customers early on, we have a few regulars that come in at around five thirty. We get busy from around seven thirty and most of our customers are gone by ten thirty, but apart from taking away plates and cutlery, he doesn’t allow any clearing up while patrons are still in the restaurant. So after service finishes, there’ll be about half an hour of work; we’re usually out of here by eleven-thirty.”

Astrid shook Zita’s hand. “See you tomorrow.”

The crash course in waitressing that she had received from the Army catering corps had served her well today; she hadn’t needed it at The Mid-Town Grill, but The Silk River was an altogether different proposition, and she would need all of her acting skills in the coming days and weeks.

Janie fitted in well at the Silk River and was well liked by the staff and customers. She deferred to Zita and the two worked well together. Once the regular patrons had got to know her, she would alternate with Zita at the front of house, seeing guests to their tables and taking the initial drink orders. She would return to take their food orders, make suggestions, smile and help them relax. On the third Friday, she looked at the diary and saw ‘Eight o’clock, table for two, Major Berg’.

“I’ll do front of house tonight if you want,” she said to Zita. Who looked at the diary over Astrid’s shoulder. “Ah, Major Berg and his wife, they haven’t been in for a few weeks now; he likes table eight in the corner.”

“As he hasn’t met me yet, I’ll look after him. Is that okay with you?”

“Yeah, fine with me. You do tables five to eight and I’ll do one to four. And I’ll tell you exactly what Major Berg will order. He’ll have a litre of porter ale, then order the Seabass and a bottle of Sagrantino.”

"Porter ale! Sagrantino; dark beer and a heavy red wine with fish!"

"Yep, and his wife will have the Gammon steak and a glass of water, and they'll sit and hardly say two words to each other. They won't have starters or desert and he'll ask for the bill pretty much as soon as they've finished; she won't speak to you at all."

"Hmm, that sounds a little bit awkward."

"Yeah it is, they're always the same, always have been."

"Major Berg, my usual table please."

"Certainly sir, table eight is ready for you." Astrid ignored Berg's wife and looked directly into his eyes and smiled.

"You're new, here aren't you? I've not seen you before," he said as she led them to the table. Berg was immaculately dressed; he had rugged good looks and a charming smile that was at odds with everything that Astrid knew he was capable of.

"Yes sir, I started three weeks ago." She pulled out a chair for him and ran her hand lightly across his back as he sat. Then stood behind his wife after she had sat down. Astrid pulled her shoulders back, pushing her chest out as she took out a notepad and pencil.

"A litre of Porter ale sir?" she said sweetly, smiling, looking into his eyes and noticing a little sparkle.

"Yes please."

"And will you be having the Seabass sir?"

"Of course."

"And with a bottle of Sagrantino sir?"

"Yes. I see they have you well trained."

"Yes, sir, Zita told me of your favourite dish." Astrid turned to Berg's wife who had a barely concealed scowl. "I suppose you want the Gammon steak and a glass of water," she said flatly. Berg's wife said nothing and just nodded.

Throughout the night, as Astrid worked the other three tables, she would occasionally glance and make eye contact with Berg, and he made no effort to hide his glances at her. She would smile at him, then get a little coy. He paid the bill with cash and she stroked his hand with the tips of her fingers as she handed him his change.

"Will we see you again next week, Major Berg?" she said as they left.

"Oh yes, same time, same table, but let's make it Thursday instead of Friday." Berg's wife was already out of the restaurant and walking briskly to their car. "Will you be on duty?" he asked, nonchalantly.

"I'll be here, I look forward to seeing you again, sir."

Berg's wife was as stony-faced as the previous Friday as she sat down at table eight. Again, Astrid stood behind her and pulled her shoulders back, this time making it obvious to him that she wasn't wearing a bra. "The same as last time sir?"

"Yes please."

Astrid placed the meals down in front of them, then turned to face Berg.

"Would you like me to pour your wine, sir?"

"Yes, I think I'd like that."

As Astrid poured his glass, she bent forward, letting the top gape open and expose her breasts. "Would you like anything else, sir?" she said as she looked up at him, as he looked down her top.

"I think I would like something else," he said, knowingly.

She looked into his eyes then mouthed the word 'later' and glanced towards a corridor that led to the rest rooms. Berg's wife scowled at her but said nothing.

A little while later, when all the patrons were eating, Astrid stood in a doorway behind Berg's wife that led to the rest rooms. She had no difficulty catching his eye and surreptitiously nodded sideways, beckoning him over.

"Excuse me dear, I must use the facilities," he said to his wife, who didn't respond, and who knew perfectly well what was going to happen.

As he moved out of sight of the seating area, Astrid was waiting for him. He grabbed her and pushed her up against the wall. She put her arms around him and kissed him passionately. She took his hand and placed it on her breast, then undid a couple of buttons on her blouse and made no effort to stop him slipping his hand in and fondle her. He lifted her skirt and put his hand between her legs then slipped his fingers inside the material of her panties.

"I want to fuck you," he whispered in her ear.

"I want you to, but not here. It's my day off tomorrow, meet me at the corner of the road at mid-day. We'll go to my place." She gasped a few times. "You better get back to your wife before we get too carried away," she said, breathlessly.

"You're right. Tomorrow then," he said as he pulled away and went back to the table. Satisfied that they hadn't been seen, she straightened her clothes and went back to serving tables.

As before, as soon as the bill was paid, Berg's wife got up to leave without saying anything. "Goodnight Major Berg see you soon, I hope," she said to him with a lascivious look in her eye as he left.

He smiled. "Oh yes, very soon," he smirked.

A Date with Berg

Berg pulled up at the junction and Astrid got in his car. They kissed for a few moments then he drove off. She put her hand between his legs, unzipped his trousers, put her hand inside; pulled out his erect penis and gently stroked it.

"Where to?" he said, trying to concentrate on his driving as she started to masturbate him.

"There, down that side road. It's about another five kilometres."

He turned left off the main road and onto an underused road. He reached over to try to fondle her breasts, but the awkward angle of his arm made his driving erratic. She hurriedly undid her jeans; pulled them down, opened her legs and pulled her panties open. He slipped his hand inside and fumbled between her legs, as he did that, she leant forward to take him in her mouth.

"No, don't do that yet, it's not that I don't want you to, but I might crash if you do."

"I don't know how much longer I can hold on," she gasped.

"How much further?"

"Not far," she gasped. "Oh God, turn in here, stop the car," she said breathlessly. Berg turned into an old commercial site that had a couple of disused industrial buildings. "I can't wait any longer, fuck me here, fuck me right now, fuck me up against the car."

He yanked on the brake; the car screeched to a halt, he got out and moved around to her side. She quickly pulled up her jeans and got out but picked up the lead pipe she had been carrying in her bag and held it behind her back, out of his sight. He was frantically undoing his trousers, and as he bent over and pulled them down to his knees, she struck him on the side of the head. He fell to the ground, unconscious.

She dragged him into the derelict building that she had prepared that morning. She removed all of his clothes and hauled him into a chair. She bound his arms and legs with thick nylon zip ties, took some rope and ran two turns around his chest, then put tape over his mouth. Certain that he was completely immobile, she went back out and moved the car around to the back of the building, so it was not visible from the road. She went back in just as he was starting to come around. She slapped his face a few times to wake him; he grimaced, tugged at the restraints then glowered at her.

"I know you commanded the special operations squad that killed Arralan civilians at Dantu, and you are going to answer my questions." She ripped the tape from his mouth.

"Fuck off, do you think I'm going to answer questions from a slutty little waitress like you. What are you? a fuck toy doing it for kicks, or a whore? How much do you charge? Now let me out of here now and I promise I'll kill you quickly."

She leant forward. "I am an officer in the Arralan army and if you hadn't been thinking with your dick, you'd have realised you were being trapped, and you *will* answer my questions."

Surprise flashed across his face, but he quickly recovered and sneered at her. "You'll get my name, rank and serial number, but nothing else from me."

"I don't want your name, rank and serial number, I already know them."

"Fuck off then."

"Okay, so we'll do it the hard way shall we?" She moved around behind him and rolled up a newspaper. "I have some good news and some bad news for you; the good news is that I am only going to hit you with a piece of paper." She moved back in front of him. "The bad news is that it's going to feel like this." She hit the side of his face full force. He gasped at the pain.

"Hurts, doesn't it?" Before he could answer, she grabbed his hair and held his head still while she struck his face over and over again. By the time she finished, the roll of paper was soaked in blood. He opened his mouth to speak, but she just rammed the paper into it.

"Forty-nine," she hissed. "I hit you forty-nine times, one for every corpse I found in the barn at Dantu. The forty-nine women and children that you and your men shot." She stood back and wiped away the flecks of his blood that had landed on her face.

His face was covered in blood and already swollen. His left eye was puffed up and almost completely shut. He managed to spit the paper out of his mouth. "Beat me as much as you like, I don't answer questions from Arralan officers," he said contemptuously.

She knew that in all probability he was not bluffing; Correlan soldiers are trained to resist physical abuse during interrogation. This is achieved through the simple expedient of asking questions and then beating the trainee until they answered. Only those who refused to answer would ever become officers. A different tactic was needed to get him to talk.

She put the tape back over his mouth then picked up his jacket, felt inside the pocket and pulled out his wallet. She opened it and took out the contents. There was a recent picture of himself, wife and daughter, the girl looked to be in her early teens, possibly younger, twelve maybe thirteen. She was pretty and had a beaming smile; unlike her mother whose forced smile was obvious. He had his arm around his daughter and was smiling effortlessly and with unmistakeable pride. There were a few other bits of paper including his military driving licence that had his home address a phone number. She left him and went outside, took her phone and keyed Berg's home number; it was answered by a woman with an abrasive voice. "Who is this?" The woman demanded, gruffly.

"Hel-lo. My name is Yola, Yola Travic, I'm from the ministry of education. I've just got a couple of questions for you," replied Astrid in the forced cheery style that officials often use. "Am I speaking to Mrs Berg?"

"Yes, what do you want?" Demanded Berg's wife.

"I'm afraid there's been a bit of a mix up and we don't have the name of the school your daughter goes to."

"What!"

"I'm afraid there's been a clerical error, the name of the school hasn't been filled in. Can you tell me what school she goes to, please?"

"She goes to the local high school for girls, she's been going there for a year and a half now. Are you telling me that this error has only just been discovered?"

"I'm afraid so, yes."

"Incompetence," grumbled berg's wife.

Astrid knew that education officials had training to deal with rude parents and adopted the fake apologetic tone that they were taught to use in these situations, raising her voice at the end of her sentences. "Would that be Balssen High school?"

"Yes of course it is," she snapped.

"And she is in the second year?"

"Well obviously she is if she's been there for a year and a half, you fool. What a stupid question," she snarled.

"I am only doing my job madam. Now I've corrected the file and you will get a letter confirming the detai…"

The woman hung up before Astrid had finished speaking, but it was not important, she had the information she needed. Now he would answer her questions. She went back to the building, drew up a chair and sat facing him. Again he glowered at her. She opened the wallet and held up the picture of his family and said nothing for a couple of minutes while he looked back and forth at her and the picture, snorting and grunting through the tape over his mouth.

"I know where you live and I know that your wife is at home right now," she said, menacingly. "So, how about I take your car and go to your house and collect your wife. It would be easy for me, I'd just find a female soldier, kill her and take her uniform. Then go to your house, knock on the door and beat your wife unconscious before she had time to realise that I wasn't a genuine Correlan soldier. I'd gag her, tie her up and shove her in the boot of the car."

Astrid kept her matter-of-fact tone and stared directly into his eyes, not breaking the eye contact and not blinking. "Then I could go to Balssen High School for Girls and get your daughter, that is her school, isn't it?" she asked rhetorically.

His eyes opened wide with at the mention of his daughter. She looked at the picture. "Oh, now she *is* a very pretty girl, you must be so proud of her. She's in her second year there, isn't she?"

He flinched and looked shocked; Astrid new she had him now. "I guess you've told her that you would always love her." She ripped the tape from his mouth.

"Every day, you bitch," he snarled defiantly.

"And I suppose you've told her that you would always protect her."

"Oh course," he snapped. "What father wouldn't." Then he sneered at her. "I can tell that you don't have children, so you have no idea of the feelings." He closed his mouth tight and held his head up in defiance. She knew that he would be silent now, training would have taught him to not say anything. She pressed home her advantage.

"I could drive to the school and tell them that your daughter was needed, they know better than to argue with the military so they would comply. I could bring your wife and your daughter back here, strip them both naked and tie them into chairs and sit them in front of you."

His expression changed slightly from defiance to concern.

"I will tell them both that I need information from you, and that I am going to hurt them, and all you have to do to stop me is to give me the information that

I want. And when you don't…" Astrid held up a pair of pliers "… you will have to listen to your daughter's screams as I slowly pull out her fingernails. You will have to listen to her shrieking and begging you to answer my questions. Your wife will be screaming at you to tell me what I want to know. Then I will start on her."

She held up a cigarette lighter, lit it and stared into the flame. She cocked her head to one side. "Burning, it's so painful," she said, maintaining the calm menace in her voice. "Maybe I'll use it on your daughter as well."

"You won't do that, you're an Arralan and all you Arralans have your superior morals that you like to boast about," he said. His expression of defiance returned, but his words were more in hope than certainty and the tone of his voice gave a lie to his defiance.

She leant forward, close to his face. "Oh yes, yes, I will hurt your wife and daughter, and I will show them the same level of mercy that you showed the civilians at Dantu." She could see his expression turn from defiance to anguish.

"I don't care what you do to my wife, just don't hurt my daughter, please, don't hurt her," he said desperately.

"Why not?" she said blithely.

"Why not?" he gasped. "She just a child!"

"I counted the bodies of twenty-two children at Dantu, eight of them were girls about the same age as your daughter. They didn't die quickly, they suffered, but you were there weren't you, so you know that don't you? So why should I spare her?"

Anger flashed across his face. "Oh, you Arralans, you're so fucking arrogant, looking down on us Correlans with your high and mighty liberal views. You think we're scum. I know the things I've done, and I know the things my soldiers have done, but now I know that you and me, deep down, we're not so different after all, are we?" He coughed up some phlegm and spat it at her, she knew he would do this at some point and was ready, she dodged to one side; it missed her.

"So, what's it to be?" she demanded, holding up the car keys. "Do I go and get them or not? It's up to you now."

He hung his head and struggled with his emotions for few moments. Eventually he lifted his head and resigned himself. "Okay, I'll tell you what you want to know," he said, defeated.

"I will check the things you say, and if they are wrong, it will be very bad for your wife and daughter." She held up the pliers and the cigarette lighter; she clicked the pliers together a couple of times then flicked on the lighter. He stared in horror at the flame. "Their fate is in your hands." She touched the raw skin on his cheek, making him flinch. "You know I'll do it!"

"You utter fucking bitch. What sort of woman are you?" he gasped.

"I do what has to be done to stop men like you. Now, how many more bodies are there at Dantu?"

"I don't know, fifty, one hundred maybe. Does it fucking matter anyway how many there were? There's lots, and they're all dead."

"How many?" she demanded.

"Two hundred, three hundred." He glared at her. "I don't know, because I wasn't really counting, because I didn't fucking care. I didn't give a fuck about them."

"Why were there only women and children in the barn, where were all the men?" she shouted.

He hung his head again. "There's a mass grave, we got the men to dig a pit then put them in it along with their families and we shot them. We filled it in then another bus load turned up, just women and children; we couldn't be bothered to dig another hole in the ground, and they certainly couldn't do it, so we put them in the barn, shot them all and just left them there."

Astrid swallowed the anger that was rising in her. "Have there been any other massacres of civilians?"

"Just one more before Dantu, it was at Kindala."

"How many died there?"

Berg grunted and appeared to be disgusted with himself. "I stopped counting after we got to seven hundred."

Astrid swallowed hard to calm herself, if she let go of the rage that was building in her, she might not get the information she needed.

"Foreign NGO's reported that they can't get access to three of the prisoner of war camps, and families of the internees haven't received any mail for months. Why is that?"

"They're all dead, that's why."

Astrid sat bolt upright, of all the things she had heard from Berg, this hit her hard. "Dead? Why and how?" she demanded.

"There's not enough food in the country, their rations were reduced. In the end they were only getting about six hundred calories a day, just thin soup, no vitamins. Then when it's winter, a disease happens along, 'flu or something, I don't know, I'm a soldier, not a fucking doctor, but they were all too weak to fight it."

"And you did nothing to save them."

"I was following orders," he shouted.

"You don't have to follow an order when it involves a war crime," she shouted back.

"You do in the Correlan Army," he said wearily.

"Why were the civilians killed?"

"There was not enough food for them either. At Kindala, they were down to less than a thousand calories a day. Then the order came through to get rid of them."

"Was the order specifically to kill them?"

"Yes."

"Who gave the order?"

"Colonel Malaya."

The hairs on the back of Astrid's neck stood up as a cold shiver ran down her spine. Malaya had been the name of the person who sent the assassin that killed Riedel.

"A female officer, Brigit Malaya?"

"Yeah, her."

Again, she swallowed hard and tried not to let Berg see her shock, if he did, it would change the dynamic of the interrogation and he might withhold a vital piece of evidence.

"What about Dantu, the civilians were being transported out of the country, why kill them?"

"That was the order from Colonel Malaya. It was made plain to me that it was not in my interest to question any of it."

"Is Malaya a member of the special operations group?"

"No, Nillzen was the boss, but Malaya was my commanding officer once, she contacted me after I joined the SOG."

"And you followed her orders rather than Nillzen's?"

"Yes. She's very…" he paused for a moment, "…persuasive." Berg shook his head, recalling the threats and intimidation that he had received from Malaya.

"Did Nillzen know about the murders?"

"Yes, but not all of them, and only afterwards, if he had known about all of them, he would have done something."

"Does anybody else in the army hierarchy know?"

"No, though the troopers who took part will probably shoot their mouths off about it sooner or later."

Astrid thought for a moment. "And Nillzen didn't do anything about it, because that would show that he wasn't able to control the SOG."

"That's right. It would have weakened him, and the SOG would have been disbanded."

"Why didn't he go after Malaya? She is only a Colonel, he's a two-star General. He could have crushed her."

"She's untouchable. Everyone knows that she's a favourite of Hallenberg. He wouldn't have let her be promoted to Colonel if she wasn't."

"Why were these people killed when other Arralan citizens have been allowed to leave?"

"They all had some connection to the Correlan government, they either worked for, or were families of people who had jobs paid for by the government. So they had to be eliminated, Malaya said something about some of them may have some knowledge that could be used against us and it was better to kill them all."

"Even the children!" she snapped.

"Yes, even the children!" he snapped back, his anger disguising the loathing he felt for himself.

Astrid sat breathing deeply to calm herself. "How do you know about the rations being reduced in the POW camps?"

"I was there, I did it."

Astrid was finding it harder and harder to contain her anger, but she knew she couldn't let emotions take over. It was getting difficult though.

"The Kindala massacre, were you there too?"

"Yes."

"And you readily took part in the killing of civilians, knowing that it was a war crime."

"God damn it woman, I was following orders," he shouted in desperation. "Malaya ordered me, she said I'd be promoted if I followed the orders and if I didn't, I'd be shot, and my family thrown in prison. What was I supposed to do?"

He hung his head in shame and started crying. "I've told you everything, now please don't hurt my daughter," he begged as tears streamed down his face. "Please, just tell me you won't hurt her."

“I had no intention of hurting your daughter.”

His head snapped up and he glared at her, as he suddenly realised that he had been fooled. She poked the raw skin on the side of his face, making him wince. “I just had to make you think that I would. You see, while you willingly take part in horrific war crimes, I don’t. So when you get down to it, you and I are not alike at all. I don’t hurt or kill little girls.” She looked deep into his eyes. “I just make them fatherless.”

Astrid moved behind him, she reached around and clamped her hand over his mouth, then pinched his nose shut. He strained at the ties holding him in the chair, thrashing his body as he realised that she was about to kill him.

She leant down and whispered in his ear. “Accept it, you knew I would do this at some point.”

He screamed a couple of times, his cries stifled by her hand. His body twitched as he started to panic, then he relaxed, his shoulders dropped and he stopped struggling. His head suddenly felt heavy, but only twenty seconds had passed and he could be faking unconsciousness. She kept her hands in place to prevent him breathing and counted slowly to three hundred. She heard his bladder emptying; colour had already drained from his face. He was dead.

Using a pair of heavy cutters, she cut the chain on his dog tags, and put them in a bag along with the pliers and the lighter. She would dump them far away. She took the magazines from her bag; they were the specialist pornographic magazines that featured heavy bondage with masochistic men being restrained and dominated by women. She opened one to a page that showed a man tied in a chair being beaten across the face and another magazine open at the page where a naked man was tied to a chair and naked woman was holding her hand over his mouth and holding his nose shut. She laid both on the ground beside him.

She opened the contact magazine to the page where she had circled mistress Zelda’s advert and left that on the floor as well. When his body was eventually found, it would be assumed that this was just a sex game that had gone badly wrong, and if anyone had seen the woman who got in his car, it would be also be assumed that she was a dominatrix prostitute who had taken it too far.

In keeping with other deaths occurring in the Correlan sex trade, whether it be prostitutes or their clients, the police would shrug it off and very little effort would be made to find her. The worst that would happen is that the police might visit Mistress Zelda and she could face a couple of hours of some difficult questioning.

Viktor and Desi

Viktor and Desi should have been at school, Viktor was no stranger to skipping lessons, but it was the first time for Desi, and he was nervous.

Desi was fearful as they approached the buildings and hung back. "Why are we here?"

"Why are we here?" Viktor mocked Desi's timid voice. "To see what's here you idiot."

"Why, what for?"

"I dunno, it's just a bit of fun, there might be something we can take."

"Like what?"

"Something, anything, what are you worried about, this place has been empty for years."

"What if we get caught?"

"We won't get caught, there's no-one around. Don't be such a pussy. Now come on."

"My mum will kill me when she finds out that I didn't go to school."

"My mum will kill me when she finds out that I didn't go to school," mimicked Viktor, putting on a high-pitched feeble voice. "Oh shut up and live a bit. You've got to learn to break the rules, that's what they're there for." He pushed against the door. It opened easily and he strode in confidently, Desi followed nervously. There was nothing inside, just an empty building with dried up pigeon droppings and twigs on the floor from nests in the rafters. Dust kicked up as they walked in, making them cough.

"It's just an empty building, why is this fun?" said Desi.

"Okay, there's nothing here, so we'll see what's in the other one," said Viktor defiantly. They walked over to the second building; Desi held back again.

"What's that horrible smell," said Desi, pulling his T-shirt top over his mouth. "It stinks like something's dead. We had a dead rat in our garage once, and it smelled like this."

Viktor turned to Desi and grinned, he opened his eyes wide. "Maybe there's a dead body in there," he smirked, waving his hands like a ghost. "Ooooh, ooooh, a dead body."

"Shut up Vik, I don't want to go in."

"Oh, you're such a baby." Viktor elbowed the door which opened with a creak; he turned to enter just as a shaft of light fell across Berg's decomposing body.

A police car responded to a call from a motorist about a couple of boys that ran screaming into the road and were nearly hit. Viktor was shaking violently and could only point; Desi was frozen and just sat staring into space. The police officer went to the building, took one look then went back to his car. He grabbed his radio. "We're going to need a crime scene team here. One dead so send the ambulance crew as well." His voice was dead pan, he'd seen plenty of corpses before, and was even used to the smell.

Three police cars arrived, followed a little while later by a CSI van. Police ran tape to form a perimeter while technicians donned white overalls, face masks and gloves then entered the building. They set up a couple of floodlights and began taking photos. An unmarked police car pulled up; a detective and his young partner got out.

"Okay. What have we got?" he asked the officer.

"So far, one dead, looks non-accidental sir."

"Show me."

The officer and two detectives went into the building; the officer ignored the smell, the detective put a tissue over his mouth and nose. His partner was not used to the stench of Putrescine, he gagged and almost threw up, swatting at the flies that filled the air. The detective looked at Berg's badly decomposed body then turned to a technician.

"Dead for about what, two weeks?" he suggested.

"Yeah, about that, given the number of flies in here," she said, taking off her face mask. "It's going to be hard to find out who it is." She looked at Berg's head. "Not a lot of meat left is there?" She gestured to the face, looked back at the detective and shrugged. "Nobody's going to be able to identify that, are they." Then she pointed to the skeletal hands. "And all the flesh has dropped off the fingertips, so we're not going to get any prints now."

"Is it male or female?" he said, looking at the bloated body and focussing on what was left of the face.

The technician pointed between Berg's legs. "Oh, it's male, what's left of his dick is sitting there, have a look." She took a couple of photographs of it.

The detective decided not to look. "His age?"

"Hard to tell, obviously adult, there's a lot of body hair still visible. My guess is thirty-five upwards," she postulated. "They'll be able to be a bit more specific once he's on the slab, but only a bit."

"Look at these," said his partner, as he gestured to the pornographic magazines, the technician took some pictures of them, then he put on some latex gloves, picked one up and showed the detective the picture of a man being suffocated.

"This might explain why he's tied into a chair."

"Okay, I've seen shit like this before. A guy gets a whore to cover his mouth, then she holds his nose shut while she jerks him off. She waits 'till the last moment; releases and lets him breathe, then he blows his load."

"That's fucking sick, why would anyone want to do that?" said his shocked partner, still unaware of all the disgusting things he was yet to see as his police career progressed.

"Yeah, I don't get it either. It's supposed to make the orgasm more intense; apparently they have to go right to the edge, but it looks like it went too far and whoever took it too far, left in a hurry."

The technician bopped down in front of Berg. "Well his hands are still tied to the arms of the chair, so she must have been doing the deed with one hand and holding his nose closed with the other. I think it's safe to assume it was a female doing it," she said, looking up at the detective who nodded in agreement.

"Though you can never be too sure these days," she muttered under her breath.

The detective pointed down beside the chair. "There's a bit of tape on the ground, that could have been over his mouth."

"Yeah, and it fell off as his skin decayed," said the technician as she took some pictures of it. The partner grunted and rubbed his stomach to try to make the nauseous feeling go away.

The technician squatted down and closely examined the seat between Berg's legs then traced a line in the air with her finger from the end of his penis to the floor. She studied the area immediately in front of the chair for a few moments. "There's no evidence of any ejaculate." She looked up at the detective and pointed to the floor just in front of Berg's feet. "It would have landed about there," she said in a matter-of-fact tone. "The timing must have been off."

The partner was not used to the dispassionate way forensic teams worked, or the blasé way they discussed the details of a death and he gagged at her visualisation, then looked around for something to distract himself from what she had just said and done. He spotted the contact magazine and passed it to the detective. "I guess this might be the perpetrator," the partner stated confidently, pointing to the circle around Mistress Zelda's advert.

"Okay, you'll have the job of finding her, while I see if I can find out who he is."

Just then, the boys' parents arrived, Viktor ran to his mother and burst into tears, clinging to her waist. He buried his face and sobbed while she stroked his hair and made soothing noises. "It was Desi's idea, I didn't want to come," he lied.

Desi's mother heard what Viktor had said, she turned to Desi, scowled at him, then slapped him across the back of his head. "How dare you miss school, and get poor Viktor in to trouble," she snapped. "What am I going to tell the teachers?" she demanded, her embarrassment making her completely miss the point of the situation. Desi cried but was too afraid to say anything. Desi's mother apologised to Victor's mother who ignored her and turned her face away in disgust. The detective ignored the women and went to his car. He picked up his radio and asked about any males in the area that had been listed as missing.

The detective went back to the parents. "This is a serious criminal investigation. You and your boys cannot speak to anyone other than the police about it. Anybody that does will be charged with perverting the course of justice, and that carries a mandatory prison sentence. That goes for all of you, including your boys," he ordered.

This wasn't true, but he had to make sure that his investigation wasn't clouded by people who always speculate and come up with theories of their own. He pointed to their cars. "Now you need to leave."

Viktor's father picked him up and carried him to their car while his mother stroked his hair as he sobbed. Desi's mother dragged him to their car by the scruff of his neck, his father walked on ahead, stony faced and silent. The detective watched as they left and knew that Desi would get a beating once he was home.

Ten minutes later, the detective got a call back with details of five male individuals recently reported missing in a radius of twenty kilometres around Balssen. Four were teenagers, he discounted them and was left with the name of an army Major who was absent without leave. Twenty-four hours later, dental records confirmed the body to be that of Major Aran Berg; listed as absent without leave for fifteen days.

<<<◇>>>

Berg's wife didn't cry when she was told, instead she just sat scowling. The detective didn't say how he had died, or where he had been found, just that he had been killed. She didn't ask any questions; she didn't seem interested, and just sat with a blank expression that had slowly hardened as the detective had been speaking.

Eventually she spoke. "I thought he had run off with one of his fancy women," she snarled.

"I know this is hard for you but…"

"Oh, for God's sake spare me the preamble, just ask the damn questions and stop pussy footing around," she snapped.

"Do you know if he was seeing anyone on a regular basis?"

She lit a cigarette, took a deep drag and blew smoke into the air. "He never saw any of them on a regular basis," she sneered.

"Did you know any of them?" asked the partner.

"I didn't know any of them, but I always knew when he had seen them." She scowled as she spoke. "And I always knew when he had a new one. Different perfume: you see, women will find a perfume that they like and usually stick with it. So, I could always smell when he had a new woman," she spat the words out contemptuously. "The latest one was probably that flirty little bitch from the restaurant. I saw him making eyes at her, she was all tits and no bra. And I saw the way she looked at him," she looked away and glowered at the floor. "Slut," she said quietly to herself.

The detective took out a notepad. "What restaurant is that?"

"The Silk River."

The partner turned to the detective. "I know it, that's the new up-market place out of town."

"Yeah, but you won't find her there. It's the first place I looked, she's left," said the wife, stubbing out the cigarette and lighting another.

The detective and his partner looked at each other.

"Thank you very much, we'll leave you now and we'll let you know when we find anything."

As they got up to go, the partner turned to her. "We're sorry for your loss."

"Why? I'm not." She huffed. "Good riddance, that's what I say." She opened a drawer and pulled out a sheaf of papers. "I can fill out these forms now." She pointed to a document requesting transfer of his Army pay to her. "And as he wasn't killed on active duty with the Army, I can claim on his life insurance. I know you'll check, so I'll show you."

She selected the insurance document and handed it to the detective who scanned the salient points and showed no reaction, then handed it to his partner to read. The policy was a joint insurance on both their lives, and the sum of quarter of a million Dhat was payable in full on the first death.

"So I'd say that someone's done me a big favour, wouldn't you?" she quipped facetiously, and without a trace of emotion.

The men stepped outside. The partner spoke first. "Here's what I think. She did it. He had humiliated her once too often and she snapped. She had opportunity and she had adultery for a motive, not to mention the money. She clearly hated him; you could see it in her eyes."

"Yes, she hated him, yes, she had a motive, yes, she had opportunity, and yes, she'll get half of his Army pay, then eventually his pension which she'll get for the rest of her life and she'll also get a life insurance pay-out equivalent to twenty years of his pay."

The partner blew out his cheeks in surprise. "Wow, this has made her rich."

"Yes it has. But she didn't do it."

"No?" The partner frowned. "Revenge for sexual reasons is common, and money issues are always a pretty clear motive for murder. She made no effort to hide the insurance papers, and she'll get an awful lot of money."

"Exactly, that tells us that she's literally got nothing to hide when it comes to a money motive. If she was guilty, we'd have never seen the paperwork. Anyway, why go to all that trouble? Do you really think that she's going to get him in a disused industrial unit, tie him in a chair then suffocate him—if that's how he actually died. And where would she get those magazines from?"

"Maybe she found them; realised what he was into and promised to do a trick for him. Then suffocated him when he was tied up."

"Maybe," the detective agreed, but in a way that suggested he didn't agree.

The partner persisted. "Perhaps she got someone else to do it? After all, she's going to have plenty of money to pay them off with."

"Possible, but humiliated wives like her will usually poison their husbands. They want to watch them get sick and suffer over a period of time before they die."

"Maybe she drugged him." As soon as he said it, the partner realised it was a stupid thing to say. "Okay, that was a daft thing to say. If she had drugged him, she could have done him in anywhere," he said, embarrassed by his comment.

"Well drugs may have been used, but toxicology will be difficult now that the blood has degraded. We'll see what the morgue says." They got in the car and the detective lit a Cavana cigarette. "You saw the house, full of nice things, new TV, nice furniture. It's pretty obvious that they didn't have money problems, so killing him for a pay-out is unlikely."

"They may have been in debt though, bank loans, credit cards. He may have been buying stuff to keep her quiet."

"Well, that's true. We'll check the bank." He flicked the cigarette out of the window and started the engine.

"Let's see what we can find at the Silk River, then you track down that Mistress Zelda." He let out a slight laugh "You know, I don't think that is her real name." The police humour being a way to alleviate tension in a situation like this. "We'll gather as much information as we can, but we've only got another twenty-four hours on this case."

"Do you really think we'll catch the killer in the next twenty-four hours?" the partner asked in disbelief.

"No, of course not. I'll write a report based on what we know, and it'll get shelved. We've got more important things to do than waste time on some pervert who got himself killed. He was an army Major, so the military police will want to take over, let them sort it out."

Suspicious Deaths

Colonel Brigit Malaya sat in one of the officer's mess halls in Talena, the vast sprawling army base in the north-east of Correla. She was now the highest-ranking female officer in the Correlan army, and the youngest ever Colonel. She had earned the respect of the male officers that she had worked with, though respect from some was given grudgingly.

She was waiting for her coffee to cool and was thinking about a tactical scenario in a written test she had just taken; wondering if she had answered correctly. She lit a cigarette and stared into the smoke. One question had been deliberately ambiguous, with three possible interpretations and she had quickly realised that this question was not so much about how it was answered, but how it was understood.

Future promotions depended on grades in this exam and the tests that took place here, as promotions would eventually lead to the rank of Major General and the command of Kandalan, the Correlan Army's base number one. It was the pinnacle of an officer's active career and carried with it a guaranteed seat on the army council to follow. She wanted that seat.

Colonel Aster, a fellow officer sat down opposite her. "Mind if I join you?" he said, cheerily.

"No, please, go ahead." She smiled and gestured for him to sit, grateful for the distraction, then offered him a Cavana cigarette.

"How's the assessment going?" he said as he took the cigarette and lit it.

"Tough, I had the medical last week; eyesight and hearing were okay, but I had to ride an exercise bike while they reduced the oxygen level to simulate rising altitude. I managed sixty kilometres until I passed out and fell off. But before I started, they told me that the record is sixty-one kilometres, and I am a little bit pissed that I couldn't make that extra kilometre. I did the written test this morning and I've still got the physical test to do, it lasts five days and apparently, it's a bit gruelling. That starts tomorrow," she said, shaking her head, daunted at the thought of the notoriously harsh tests of courage.

Aster drew deeply on his cigarette and blew the smoke out of the side of his mouth, away from her. "No one who takes the test is allowed to say what happens, but I've heard that the physical test is brutal; the thing to remember though, is that however tough it gets out there next week, they're not going to let you die."

"Are you sure about that?" She half laughed but with a touch of anxiety.

He smirked, "Well, okay then, they'll *probably* not let you die."

She smirked nervously. "You're not reassuring me."

He tipped sugar in his coffee and got serious. "I've been thinking about that business with Nillzen. What do you think about it?" He asked her in a way that suggested that he already had a theory.

"General Nillzen? The army council report says that he tripped on the corner of a rug, fell, banged his head and is in a coma. The doctors relieved the pressure on his brain but say that he'll be a vegetable if he ever comes out of it," she replied, recalling the precis of the report into his accident. "The doctors want to turn off life support, they say that the brain damage is too great, but his family are refusing to let them do it. They're convinced that he'll make a full recovery."

"Yes, that is understandable, theirs was a close family, and it was a tragic accident, wasn't it? He went to answer a call in his private office, which could have only come from headquarters, and yet I've been told that no call to him appears on the log in headquarters for that day. I was under his command for a while, and I knew him as well as anyone can know their commander. He was a gifted officer, destined to join the army council. It's surprising then that he could be so careless…" he stirred his coffee nonchalantly and looked at her quizzically, cocking his head to one side a fraction. "…don't you think?"

Malaya looked at him askance, and frowned, puzzled by the tone of his voice.

He paid no attention to the confused expression on her face and continued.

"And there were three guards on duty in the gatehouse at his home. All killed, one with his throat cut, one with his head very nearly cut right off and one with his face smashed in and a stab to the chest with a blade long enough to go right through his body. It pierced his heart and came out of his back."

"I read the report on their deaths," she looked down and shook her head in shock. "They were horrific, and it was a very strange business; they were the only ones targeted in the attack, nothing was taken, and no-one saw anything. Why kill just those three guards?"

"Hmm, yes indeed, why kill just the guards and disappear?" he asked rhetorically. He sipped his coffee while keeping his eyes on her. "All those people there that night, and no-one saw anything. Granted, the gatehouse is some distance from the house, but still…" He let his words trail off.

"Why would the guests be paying any attention to the gatehouse?"

He ignored her comment. "No motive has been established, nothing was taken, and no suspect identified."

"Suspect?" she shook her head. "No, you mean suspects. Surely there had to have been more than one assailant to take out all three guards."

"Or one very good one," he said, confidently.

"No," she said firmly. "No, I can't accept that."

"Okay, but then there was the mysterious waitress who turned up; the awkward, slightly simple looking one who walked with a limp and had bad glasses. She claimed that a catering agency had sent her, but nobody knew anything about that, and the agency has also denied any knowledge of her. She was caught upstairs and challenged by one of the house staff; he suspected she had gone up there to steal something. She attacked him, knocked him out, tied him up and then, poof, just disappeared." He waved his hands to exaggerate the sarcasm in his voice.

"It's not unheard of for brazen thieves to take advantage of social situations, pretend to be a guest or an employee and get violent when discovered. She was almost certainly in disguise. She would have been looking for jewellery. I read that she had also attacked a guest and had taken her clothes."

"Yes. The poor woman was knocked out, dragged into a toilet cubicle and stripped, but none of her jewellery was taken. And do you think a jewel thief would pass up a chance like that?"

"The woman's car was stolen. A thief would do that," she said firmly.

"It was an expensive foreign sports car, and it hasn't been found. If a car is stolen and used in a getaway, it's usually dumped after a few kilometres, as the thief would not want to take the risk of being seen in it, and the further they go, the more people see it. They would then want to distance themselves from the vehicle as soon as possible—not waste valuable time trying to hide it."

"What are you getting at?"

"Major Pell, did you know him?" he said, deliberately not answering her question.

"No. I knew of him, but I never met him."

“Another ‘accident’,” he said with derision. “He slipped on a bar of soap as he got into a bath, banged his head on the tap, knocked himself unconscious and drowned.”

Malaya frowned slightly. “That’s what the police report concluded. There was no evidence of anyone else being in the building, no murder weapon. Plus, they found the door locked from the inside and with the key still in it.”

“Really?” he said unconvincingly. “The report also left out the part where his wife said that he hated taking baths and would only ever shower.”

“Okay, that is odd, but an accidental death and Nillzen’s injury don’t make a conspiracy, if that’s what you are getting at. They’re probably just coincidental. Besides, the report also states that his wife had never been to the house Pell was renting, the shower may have been crap.”

“Well, I agree that is possible, but could it be coincidental that two gifted officers are removed from the Army, one dead and one in a coma, both in odd ‘accidental’ circumstances? What about Major Berg, you knew him, didn’t you?”

Malaya half laughed and sighed, shaking her head. “Yes, I knew him, I was his superior officer for a while. He could not ever be called ‘gifted’. He was loyal, but just a machine for taking orders and carrying them out. He was never going to rise above Major.”

“Yes, that’s true. I knew him reasonably well, and I don’t think he was a pervert, do you?”

“Well, who knows?” She shrugged, “Nothing surprises me anymore.”

“He was a Correlan man from the north east, and up here, they don’t let themselves get stripped naked, tied up by a woman and then play asphyxia games to get a buzz. If anyone had ever found out, he’d have been a laughingstock. It would have ruined his career.”

Malaya shuffled awkwardly in her seat and avoided eye contact. “Well, plenty of people have secrets that they hope no-one will ever discover, things that would destroy them if they ever got out.”

“Oh, come on, do you really think that there are actually guys that do that breath-play thing to get turned on, or whatever it is they call it?”

“Given the material that was found near his body, it would appear that it’s relatively common. They included pictures from the magazines in the report, those men couldn’t all be actors. And there was that contact magazine.”

"Oh yeah, and when they found 'Mistress Zelda', she was living in Balun, a couple of hundred kilometres away. Do you think she's going to travel all the way across the country to toss a guy off? Because I don't think so. Besides when the police tracked her down, Mistress Zelda turned out to be a sixty-eight-year-old and had been in hospital for a month being treated for an infection in her knee. She may be a dominatrix, but she wasn't there."

"Military police carried out an investigation, they concluded that it was a sex game that had gone wrong." She shrugged her shoulders. "We have to accept their findings."

"No we don't have to accept their findings. Civilian police investigated it first and they said that it was a sex game that had gone wrong, then the military police took over the investigation and came to the same conclusion."

"So, doesn't that prove it then? Two independent investigations getting the same result?" she said, firmly.

"Independent!" Aster laughed sarcastically. "The military police report was word for word the same as the civilian police report. It was a direct copy." He took a deep drag of his cigarette and blew smoke into the air, then pointed at Malaya. "There was no investigation, the report was a fudge."

Malaya frowned. "Why would they do that?" she snapped.

"Do you really think that it's in the army's interest for it to be known that an assassin is so easily able to kill an officer? No, it's much better to destroy a man's reputation by branding him as a deviant who died while being jerked off by a whore." Aster sneered contemptuously. "And why did they need to include those pictures in the report? what purpose did that serve, other than to humiliate the wife of a good soldier? Berg's wife didn't deserve that."

"Okay," said Malaya sharply. "What is your point?"

"My point is, my dear doubting colleague…" said Aster, stubbing out his cigarette for emphasis. "…that we are losing too many talented people to 'accidents'. There have been others, but they have been kept quiet. Too many people with new ideas are being lost. I don't know if Berg is any part of it or just an aberration. But I think we are dealing with a very skilled assassin, someone very skilled at making a murder look like an accident."

Malaya thought for a moment, weighed up all that he had said. "Maybe there is something in what you say, but if there is, the military police would be on to it."

"No they won't be 'on to it' as you say, they'll do nothing," he said, disdainfully. "The army council controls the military police, and they don't want to admit that this could be happening. Much better to go with the simple explanations."

She found herself getting irritated with him now. "That's quite a risky thing for you to be saying. Doubting the army council could get you in a lot of trouble."

"Yes, I know."

"So why are you telling me this?"

"Because you are smart!" he said firmly, then softened his tone. "Look, you're a really good officer, and if I'm right, then that makes you a target and the Army needs you. Just be careful and don't have any accidents, I don't want to read about you slipping on a bar of soap or tripping over the corner of a rug."

She ignored his obtuse compliments. "How do you know all this?" she demanded.

"I have a friend, she is a civilian and works at army headquarters, she gets drunk and tells me things."

Malaya frowned deeply and angrily pointed her finger at him. "I'll pretend I didn't hear that," she said forcefully. "You and your friend need to be very careful of what you say and who you say it to."

"It's not '*what you say and who you say it to*'. "It should be '*what you say and to whom you say it'*. Sorry to correct your grammar, but if—when—you get promotion, you'll be making a lot of speeches and writing a lot of reports, and they'll like you to use the correct form of words." He got up and nodded respectfully. "Good luck with the physical tests, I will be thinking about you," he said and left.

Malaya lit another cigarette and went back to her thoughts on the written test, but her mind kept drifting back. She kept telling herself it was just coincidence and she had better things to do than worry about his paranoid delusions. But there was a little nugget of doubt in the back of her mind; it was his turn of phrase and the conviction in his voice. There was nothing she could do though; this was military police territory, and she could not interfere.

The Test Day 1

As commanded, Colonel Malaya reported to the guard house at six-thirty in the morning. She was with a group of seven men. They were all from different branches of the military, she didn't know them and only met them the previous day in the written test. All were nervous, including her, and being nervous was not a feeling she was used to. Three-star General Kedara entered the room, he looked stern and serious. All stood to attention and saluted. He acknowledged them but left them standing.

He spoke with an aggressive edge to his voice. "This trial will take five days, it will test your courage in very harsh conditions, and do not underestimate just how difficult it will be. You will each be given two, six-digit numbers; you will have ten seconds to memorise them. You may not write them down or keep them in any way. Over the next five days, you will be coerced into revealing your numbers. Those who do will immediately fail the test and will be removed, anyone who interferes or tries to stop another candidate's test will fail and be removed. After five days you will disclose your numbers to me, and me alone. That is an order."

He gestured to an aide who took some envelopes from a box. "After the tests are over and you leave the test centre, for the rest of your life, you are forbidden by military law from ever revealing any aspect of the tests, regardless of whether you pass or fail. The law applies even after you leave the military. Is that absolutely clear?"

"Yes General," the group answered in unison.

An aide passed envelopes to the contestants; each had their name on it.

"Inside the envelopes are your numbers, they are unique to you; do not discuss your numbers with any of the test subjects. Your ten seconds starts now."

Malaya opened her envelope and saw 182571 589647. She closed her eyes and visualised the numbers.

The General checked his watch. "Close your envelopes now." Malaya had already closed hers, and Kedara had noticed it. "You will now be taken to a location within the base. You will all face the same tests, but at different times.

You will be temporarily demoted to the rank of private second class for the duration of the tests, so you cannot question or refuse any orders given to you by anyone. I wish you all the very best of luck."

They saluted as he left the room. A cheery Sergeant from transport entered the room. He rubbed his hands together. "Now my lucky lads and lass, who's for a little ride?" he said, as he nodded towards the door. "Come on, this way."

He hummed a cheery tune as he led them out of the building to a waiting troop truck. Just before they reached it, he turned to them and smirked. "Look." He glanced over their shoulders towards the guard house. "Good, no one can hear me from here." He grinned at them and half-laughed. "Look, you do know you all have the same numbers, right?"

"Really?" said one of the men, then turned to the man next to him. "What have you got? I've got 9657…."

"Shut up, you stupid fucking arsehole," yelled the Sergeant. He pointed back to the guard house. "Get out." The first dejected failure walked slowly away. "You lot, get in," he shouted. "You're all going to fail. Fuck knows why I'm even driving you out. I've seen hundreds like you, and you've all lost already, I can see it in your eyes. You're pathetic."

One of the men approached him. "Remember we are your superior officers and…."

"Shut up… 'Private'," shouted the Sergeant. The man stood, shocked, as the realisation of their situation dawned. "What are you waiting for 'Private', get in now," the Sergeant yelled in his ear. They sat in silence as the truck made its way across to the far side of the base.

They arrived at a remote collection of buildings, all got out and were directed into one where they sat for an hour. Nobody spoke, all were just waiting for the tests to start. Malaya was taken first; two hooded guards walked her into a room where the Major in charge of the tests was standing holding a neatly folded prison uniform. Four lecherous young troopers were lolling around in chairs, smoking. Their ties were off, shirts were undone, and empty beer cans littered the floor. They looked her up and down lasciviously and kept their gaze lingering on her. The Major placed the uniform on a table in front of the troopers, then pointed to the wall on the other side of the room.

"Stand over there," he ordered. She walked over and stood where he commanded. He pointed to the uniform, it only had two parts; a thin jacket—little more than a thick shirt- light grey and with the word 'Prisoner' printed repeatedly all over it. There was a pair of trousers with the same pattern, but nothing for her feet. “You have to wear this uniform during the tests; you must take off all your clothes including your underwear and put this on. And you now have a choice, you can give me the numbers, which would mean that you fail the test, or you can take off all your clothes now and put the prison uniform on while these men stare at you.” He gestured to the troopers. “They’ve been up all-night drinking and waiting for this.”

Malaya gritted her teeth as anger flashed though her. ‘So this is how it’s going to be’, she thought to herself. She knew that having a prisoner naked during serious interrogation was common, as it greatly enhances the sense of vulnerability. This is particularly so for a woman, where the humiliation of being intimately exposed in front of predominantly male tormentors is often the crucial first step in breaking her spirit and extracting the information required. She refused to let them use her own body as a weapon against her, and if she had to be naked, then so be it.

Without hesitation, she started to unbutton her tunic. She gritted her teeth and fixed her gaze on the Major, scowling at him; the troopers leered at her.

“We’re gonna see your tits, we’re gonna see your tits, we’re gonna see your tits,” the troopers started chanting as it became obvious that she was not going to reveal her numbers.

“And your muff,” said one, pointing at her crotch. “If you’ve got one that is, do you shave it all off, or just trim it up, darlin’?”

“We’re gonna see your arse,” said another, downing his drink and throwing the empty beer can across the room. “So you’ll have to give us a twirl, and you’ll have to bend over and show us your arsehole, love.” He lolled back in his chair, spreading his legs, pulling his trousers tight and showing that he had an erection.

The troopers laughed and pointed; a couple rubbed their hands together as they ogled at her. She felt herself blush slightly as she removed her blouse and skirt.

“At any time, you can give me your numbers and we will all leave the room,” said the Major calmly.

She gritted her teeth again and looked him straight in the eye as she removed her bra and stepped out of her knickers. She stood naked for a moment, her head held high, her hands by her sides and making no effort to cover her modesty before walking to the table and taking the uniform.

“I could have you,” said the trooper, quietly and ominously, as he sat in his chair rubbing his erection through the material of his uniform. He sneered at her. “We could all fuck you and no-one would ever know, ‘coz you can’t tell anyone, can you?”

Malaya glared at him, she would kill him if he tried, but she couldn’t take on all of them. She put on the clothes and turned away. She stood barefoot on the cold concrete floor, silently defiant in the prison uniform, her unblinking gaze on the Major who beckoned the guards over to take her away.

“Maybe another time, eh? ‘Private’,” shouted the trooper as she was led out of the room. “There’s plenty of time; you’re here for a few more days and we know where your cell is.”

Malaya returned to the rest of the contestants, aware that they would not have to suffer the same degrading test. At first, she was certain that she wouldn’t be raped, but this was just the first test, and it had shocked her. A little unease crept into her mind as she waited for whatever was coming next. The young trooper was right, law forbids her to say what happens in the tests, and they could do whatever they wanted to her.

She felt cold and vulnerable and fought hard to stop herself shaking; and not just because of the cold, but because of the helpless feeling she had in front of the troopers; a feeling that was still lingering inside her. It had been distressing being so exposed while having no control over the situation. It was still morning on the first day and she worried about the coming days and what they would hold for her.

One by one they were taken away, two huge guards wearing balaclavas would come in, grab them by the arms and drag them out. Malaya was last, she was taken to a room and thrown in. The door slammed behind her and she heard a key turn in the lock. The room was light grey, the walls, ceiling and floor were the same shade. There were no furnishings in the room and no windows. The ceiling was high with six large fluorescent light fittings that were the width of the room. Each fitting had six tubes; far more than was needed for a room this size. Only one tube in one fitting was on. Suddenly she realised that it was very quiet and knew what was about to happen. Sensory deprivation, a prelude to coercion.

The light went out and she was plunged into absolute darkness, she held her hand millimetres from her face but could not see it. Her eyes could never adjust to total darkness but as her body tried to, her pupils would become fully dilated.

Minutes passed, then all thirty-six tubes suddenly came on, filling the room with blinding white light. She covered her eyes and put her head down.

She hadn't noticed the speakers in the ceiling, but became very aware as at the same time, deafening heavy rock music blasted out, with screaming, screeching vocals and sharp, distorted guitars, powerful sub-bass that she could feel in her stomach and a bass drum that felt like it was punching her in the chest. She couldn't cover both her ears and her eyes, so she moved and faced into a corner of the room and put her fingers in her ears.

She did not know the music but recognised its underlying rhythm of one hundred and twenty beats per minute. If she counted every other beat, that would give her seconds; if she then counted sixty, that would be a minute and if she counted to three hundred, that would be five minutes.

Training had taught her that sensory deprivation works by removing all points of reference, then saturating the primary senses and wearing down the subject, but now she had figured out how to keep time. At exactly three hundred, the lights went out and the music stopped, plunging her into darkness and silence. She started counting from zero again and when she got to three hundred, the lights came back on, as did the music. She was elated, and as unpleasant as the experience was, she had something to occupy her mind and focus on.

After six bouts of light and sound, silence and darkness, the door opened the Major walked in. "Tell me the numbers." She stared at him and said nothing. 'Two can play mind games' she thought to herself.

"As you wish."

He left the room and the show started again. After three one-hour sessions her eyes were bloodshot and her ears ringing; she felt sick from the constant ultra-low frequencies that seemed to affect her abdomen, but she had not revealed her numbers. She was taken to another room and locked in. This room had a thin mattress on the floor which did precious little to mitigate the rough ridges in the concrete.

There was no blanket and no pillow. There was a plastic jug with a small amount of water and a bucket to use as a toilet. A small, barred window high up let in some light, and with this she could judge the passage of time. It became obvious that she would not get any food and despite her hunger, she knew not to ask for any. Asking created a need which could be manipulated. Eventually a hatch at the bottom of the door opened and plate with some stale biscuits was slid in.

The Test Day 2

The door crashed open, and the two hooded guards came in, dragging her to her feet and hauling her into another room. They shoved her into a chair and secured her with leather straps around her arms and legs and another around her waist, then left her. She guessed the time to be about six thirty; she started counting at one second intervals. An hour passed, and the guards re-entered the room, one stood behind her and grabbed her hair, yanking her head back, the other stood in front.

"What are the numbers?" he shouted.

She looked beyond him and focused on a mark on the wall. She determined to keep looking at that spot and not at him. He slapped her face, not too hard, but hard enough to make her wince, again shouting, "what are the numbers?" He slapped her face again. "This will continue until you've told us the numbers," he snarled.

She had experienced treatment like this before in training, but that was nowhere near as severe as she was getting now. She remembered what the instructors had taught her; don't make eye contact, focus on a spot on the wall opposite, and never let them see that you are afraid.

"Name: Brigit Malaya. Rank: Private second class. Serial number: YK 18 79 56 48 F," was her reply.

The slapping eventually stopped, but the shouting didn't. She watched as the sunlight moved across the floor. Abruptly, the shouting stopped, and the guards left the room. She estimated that her ordeal had lasted over three hours. She knew that the guards could return at any time and that this gap was to give her time to think about what else was in store. The door opened, and the Major walked in. He put a small table down in front of her and placed a tray of sandwiches on it. He removed the straps on her arms, and she resisted the urge to touch her face or show him in any way that she was hurt.

He drew up a chair and sat opposite her. "You've not had anything to eat today, and precious little yesterday, just breakfast and a couple of biscuits. You must be very, very hungry."

She glowered at him and avoided looking at the food, but the aroma of the fresh bread made saliva flood her mouth. She could have easily reached over and taken something but knew that this is exactly what he wanted her to do. He picked up a sandwich and peeled it open a fraction.

"Oh, look. Smoked Salmon and Cucumber. I know some people don't like smoked Salmon, so let us see what else there is. Beef and Horseradish, Tuna and Mayonnaise, Salami, Ham and Cheese. Oh dear, they'll be a little bit bland, as will the plain Chicken, but a little bit of salt and pepper soon will improve that." He held up a sandwich. "You can have whatever you want. All you have to do is give me your numbers."

She gritted her teeth and ignored the hunger pangs.

"Name: Brigit Malaya. Rank: Private second class. Serial number: YK 18 79 56 48 F," she said, staring at the wall behind him.

The Major bit into a sandwich. "Mmmm, Tuna and sweetcorn, a classic, and I must say it is delicious. Give me your numbers and you can have any or all of them."

She looked him in the eye. "I'd rather eat my own shit," she snapped.

He shrugged. "Well that happens from time to time, you wouldn't be the first."

He put three packets of cigarettes and a lighter on the table. "You are a very heavy smoker, and you've not had a cigarette since yesterday morning, by now you would have got through all of these; you must be getting a bit twitchy. As you can see, they are Cavana, your favourite brand and given a choice between smoking or eating, people with a serious nicotine addiction like yours will almost always choose a cigarette over food." He waved his hand dismissively. "I don't smoke, so I find it to be very odd to deny your body the nutrition that it needs and take the drug that it wants instead. But then that's addiction for you."

He opened a packet and slowly took one out and held it out to her. She looked at it and felt a strong desire to take it but forced herself not to and looked away. She knew she was in the first stage of nicotine withdrawal; her craving was intense, and a dull headache was just starting. She had tried to give up smoking before and knew that by the end of the day she would start to get irritable and anxious. By the end of the next day she would start to feel depressed.

Without realising it, Malaya had rubbed her forehead while he was talking about smoking, the Major knew that this was a sign that she was weakening.

“Go on, take it, light up now.” He flicked on the lighter; the flame shimmered hypnotically. He placed the cigarettes and lighter on the table within easy reach of her. “Just give me your numbers, that’s all you have to do.”

“I’ll give up smoking then,” she said as firmly as her craving would allow.

He got up and left the room. The guards entered, and she braced herself for more abuse, but instead they removed her restraints and took her back to her cell. After a couple of hours the hatch opened, and a bowl of lukewarm porridge appeared along with a bottle of water, but no cigarettes.

She laid on the mattress, trying to ignore what might be instore for her by focussing her mind on the written test. She heard screaming from another cell and the sound of generator being cranked; a man’s voice begged the guards to stop. But the screaming continued.

It was dark when the guards entered her room again. “The numbers,” yelled one of them.

“No,” she yelled back.

They grabbed her by the arms and dragged her along the corridor. The Major was standing by an open door to a cell. They dragged her into the room, it was cold and damp. In it one of the other men was hanging by his wrists from the ceiling. He was naked; his face was bruised around his left eye. Deep red weals covered his torso where he had been whipped with leather straps. A guard threw a bucket of cold water over him.

“Numbers,” yelled the other guard.

“Name: Deni Papalous…. Rank: Private second cla…” was all he could say before he was punched in the face, the force of the blow splitting his bottom lip open.

Malaya looked on in horror, these were her own people and everyone in the room was from the Correlan Army. She knew that the tests were extreme but struggled to understand how they could beat a colleague so viciously.

“This will be you before the week is out, you will be treated no differently. No account will be made for your gender, you will hang there naked; you will be beaten as he has been, and facial scars do not look good on a woman.”

The Major waved his hand, directing the guards to take her to another room. She recoiled slightly at the fetid stench that hit her as the cell door opened. In there, one of the other men was hanging from a hook on the wall; he was also naked. Ropes around his wrists locked his arms straight out behind him, his feet were off the floor and his full body weight was taken on his shoulders that were twisted back. He gasped and grimaced, fighting the pain.

"This is called the Strappado, and it's effective albeit a bit mediaeval. He's been there for three hours now; the pain builds until it is unbearable. We'll have his numbers before the hour is out."

The Major looked at Malaya and saw she was shocked. "You will also have to suffer this in exactly the same way before the end of the week. Quite apart from the extreme discomfort that this causes, as a woman, how do you think you will feel as these men man-handle you, ripping off your clothes and stripping you naked? How will it affect your female psyche as they tie your hands behind your back and haul you up, leaving you exposed and defenceless?" he said calmly.

"The troopers are still here, and they could come in and do whatever they want to you."

He noticed her brief look of revulsion as her brow furrowed, then her expression harden as she scowled at him and stiffened her back.

Once again, he gestured to the guards to take her to another cell, he walked ahead and stood by the open door. "Take a look," he said, gesturing into the room. There was a freshly made bed, an armchair, a table with tea and coffee makers and a selection of bread rolls and cakes. To one side there was an en-suite shower with large towels hanging on a heated towel rail along with a white bath robe. A vase of fresh flowers filled the air with a sweet scent. "This could be where you stay tonight, you know what to do."

She looked at him, gritted her teeth, said nothing and just shook her head.

"Take her to the cage."

They dragged her outside and forced her into a metal cage. It was a one metre cube, with not enough room to stand or lay down. She sat in the corner; the bars on the bottom of the cage made finding a comfortable position difficult.

The Major appeared. "The guards will check on you throughout the night, and you can come in whenever you want and have the room I showed you, just give them the numbers."

"NO!"

He left and snapped his fingers at the guards. One pulled a rope, and a bucket of cold water emptied over her. She sat, shivering, knowing that her will was starting to falter. "They will not break me," she said to herself, trying to force the doubt from her mind.

The Test Day 3

Guards dragged her from the cage and put her in a room with the others, three were now missing and one of the missing was the man suffering the Strappado. She was shivering and exhausted, rubbing her hands together to try and generate some warmth and subconsciously looking around for a source of heat.

Nobody spoke, three of the men looked drawn, their faces grey and with signs of bruising. Papalous had received a serious beating, his left eye was swollen and almost shut, he had multiple bruises on his face and a ligature mark around his neck. He tried to hold together the split in his bottom lip. Eventually he spoke.

"They used electricity on me," his voice was weak and fearful. He wiped tears from his eyes. "They have a machine, they call it Mr Sparky, or something like that. The beatings were bad enough, but I can't take any more electric shocks, I just can't." He bowed his head and sobbed quietly.

The door burst open, and the guards walked in, they grabbed him by the arms, hauling him to his feet. "Time for your follow-up appointment with doctor sparky."

"NO" he screamed, "NO, I can't take any more, please no, I'm begging you, please, no more." He collapsed in their arms. Malaya went to stand, but one of the men put his hand on her arm. "We can't interfere," he said.

One of the guards put his hand on her face and shoved her back in her seat. "Go on then, try to stop us, what are you going to do?"

Papalous was crying uncontrollably. "I can't take it; I can't take it. I'll tell you my numbers," he cried out through sobs. He looked at the rest of the contestants. "I'm sorry, I'm sorry, I've let you down. I know I should be stronger, but I'm not." The guards looped his arms around their shoulders and carried him out carefully, in stark contrast to their previous behaviour.

Malaya felt sorry for the men who had failed but was also envious of them. She was jealous of the comfort they would receive from their wives, for the law in Correla prevented her from ever having the partner she so desperately wanted. She would never have the joy of a companion to spend the rest of her life with, to come home to, to care for, or to be cared for. She would never feel complete, but the law was the law and she had long come to accept that a lifetime of loneliness would be her fate.

The Major entered the room. "Well it's day three, and there's still four of you left. I will have to instruct my guards to work a bit harder." He looked at her. "Private Malaya, you were cold last night, let's see if we can do something about that."

One by one, the men were taken away. Then they came for her, she was taken to a different building and once again shoved into a room and locked in. On one side behind a metal grille, were coils of wire. She heard an electrical relay click, there was a loud buzz, and the coils began to glow, they were heat coils and in seconds the room started to warm up, at first it was pleasant, but quickly became uncomfortable.

A dial on the wall showed the temperature rapidly rising through twenty-five degrees centigrade. It rose to thirty degrees and stayed there. She turned away to shield her eyes, but felt the radiant heat on her back, she arched her back so less of the hot cloth from the uniform would be in contact with her skin, but this was a hard position to maintain, and she quickly realised that she would just have to move every few minutes.

After a while, she checked her pulse, her normal resting heartbeat was fifty, it had already risen to over one hundred and thirty. She tried to count seconds to get a sense of the passage of time as she had done before but felt dizzy and found it hard to concentrate. Sweat had now drenched her uniform, adding to the discomfort. Time passed, and her head began to swim, she felt nauseous and sweat was running into her eyes, stinging them. She had no idea how long she had been in there, when a voice came over a speaker in the ceiling. It was the Major.

"You are seriously dehydrated and in about ten minutes you will have heat stroke, you could die from that. Outside there is a glass of iced water. Tell me your numbers and you can have it."

"Name: Brigit Malaya… Rank: Private second class… Serial number: YK 18… 79 5… 6 48… F," she gasped. Five minutes later she collapsed.

<<<◇>>>

It was mid-afternoon before Malaya woke in her cell; her uniform stained with the white marks of dried sweat. Four large bottles of iced water were beside her mattress. She sipped one third of one bottle over the course of ten minutes, then waited. The water was too cold, and she could get painful stomach cramps if she drank too much too soon, and she knew that this was deliberate, just another nasty, cynical way to torment her.

"Day three," she said aloud. "Two more days to go, how much worse is this going to get?"

The tests were far harsher than she had expected, and she had felt anxiety rising in her today. Occasional despairing thoughts flashed through her mind, and they were getting more frequent.

The door burst open, and the guards came in. "Doctor sparky will see you now."

She froze in terror; she had received an electric shock as a child and remembered the pain. For the first time in the tests, she felt her willpower slipping away. "No, no, no," she said. It was quiet and involuntary, but the guards heard it.

"You are going to tell us your numbers today," one of them snarled.

She struggled and shouted at them as they strapped her into a chair, her quiet defiance replaced by yelling and abject fear. Bare copper wire was wound around her ankles and wrists, and the other ends plugged into doctor sparky. This was a large box with a crank handle on the side with two knobs and a button on the top. A guard pointed to them.

"Intensity, duration, and go," he said and turned the knobs to their minimum setting. He cranked the handle and pressed the button. She felt a jolt; it hurt, but was not too painful, though it was extremely unpleasant. She looked down at her arms and legs to see them shaking with the frequency of the current. Five seconds later, the current stopped, and the guard cranked the handle again. She gritted her teeth to stop herself from biting her tongue as he pressed the button and the next jolt hit.

The guard stepped away and the Major appeared; he stood silently in front of her for a few minutes, then spoke softly. "I had hoped that we would not have to use this on you, but you leave us no choice. I have told the guards to go further than we usually do." He gestured to the controls. "First, we will increase the intensity until we find your upper pain threshold and we will go past it. Then we will set the duration, this will slowly increase, and every shock will last longer than the preceding one." His voice, as ever, was calm and unconcerned with the suffering that tests were causing. He got close to her face.

“We *will* find your threshold and we *will* exceed it.” This time, his voice had an air of menace, a tone that he hadn’t used before. He noticed the worried look on her face and the fear in her eyes; he stood up straight and sighed, the harshness in his voice faded a fraction.

“Look, we don’t have to do this to you. I don’t want to do this to you, I know how bad it is, and I can see that you are frightened. So please, just give me the numbers and you can go back to the room I showed you, please, your numbers.”

She looked back and forth at the machine and the Major, breathing through clenched teeth, her look of fear slowly replaced by anger. “NO,” she shouted. “Name: Brigit Malaya. Rank: Private second class. Serial number: YK 18 79 56 48 F.” She braced herself and closed her eyes. The guard turned the intensity up one notch. “Last chance,” he said.

Malaya shook her head. The Major turned to leave the room but stopped as he got to the door and looked back at her. “The pain from the shocks eventually gets so bad, that some test subjects have been known to bite part of their tongues off. Try not to do that.”

The Major left the room and heard her first yelp as he walked away. He could hear her shrieking as he walked down the corridor to his office. He shut the door, unwilling to hear her screams. It wasn’t long before the intensity reached the point where her diaphragm went into spasm, preventing her from crying out. Instead, her body locked rigid as electricity coursed through her, then collapsed, trembling when the current stopped. Two shocks like this knocked her unconscious.

The guards removed her restraints and dragged her limp body back to her cell, laid her on the mattress then broke an ammonia capsule under her nose and slapped her face. She woke immediately, then, satisfied that she was conscious, the guards left her, locking her door as they went. Usually they left all the lights on to prevent her from getting any proper sleep, but this time they turned them off, plunging the room into total darkness. She groped around in the dark to find a bottle of water, then heard the voices of young men outside her door. She recognised the voice of the trooper that had threatened to rape her. Someone banged on the door, probably him.

“You alright in there, love? A bit lonely are you, do you want some company?” His voice was harsh and sarcastic.

She backed into a corner and curled herself up in a ball, trembling, she would be too weak to fight them off now.

"Or shall we just come in and fuck you anyway?"

There was nothing she could do; tears rolled down her face as she waited for the door to burst open and the four of them come in to hold her down and take turns on her. But it didn't happen.

"Maybe tomorrow night, eh?" came the voice, then the sound of laughter.

The Test Day 4

She woke and had no recollection of how many shocks she had received or how long they had lasted or when she ended up back in her cell. She did recall the troopers outside her door and shuddered as she remembered. Tepid watery porridge appeared through the hatch along with some more water. It was late morning and there was still one-and-a-half days to go. She was frightened—terrified. For the first time in her life she knew sustained fear, and she now doubted whether she could resist any more. The horror of what her own people were doing to her was beyond her comprehension. She put her head in her trembling hands and started to cry.

The door opened, and the guards came in, her heart sank, what more could they do to her. They grabbed her by her arms, dragged her to her feet and held her firmly. The Major entered, his expression hard and pitiless. He slowly and deliberately took his sidearm from its holster, drew back the slide, then held the weapon so she could clearly see him flick the safety off. He nodded to the guards who grabbed her face and forced her mouth open. He rammed the muzzle in her mouth.

He looked unblinking into her eyes and waited for ten seconds before speaking. "There's nothing special about you," he hissed through clenched teeth. "There'll be plenty more through these doors after you, so it really doesn't matter if you die."

He looked deep into her eyes. "A certain number of test subjects are expected to perish, and in here, we have immunity from prosecution."

She started to shake and a feeling of cold flooded through her body, her teeth chattered against the barrel of the weapon as she tried to calm herself, but it wasn't working. She could taste the metallic tang of the weapon, and the aroma of gun oil filled her head. Her breathing had reduced to short panting and she was getting dizzy through her hyperventilation. The gun was a Nagler twelve-point five, the most powerful pistol in the Correlan military, a single shot would tear her head off.

"Numbers." he yelled.

Unable to speak, Malaya summoned all her courage and shook her head as far as the weapon would allow. He let out an irritated grunt, then pulled the trigger, the hammer clacked against an empty chamber. She gasped, and her knees gave way, she slumped down and was held by the guards. The Major left her cell and the guards dragged her to another room. In the centre of the room there was a large oil barrel with its top off; it was full of water.

The Major stood in front of it. "This is getting tiresome. For the last time, the numbers, please."

"Name: Brigit Malaya. Rank: Private second class. Serial number: YK 18 79 56 48 F."

The Major pointed to the barrel. "This usually works, and you know your options." She looked at the barrel, eyes wide open in dread. He looked at the guards. "You know what to do." He left.

The guards tore off her clothes, stripping her naked, then tied her hands behind her back. She struggled and fought them as hard as she could, but she was too weak. They dragged her to the barrel.

"The numbers," one shouted.

"No."

They pushed her head under the water and held it there, she was too weak to stop them. After about ten seconds, she started to panic, they pulled her out and she gasped for air, but they immediately pushed her head under again, this time holding it down for longer. They pulled her out and shouted, "Numbers."

"Name: Brigit Malaya. Rank: Private second class. Serial num…" was all she could say before they pushed her under again. They pulled her out; they sensed her fear and pushed her under again. They pulled her out quite quickly, her stress was doing the work for them.

"Numbcrs," thcy shouted in unison, both millimetres from her ears.

In she went again, and panic rose in her like never before, she fought the breath reflex as carbon dioxide built up in her blood. They sensed she would soon not be able to stop herself from trying to breathe, and pulled her out, but as she emerged from the water she had just inhaled a small amount. She coughed out the water, and stood, gagging and spluttering, her throat burning, and her body racked with terror at the primeval fear of drowning.

"Numbers, or it's longer this time."

"NO, please no," she cried as they slowly pushed her head down and into the water. She breathed in as deeply as her fear would allow.

Twenty seconds passed, and she felt water start to flood up her nose. Sounds were muffled, but she heard the door being kicked in, the guards pulled her out and she collapsed on the ground, coughing, crying, and gasping for air.

"Stop what you are doing," shouted a military police Captain. "Arrest those two, untie her and someone find some clothes for her."

Burley policemen grabbed the guards and dragged them out. An elderly nurse ran in with a large towel and put it over her. The police Captain bopped down to Malaya. "You're going to be alright; the test has been cancelled. There's been… an incident."

The nurse helped Malaya to her feet and led her out of the room. "I thought I was going to die," she said through tears.

"It's alright my lovely, you're safe now," said the nurse in a soft country brogue.

In the corridor, the Major sat with two military policemen standing either side of him. He was ashen faced and trembling, he looked up at her, he was a pathetic sight. "There's been a death, and it's my fault, I told the guards to use more force, but they went too far, I couldn't control them." He put his head in his hands and started to cry. Medics wheeled a gurney out of one of the cells, a sheet covered a body; an arm dropped out from beneath the sheet; blood was dripping off the fingers. A medic quickly put the arm back. Malaya was overcome with anguish as she remembered Aster's words. "*They 'probably' won't kill you.*" Her knees buckled; the Captain caught her and supported her until she regained her balance.

The nurse led her to the room with the bed and shower, she washed her, dressed her, and put her to bed; Malaya was incapable of doing any of this for herself now.

"Just you have a little sleep my lovely, the Captain will have a word with you after he's dealt with them arseholes out there." She stroked Malaya's forehead until she dropped off to sleep.

Three hours later Malaya awoke to find the nurse sitting patiently beside her and the military police Captain standing at the end of her bed. The nurse handed Malaya a mug of tea.

"I saw you were stirring, so I made you a drink."

"Thank you," said Malaya, her voice hoarse from the water she had taken in. She noticed that her pillow was wet.

The nurse smiled. “You coughed most of it up in your sleep. I stayed here to make sure you were alright. You’ll be groggy for quite a while though.”

“Thank you, you are very kind,” she said weakly.

“Unlike the Major and his guards,” said the Captain, smiling at Malaya, who went to get out of bed. “No, please don’t get up, you’re still very weak.”

He pulled up a chair. “Despite what the Major may have told you, they do not have immunity from prosecution. The guards have been charged with murder and will get life, no question about that, even though they’re keeping their mouths firmly shut. The Major hasn’t said what has been done to you but has admitted that he ordered more force to be used on all of the test subjects. He’s been charged with conspiracy to murder, he’ll get fifty years, minimum. And we haven’t yet charged them all with your attempted murder.”

Malaya sat bolt upright, as suddenly the full horror of her situation hit home. “You don’t think that they were intentionally going to kill me, do you?”

“Oh yes,” he said dismissively. “Two men holding a woman’s head under water seems pretty premeditated to me.” He paused, wondering what to say, worried about her state of mind. He glanced at the nurse for guidance. She nodded at him then squeezed Malaya’s hand to comfort her.

“You’d already inhaled some water, a few more seconds and you’d have gone past the point of no return.”

“Them fuckers,” muttered the nurse.

Malaya gasped and looked up at the ceiling, the horror of it all racing through her mind. She’d been in life threatening situations before, but that was in combat and she’d had some degree of control. But she had been powerless to stop these two men from trying to drown her, and the thought that they had nearly succeeded affected her more than she wanted it to.

“Then, of course are the assault charges for the beatings to the other contestants,” said the Captain.

“But isn’t that part of the test, to see who can withstand the coercion?”

“No, most definitely not. They’re not supposed to do any physical harm, and as for the electric shocks the guards gave you.” He looked down shook his head. “Disgusting,” he muttered. “These guards are new and they’re psychopaths—head cases, it doesn’t matter that the Major said he couldn’t control them, he gave the orders.”

“How did you find out?”

“We intercepted a call to his medical team that there was a problem, and that one contestant was dying. We got here as soon as we could. I’ve never been here during the tests before and I had no idea of the level of brutality. I am shocked, and I am determined to make them face the full force of the law,” he said angrily.

“I can’t thank you enough.”

“All part of the service ma’am,” he said, then smiled at her and tugged the peak of his cap, injecting a little bit of humour. Malaya smiled for the first time in four days.

“Okay, now for the dull police stuff.” He pulled a notepad from a briefcase. “This may be hard for you, but we only have a vague idea of what has happened here, but what is certain is that serious crimes have been committed, so we do need to know, and as this is now a criminal matter all rules of disclosure are void. Are you up to telling me what happened to you?”

“Yes, I’m okay, the shock of it all is easing a bit.”

“The shrinks will soon have you sorted out my lovely,” said the nurse. Malaya knew she was only trying to be helpful but laying on a psychiatrist’s couch answering questions about her childhood relationship with her father instead of the tests, was not what she was planning for the near future.

Malaya worked through the events of the past four days, watching the Captain and nurse wince and muttering disapproving noises as she recalled the things she had endured. A couple of times she became emotional as she recalled what they had done to her. They waited patiently as she calmed herself before continuing. The Captain made copious notes and finished with a flourish.

“Well that’s about five new charges we can bring, now there’s just one more thing, it’s just routine. I need your numbers.”

Malaya opened he mouth to tell him, then stopped herself. “Why?”

“Oh like I said, it’s just routine paperwork, you know how it is, modern police work is ten percent work, ninety percent writing about it. So, let’s have them.”

“No.”

“Come on, you know that the test has been cancelled.”

“So why do you need my numbers, and how did you know about the electric shocks? I hadn’t told you, and you said the Major hadn’t said what they’d done to me and you said the guards haven’t said anything. Your exact words were *they’re keeping their mouths firmly shut.*”

His expression changed to anger. “Give me the numbers,” he shouted.

“You’re not a real military policeman, are you? And no-one’s died have they.” She turned to the nurse. “And you’re not a real nurse, just a crass caricature. I didn’t inhale that much water, you put that on my pillow.”

“Yeah, I did, now give him the fucking numbers,” the nurse sneered, her easy country accent being replaced with a harsh city one.

“No.”

The Captain pointed at her aggressively. “Let me remind you that you are a private second class and I am an officer, and I order you to give me the numbers.”

“NO,” she said firmly.

“If you continue to disobey my order, you’ll be court marshalled and go to prison for a long time. Now give me the numbers, that is an order,” he shouted.

“NO!”

“Do you really want to go into the cage again?”

“If it’s that or giving you the numbers, I’ll take the cage.”

He threw the prison uniform at her.

“Fuck you,” she shouted.

“Guards.” Two men entered the room. “Put her in the cage.”

The Test Day 5

At six thirty Malaya was taken out of the cage and led to the room that she had been in the day before. She showered and had a breakfast of cereal with warm milk, pâté on toast, a glass of orange juice and a mug of tea. She got into bed and was allowed to sleep for four and a half hours. She awoke to find her freshly washed and pressed uniform was hanging on the back of the door. Clean underwear was on the chair and her shoes, polished to a mirror finish, were beside the bed. She dressed and did her hair.

She checked the bruises on her face from the slaps she had received; they had started to fade and were still a clear blueish yellow; she would not try to hide them but would wear them as a badge of honour. She left the building and walked with her head held high to the car that was waiting for her.

She walked into the guard house, General Kedara was waiting for her, he had her envelope in his hand; he opened it and looked at the numbers. "Your numbers please."

Without hesitating she replied. "182571 589647, sir."

He smiled, then opened the results of the written tests and read them. He put that down, opened a packet and took out two embroidered epaulets. He took her old epaulets from her shoulders and attached the new ones. He saluted her.

"Well done, General Malaya."

"Thank you, sir," she said, swallowing hard and barely holding back the tears of joy. She saluted him and couldn't resist looking at her new rank badge on her shoulders, her pride momentarily dulling the pain that she still felt.

She looked around, none of the other contestants were there. The General noticed. "You are the only one that passed, the others all cracked yesterday."

She felt conflicted, proud that she had passed, but concerned for the other men and what must have been done to them to make them reveal their numbers.

General Kedara smiled and took her by the arm. "You now get access to the senior officer's club. There will be an official ceremony there tonight, eight o'clock sharp. Now, my driver will take you back to your quarters."

"Thank you, sir, but no thank you. I will walk."

"As you wish."

She turned and strode purposely out of the building. Her quarters were on the other side of the camp and it would be a long walk back, but she didn't mind. She was elated as she breathed in the warm air, and despite the rigours of the past few days, felt more alive than she had ever done.

As she approached the building that housed her quarters, she saw a young trooper walking towards her, she recognised him from day one of the tests. He suddenly recognised her and stiffened. As they got close, he stopped, stood to attention, and saluted. She returned the salute.

"Permission to speak ma'am," he said nervously as she passed. She stopped and turned to him. "Permission granted."

"About the tests ma'am. I…"

"Stop there," she said firmly. "Were you following the orders of a senior officer?"

"Yes ma'am, we all were but we all hated doing it and we hadn't been drinking ma'am," he said, anxiously.

"Were you carrying out the orders of a senior officer exactly in accordance with that officers' instructions?" Malaya calmly replied.

"Yes ma'am. The Major told us what to say and how to act."

"Then you were doing your duty and I would expect nothing less from you."

The trooper blushed and got flustered. "But ma'am, we saw your breas—"

"Think no more about it, that is an order," she interrupted.

"Yes ma'am. I will ma'am, err I mean I won't ma'am. Thank you, ma'am." He stood frozen in place.

She smiled. "You can go now," she said softly.

"Yes, ma'am, I'll go now, thank you, thank you ma'am." He saluted again, turned and walked briskly away.

Celebration

At precisely eight o'clock that evening, General Malaya crossed the threshold of the building that she had walked past so many times but had not been able to enter, the senior officer's club. As she entered the lobby, a staff member approached her.

"This way please ma'am." She followed the staffer into an ante room. A uniform was hanging on a rack. "This is your new dress uniform ma'am; you can't enter the club without it."

Malaya looked at it for a few moments. The cut of the jacket was subtly different, beautifully tailored and somehow classier. The epaulettes were the same as the ones General Kedara had presented to her, but the lapels were different, the main body material was Grey/Green cotton. The lapels on her old dress uniform were the same colour, but satin. On the new uniform, the lapels were red satin with a seven-point gold star embroidered on each one. She put it on and swelled with pride.

She entered the main hall of the club to rapturous applause from the generals gathered there. All stood and clapped as she walked confidently to General Kedara. He beckoned her to stand by his side. A waitress handed her a glass of champagne.

"Gentlemen, this is a great day. All of us have taken the stamina test, so we all know what General Malaya has endured. So let us toast not only our newest general, but the first female ever to become a general in the Correlan Army. Raise your glasses to General Brigit Malaya."

"General Brigit Malaya." Came the unison response. Kedara turned to her. "Would you like to say something?"

"Yes, sir, I would. Thank you." She cleared her throat. "Gentlemen, my colleagues, I can assure you all that there was one test that none of you had to endure." She waved her hand dismissively. "But that is of no consequence now. The only thing that matters is that we are all part of the same team. I may be the youngest general in the Army and I may be just a woman, but I will always have your backs, I will always fight for you, and if necessary, I will die for you. I will fight for our country with every fibre of my being, and if duty requires it, I will die for our country." She held up her glass. "The army," she shouted. "The army," came the reply from all in the room.

The generals looked around at each other, nodding with approval and started clapping. The applause died down and she set about moving through the assembled crowd, shaking hands, accepting congratulations, and exchanging pleasantries. She came face to face with the Major in charge of the tests. There was a moment as their eyes met and he shuffled awkwardly. She suddenly realised that she had no ill feelings about him.

"I have no animosity towards you," she said magnanimously. "We all have our roles to play in service to our country, and many duties are onerous; you were carrying out your duties." She smiled, and he relaxed.

"Thank you. Not many people see it that way when I meet them again." He laughed nervously. "General Kedara always invites me to these events so that the contestants can meet me again. He likens it to them falling off a horse and getting back on again, because it's not the horses' fault that they fell, the horse was just doing its job, just as I was doing mine."

"There is just one thing I'd like to say, though," she said, frowning.

The Major looked worried. "What is that?"

"Maybe you could be a little less good at your job."

He laughed. "I'll bear it in mind ma'am." They shook hands and she was about to move on, when he stopped her. "There is one thing that you should know. You are the only person who has ever remembered all of the numbers given to them. Everyone in this room has passed the coercion tests but they have all failed to remember all their numbers."

"But it's not about the numbers, is it."

"You are right, it's never about the numbers. They are just the focus, without them, the test would have no meaning. However, the fact that you remembered them is remarkable. Now, there are some people here that you should meet."

On the other side of the room, she saw the men that were the other test subjects. He led her over to them. She shook hands with them and accepted their toast as they raised their glasses to her. She looked at Colonel Papalous, the man who had broken down at the prospect of another session with the shock machine.

"The stitch in your lip looks painful, and how's the eye?"

"Everything is fine, it's just a scratch really. I'll have a small scar, no big deal about that, it'll make me look a bit more macho, women like scars—or so

I'm told. And the eye, well that was never going to be permanent," he said with a wry smile.

She looked at the other men. "You all look very cheerful considering you've just failed a crucial promotion test," she said, with a hint of suspicion in her voice.

"Yes, remarkable, isn't it?" said one, smirking.

"And why are you here if you failed promotion…" She closed her eyes as it dawned on her. The Major spoke and confirmed what had just become obvious to her. "You were the only test subject."

Malaya pointed at the men. "And you lot were stooges. And your bruising was make-up."

"Yes," said Papalous. "We were all part of the illusion."

"But your injuries, they were real. I saw them hit you and split your lip."

"Yes, they are real. It was my idea, we realised that you would be a tough nut to crack, and we needed to get a lot more convincing, so I volunteered to take a beating that you would see. A few jabs of local anaesthetic and I didn't feel a thing. Even the other guys didn't know." He paused and rubbed his chin. "Bloody well hurt the next day though."

"That is uncommon dedication," she said. "I'm impressed."

"Yes, dedication, a month's leave plus two thousand Dhat to take my family on holiday."

"Ooh, lucky bugger," laughed one of the men. "Why can't I get a beating like that, I could do with a couple of thousand Dhat."

"Well that's you next time, then," said the Major.

The man's expression changed, "What! Err, no, I didn't mean it, I was just having a laugh."

"Too late old boy."

The Major took her to one side. "Now, due to your rank you have to assume that if you were to be captured you would be harshly interrogated and depending on who captures you, torture would be a definite possibility. If the Arralans get you, you may get shouted at, but there would be no mistreatment. However, there are factions within the Northern Alliance who use torture as a matter of routine, and despite claims to the contrary by the leadership, its use is widespread.

"In a real situation where you are captured and interrogated, two techniques would be used depending on what information the enemy wanted from you. If the information was urgent, you would be physically tortured, it would be brutal, agonising, and completely without mercy. But if you were just being held, they would grind you down with psychological torture, with the fear of pain often being worse than the actual torture itself. What we do is to approximate both techniques. Thinking back, did the electric shocks really hurt as much as you thought at the time? if they did, you'd have burns on your wrists and ankles."

She looked at her wrists, there were no marks. She looked back at him, astonished. "But I..."

"That's the psychological element, your anxiety caused your brain to exaggerate everything. It was a very low current. We couldn't risk giving you shocks that were as strong as you imagined, it could have killed you. Remember that, if you ever get captured."

"And the water at the end? I nearly drowned."

"There was never any chance of that. The guards are trained diving instructors. They are life savers who work in the marine training division. They know exactly how long someone can stay under for."

"You took me to the point of despair, then gave me hope in order to get me to reveal my numbers."

"Yes, that's classic emotional abuse, it only works when the subject is at their absolute lowest. Most subjects crack on the morning of day four, but you clearly hadn't reached that point. When did you realise the test wasn't over?"

"As soon as he asked for the numbers. The comely old nurse holding my hand, the Captain trying too hard to be sympathetic. It suddenly became obvious."

General Kedara approached and took her to one side. "You were still a private second class and you disobeyed a direct order from the Captain to reveal your orders. Why?"

"You had ordered us to give our numbers to you and you alone, sir. Only a Major general, the army council or grand field marshal Hallenberg can countermand your order, and he didn't look like any of them, sir."

Kedara laughed. "Good, very good. Now speaking of the grand field Marshal, I have a letter for you."

She opened the letter:

General Malaya, I wish to congratulate you on your promotion and look forward to your years of service to me and the great nation of Correla in the struggles that we face.

GFM Godin Hallenberg

“Hmm,” murmured Kedara. “Hand-written and signed by Hallenberg. These letters are usually typed by his aide, Marek.”

He paused and looked at the lapels on her jacket, then looked her up and down, admiring her uniform. “You know, I doubt that this uniform will ever need to be cleaned.”

“Sir?”

“Your potential was spotted while you were still in basic training. Keep up the good work and I don’t think it will be long before your lapels are blue with two gold stars. And then…” Kedara tapped his white lapels, each with three gold stars. He let this gesture sink in for a few moments.

“Because of your success in the tests you will now be granted three week’s leave. But for the first week you must stay here so that you can be checked by the doctors on a daily basis. The test was particularly hard on you and it is important that you don’t have any lasting issues. As you are now on leave, you will have no duties and can spend the time as you see fit. Then you will have two weeks at the officer’s resort at Don-Bahlia and have full use of all the facilities. The beach is stunning there, so get some sun, you’ve earned it.”

He smiled, took her arm and led her away from the main group then with a twinkle in his eye, lowered his voice.

“What happens at Don-Bahlia, stays at Don-Bahlia, you can do anything you want there, absolutely anything! You can have whatever liaison or assignation you desire—with anyone.”

He looked at her with a slight smile and an odd expression that she found hard to read. “A lot of women are there on their own; the staff are very discrete and if they see anything, they are paid enough to not ever mention it—if you understand what I mean. So make sure you enjoy yourself to the full. That’s an order.”

“Yes, sir, understood sir.” Though she didn’t fully understand what he actually meant.

<<<◇>>>

In a base on the far side of Correla, Colonel Lothar Valerian sat at his desk, enraged. He had just read the notification of a promotion within the army. His heart had skipped a beat when he saw the name Brigit Malaya, the focus of his hatred for his entire military career, now with the rank of one-star general, and now, for the first time she seriously out-ranked him.

"Damn you woman," he fumed as he banged his fist on his desk. "You may be a senior officer now, but never will you be superior to me. I am better than you in every way, I always have been, and I always will be."

He clicked a file on his computer bringing up her picture.

"Because you are a woman, they must have gone soft on you during the selection tests, did you fuck the examiners, or did you simply suck the right number of cocks?" He said sarcastically as he closed the image, then opened and printed out the selection test application form.

He muttered to himself as he filled out the form. "I am told that these tests are the harshest in the army, and I fail to see how a mere woman could pass them. I will pass them, and I will get promoted higher than you and then I will put you in your place… General Brigit Malaya."

Malaya sat on a couch in her quarters, reliving the pride she had felt this evening as she had moved through the crowd in the senior officers' club. She had taken her uniform off and hung it on the back of a door. She put her feet up on the couch and tucked them in under the soft bath robe that she was wearing. She poured herself a large brandy and while she drank it, she sat looking at the red satin lapels, each with its single seven-point gold star.

She thought about all the things that had been done to her over the past five days. The noise, the bright lights, the heat, the cold, the hunger. Then there were the electric shocks, the beating, the gun in her mouth and the near drowning. She poured herself another large brandy and downed it in one. She now knew that the other contestants where fake and just a form of psychological torture. But she hadn't known that at the time, and their treatment, beatings and the apparent death had seemed very real and the effect on her had been profound.

She lit a cigarette, stood up and paced around the room excitedly. "But they didn't break me, they didn't, I beat them," she said, loud and proud. But inside, she knew the suffering she experienced had changed her, she had often wondered if she could do those same things to others; to deliberately hurt people to get what she wanted. She was well aware of her propensity for violence as a first resort, that had always been with her, and she liked that she could intimidate people bigger and stronger than her to get her way.

She liked the fear she saw in their eyes as she grabbed them by the throat and slammed them to the ground. But would that violence ever morph into sadism; to bring out that thing inside her that she had always suspected was there and allow her to inflict pain on someone just for the sake of it. She wondered what else would be needed to push her over the edge and cause her to actually enjoy causing suffering to another human being; someone restrained and not able to fight back or resist. What fear would she then see in their eyes?

"What would it take for it to not be a problem for me?" she asked herself.

She poured herself another large brandy and paced around the room, thinking about the humiliation of being naked in front of the young males, their leering looks and taunts as she undressed. She remembered the sickening feeling of degradation as she removed her underwear and walked across the room to take the prison uniform, knowing that they were staring at her naked body and judging her.

"If they were girls, I might have even enjoyed it, I'd have taken my time, perhaps I would have put on a bit of a show," she muttered as an unlikely scenario entered her head.

A magazine on a coffee table had a picture of a minor female TV celebrity on its cover. She picked it up and looked at the woman: a pale but pretty twentysomething peroxide blonde with piercing blue eyes, blood red lipstick and impossibly white teeth.

"Oh, you are gorgeous, do you want someone to keep your bed warm at night sweetheart? a woman maybe? How about me?" she mused. She grunted contemptuously and tossed the magazine down, finished her drink and went into her bedroom.

She got in bed and set an alarm for five hours. The bed was a double, all officers were assigned quarters with double beds as it was assumed that they would all be married. She could spread out, sprawl across the whole width if she wanted to, but for some reason she always slept on the left. Before settling down she looked at the empty space next to her and sighed. She yearned for a woman to be lying beside her, someone to share her triumph of promotion, someone to talk to, someone to love. To feel someone's hands touching and caressing her, to feel her hands on someone, someone to have sex with. But she knew it was out of the question.

"Maybe one day," she said quietly as she closed her eyes and drifted into a dreamless sleep.

Astrid's Return

"The Dantu massacre was ordered by Colonel Malaya sir." Astrid could barely suppress her anger as she spoke to DeSalva.

A look of shock flashed across his face.

"But there's more sir, and it's bad, really bad."

"Go on," he said, apprehensively.

"There was a bigger massacre before Dantu. At Kindala, sir."

"How big?"

"In excess of seven hundred."

"My God!"

"And the men in the prisoner-of-war camps; they're all dead. Sir, they were starved to death."

"We thought something was up, but not anything like this." DeSalva put his head in his hands. "Barbaric," he said quietly, "we're not in the middle ages anymore."

"All of it was ordered by Colonel Malaya sir, all of it." Astrid's voice descended to a whisper as emotion got to her. "I want to go after her sir."

"No."

"Sir, I must."

"No."

"Sir, I must have revenge," she said angrily.

"NO," shouted DeSalva. He banged his fist on the table. "That is precisely why you will not go."

There was a minute of silence, eventually he spoke. "Listen to us, listen to what she is doing to us, we've never argued before; we are better than this."

"I'm sorry sir."

"An apology is not required, but look at what she has done to you, you are shaking. Your anger at her could cause you to make a mistake."

Astrid knew he was right, and deep down she knew that she was not emotionally ready to go after Malaya. "She killed the only man I have ever truly loved," she said and hung her head.

"Five years ago, I promised you that you would get your chance at her, and you will, but despite all of this, not yet."

He opened Malaya's file on his computer and studied it for a while. "I agree that she is dangerous and needs to be dealt with, but we simply don't have enough information on her."

Astrid calmed herself and nodded to accept DeSalva's logic. "I meant no disrespect sir, and I apologise for getting angry, it was inappropriate. I accept whatever disciplinary action you want to give me, and I hope it hasn't damaged our relationship."

"Since we first met our relationship has been frank, honest and professional. It would take a lot to damage that. There will be no disciplinary action this time." He looked her straight in the eye. "Astrid, I do understand your feelings. Riedel was a good man but give it time."

She sighed as she remembered Riedel.

"I want a full report on the Nillzen mission and everything about your subsequent activities in Corella; and I mean everything. After that, I want you to work with the intelligence teams again, your collaboration with them was very productive last time. There are no missions planned, but if any arise, I'll be giving them to other members of the team."

"Hmm, you're giving me a desk job," she said quietly, then looked at him and smiled.

He was pleased to see her sense of humour return, albeit slightly. "You are not being side-lined." He opened a map of Corella, "We have recently received information that the Correlans are focussing their efforts in the north." He pointed at a mountainous region. "They have uncovered a plot by the Northern Alliance to assassinate the prime minister. Hallenberg has decreed that they must deal with the NA once and for all."

"Nobody has ever been able to keep the northern tribes under control sir. That area is vast and will require a huge amount of manpower."

"Which is good news for us. A lot of troops have been quietly withdrawn from the border and re-deployed to the North, so the harassing raids should decrease significantly. We never thought that there would be an invasion, not for a while anyway. The Correlans just wanted us to think there would be an invasion. It will come though, one day, when they have perfected whatever it is that they are working on." He shook his head, "Riedel knew what it was, and this is what I want you to work on, and by doing so, you will honour his memory. Dismissed."

Astrid sat in silence opposite DeSalva as he read her report on the Nillzen mission. He opened his eyes wide as he turned successive pages. He put down the file and cleared his throat. "Creative…" he said, slightly alarmed at what she had done. "…even by your standards. But why did you kill that Zappan character? He was just a trooper."

"As you can see sir, it was through him that I learned of Berg's part in the atrocity and subsequently of Malaya's involvement."

"And nothing to do with the fact that he was the one that killed the civilians at Dantu?" He raised his eyebrows, then frowned slightly and stared at her.

"He was a target of opportunity sir. Plus, he could have compromised me," she said unconvincingly, fidgeting in her seat as she spoke.

DeSalva looked her in the eye. "Captain Peterman," he said firmly. "Revenge is not what we do, remember that. The risk you took with him was too great for far too little return."

"Duly noted sir."

"We're not going to risk another mission like this, you were gone for over two months and were far too exposed. There was no chance of backup or rescue. By now, someone in Corella should have worked out that these are not accidents. We are going to have to be very careful from now on, and we are running out of ways to get you in and out of the country. Fortunately, given the information provided by our asset at the Correlan Army headquarters, we think we have eliminated enough people for the time being. So a lull in our activities will be to our advantage."

"Can the asset be worked any harder sir? Could we use the asset to find out what their master plan is?"

"No, she's a civilian and works in a different department. We've not been able to recruit anyone who has the right security clearance. The supply of information from her is sporadic at best. She supplies us when she can, and we can't dictate what we want other than in broad terms."

"I will work with intelligence to gather information by other means sir."

"Their internal internet, or intranet if you like, is a closed fibre optic network that is impossible to penetrate from outside and has very sophisticated login procedures that we have never been able to crack. The network has multiple mainframes and multiple backup systems. But their phone system is old and primitive, so it's wire taps, radio intercepts and interrogation of defectors and captured Correlans. Most of whom give up information readily when they see how much better life is here."

"Do you want me to do some of the interrogations sir."

"No, I want you to do all of them for the foreseeable future. You speak Correlan fluently and have a good knowledge of the different regions of the country, and I've heard you using the regional accents as well as the high form of Correlan. We captured a General quite some time ago; he is being held at a manor in the south. He is known as an honourable man, so in exchange for giving his word that he will not attempt escape or harm any of the guards, he has free reign of the house and grounds. The guards have been told to always stand to attention and salute when they see him."

DeSalva handed Astrid a photograph of the man. "We are pretty sure that he doesn't know who you are, and even if he did, he would certainly not expect to see you in person, so I want you to go there and make friends with him. He's from the south west, so you will have a lot in common.

"From time to time we'll give you un-redacted Correlan newspapers to give to him, that should help build a relationship. Always address him as 'sir' and always salute when you meet him. He hasn't given us anything yet, but analysts think he will if the right approach is used. Obviously, the house is bugged, and he will certainly be aware of that, but there are microphones hidden all around the grounds, and all of them record twenty-four hours a day. We'll tell you where the microphones are, so you can stroll in the garden chatting to him."

"I should let him lead the way, so that he doesn't become suspicious, sir."

"Correct, and don't rush, build a relationship over time and let him lead the conversations; don't ask questions about their tactics or strategy. What we want is casual chat, this is often the most revealing."

"Sir, what if he decides to stand in the middle of a lawn and talks quietly."

DeSalva smiled. "Don't worry, the microphones will pick it all up, they are very good."

"I'm guessing that my visits won't be too frequent, sir."

"That's right, once you have established a relationship, long gaps between visits will make him more likely to talk when you do see him."

"What do I be doing between the visits, sir?"

“You’ll be working with intelligence analysts; transcribing wire taps and radio intercepts, de-briefing defectors etc… Spend time on the range; I want you to hone your sniper skills and I also want you to do some teaching.”

Astrid was taken aback. “Teaching what sir?”

“The skills that you have, fieldcraft, initiative, improvisation, loyalty, comradeship, leadership, everything. All the qualities that I saw in you five years ago, all the things that come so instinctively to you; including the things that you don’t even recognise in yourself. Analyse what it is that makes you so good and write about it, and don’t be modest. I know your history and I know you can stand on a stage and talk to people. Give lectures, inspire people, give them the same sense of self-belief that you have.”

She smiled but with a tinge of sadness. “I got all those qualities from Riedel, sir.”

Pell's House

The daily checks at the base hospital were starting to irritate Malaya, she knew they were important but wanted the week to be over. Four days in and she was restless, unused as she was to the lack of activity or mental stimulation. She tried reading books and newspapers but couldn't concentrate. She turned on her TV but found the banality of daytime television stultifying and after a few minutes hopping through the channels, turned it off and refused to watch any more of it.

She still ached from the rough treatment; the bruises on her body had almost completely gone, but her mind was as sharp as ever and Aster's words nagged at her. She got in her car and drove to the house that Major Pell had rented.

The house was old and had been unoccupied since the death. The landlord was superstitious and wouldn't go near the place now, and in keeping with traditional practice in Correla, houses where death had occurred were abandoned and just left to decay. The ground around the building was dotted with trees and overgrown shrubs from what was once a very large and ornate garden.

Walking up to the front door, she saw the marks around the lock where the sledgehammer had hit. She pushed, it opened slowly, its hinges creaking from lack of use; the stale air inside smelled of damp. There was a light film of mould on everything; a bowl of fruit contained only husks of blue and brown. She moved slowly from room to room, not sure what she was trying to achieve. Newspapers and magazines were folded and placed neatly on a coffee table. She entered a room directly below the bathroom, the smell of damp was particularly strong here. The bath had been overflowing for hours before Pell's body was discovered and the ceiling had caved in from having been soaked. Fungus was now growing on the soft furnishings.

In the kitchen, mice had found boxes of cereal, nibbled away the corners and removed all of the contents. Ants had found a bag of sugar, and this was still sustaining their colony as they swarmed all over it, each ant carrying away an individual grain. In a bread bin there was a shrunken loaf, dried out and covered with a thick layer of blue-grey mould. She opened the fridge, the power had been off for months and the tomatoes, cucumber and salad had reduced to a watery slime. A half empty bottle of milk had separated into thick creamy curds floating in orange-yellow liquid. A thick layer of black mould coated the inside of the fridge and a smell of rotting meat was coming from packets of sliced ham, one of which was open and had completely rotted away, the other was still sealed in a plastic pack that was inflated like a balloon; the meat inside having turned to a foaming liquid. She closed the fridge and moved on.

In a small cupboard she found medicines: pain killers, anti-inflammatory tablets, antihistamines, cough syrup, plasters, and tubes of antiseptic cream. There were vitamin supplements and eye drops; all of the items in the cupboard were neatly arranged and in date at the time of Pell's death.

In a drawer was a domestic tool kit, with screwdrivers of different sizes, pliers, cutters, a tape measure and a small hammer. All had the same light blue rubber on the handles, and she recognised them as being sold by a chain of hardware stores across the country. She had bought the same kit herself. The tools had been removed from the blister pack and placed in the drawer, and it looked like some items had only been used a few times.

Beneath the sink were bottles of bleach, sprays of surface cleaner, aerosol cans of polish, dusters, packets of toilet rolls. Again, all neatly arranged. It all spoke to Malaya and confirmed Pell's personal profile of being well organised and disciplined.

"And yet he slipped on a bar of soap," she said to herself.

She went upstairs and found the bathroom. The bath had a mixer tap, a large block of chrome plated, machined brass. On it was a button, the press of which would direct the water up through a shower hose. She examined the rounded water outlet and compared it to a picture of Pell's head wound that she had brought with her. It was the same size and shape.

"Possible," she muttered to herself.

She called to mind the report.

'...The door was locked from the inside with a key. The key was still in the lock, but the bolts top and bottom were still drawn back... All the other doors and windows were locked with a key and further secured with bolts.'

She went to the door and examined it, she could see where the military police had forced the door and smashed off the striker plate on the door surround. The key had been left on a shelf nearby. The key was quite simple, and the keyhole didn't have a metal plate around it and was enlarged through years of use. She tried it in the lock; the mechanism was well worn, and the lock engaged with very little effort.

"Why lock the front door, but not slide the bolts? Maybe he didn't feel the need to," she mused. "But if he really was murdered, how come all the doors and windows were locked from the inside?"

She looked at the key and noticed a small crust on the very end. Looking closer, she saw the characteristic white bloom of superglue. "Why put superglue on a key? A key is the last place you want glue," she said aloud. She studied it closer and noticed some small fibres in the glue residue, then it occurred to her. "Unless you use it to attach a bit of string and use that to pull the key into the keyhole from outside. You lock the door with lock-pick tools, then pull in the key with the string, and you could keep trying until it was in place then yank out the string leaving the key in the lock, and that's why the bolts weren't drawn; it would not be possible to do that."

She went back into the kitchen and opened the drawer containing the tools. She remembered that the tool kit she purchased included a tube of superglue; there was no glue with the kit in the drawer. It was possible that it had all been used, but it was far too much of a coincidence to ignore.

"Could Aster be right? or am I just seeing what I want to see?" she said quietly, aware of the danger of making evidence fit a theory instead of the other way round.

She went outside and stood by the front door scanning the garden. Fifty metres away there was a ditch that ran along the line of a hedge. She walked over to it and noticed that some of the branches on the hedge were damaged in one spot and that grass in the ditch was shorter below the damage. To her it looked like an improvised surveillance foxhole, but it could have a more prosaic explanation. She looked back at the house. "But if this was a foxhole, he had a clear view of the front door, the bedroom and the bathroom. He watched Pell, then made his move when Pell was in the shower."

A buzz of excitement filled her. "If this was a murder and not an accident, then this assassin's good, he'll be hard to catch, and when we do, he'll pay for what he's done," she said aloud.

But she also knew that she couldn't take this to the military police, it was just too far-fetched for them and they wouldn't take kindly to someone challenging their conclusions. She decided not to tell Aster but would quietly investigate the other deaths whenever she had time.

Don-Bahlia

Brigit arrived at the hotel complex at Don-Bahlia early in the afternoon. A porter took her cases as she checked in.

"You have the best room in the hotel," said the receptionist. "It is always given to officers who have taken the selection test." She programmed a key-card. "You are on the top floor, so no-one will be walking past your door at night. Use this card to get into your room. I think you'll like the view."

"Thank you."

"I hope you don't mind me asking," said the young woman. "But I've heard that the tests are harsh, are they?"

"They are, but I'm not allowed to say exactly what happens, so let's just say that I never want to do them again."

"Oh, you're so brave, I don't think I could do them."

She handed Malaya the key-card, and as Malaya took it, the girl brushed her fingertips across the back of her hand. It was a subtle gesture and Brigit was not sure if it was accidental or not. The receptionist made eye contact as she did it but did nothing that suggested it was anything more than a slip of the hand, but it was a strange thing to do.

"I should warn you that the beach does get very hot at this time of year, so you'll need some high factor sun cream," the receptionist said, pointing to some shops along the corridor.

"Oh, okay. I'll need some more money then, is there a cash machine here?"

"You won't need any money while you are in the complex. It's all free for you, just show them your key-card."

She went to the shop and picked up a bottle of factor twenty sun cream. She handed over her card to the girl behind the counter who swiped it through the till, then smiled as she handed it back. 'Very nice.' Brigit thought as she left the shop and went to her room.

The porter was waiting with her bags and followed her into the room, placing her suitcase on a low table and the bags on the floor beside it. She tipped the porter and he turned and left. She opened the shutters and walked out onto a balcony. The view took her breath away. The beach of golden sand curved gracefully between two large rock outcrops. Palm trees lined the paths that cut across manicured lawns. Flower beds were stuffed with brightly coloured plants, all in bloom and giving off a sweet perfume. Waves of crystal-clear water broke gently on the shore; she could see people swimming in the sea. The beach was wide and deep, but there were few people on it.

There was still time to get some sun, so she quickly changed into her bathing costume and went to the beach. She found a sun bed and put some sun cream on her arms and legs then laid down and pulled out a book to read. Occasionally she looked up from her book and slowly began to feel self-conscious. There were plenty of women her age and older that were wearing bikinis, yet she had a frumpy, flowery bathing suit on that covered everything except her arms, legs and head. She had never felt awkward like this before and realised that she had never been on a beach holiday. She knew she had a good figure, so why not show it off, she was, after all, on holiday.

After breakfast the next morning, she went to a parade of shops in the complex and obtained a pair of stylish sunglasses, a sarong and blue bikini, then went back to her room. She was exited as she put the bikini on, she had never felt exited by clothes before and stood looking at herself in a cheval mirror. She put her hands behind her head and admired herself, and for the first time in her life, she felt feminine. She wrapped the sarong around her waist and walked proudly to the beach, and for once she wanted to be looked at.

She found a sun lounger, opened the bottle of sun cream and rubbed it on, then started to read her book and realised that she had not thought about the army, her promotion, Pell's death or Aster's words since leaving the base. And she was determined that it should stay that way while she was at Don-Bahlia. Warm winds blew off the sea and dried the sweat on her body, it felt good, this was going to be the best holiday ever. She closed her eyes and quickly fell asleep.

She woke after about half an hour and rolled onto her front and struggled to put on the sun cream on her back. A woman approached her.

"Do you want a hand putting that on, you'll get awfully burned if you miss a bit, and that'll really spoil your holiday."

"Oh, okay, thank you."

The woman squirted cream onto Brigit's back and started to rub it in.

"Oh, that feels very nice," said Malaya.

"I studied beauty and fashion at university, part of the course was massage techniques. I even thought about becoming a masseuse."

"What do you do now?"

"I'm a housewife. My name's Anna, Anna Pradova."

"Pleased to meet you, Anna. I'm Brigit Malaya."

Anna opened her eyes wide. "*The* Brigit Malaya," she said, excitedly.

Brigit looked up at Anna. "I'm sure that there is more than one Brigit Malaya in the country," she said, feeling slightly embarrassed at Anna's reaction.

"General Brigit Malaya, the youngest ever Colonel, and now, the first ever female General in the Correlan Army."

She rolled onto her back to face Anna. "Yes, that's me, but how do you know about me?"

"My husband is General Ulrich Pradova he's an air force commander. Uli told me about you."

"Nothing bad, I hope," said Malaya, still feeling a little self-conscious as Anna gushed.

"Oh far from it, Uli was really impressed that you passed the tests. He took them last year. He's never told me what happened to him, but he was very quiet for a few days afterwards, and I couldn't help but see the bruises."

Brigit look around at the beach. "Is he here? I'd like to meet him."

Anna sighed. "Sadly not I'm afraid. He got called away on a mission just after we arrived here, he'll probably be away for the whole two weeks. He insisted that I stayed, but I'm going to be lonely without him."

"Do you have any children with you?"

"No, we don't have kids, we didn't want them. Unusual I know, but we like to think we're a little bit unconventional."

"Well I'm on my own for the next two weeks, so let's hang out together. Besides, this book is really dull." She laughed and threw the book at a rubbish bin and to her amazement, it went in.

"Good shot." Anna suddenly checked herself. "You're the woman who was engaged to that politician, the one that was killed."

"Yes, I am."

Anna put her hands up to her face. "Oh I'm so sorry, I didn't mean to pry or bring up bad memories," she said as she reached over and squeezed Brigit's hand.

"That's okay, it was a long time ago and I've got over it." She took Anna's hand and held it for a few seconds.

"It's just that I read your speech when it was printed in the newspaper, you must have loved him a lot."

"He was a special man, was Karl Davat. I saw things in him that no-one else saw, but like I said, I'm over it and I don't mind talking about it."

"Do you mind if I sit here?" said Anna as she pulled up a sun lounger.

"No, please do, I don't get the chance to talk to many other women outside of the Army."

"Can I call you Brigit?"

"Of course you can Anna."

"What struck me in your speech was when you said you could never love another man. Is that true?"

"Yes, it is."

"Wow," said Anna "I hate it when Uli goes away. Sometimes he's away for months and I miss him so much. I can't imagine what it's like for you."

The two women sat and talked for hours, Brigit found the combination of Anna's bubbly enthusiasm for everything in life and her sense of humour very relaxing. Every now and then they would rub sun cream on each other. Occasionally they would drift off to sleep, only to wake and go for a swim to cool off. Brigit found herself laughing at stupid things and realised that she couldn't remember the last time she had laughed at anything.

"Let's have dinner tonight," said Brigit.

"Great idea. Then tomorrow we'll go shopping for a new bikini for you."

"But this one is new."

"Yeah, and it looks really good, but I think you can do better. You have a fantastic body, and you need to show a bit more of it off."

"Oh that sounds interesting." Brigit blushed a little, she was not used to getting compliments, and this sincere praise coming from another woman—a woman that she found very attractive—gave her a strange feeling inside.

It was late, and the meal was finished, as were the two bottles of red wine; they were the last ones on the terrace, and the only sounds were from the cicadas and the quiet classical guitar music from speakers hidden in the foliage. Brigit sipped a brandy and studied the beautiful woman sitting opposite her, Anna was wearing an elegant evening dress with a deep neckline that enhanced her figure. Two stylish earrings were complimented by a matching delicate cleavage choker necklace.

Every now and then the gentle breeze would waft Anna's perfume towards Brigit, it filled her head and intoxicated her in a way that alcohol could never do. Anna was elegant, eloquent and educated, everything that Brigit admired in a woman. Eventually Anna yawned and stretched.

"It's been a lovely evening, but I really must go to bed now."

"Yes. Let's go."

The two women stopped outside Anna's room. Brigit fought the desperate urge she had to take Anna in her arms and kiss her.

"I'm really pleased to have met you." said Anna. "See you tomorrow."

"I'm so glad we met," said Brigit, then to her surprise, Anna leant forward and kissed her on the cheek. Anna went into her room, leaving Brigit in stunned silence. She walked to her room unable to comprehend what had happened today. All she really knew was that she was happier than she had ever been in her life. She swiped the key-card in the lock and entered her room. The aroma of Anna's perfume still filled her head, almost making her feel dizzy. She glanced at the double bed, and for a split second in her mind's eye, she saw Anna in the bed, pulling back the sheet and beckoning her in.

"This one?" said Brigit, holding up a black bikini.

"No, it's nice, but it's not classy enough for you. You need something with wow factor one hundred, like this." Anna held up a skimpy yellow bikini that had clear plastic straps. "You'll look fantastic in this."

"It's a bit brief!" said Brigit, slightly alarmed as she looked at the tiny patches of fabric. "And it's a thong back, not much thicker than string!"

"You can carry it off. Trust me, you'll look great."

"Okay, then I'll trust you." Brigit handed the bikini and her key card to the store assistant.

"Don't get me wrong, I love what you are doing for me, but why are you doing it? I've never had someone pick clothes for me before, and I must admit, I could get quite used to it."

Anna looped her arm through Brigit's as they walked out of the store. "I studied fashion and I found that I loved dressing women, even more than I loved massaging them. The female form is so beautiful, you know, soft curves and clear skin. I'm going to get as much pleasure from seeing you in it as you will get from wearing it."

They went to Brigit's room. Anna sat on the bed and Brigit started to undress.

"No" said Anna. "Change in the bathroom, I want it to be a surprise."

After a couple of minutes Brigit stepped out. "What do you think?" she asked, slightly nervously and subconsciously biting her lip.

Anna put her hand to her mouth in shock. "Oh my God, you look so good. Wow."

"The top doesn't cover very much of my breasts," said Brigit, looking down at herself, and fiddling with the fabric, anxious at wearing such a revealing bikini.

"That's the idea, it makes your boobs look fabulous."

The bikini bottom formed a shallow 'V' down from Malaya's hips, exposing a lot of her body below her navel. "And the bottom only just covers my you-know-what."

"Again, that's the idea. You'll knock them dead when they see you on the beach. Turn around."

Brigit turned and heard Anna gasp, then laugh.

"What is it, what's wrong?" she asked, concerned.

"Nothing's wrong. It's just that the straps are clear; I can't see them, and from the back you look naked. Stunning, just stunning."

Anna could see Brigit was a bit self-conscious and nervous at the prospect of going to the beach. She took hold of Brigit's hand and led her to a full-length mirror in the bathroom. "You are beautiful, just look at yourself," she said as she ran her hand gently up and down Brigit's back.

Brigit studied her reflection for a few minutes, and an awkward smile gradually broke on her face, melting the look of concern. "I suppose I do look good. My nipples are visible through the material, but you know what, I don't mind that. I actually quite like it."

Anna moved a cheval mirror so Brigit could see her back reflected in the bathroom mirror. Brigit burst out laughing. "Yes, I see what you mean, I hope I don't get arrested."

"Oh God, look at your flat stomach, mine's all flabby. I hate you now," laughed Anna.

"In no way are you flabby," said Brigit.

Anna lifted her shirt and rubbed her stomach, grabbing a bit of flesh. "Compared to you I am. Look at you." She put her hand on Brigit's abdomen and stroked gently, letting her touch linger as her hand went down below Brigit's naval. "Flat, and with perfect abs." Anna ran her finger lightly around the outline of the muscles of Brigit's Abdomen. "How do you get them so tight?"

"A five-kilometre run every morning, followed by fifty lengths in the pool, followed by two hundred press-ups and two hundred sit-ups." Brigit turned to Anna and grinned. "Sometimes I do the sit-ups in the nude."

"Ooh kinky. I don't know how to do sit-ups properly; you'll have to show me sometime."

Brigit laughed. "Do I have to be naked?"

"You can be if you want. I could be naked too. That'll make it a bit more interesting."

The women made their way to the beach and a soon as Anna's feet touched the sand, she took off her bikini top, and heard Brigit's slight gasp.

"Aren't you going to?" Anna asked.

"Well I hadn't planned to," said Brigit, then she looked around the beach and saw that most of the women were topless, she hadn't noticed it before.

"You can go topless on this beach, so go topless."

"You weren't topless yesterday."

"I wasn't with you then." Anna glanced at Brigit's chest. "Go on, pop it off."

"Okay then." Brigit undid the clasp and removed her top, unable to stop from glancing around to see if anyone was watching.

"It's your first time topless, isn't it?"

"Yes, it is."

"Feels good, doesn't it?"

Brigit thought for a minute. "Yeah, actually, it feels really good, come on, lets walk along the beach for a bit."

She took Anna's hand and they strolled from one end of the beach to the other. They walked in the surf line as the warm sea foam babbled over their feet. Brigit had her shoulders back and held her head high. She knew that people were turning and looking at her, she could almost feel their eyes on her, but she didn't care; she relished it. They played in the water for a while then found a couple of sun loungers. They put on sun cream on each other's backs, and Brigit found that her hands were trembling slightly as they moved across Anna's skin. She shuddered as Anna smeared some cream onto her bottom.

"Nice bum," said Anna to herself quietly. "A beautiful woman with a nice bum, flat stomach, fantastic legs, slender hips, and really great boobs. What I wouldn't give to have a body like yours."

Brigit laid down on the lounger and closed her eyes, and despite her heart thumping in her chest, the moment was serene; she felt a calm that she had never felt before. She turned to Anna and slowly looked her up and down.

"You are beautiful," she said, her voice breaking into a whisper.

"So are you," said Anna as she reached over to hold Brigit's hand.

They chatted over the meal that night, laughing and giggling like schoolgirls. Brigit wondered how they had so much to talk about, but words just seemed to flow easily between them, with neither dominating conversation.

Anna looked up in wonder at the clear night sky. "The stars are so bright tonight; my mother was very superstitious; she always said a clear night sky was a sign of good things to come."

"Let's hope she was right," said Brigit as she too gazed up the stars.

Anna pointed to a meteor as it burned up in the atmosphere. "Ooh look, a shooting star, we should make a wish," she said excitedly.

"I already have," said Brigit as a waiter handed her a glass of Brandy.

They finished up and went to their rooms, and there was a moment of silence outside Anna's, where they stood facing each other, holding hands and looking into each other's eyes. Brigit, emboldened by Anna's kiss the previous evening, moved forward, put her arms around her and kissed her on the lips, moving her hand up and stroking the back of Anna's neck then pulled away. There was no negative reaction from Anna, just a moment where they were looking at each other. Brigit leant forward and kissed her on the lips again, lingering slightly longer this time. Again, there was no negative reaction as Brigit pulled away, just a smile and curious look from Anna that she found hard to read.

"Goodnight Anna," she said then turned and went to her room.

"Take it slowly, let her make the moves now," she said to herself while she got undressed. As she got into bed, she looked at the empty space beside her, she smoothed out some wrinkles in the fabric as she imagined Anna laying there naked.

<<<◇>>>

"I spoke to the receptionist, she said it's going to be too hot on the beach today," said Anna over breakfast. "So what do you want to do?"

"I'd still like to catch a bit of sun, so why don't we stay here and use the pool and then go to my room and lounge around on my balcony when it gets too hot outside."

"Good idea, besides, we can't go topless around the pool."

"You're really into the topless thing aren't you."

"Yeah, I love it—and so do you. Go on, admit it, I saw the look on your face at the beach yesterday, you were all 'look at these two, check me out'. You were loving it."

"Yes, you're right. It was a first for me and I liked it—I liked it a lot."

"And do you know what I liked best?" said Anna

"No, what?"

"I liked that people were seeing me holding hands with you." Anna leant forward and took Brigit's hand, squeezing it gently. "I don't know why, but that meant a lot to me."

By midday it was too hot to sit by the pool and both women had swum enough. So they collected their things and went to Brigit's room. The balcony had a waist high brick wall and was large enough for two sun loungers and a table, with plenty of room to spare. Brigit pressed button in the room and a sun blind motored out of the wall. Anna put out the loungers then leant against the wall, admiring the view.

Brigit stood behind Anna, put her arms around her and nuzzled into her neck. "We won't get any direct sunlight now, but it will still be bloody hot and there's enough UV reflecting off the wall for us to get a tan," she said.

Anna looked all around the balcony. "We're not overlooked at all, so there's only one thing for it."

"What's that then?"

"This." Anna took off her bikini top, Brigit was expecting that, but she didn't expect Anna to remove her bikini bottom as well. "We get naked."

Brigit stared in disbelief.

"The more skin, the more vitamin D is made and that's good for you, it boosts the sex drive." Anna said as she put her hands up behind her head, running her fingers through her long auburn hair. She closed her eyes. "Not that mine needs boosting though." A sinuous wave rippled through her body. "God, I need a bit of sex right now." She seemed to daydream for a moment, then snapped out of it and sat on a sun lounger.

"Your turn," she said. "Go on, be daring, you need to be more daring, and I want to see you get naked."

"Okay then, you just sit there and watch." Brigit took off her top, then slowly slid off the bottom, then mimicked the move that Anna had made. "Is this daring enough?" she said, swaying her naked body from side to side.

Anna swallowed hard. "I know I've said it before, but wow, you are beautiful."

"I'll call room service and get some wine sent up."

"Good idea," said Anna as she laid back.

Brigit walked over to her and stood close. "White or red?"

"Two of each. Let's stay here for the rest of the day, we can always get some food sent up later."

Brigit made the call, and as she walked back to her lounger, Anna reached up and ran her hand across Brigit's thigh. "This is so nice."

After about ten minutes, there was a knock on the door. 'Room service' came a female voice. Brigit stood up and went to put on her bikini.

"No," said Anna. "Just wrap this around you." she said with a mischievous look in her eye as she held up a sarong.

"It's completely see-through!"

"Go on, I dare you."

"I just can't say no to you, can I?" said Brigit as she wrapped the sarong around her like a toga. "Whoever is at the door is going to see everything!"

She opened the door and a waitress entered and placed a tray with four bottles of wine on the table beside Anna. She looked only at the bottles as she opened them, then curtseyed and left. Brigit burst out laughing.

"You had nothing covering you. At least I had this flimsy thing on. You little devil, she must have seen your… seen your…. she must have seen your… chuff."

"I bloody well hope so. There'd be something wrong with her if she didn't have a little look, it's only human nature. I don't mind people seeing me naked,

I actually quite like it. I used to earn a bit of money when I was at university by doing life modelling for the art classes."

"Life modelling, what's that?"

"You take all your clothes off and sit there for a couple of hours while they paint pictures of you, or take photographs, or make sculptures out of clay. Fifty Dhat for just sitting there in the buff—easy money. Mind you, I think some of the guys just sat and looked at me."

"I can't say I blame them," said Brigit quietly, as she looked at Anna's body.

It took until the third bottle of wine was nearly finished before the women were drunk enough for the conversation to drift away from the trivial to the personal.

"Will you really never have another man in your life?" said Anna.

"No, never."

"Have you had anyone since? There must have been someone special"

"No, there's been nobody."

"When I said I miss Uli, I meant I miss the sex. What do you do for sex?"

"I don't do anything."

"What!" exclaimed Anna, a little bit louder than she intended. She held out her hand and wiggled her middle finger. "You must masturbate though, surely you do."

"No, I've never done that."

"Oh you must, it's great, though not as great as when someone does it to you."

"Maybe I'll try it, and maybe you can show me how."

Anna seemed not to hear what Brigit had just said. "Oh, I can't imagine life without sex, I crawl up the walls if Uli is away for more than a week." She laughed. "Uli says I'm over-sexed, he says he can't keep up with me."

"Does he feel inadequate then. Is he bothered by that?"

"No, not at all. And anyway, it's not that, it's more that he knows I want more and worries that he doesn't satisfy me. He does, but he has the distraction of work. I stay at home now and I think about sex all the time."

"You have a high libido."

"Yep, off the scale." Anna poured herself another glass of Malbec. "It's a blessing and a curse." She sipped the wine and grinned an impish smile. "But mainly more of a blessing."

"Do you masturbate a lot?"

"No, not really, I think of it as an emergency reserve." Anna's voice became a little sleazy as she ran her hands up her inner thighs. "What you really want is someone else's hands on your body, someone else's fingers getting you off." She ran her hands up her body and gently squeezed her breasts. "And you want to know that they are also getting off by seeing what they're doing to you."

"Have you ever had an affair?"

"No, never. Although I did think about it once. Uli was away for six months, and I found that really hard, but I just couldn't cheat on him with another man."

"You said 'with another man'. What about with a woman?"

Anna pushed herself up and looked quizzically at Brigit for a moment then flopped back down. "I dunno, I really don't know about that."

"Have you ever thought about it?"

"Oh yeah, I've thought about it a lot, you can't work in woman's fashion without being surrounded by beautiful girls. And every now and then I'd see one and there'd just be something about them and then I'd think about it. Particularly when my job was to make them look as alluring as possible."

"Do you think you ever will have sex with a woman? after all, legally, it's not adultery."

"Isn't it?"

"No, adultery is only between a man and a woman, and then only the physical act of penetration."

"But girl on girl sex is illegal."

"Yeah, but it goes on all the time."

"Does it? I've never heard of anyone doing it."

"Exactly. Because it's illegal, no-one would ever admit to it, would they?"

"I suppose you're right; I've never thought about it that way."

Brigit rolled onto her side and propped herself up on one elbow. "It beats me why it's illegal anyway. And you know what, I think that some laws should be broken, after all, if two women fall in love and want to have sex, what harm does it do to anyone else? how does that affect anyone else? I can't see what the problem is."

"That's true. It's nobody else's business, is it?"

Brigit reached over and held Anna's hand. "So, do you think you ever will?"

"Yeah, probably. Because for so long now I've been curious about what sex would be like with a woman. I suppose it's inevitable."

"You could have a long-term relationship with a woman, and because you are married no-one would ever suspect anything." Brigit put her head down but looked up into Anna's eyes. "If you decide that's what you want, then a woman would know it's your first time and would want to give you as much pleasure as possible. You could have the best of both worlds," she said softly.

"That's true, and it is very tempting. But I worry about Uli, if he found out, it might hurt him, and I love him so much."

"Talk to him, tell him that you love him, but you need this. You said that you are an unconventional couple, you also said that he told you that he can't keep up with you, so he might even be pleased for you." She reached over and brushed a lock of hair away from Anna's face, guiding it behind her ear, and stroking her face as she drew her hand away. "It's quite common in other countries for a couple to have an open relationship like that. People are the same the whole world over, so I think it's probably quite common here in Correla. We just don't hear about it."

"I really should try it, shouldn't I, because deep down I know that I want to. But I do need to think about it, it's a very big step."

"I think a free spirit like you would come to see it as completely normal. In fact, if you are curious already then if you didn't at least try, you'd be lying to yourself."

Anna reached over and took Brigit's hand. She held it for a few moments, staring up into the night sky, deep in thought then turned to face her. "I just need to find the right woman, don't I," she said softly.

Brigit lifted Anna's hand and kissed it. "Who knows, you may already have."

Anna looked into Brigit's eyes. "Yes, I think I have found her." She held Brigit's hand to her face and kissed it. Anna stretched and yawned. "But I need to go to bed now, though I doubt I'll sleep, I've got so much going on in my head." She stood up and got dressed, then lent down and kissed Brigit on the lips, lingering for a bit, then moved so their cheeks were touching. A shiver ran down Brigit's back as she felt Anna's breath on her neck. It was hard for her to resist holding Anna and pulling her into the passionate embrace that se so desperately desired.

Anna stroked Brigit's face with the back of her hand. "Thank you for a lovely day, and for opening my mind to new possibilities." She looked down at Brigit's naked body, and slowly drew her hand down from Brigit's neck, between her breasts and placed her hand low on her abdomen. "The female body is so wonderful, and you are so beautiful." She slowly ran her hand back up, her fingertips briefly touching Brigit's breasts, then she leant down and kissed Brigit on the lips again.

Anna left, and Brigit went into her room and laid on her bed, emotions churning inside her as she thought about everything that had happened today and all the conversations. She had tried hard to not come on too strong, to not scare Anna off, and was confident that she hadn't. She remembered the rush inside when Anna stood nude in front of her and the excitement she felt after taking off her bikini and displaying her naked body and being unable to stop the feeling of pride as she did so.

"Oh Anna, you are so gorgeous, and I want to have you, oh God, I want to have you so much." she said as she drifted off to sleep.

Brigit woke late; it was nearly nine and her head throbbed from the previous night's wine. She thought about Anna; she thought about everything that had happened yesterday and hoped that the alcohol wasn't distorting her memory, but she had drunk a lot more wine than normal and she wasn't used to wine.

"Today, it's got to be today," she said aloud. "It's today or never."

She stood cleaning her teeth and felt herself trembling slightly in anticipation, then a rush of adrenaline flooded through her body as she glanced over to the bed and imagined the two of them making love.

She showered and put on her bikini. Beachwear was not allowed in the restaurant, so she put on a pair of shorts and a white cotton shirt and checked herself in a mirror. The bright yellow of her bikini top was visible through the thin cotton. "No, fuck it," she said, "I'm going to take my top off anyway, so why even put it on." She took off the shirt, removed the bikini top and put the shirt back on. She checked herself in the mirror again, the material was opaque where the cloth fell away from her body. But where it touched, it became slightly see-through, and she liked that she could just see the dark skin of her nipples.

There was a knock on her door, she opened it to see an exited Anna, who rushed in and put her arms around her. "I've got some great news," she said, then stopped herself, pulled back and looked at Brigit's breasts. "Ooh look at you and your boobs." She pulled the shirt tight across Brigit's chest. The material became completely transparent. "Wow, nothing left to the imagination now, is there. Are you going to wear that down to breakfast?"

"Yeah, you said I should be more daring, so here I am." Brigit pulled her shoulders out and thrust her breasts forward. She looked down, admiring herself for a moment, then looked back at Anna. "So, what's this great news you've got for me?"

Anna took hold of Brigit's hands, she paused for a second, smiling and looking deep into Brigit's eyes. "We're going to have sex tonight!" she said proudly.

Brigit's heart skipped a beat and more adrenaline surged through her. She felt her mouth go dry and her knees tremble a fraction.

"Now, isn't that great news?" said Anna.

Brigit swallowed hard. "Yes, it is really good news, but why wait until tonight, why not now?"

"Because that's when Uli is coming back. He just called me, he wasn't on a mission after all, he just had to deliver a report in person to the air force council. As soon as he's back we're going to have sex and I'm going to fuck his brains out, I'll tell him that he can do whatever he wants to me."

Brigit's heart sank, she had completely misread everything that Anna had said and done. She was crushed and couldn't hide the disappointment on her face.

"What's wrong?" said Anna. "Are you not feeling too good?"

Brigit pushed away, there was no way she could let Anna know the real reason. "No, I'm actually not feeling too well, I've got a bit of an upset stomach. I think it's best if we don't spend any time together today. I wouldn't want you to catch something and spoil your time with Uli."

"Oh, I'm sorry to hear that. I enjoyed myself so much yesterday."

"Me too, but I think I'll stay in my room today." Brigit rubbed her stomach to lend credence to her lie and felt pathetic as she did so.

"Well I hope you feel better soon. Is there anything I can get you?" Anna was totally oblivious to Brigit's true feelings.

"No, I don't need anything, but thank you anyway."

Anna grinned. "If you're better tomorrow, I'll tell you all the dirty things that Uli did to me."

Brigit forced a smile and closed the door as Anna left. She sat and looked at herself in a mirror; gone was the smile, the wide eyes, the glow of love and the anticipation of intimacy. Back was the stern frown, furrowed brow and tight lips.

"You, stupid, stupid, stupid little bitch," she said to her reflection. "What the fuck were you thinking," she yelled, then punched the mirror, shattering it and ripping her skin open. She ignored the blood flowing from her knuckles; picked up a shard of glass and used it to shred the bikini, throwing the tattered ribbons of cloth into a bin.

Only when her rage subsided did she pull a sliver of glass from her hand. The cuts were superficial, despite the amount of blood. She rinsed her hand with some bottled water, then took a plaster from the first aid kit in her bag and put it over the cut. She got dressed in the clothes that she arrived in, packed her bags then picked up the phone and dialled reception. "This is General Malaya. Send a porter to my room, I'm checking out now." Five minutes later she threw the key card on the reception desk and left the hotel without speaking to anyone.

Malaya's Assignment

"Ah, General Malaya, back so soon?" said Kedara. "Did you not like Don-Bahlia?"

"It was wonderful sir, but I'm not used to holidays and I missed the mental stimulation of work," she said, trying hard to not show her true feelings.

"And you were on your own, yes, I can see how that could get boring, particularly with your famously celibate lifestyle."

Malaya avoided eye contact. "I'd had enough sun and just wanted to come back and get stuck into whatever the army has in store for me sir."

"Well good for you. Now, I want to talk to you about a project that I want you to work on. You are not going to get a command just yet, because I want you to work for me."

"Sir?" Malaya tried and failed to hide her disappointment, and Kedara noticed.

"You will get a command at some point, but right now this is far more important and crucial for the development of the army. I want you to inspect all the army bases in Correla. Some are sloppy, and you are known for your precision. You'll be travelling the length and breadth of the country and writing a lot of reports; you will be based here in Talena and you will report directly to me.

"I'm afraid to say, that despite the astonishing way you dealt with the test and the courage that you showed, the rank of a one-star General doesn't bring with it much power. But working for me, you will be able to exert some influence for the better."

He put his hand on her shoulder. "Brigit, I know you are disappointed, but this is vital work, and there have to be changes. Major General Mikos is retiring soon due to ill health and I am unopposed to become Kandalan base commander. I will eventually end up on the army council, and then I can order changes, but I need ammunition, I need to plan and prepare. And what is it that all good soldiers need to remember?"

"The three P's sir. Planning, preparation and plenty of ammunition."

"Correct. You'll have an expense account that clears through my office; I will sign off on it, so it won't be independently audited, and I don't care how much you spend or what you spend it on. Staff cars are at your disposal twenty-four hours a day, seven days a week. Your rank now gives you access to level one of the mainframe, and I will give you a password which means your use will not be monitored, and as you are taking your orders from me, no-one will question your actions. Take your time, accuracy is important and there is no rush, and don't worry, you'll make two-stars soon enough, then you'll have some power."

"Sir, I volunteered for the army and signed for a life term. I will do whatever is best for the army and Corella, regardless of my personal feelings."

"I know, that is why I have chosen you for this. The army does need to modernise, but it has to be done the right way and that it a slow process. Some people are trying to rush through changes, and the more they push the harder the army council will push back. I will end up on the army council sooner or later, and then I will give you more power than you can imagine, so just be patient."

Despite her 'regardless of my personal feelings' statement, a buzz of excitement ran through her, and she couldn't stop a little smile. "Thank you, sir."

"All good things come to those who wait, Brigit." He smiled and slapped her lightly on the arm.

With no command and no active operations, Malaya now had the means and the opportunity to carry out her own investigations into the deaths. Freedom to travel anywhere in the country gave her the opportunity and having access to the mainframe would give her the means.

Sitting at her desk in her quarters, she typed her username and the special password into her computer. A dialogue box opened. Of the five levels indicated, only level one was enabled. She clicked this and a menu appeared displaying a wealth of available information. Two items caught her eye, personnel files and military police reports.

"Perfect. I can look at whatever I want," she said aloud, "And not monitored. I think I'll have a little drink to celebrate." She poured herself a brandy and lit a cigarette, then closed her computer and sat on a couch feeling particularly self-satisfied. "And I think it's time to find out who Aster's girlfriend is."

Aleska

Aleska Mireille was sitting on the park bench reading a book when Malaya sat down next to her, close, almost touching, even though there was plenty of room on the bench. Aleska frowned, and without realising it moved away slightly. Malaya moved to maintain her closeness.

"Aleska Mireille, you and I need to have a little chat."

"How do you know who I am?" Aleska demanded, trying to sound tougher than she was.

"It wasn't too hard to find out. After all, there can't be many female civilians working at Army headquarters, but it doesn't matter how I found out your name and where you work."

Aleska stood up to leave.

"SIT DOWN!" snapped Malaya.

Aleska sat and turned to face her. "Who are you and what do you want?" she said forcefully.

"I am General Brigit Malaya, and I wanted to meet you, so we could talk about a few things, face to face."

"What things?"

"I need you to do something for me."

"How do I know you are who you say you are?" Aleska demanded. Malaya produced her military ID card. Aleska studied it then handed it back. "What do you want?" she asked, suspiciously.

"You work at the army headquarters, what is your job there?"

"I have to read reports and correct spelling and grammar before senior officers' see them. The high command is very picky when it comes to the correct use of the Correlan language."

"Why is a civilian working at military headquarters?"

"I have a double master's degree in the Correlan language from the Godin Hallenberg university, you must know it, it is the most prestigious university in the land," she said pompously. "You see, the language used by all military types is, well how can I put it politely, the reports are a bit basic, full of contradictions, idiotic punctuation and profanity. The army council doesn't like profanity in reports." Aleska's tone was deliberately condescending.

"So you have to paraphrase certain passages, I assume."

She sighed for effect. "Oh yes, far too often."

"And you do this without losing context."

"Of course. I do it all the time, it's a highly skilled job; I doubt that there's anyone in the whole of Corella that could do the job as well as me. I am very highly thought of, that's why I have level one clearance. When it comes to Correlan grammar and syntax, I am second to none." Aleska raised her head arrogantly. "Why else would they give me level one access?"

"So you are aware of the contents of the reports."

"Well obviously I am. What an idiotic question," Aleska replied firmly and with a hint of irritation.

"And do you tell anyone about the contents of the reports?"

"NO," she protested. "Of course not, they're restricted documents."

Malaya smiled and shook her head. "Oh, you little liar."

Aleska stood up. "I don't have to talk to you." She turned and walked away. Malaya let her take a couple of paces then spoke, raising her voice. "You're fucking Colonel Aster, and you know he's married."

Aleska stopped and froze.

"You get drunk and tell him things, don't you? Don't try to deny it, Aster told me himself."

Aleska turned, her face white. Malaya patted the bench seat, then beckoned her over. "Come here, sit next to me. Let's talk about it."

Aleska sat down. "How did you find out?" she asked, her former arrogance replaced with timidity. Malaya turned and sat side-on to Aleska. "I followed the two of you to that grubby little hotel out of town that you go to on a Wednesday night. Tell me, what makes it so exciting? is it the seediness of the place, or the fact that he's married? I'd really like to know."

Aleska shook her head wearily. "It's neither of those, and yes, I know he's married, but you know what it's like when you love someone, you can't help what you do. Oh God, we thought we were being so careful." She took a tissue and wiped away a tear. "Are you going to tell his wife?"

"No, that is provided you do what I want."

"What do you want me to do?"

“I want to see reports on the non-combat deaths of all senior officers over the past five years. Everyone at the rank of Major and above.”

Aleska’s jaw dropped open. “I can’t do that, the files are classified, they’ll kill me if I take them.”

“No, they’ll accuse you of being a spy, they’ll brutally torture you, then they’ll kill you,” said Malaya coldly.

Aleska gasped. “But I don’t have access to them, they are on level two. I told you, I only have access to level one.”

“I know that there are paper backups of all the files, get them and copy them.”

“I can’t do it; I can’t take that risk.” Aleska was starting to panic, and Malaya pressed home her advantage.

“In that case, I’ll tell them that you have revealed classified information to a third party. It doesn’t matter that it was to an army officer.” Malaya sneered. “Pillow talk, was it?” She moved close to Aleska, intimidating her. “They’ll take you, torture you, kill you, then shoot Colonel Aster for not reporting your actions. Now, are you going to take the risk?”

“Oh God, please don’t tell them, please. But I can’t see how I’d get the files out, even if I scan them to a USB stick, our bags and pockets are searched as we leave.”

Malaya rolled her eyes and let out an irritated sigh. “You scan the files and copy them to a USB stick, put it in a condom then shove it up yourself, you stupid little bitch. Do they do cavity searches?” she demanded.

Aleska shook her head and tried to hold back tears. “No, they’ve never done that.”

“Do it then.”

“I can’t, please don’t make me do it.”

Malaya turned and looked into the distance. She lit a cigarette and blew smoke up into the air, pausing for a few moments, then spoke calmly. “They’ll take Aster first; he’ll give you up fairly quickly. Then they’ll come for you; you’ll be beaten, and gang raped to start with.”

She turned her face away nonchalantly, so that Aleska couldn’t see her close her eyes as she remembered the sheer terror she felt during the tests when she thought she was going to be raped. She shuddered inside but didn’t show it, and she knew just how much fear she was instilling in Aleska.

“Then the torturers will come in, and some of them are female, they’re the worst you know, much worse than the men. My God, the things they do to people, particularly another female. You see, being women, they know what a woman fears, how to debase and degrade her, how to ruin her, where on her body to cause the most pain, how to abuse and mutilate her most intimate parts. How to hold her screaming in agony for hours at a time."

Malaya paused to let her words sink in and could see Aleska trembling slightly. She looked up and down at Aleska. "You are a good-looking woman." Aleska flinched as Malaya reached over and stroked the side of her face. "But I've seen what's left of pretty girls like you after a few days with them. You won't be good-looking anymore." She grabbed Aleska's chin and turned her head, so they were face to face. "You'll beg them to kill you," she snarled, and shoved Aleska's head away.

Aleska started crying. "I'll try to do it." she sobbed.

"No, you will not try, you *will* do it." Malaya handed her a USB stick. "Use this, it's got no sharp corners. Drop it in this hole here and be discrete." Malaya pointed to a small hole in the side of the bench. "Thursdays in the afternoon between twelve-thirty and one o'clock; you won't see me, but I'll be watching you. Do this and no-one will hear about it from me, and you can carry on with Aster. I don't care what you get up to with him, just don't let me down."

Aleska sniffed back a tear then nodded in acquiescence.

Malaya stood to leave and glared down at the terrified woman. "You have loose tongue when you're drunk, and I would suggest you give up the booze, because if I find out you've told anyone about our little arrangement, even Aster…" She opened her bag to show her service pistol. "…I'll blow your stupid fucking head off."

Three weeks later, Malaya sat in her quarters, poured herself a large brandy, lit a cigarette and downloaded the final set of files from the data stick to her computer. The last file was a document from Aleska.

These are the last reports of deaths that you requested. There are no more. I have done what you asked, and I am begging you not to tell anyone. I am not seeing Colonel Aster anymore and I have given up alcohol. Please, I can't stand the stress of what you made me do for you.

Malaya downed her drink and scoffed as she read the note. "You should have thought of that before you got pissed and blabbed to Aster. You can sit and stew about it for the rest of your life, a suitable punishment for your stupidity, I think."

She clicked the file shredder and destroyed the note. "You're my little pet now," she said as she poured another brandy. "Who knows, I might need some more information at some time in the future."

She dropped the files into a folder called 'Deaths' and realised that she was too drunk to do anything more with them. "Tomorrow night," she muttered as she rubbed her temples. "No brandy tomorrow night, well, maybe just one."

DeSalva gestured for Astrid to sit. "We have received some important information on Malaya; she has recently been promoted to general, and the Correlan general's exam is brutal, so she's tough, both mentally and physically, no doubt about that. She's a one-star general so doesn't have that much power, and interestingly, doesn't have a command yet. She's based at General Kedara's camp at Talena, but she travels extensively through the country and is going to be hard to track."

Astrid sat opposite DeSalva; she was at odds with her feelings. She knew that going after Malaya without enough data could be disastrous. But her desire to kill the woman still filled her thoughts. She knew she had to be patient, gather all the information she could and find a way to get close. She had already decided that this kill, whenever it came, would be the way she had promised herself on the day Riedel died, and would not ever be seen as an accident. Nevertheless, she couldn't help but think that her chance might never come.

Malaya And the Hammer

General Malaya was inspecting some vehicles being repaired in a workshop, one had a series of small round dents in the side, it was next on the list to be repaired. “What happened here? these look like impacts from low velocity rounds.” she said, pointing to the dents.

“No ma’am, they’re hammer blows,” said the technician, standing to attention and saluting. “A trainee couldn’t hack the survival course and attacked the vehicle that the instructors were sitting in.”

Malaya studied the indentations. “These are smooth and rounded, hammers have an edge to the striking face, that would leave a sharp edge to the mark, would it not?”

“Not if the ball pein was used ma’am.”

“What is a ball pein?”

“As you rightly say ma’am, hammers do have an edge to their face, but the other side of a metalworking hammer has a rounded end, it’s called a ball pein hammer. Like this ma’am.” He opened the tool chest and pulled out an engineering hammer and handed it to her.

She studied it for a moment, tapping the ball into the palm of her hand. “Of course,” she said quietly. She handed the hammer back to the fitter. “Thank you, carry on.”

“Yes ma’am.” The fitter saluted and turned back to start work on the vehicle.

Malaya pulled up outside Pell’s old rented house, several months had passed since her last visit and the grass had grown long. She entered and went to the kitchen where she knew there were some keys, took them and went into the garden. The shed door was hard to open, its hinges were rusty and long grass bound against the bottom edge. She got inside and saw a ball pein hammer on the bench, she picked it up, noting that it was heavier than the one the fitter had shown her.

She pulled out the picture of Pell's head injury, the impact site was clearly visible and was a well-defined circle. Using his ear as a size reference, she estimated the wound to be twenty-five millimetres across. She went inside, taking the hammer with her. She held it up to the water outlet in the bath, it was exactly the same size. "This is the murder weapon," she said to herself. "Aster, you are right."

She replaced the hammer, locked the shed and went to her car. She sat, thinking, Aster was not paranoid after all and now she would have to investigate the other deaths, but as a newly promoted one-star general, she would have to do it secretly.

Back in her office, she took a USB data stick, plugged it into her computer, entered the password and created a folder and named it 'The Assassin'. She created a file called 'Pell' and typed in all that she had learned at the house.

Connections

Printouts of the files supplied by Aleska sat neatly stacked on the table, with the names of each deceased man on top. She wrote the names along with their official cause of death on sticky notes and stuck them on the wall. Major Pell she knew about, as did she Major Berg. But Colonel Allman, General Tyke and General Lashay, she did not know about. There was a stack of names of officers that had died of natural causes, mainly from lung and liver cancer and heart attacks, due to the vast amounts of alcohol and cigarettes these individuals consumed. There were a few strokes and an embolism, some had died as a result of the effects of dementia, and several were listed as 'clinical frailty', the modern way of saying death from old age. One death, General Tyke's, was listed as a suicide.

She had disregarded all these other deaths, but then remembered something. "Heart attacks," she said quietly as she recalled a school lesson about the dangers of some wild plants when playing in the woods. "Some herbs can cause heart attacks but be undetectable in the bloodstream," she said aloud as she reached for a medical textbook and flicked through to the section on poisons. Within a couple of minutes she found something.

Plant based poisons: Aconitum, also known as Wolfsbane, Devil's Helmet or Monkshood.

Aconitum is a poisonous plant found all over the world, all parts of the plant are toxic, especially the root. Detecting the alkaloid toxin Aconite is difficult and is only possible using highly sophisticated equipment not normally available to forensic labs. As a result, death resulting from Aconite poisonings are often erroneously ruled as accidents or natural causes.

Case study: An extract of the root had been dissolved in alcohol creating an Aconite tincture, a small amount of this was added to the victim's alcoholic drink, and as this drink was highly aromatic, the tincture was not noticed by the victim when the drink was consumed. Death from a heart attack occurred quite quickly. Post-mortem examination ruled the death as natural, but the victims' family did not accept the findings and paid for a private laboratory to test the victims' blood. Only then was the poison discovered and the cause of death changed to homicide. No perpetrator has been identified and the case remains open.

She grunted, "No-one could accuse our labs of being sophisticated, so how many of these heart attacks were natural, and how many from Aconite poisoning?"

She scanned though the heart attack deaths and discovered that two victims, Colonel Van Loewen, and Colonel Rickard lived off-base. "Doesn't prove anything," she muttered, but decided to read their personnel files anyway. Both men were considered to be dedicated soldiers of above average intelligence and who would pass the general's exam. Both were also known to be heavy spirit drinkers and preferred a local brand of highly-flavoured whiskey. Both died within a couple of weeks of each other.

"So, the killer breaks into their homes, he finds half empty bottles of whiskey, he adulterates them with Aconite, exits the property and leaves no trace. It could be days or weeks before the target has a drink, by which time the killer is long gone."

She lit a cigarette and sat back in her chair looking up at the ceiling, trying to focus her thoughts. "Or maybe the killer had access to their homes; a gardener or handy man, someone servicing a washing machine."

She rubbed her forehead. "Is this possible? Is it even likely?" she asked herself, trying hard not to think herself into a scenario and confirm something that was just a theory.

"Keep an open mind, Brigit," she said as she wrote 'Poisoning, definitely plausible?' on a sticky note and placed it next to Van Loewen and Rickard.

Even though he wasn't dead, she added General Nillzen's name. She remembered reading the report on Dodi Zappan's unusual death and included his name on the grounds that he was military and had died in an accident. "What connected all of these men?" she mused as she reached for the brandy bottle. Remembering that she was only going to have one tonight, she poured herself a double. "It's still only one drink," she said quietly.

She took Nillzen, Berg and Zappan, and placed them in a row separate from the others. She wrote SOG on another sticky note and placed that above the three. "Nillzen ran the SOG, but never went on operations. Berg was in charge of the squad and Zappan was a private first class in the squad. This is the only connection between the three of them."

Malaya opened Dodi Zappan's personnel file; it showed that he was an only child and that his mother had died shortly after giving birth to him. Alois, his father, had been a violent alcoholic and neighbours had always said that he had beaten her to death for not getting an abortion, then intimidated the local doctor into lying on the death certificate.

Dodi was brought up by his father and had no female influence during his formative years, except for the prostitutes that his father brought home. He had little care from his father as he was growing was frequently beaten. During his school years it was discovered that he was slightly above average intelligence but had also inherited his father's violent tendencies.

A favourite trick he used was to come to school wearing his father's old trousers cut down into poorly fitting shorts. Any other child would have been humiliated by this, but Dodi would stand in the middle of the playground and wait until one of the children made a derogatory comment, then viciously beat them.

At age fifteen, his father gave him one hundred Dhat and threw him out of the house. Dodi went straight to the army recruiting office and signed on for a full life term. In the army he found the camaraderie and friendship that had eluded him all his life and seemed to relish the discipline as his commanding officers finally gave him figures of authority that he could look up to.

A few months after Dodi signed up, Alois Zappan was found beaten to death in what appeared to be a sustained attack over the course of several hours. Both of his arms were broken as were all of his ribs; the bones in his feet had been crushed and drag marks in blood indicated that this had been done to prevent him from getting away.

The pathologist suggested that an iron bar or something similar had been used to inflict the injuries before a final series of blows to the head killed him. Dodi had revenge for a lifetime of abuse as a motive and was the only one with the strength and ability to take him on, but his army comrades provided an alibi for the time of the attack. Nobody was ever in any doubt that it was Dodi that had tortured and killed Alois Zappan, but so hated was the old man that no serious investigation was ever launched.

The files' conclusion stated that while Dodi Zappan was clearly a psychopath capable of extreme violence, he would never rise above the rank of Corporal, but it was also noted that he responded well to orders and carried them out quickly and efficiently.

"Perhaps she was a prostitute and he got rough with her and she pushed him down the stairs. Maybe it was an accident after all. Maybe it was as the report says, that the woman left him sleeping and that he had gone home too drunk to know what he was doing, then fell," Malaya said to herself. "Do I believe that? No, I don't, but the only connection is with Berg and Nillzen." She shrugged her shoulders, wrote 'accident?' on a sticky note and put it next to Zappan's name.

She sat staring at the names for a while, then she remembered Aster's words about her. *"Because you are smart... that makes you a target."*

"What if they were all smart?" she mumbled to herself. Again, she recalled something else Aster had said. *"We are losing too many talented people to 'accidents'."*

She would need to research their backgrounds. But first, she needed to convince herself that these were not accidents. She picked up Allman's file. "He died in a car crash," she muttered.

The report stated that the autopsy did not find any alcohol in his blood but did find a high level of opiates; enough to seriously impair concentration and reaction times. Once this had been discovered, a hair test was done; hair absorbs and retains trace amounts of any drug that is consumed, and a hair test is the army's standard method to determine a history of drug use. A lock of Allman's hair was taken, and individual strands were cut into small pieces, each piece equivalent to one week's growth. Each piece tested positive for opioids.

He received a posthumous dishonourable discharge and was denied burial in a military cemetery. This also meant that his wife would not be able to receive any of his salary or pension and had to bear the full cost of his funeral, and as he was on duty at the time of the crash, his life insurance was automatically void. She would live in poverty for the rest of her life.

"I don't accept this, I can't believe he took drugs," she said aloud, as she put down the file and picked up Lashay's file.

"General Lashay and his wife died in their sleep from carbon monoxide poisoning at their holiday home. Let's see what the report says," she said, as she opened the report. It stated that a gas heater had been serviced that day and the engineer had created a blockage in the flue which lead to a fatal accumulation of carbon monoxide. The engineer's name was Tillerman, and he is serving a thirty-year prison sentence for double manslaughter and criminal negligence.

<<<◇>>>

Tillerman glowered at Malaya as she sat opposite him in the huge visitor's room in the prison. It was outside normal visiting hours, and they were the only ones in the room except for a guard who stood by the door on the other side of the room. Eventually he spoke. "I've not seen you before, are you another distant cousin?" he sneered.

"So, when are you going to start verbally abusing me, huh? Spending an hour accusing me of murdering them, shouting at me, swearing at me, spitting at me, like you family members always do. I don't get any choice over visits, if someone wants to see me, I can't say no, and I just have to sit here and take it," he snarled.

"I'm not a family member, I'm General Brigit Malaya."

"Humph," he grunted. "I suppose you're going to accuse me of incompetence, accuse me of being a disgrace to my unit. That's what usually happens when the army visits."

"Why would the army come say you were a disgrace to your unit."

"Because I was in the army. I signed up when I was fifteen. I did thirty-five years." His anger couldn't hide the pride he felt in his military service.

"There's no record of you being in the army. I checked."

"That's because you bastards took it away from me," he shouted as he lunged forward, the manacles around his wrists and ankles stopping him short. The prison guard drew his riot baton and took a step towards Tillerman. Malaya waved him away.

"When I was fitted up for this, they deleted all my records. I was in the vehicle maintenance corps. Sure I wasn't a combat soldier; I didn't shoot people or blow them up or stick bayonets in them, but I did my bit for THIRTY-FIVE YEARS," he said, raising his voice to a shout again.

"I repaired armoured personnel carriers in the field, under fire. I fixed tanks in the field, under fire. I kept everything working and I was fucking good at it. When I left, I got a gold watch and a handshake from grand field marshal Hallenberg along with a personal 'Thank you' from him. It was the greatest day of my life."

He sat back, still seething. "I was framed for this, and you lot have taken all my commendations, all my certificates from exams that I passed, all of them with A1 pass rates, I'll have you know. You lot even took my gold watch and the picture of me with Hallenberg. And on the advice of the army personnel department, my wife has divorced me, it would have been our thirty-seventh wedding anniversary next week." He calmed down, relaxed his shoulders and sighed. "There was no blockage in the flue when I left."

He looked around at the prison walls. "I'm doing thirty years, twenty if I get parole. Either way, I'm going to be an old man by the time I get out, if I ever get out." He moved his eyes to glance at the guard without moving his head.

Malaya noticed a feint remnant of a bruise around his right eye. "How did you get the bruise?"

Tillerman lowered his voice. "From the guards. They do that if you protest your innocence too much. I'll get a beating later for just talking to you." Again, he glanced at the guard. "It's usually him," he whispered, but just loud enough for the guard to hear. "It's a rough prison." Malaya looked at the guard, he was smirking and tapping the handle of his baton.

"After leaving that army, I retrained as a gas fitter, passed all of the exams with A1 grades. Due to my diligence I quickly became an instructor. Diligence, that was the reason I became an instructor, you can check with the gas company if you like. Diligence, it was written in my personal record," he said, angrily.

"Tell me about your work on the boiler at Lashay's holiday home, was it a routine service?"

"Yes. It had to be serviced twice a year for insurance purposes. It was an older unit, and I was familiar with the type, so I got to do the servicing, and you have to pay particular attention to the flue on those models, you have to make sure they don't get blocked." He leant forward to emphasise his point. "Which I did," he growled.

"When you say you had to pay particular attention to the flue, what do you mean by that?"

"You have to wipe it down and make sure it's clean so that dirt doesn't drop onto the burners. Soot mixes with condensation in the flue then dries out and falls down. They get dirty quite easily."

"The report states that there was a rag in the flue."

"It wasn't mine."

"I believe you."

Tillerman raised his eyebrows. "Finally," he laughed but without humour.

"How easy would it have been for someone else to put the rag there?"

"Piece of piss; you wouldn't even need to be inside; it could be done from outside. Just take off the grille on the flue outlet, stuff in a rag and off you go. The burner gets inefficient, and Carbon Monoxide starts to build up, it's heavier than air, so a layer gradually rises from the floor. They lived in a bungalow, it was late Autumn, and all the windows would have been shut. You can't smell Carbon Monoxide." He looked away and shook his head. "They wouldn't have known anything about it."

"Thank you," she said as she stood to leave. "This is a civilian prison so there's not much I can do to help you, but I will try to put a word in with the parole board. Keep your nose clean and I'll see if I can get it reduced down to ten."

"Thank you."

Malaya walked to the door, as she drew level with the guard she slammed her fist into his stomach and grabbed his throat as he doubled up, hauling him up and banging his head against the wall.

"Now you listen to me and you listen very carefully," she hissed into his ear. "No one lays a finger on Tillerman from now on, and you are going to see to that. If I find out that he has been hurt in any way, by anyone, I will have you transferred to a military prison where the grizzly deaths of guards at the hands of the inmates is all too common. Tillerman did thirty-five years in the army and that counts for a lot amongst the prison population, so when I tell them that you used to beat him, you will suddenly become a person of very special interest to them. Have I made myself abundantly clear, or do you want me to explain it further?"

He didn't answer quickly enough, so she banged his head against the wall again. "Have I made myself clear?" she shouted. Fearfully, he nodded. She pulled him away from the wall and despite his size, easily threw him across the room. He landed heavily, then scrabbled backwards, backing into a corner as she walked towards him. "You didn't answer me; do you understand that Tillerman's safety is now your responsibility?"

"Yes," he replied timidly, then glanced at Tillerman, his usual expression of arrogance replaced by one of fear.

"Good."

The Drugs

Malaya could not bring herself to believe that Colonel Danial Allman abused drugs. She read his report again and sat pondering the possibilities. She talked to herself as she wrote down notes. "The hair test was positive for opioids; the strands were cut into sections that represented one week's growth; all sections apart from the root had the same concentration. Twenty-four sections were tested."

She flicked through a human biology textbook and read a passage about rates of hair growth in men. "This means he would have had to have been taking drugs for more than five months before his death." She closed the book and sat thinking. "That would have been noticed," she said aloud.

She read the toxicology report again and noted that the test only showed the presence of opioids and not the type, but the lab stated that the amount in the hair meant that a significant quantity of an opium-based drug or a derivative had been consumed over a long period. She lit a cigarette and paced the room trying to make sense of everything. Allman's body had been cremated and all of the hair samples had been used up, so no further testing to determine the type of drug was possible.

The word 'derivative' came to mind again. "I wonder," she said as she sat at her computer and opened a browser, not quite sure what she was looking for.

After thirty minutes of spurious web pages and irritating pop-up adverts, or requests to register in order to access information, she came across a medical web page on opioids. It was a huge technical document covering all aspects of opium.

After half an hour of trying to decipher medical acronyms, jargon, graphs and scientific text, she was about to close the page when she noticed the words 'Psudonarcotrine Hydrochloride'. A brief paragraph described an experimental drug that was similar to psudomorphine. The manufacturer claimed that the drug was almost as effective at pain relief as morphine and had all of its benefits but none of the drawbacks of addiction or personality changes.

On further reading, it transpired that the drug manufacturer had wildly over-exaggerated the drug's efficacy, and in randomised, double blind clinical trials it was shown to be much less effective than current pain medication. It had been deemed too expensive to make for such poor performance and had been discontinued, but large stocks had been manufactured and sold worldwide, with some doctors prescribing Psudonarcotrine as a placebo, simply due to its ineffectiveness. The very last sentence on the page contained a warning.

'*A secondary reason for ceasing the drug's manufacture was that although this drug had no euphoric, addictive or mind-altering properties, a drug test might have shown a positive result for opiates and could have resulted in dismissal from a workplace'*.

"That's it," she said, but without any sense of triumph. "For *might* show a positive result for opiates, read, *will* show a positive result for opiates. Somehow, he was able to take Psudonarcotrine without knowing it, and on the day of the accident, he received a fatal dose of a real narcotic, and again, without realising it."

She stood up, lit another cigarette and paced agitatedly around her room as she tried to think how it could have worked. "How would I have done it?" she said quietly. "It couldn't be in his food, not over the course of five months. It had to be something else." She suddenly stopped pacing, there was something about her use of the word 'course' that nagged at her.

"A ship's course," she said aloud, "A training course, a three-course meal, a course of medication… a course of medication!" she said excitedly. "The drug was ineffective and could have been mixed with tablets that a doctor had prescribed; he would have not known he was taking it."

She sat down and realised that this would be a ridiculous theory unless he was actually on long term medication.

"You'd better come in then," sighed the crushed Sara Allman, as she wearily led Malaya though to the dingy living room in the flat on the fifth floor of the brutalist block of flats. She closed a window to cut out the sound of a profanity laden row coming from a couple in flat a two floors above. "They've been at it for over half an hour now. It'll stop when he punches her in the face."

Sara was haggard and drawn with bags under her eyes and was painfully thin from an obvious lack of nutrition. “You’ll have to excuse the smell of piss,” she said bluntly. “The drunks do it on the landings, the whole block stinks of it in summer.”

She huffed and sneered with disgust. “These flats were supposed to be a utopian dream, cheap housing for the workers. Now look at them, each one a quarter of a million tons of rat and cockroach infested rotting concrete. They used the wrong grade of concrete, with too much sand and not enough reinforcing bars; those they did put in are too far apart and too close to the surface. Plus, they poured the concrete in winter and frost damaged it, so water has got in and the reinforcing bars are rusting and breaking up the surface of the concrete, letting more water in. It’s a vicious circle of decay.”

Sara noticed the quizzical look on Malaya’s face. “I have a master’s degree in civil engineering. Fat lot of good that’s going to do me now.” She sighed, and her shoulders dropped. “The heating doesn’t work property and it’s freezing in winter, cold and damp in spring, boiling hot in summer and cold and damp in autumn. But this is the only place where I can afford to live now. Two years I’ve been here and it’s this or the streets.”

She gestured for Malaya to sit. “I’d offer you a coffee, but I can’t afford any, so it’s water or nothing.” Sara barely hid her contempt for Malaya. “Not that you’d want to drink the water, it’s from the tanks on the roof; it’s a bit cloudy and tastes disgusting from God knows what’s in it. You have to boil it first otherwise you throw up after drinking it.”

“Nothing then, thank you,” said Malaya as she sat on the edge of an old, stained couch. Sara sat in a tatty armchair opposite; her right hand trembled and she slipped it under her leg as she sat down. She stared at Malaya for a few seconds with a look of barely concealed hatred on her face.

“So, what’s the army here for, huh? Gonna to tell me again what a disgrace my husband was, what shame he brought to his unit, are you gonna tear up the floorboard looking for needles? Because that’s what you lot did to me before,” she said disdainfully.

“No, I actually want to help you.” Malaya felt uncomfortable looking at Sara and feeling the visceral hostility in her.

“Oh, I get it. Send an army shrink around to do the whole ‘accept your husband’s secret addiction and move on’ speech. That sort of help. Well I’ve had all that and no, it didn’t help.”

"No, it's not that, I just need to know if he was on any medication."

"Oh, other than the smack, you mean?" she answered flippantly.

"No, please hear me out, I really do want to help you. Did he take any medication long term, something that the army doctors didn't know about?"

Sara sighed. "Yeah, well he did, and no, the army doctors didn't know about it."

"Why had he not declared it?"

"He was put forward for the general's test, he was convinced he would pass. So on the strength of that, he wrote to the army council with suggestions to improve performance. But it backfired, the army council were not at all pleased and he was passed over for the test for a year. Shortly afterwards he had an accident and damaged his back, not enough for it to affect his work, but enough for him to fail the physical tests. He'd heard that they are tough."

"They are," said Malaya as she took a cigarette and put it in her mouth. "Do you mind if I smoke?"

"Yes, I do mind, so don't," Sara replied flatly without blinking. Malaya put the cigarette back in the packet and was a little surprised at Sara's aggressive tone of voice, a tone she was not used to receiving.

"He was worried that if the army doctors found out he would not be allowed to take the test the following year. So he went private and got a six-month course of tablets, cost us a fortune."

"If it was ever found out that he'd withheld medical information he'd have been demoted."

"Yeah, well it's irrelevant now isn't it."

"How did he receive that tablets, in a bottle, blister pack…?"

"No, they came in these little plastic trays with a single tablet in its own little hole. The holes were dated, and he had to take them in the right order."

"What sort of tablets were they, regular pills or capsules?"

"Capsules. The paperwork said that it was a slow-release medication."

"Do you have any of the capsules left?"

"No, he'd taken the last one on the day he died."

Adrenaline shot through Malaya's veins, and she tried not to show a reaction. "Do you have any of the trays?"

"I chucked them away, what would I want to keep them for?"

"You threw away potential evidence." Though she needed to make the point, Malaya kept her tone light, as antagonising an already hostile Sara would be counterproductive.

"Look, your military police came crashing through my home, tearing up floorboards, ripping up furniture, pulling everything out of cupboards and throwing it all on the floor looking for his alleged stash of heroin; burglars would have made less mess. I showed them the trays and they couldn't give a shit about them."

Sara slumped back in her chair, rubbing her forehead as her anger turned to anguish. "I've lost everything. I had to move out of the home we rented and use our life saving to pay for his funeral, I had to sell my jewellery, my clothes, everything, even my wedding ring! I used to give to charity, now I have to go to the food bank and see what out-of-date tins there are. This shit hole is that only place I can afford, and I've only just got enough money to pay the rent."

Her expression changed as anger flashed across her face. "People see me in the street, and I can see what they are thinking by their eyes, it's the 'she must have known' look, the 'she must be one too' look, the guilt by association look." She sat forward with her head in her hands. "He wasn't a drug addict, he just wasn't."

Just then the door opened, and a surly teenage girl in school uniform walked in. "Oh Yaz, what have you done to your face?" said Sara, reaching up to the scratches on Yazmine's cheek.

"I had a fight a school."

Sara sighed. "Oh no, not another one."

Malaya noticed that the knuckles of Yazmine's right hand were red and a little swollen.

"Yeah, well this little cow called dad a junkie." Yazmine smiled triumphantly. "She won't be saying that again." She pointed at Malaya. "Who's she?"

Sara opened her eyes wide and smiled. "Oh, this nice lady is with the army," she said, sarcastically.

"Humph," grunted Yaz, as she moved to stand next to her mother.

"She says she wants to help us." Again Sara's voice was heavy with sarcasm.

Yaz looked directly at Malaya with the same look of hostility that Sara had. "By doing what? Telling us how dad was a disgrace to his uniform like all the other Army pricks do," she snarled.

"I really do want help you and…"

"Oh button it woman." Yaz interrupted. "We're sick and tired of you people trying to 'help', all you do is rub it in. We know dad was innocent." She noticed the look of shock on Malaya's face but didn't care.

Malaya was taken aback by the vehemence of Yasmine's comments. "Please don't talk to me like that."

"What are you going to do about it, huh? You can't make it any worse for us. Look at this place, we've got nothing now, you've destroyed us. When the military police came to our home, they trashed everything. I was thirteen and I had thirteen little dolls. Dad had bought me a new one every birthday, each one had a special message from him, I loved those dolls. You lot ripped them open and said that drug addict fathers always hid their drugs in their children's toys. I WAS THIRTEEN," she shouted.

Sara looked up at her daughter with a mixture of sadness and pride, she reached up and took hold of her hand. "It's been very hard on Yazmine."

Yaz looked down at her mother and stroked her hair. "It's been hard on you too, mum," she said softly, then turned to Malaya. "Some days she doesn't eat, so that I can have something. She thinks I don't know, but I do. How do you think that makes me feel huh? Like shit, that's how." All the time she stroked the back of her mother's head to comfort her.

Tears welled in Sara's eyes as she reached around Yazmine's waist and pulled her close. "I thought you didn't know," she whispered through tears.

Yaz swallowed hard. "I do know mum, and I hear you crying at night, you try to hide that from me as well, but I hear you."

Sara wiped her eyes and took a moment to gather herself, then looked at Malaya. "Because of who I am and what happened, I can't get any work around here, and Yaz is too young. The only money we get is handouts from the government, but it just isn't enough."

Suddenly Yaz opened her eyes wide and smiled with exaggerated enthusiasm. "Mum, I know how we can get some money. Remember what that man said the other day? We could go on the game together."

"Oh yes, I'd forgotten about that," said Sara, mimicking Yazmine's false excitement. "Yes, apparently men will pay a lot of money to fuck a mother and daughter at the same time," her voice descending into contempt as she spoke.

Yaz's face turned hard again. "Yeah, a whole load of money, particularly as they know I'm a virgin and under-age." She glowered at Malaya. "And don't think we haven't talked about it; we might not have any option soon. The rent man always looks us up and down and says, 'you know, there are other ways to pay'."

Sara buried her head in Yaz's side, sobbing. "No baby, you can't, not that. I know we've got nothing, but not that, maybe me, but not you, you're all I've got."

Again, Yaz spoke softly as she stroked Sara's hair. "And you're are all I've got mum. We've only got each other now, there is nothing else."

Mother and daughter stared, stony-faced at Malaya, united in their grief, but showing it in different ways, and both united in their animosity to her. Malaya opened her bag and took out three hundred Dhat and put it on the table.

"We don't want your money," said Sara as proudly as she could, but the expression on her face belied her true feelings.

Yaz snatched up the notes. "Yes we do mum, the rent man is due tomorrow."

Malaya stood and turned to leave. "I really do want to help you."

Sara and Yaz said nothing. Malaya stopped as she got to the door. "You need to get out of here."

"Really? No shit" said Yaz. "If you really want to help us, then clear my dad's name."

Malaya nodded respectfully and left, emotions churning inside her. She was shocked and more than a little humiliated. She was also impressed with Yazmine's strength of character; few people would ever get away with speaking to her the way Yaz did, but there was no self-pity, even though this would have been understandable. Instead there was a maturity in the young girl's voice, and Malaya found the love that she showed to her mother deeply humbling.

As she approached her car, she saw it was surrounded by a group of youths, one who seemed to be a leader leant against the door. "Nice car, lady," he sneered. His mates sniggered.

"It's an army staff car, get away from it," she snapped.

"Oh, army, eh? Good job we were looking after it then, I reckon that army owes us some money. What do you think lads?" The gang sniggered again.

"Get away from my car. I won't tell you again."

The youth stood up straight as she walked up to him. He glanced around to his mates and laughed, turned back to face her and moved closer, puffing out his chest. "Make me," he scoffed and sneered.

The palm of her hand hit his chin, jerking his head up and making him bite his tongue. She grabbed his wrist, twisted it behind his back, turning him around, then held the back of his head and slammed his face onto her car, crushing his nose and splitting his lip. A jab to his kidneys made him yelp in pain. She grabbed him by the hair and threw him to the ground. Then turned to face the shocked gang who backed away, then turned and ran.

"You broke my nose," he said as he laid on the ground snorting out blood, wiping his face and trying not to cry. She looked down at him. "You should have moved when I told you to."

"You made me bite off a bit of my tongue." He reached around, rubbing his back trying ease the pain in his kidneys.

"You'll live. Just be grateful I didn't decide to break your arms." She got a cloth and wiped the blood from her car and left the youth crying on the ground as she got in and drove away.

A week later Malaya returned to the flat.

"It's that army woman again mum, what do you want me to do?"

"I suppose you'd better let her in," sighed Sara.

"What do you want?" said Yazmine suspiciously, as she closed the door behind Malaya.

"Come with me, you're moving," said Malaya.

"How long are we going to be away?" said Yaz.

"For as long as you want. Grab whatever you want to take with you."

Yaz let out a humourless laugh. "Do you think there's anything here in this shit hole worth taking now? We've had to sell it all," she said.

"My photo album," said Sara. "Pictures of the family, that's all I want to take."

"I'll pack some clothes mum."

As they left the flat, a scruffy man approached. Sara looked worried. "It's the rent man, he's early," she said, fearfully pulling Yasmine behind her for protection.

"Where are you two going?" he grunted.

"They're leaving," said Malaya.

"Mind your own fuckin' business, bitch, I ain't talking to you. They owe me money."

Malaya positioned herself between the man and Sara. "Get out of our way," ordered Malaya, knowing full well that he wouldn't.

"They ain't fucking going nowhere."

"Get out of our way," she shouted.

"NO," he yelled. "You get out of my way." He pulled a butterfly knife from his pocket and flicked it open. "I've got a knife, so get out of my fucking way or I'll cut you with it, bitch," he said waving the knife as menacingly as he could.

In one swift move, Malaya drew her pistol, cocked it, grabbed the man by the throat, banged him up against a wall and jammed the muzzle against his forehead, cutting his skin. "And I have a gun. I am General Malaya of the Correlan people's army, and as you have threatened me with a weapon, I am legally entitled to BLOW YOUR FUCKING BRAINS OUT," she shouted, then paused, feeling him tremble and watching the colour drain from his face as she twisted the gun, pulling open the cut on the man's forehead; blood trickled out and ran into his eye. She slowly moved her thumb and flicked off the safety and saw the fear in his eyes as he watched her.

"Now turn around and walk away, and if you are lucky, I might not put a bullet in your back." She released her grip and the terrified man turned, walked, then ran away.

"Ooh, cool," said Yasmine, quietly.

A few minutes later they were all in Malaya's car. "It's going to be a long drive; there's some water and something to eat in a bag back there. Help yourself." Yazmine immediately snatched up one of the snack bars and handed it to her mother. Sara paused for a moment, then took it and ate it, unable to stop the look of relief. Yaz picked up a bottle of water and handed that to Sara. "Look mum, the water's clear, we haven't seen that for a while."

Malaya looked in the mirror noticing Yazmine's eyes light up as she spotted a bar of chocolate and saw her smile; she knew it was the first time in many months that Yaz had smiled.

After a while, Yazmine fell asleep. "It's just been tough for her," said Sara. "She gets teased at school and I know she gets upset when she sees other girls with things that she wants but can't have. I try to find the money, but it's so hard and kids can be so cruel. She gets angry about that. As you know, she gets in a lot of fights, but she's a good girl really."

"I know she is. She is well spoken and that must have made her stand out in the school that she now goes to, I mean went to," said Malaya, correcting herself.

Sara sighed. “Kids are wicked, they pounce on anything that’s different and it’s a rough school. She was quite rude to you; she was not like that in the past and I’m sorry.”

“Don’t be. All the crap that Yasmine has had to take has brought out the courage in her and she is not afraid to speak her mind. I respect her for that, and I admire her for it too.”

“Yes. She wasn’t like this before…” Sara struggled to find words without getting emotional. “… before the… accident, but she’s had to grow up so fast, too fast really. I don’t know what I’d do without her now. Dan would have been so proud.”

“She looks after you; she has a strength well beyond her years. When we got in the car, she made sure you had something to eat and drink before she did; that impressed me, it impressed me a lot.”

“I can hear you, I’m not really asleep,” muttered Yaz. Sara laughed, and Malaya smiled as tension between her, and the mother and daughter evaporated.

After a couple of hours they stopped at a service station and went to a café for something to eat.

“Don’t bolt your food Yaz,” said Sara, looking at the enormous plate of fried fish, potatoes, beans, peas, and a bread roll. Beside the plate was a pot of mandarin orange segments in syrup. Beside that was a glass of cola. “You’ll get tummy ache.”

“Mum, this is more food than I’ve had in a month, do you think I’m going to rush it? No, I’m going to make this last.”

The three finished their meals; Yazmine sat back and put her hand on her stomach, she blew her cheeks out and wiped away some crumbs from the corner of her mouth “I think I’m going to need a little sleep now.” She suddenly burped and blushed with embarrassment.

“Where are we going and what’s happening?” said Sara.

Malaya took some documents from her bag and handed them to Sara and Yazmine. “These are your new identities. Birth certificates, national registration numbers and I.D. cards. They are forgeries of course, but the numbers are genuine, so you won’t have any problems with them, but you need to get some passport photos taken, there’s a booth here, we’ll do it later.”

Malaya held the two halves of the ID card open. “Then slip them into these and run a warm iron over them to seal them; no-one will be able to tell the difference.

“We are heading to a village way out west; nobody knows you there and you can start a new life. The man who runs the local shop is an old friend of my family, he’ll give you a job Sara. Yazmine, you were due to leave school soon and your leaving early will not be a problem, given all the shit that you have had to put up with. You can always go to college later to finish your education if you want.”

“Why are you doing this?” said Yazmine, curiously rather than suspiciously.

“I never believed that Dan Allman, a responsible father and a Colonel in the army, would take drugs. I’ve seen his service record; it couldn’t be better. I also read the military police reports and I was appalled by the treatment you received from the army.”

Malaya paused, and for once in her life felt herself getting emotional over someone else. “It made me feel ashamed of being in the army.” She wiped a tear from her eye; Sara noticed and put her hand on Malaya’s arm to comfort her.

Yazmine leant forward, eager to talk. “What do you think happened?”

“I think there was a mix-up in the laboratory, but we can’t get a second test done, because all the hair samples have been used and your father has been cremated.” Malaya lied; she couldn’t risk letting them know that she thought he had effectively been murdered. “I fully intend to clear your father’s name and then you can both have your lives back. But it will be difficult.”

“Thank you,” said Sara as she wiped tears from her cheek.

Five hours later they pulled into the village, stopping outside a small cottage.

“This is your home now. It’s owned by the shop keeper and the rent has been paid for the next two months.”

“Ooh, it’s cute,” said Yazmine.

“Right, the first thing that the two of you need to do is work out a back story, nothing too complicated, and keep it similar to your actual experience, as that will make mistakes less likely, and it’s best that I don’t know what it is. Sara, tomorrow morning, go to the shop and say that Brigit sent you, and he’ll give you a job. My friend doesn’t know anything about you, except that you have had some problems and I am helping you out as a friend, which is what I hope we are now."

They walked to the door, Malaya took the key from under the mat and let them in. "I took the liberty of having some clothes delivered; I took a guess on the sizes, I hope they fit, I figured that you wouldn't want to take too many clothes from your flat."

"We didn't have any worth taking," said Sara as she offered up a pair of jeans to herself. Then looked around in wonder at the furniture.

"There's clean bedding, and there's some food in the cupboards and milk in the fridge. Oh, and one more thing." Malaya handed a brown envelope to Yazmine. She opened it a pulled out five bundles of notes.

"How much is here?" she said, staring in amazement.

"Five thousand Dhat."

"What! We can't possibly accept that!" said Sara.

"Err mum, yes we can," said Yazmine.

Malaya smiled and turned to face Sara. "It's from a special army fund, I can use it at my discretion, and I think you are owed it. You are going to need to buy new clothes, buy food etc. The nearest big town is a fair distance away, so you will need to buy a car and as you can probably imagine, the pay from the shop won't be a lot."

She pulled an envelope from her bag and handed it to Sara. "And this is from me, buy yourself something nice, and buy Yaz some of those things she wanted." She breathed deeply to try to control her feelings but couldn't stop a tear forming in her eye as she looked at the joy on the face of Yazmine. Sara had a look of relief, as at least part of the burden of the past two years lifted from her shoulders.

"How can we ever thank you?" said Sara, her hands trembling as she took the envelope.

"No thanks are required; I just wish I could do more."

She scribbled a number on piece of paper. "If you have any problems, call this number at any time of the day or night and leave a message, I might not answer straight away, but I promise that I will get back to you. I've got to go now; I will pass through from time to time; I can't say when though."

Yazmine put her arms around Malaya, holding her tight "I'm sorry I was rude to you."

"If the situation was reversed and I was in your shoes, I can assure you that I would have been much ruder."

Sara hugged Malaya, wiping away tears again. “Do you think you’ll ever clear his name?”

“I hope so, but it might take time, so please don’t get your hopes up too much.”

“You appreciate that my relationship with my patients is based on complete confidentiality, so the information I can give you is very limited.” Doctor Schaller’s consulting room looked more like the drawing room in a stately home than a surgery. Abstract artworks adorned the wall, and Malaya thought the modernist scribbles incongruous against the dark wood panelling and lush carpets.

“Yes, I understand that, but you can confirm that Colonel Allman visited you.”

“Yes, I can at least confirm that, but the doctor/patient relationship prevents me from saying what he visited me for. I was shocked and saddened to hear of his death, particularly with the manner of his death.” He shook his head slightly. “How a man can fall,” he said quietly.

“I know you can’t say what he visited you for, even though I do know why. I also know that you prescribed a long course of medication that had to be taken in a specific order. I am right, aren’t I?”

“That is correct.”

“How did he receive his medication?”

“It was delivered to him. Look,” he frowned, “why are you asking me this. The man died a couple of years ago.”

“It’s a matter of national security; like you, there are certain questions that I can’t answer. Can you tell me who delivered the medicine?”

“Well it’s no secret that I use the same pharmacist for all my prescriptions. Most of my clients don’t want to be seen visiting a chemist as they often have jobs that would be compromised if it was thought that they were ill.” Doctor Schaller looked over the top of his half-moon glasses to confirm without saying anything that he knew that this had been Allman’s situation.

“The pharmacy delivers them. Madden Healthcare is the company, they are very discrete, they use unmarked vans and deliver the product in plain boxes.”

Malaya stood and shook the doctor's hand. "Thank you, Doctor Schaller, you have been most helpful. Oh and one last thing, this conversation should be considered confidential as well."

"Of course General."

Madden Healthcare

Malaya sat in the office of Pieter DeBoer, the personnel manager at Madden Healthcare. He had agreed to talk to her as soon as she had shown her military ID.

"I was in the Army, did ten years in the third artillery corps. Best days of my life, demobilised twenty years ago and I still miss it. Now, you said it was of national importance." He rubbed his hands together gleefully. "How can I help?"

"I understand that one service that Madden Healthcare provides is packaging and delivery of medication."

"Yes, that is correct, we specialise in packaging tablets into date stamped boxes, some medicines have to be taken in the right order, and some people forget, so we put a date on each individual compartment."

"How often do you make deliveries to each customer?"

"It varies, if a customer is on long term medication, we will deliver six months' worth at a time. It keeps the costs down."

Malaya found DeBoer's tone of voice a bit too loud and slightly condescending, and his manner was a bit smarmy. She ignored it. "This is a bit of a long shot, but did any member of staff leave suddenly about two and a half years ago?"

"Oh no, no-one leaves here. It costs a lot to train the production staff, so they are paid very well to make sure they stay. It keeps the quality up as well. It's all about consistency, you know."

"What about delivery drivers?"

"Oh they come and go all the time, they're all young women earning a bit of cash part time. They do about fifteen drops a day and finish early enough to be able to collect their kids from school—if they have any. They're employed on a casual basis which is an arrangement that suits us and them very nicely. I can provide you with a list of names if you like."

"Thank you, and yes, I will need them. Do you personally interview the applicants?"

"Yes, that is my job," he said a bit pompously. "Tough one that, talking to pretty girls."

Malaya noticed a slightly sleazy look in his eye. "I assume that you keep records of delivery addresses?"

"Yes, of course."

"And do these records have the names of the drivers who made the deliveries?"

"Oh yes."

"Can I have copies?"

"Of course, I'll let you have the file, I doubt I'll be needing it very soon. You know, now I come to think of it, there was one girl who was only with us for one week. Rula Merka was her name. Pretty girl, early twenties, just didn't come in to work one day, normally the girls give us a bit of notice. I thought it was a bit rude, and it caused us problems with deliveries for a couple of days."

"Can you describe her?"

He stroked his chin and thought for a moment. "Average height, brunette, light brown eyes, very attractive. I can't say anything about her personality though, she wasn't here long enough for me to get to know her."

"Do you spend time with the drivers then?"

"I like to spend time with new members of staff and get to know them. I know all of the production people quite well, but we have a high turnover of drivers, so yes, I suppose I do spend quite some time in the dispatch department."

"Did Rula Merka have a good figure?"

DeBoer smirked and looked up at the ceiling. "Ooh, I can't say that I noticed." He looked back at her and winked. "Yes, a very good figure." Malaya felt herself cringe ever so slightly.

He clapped his hands together. "Now, is there anything else I can help you with?"

"No, you've told me all I need," said Malaya. 'More than enough' she thought.

DeBoer opened a filing cabinet, took out a thick folder and handed it to her. "These are all the drivers we have used for the past four years. I will need the files back though."

"Of course, I'll post them back in a couple of days. And thank you for your time."

“And you can’t tell me what it’s all about, can you?” He smirked and winked at her. “Well I fully understand. Look, if you are ever in the area, maybe we can go out for a drink sometime and talk about army things; shouty sergeant Majors and idiotic officers.”

“Are you hitting on me Mr DeBoer?” said Malaya with a wry smile.

“Oh no, nothing that crass, it’s just that the people here are all such pansies and I yearn for a bit of soldier’s banter.”

‘He *was* hitting on me’, thought Malaya as she walked to her car, ‘he blatantly looked at my hand for a wedding ring’. “Good luck with that,” she muttered.

As she went to her car, she passed the ‘Goods Out’ door and noticed a couple of the drivers loading their vans. They were both brunettes in their early twenties. “And he has a thing for young brunettes.”

A quick search for Pieter DeBoer in the army archive brought up just one name. It showed that he had been in the third artillery but had never even risen to the rank of corporal. This in itself was remarkable, as troopers would normally be promoted within three years, and he had been in for ten. There was a series of complaints about him by female soldiers for groping. Malaya half laughed as she read this.

“Surprise, surprise,” she said quietly.

These allegations were not taken as seriously as they should have been, and even though the complaints were from twenty years ago women in the Correlan army were still expected to put up with unwanted sexual touching. A fact that she found disgusting and was something she would put a stop to once she had the necessary power. DeBoer had been demobilised, and everyone knows that demobilisation is usually just an excuse to get rid of someone when there wasn’t a specific reason for a dishonourable discharge. And it appeared that his demobilisation was less than a week after an incident that was reported as:

‘Inappropriate actions and comments to a senior officer’s daughter.’

“A bit of a handy man then,” said Malaya as she closed the file. She scanned through the folder that DeBoer had given her and found Rula Merka’s file. She had started on a Wednesday and didn’t turn up for work the following

Wednesday, in that time she had made seventy deliveries. A tingle ran down Malaya's spine as she noticed that the last delivery was to Allman's home, and was for six months' supply of a powerful anti-inflammatory drug. She put the file down, stood up, lit a cigarette and paced around the room, thoughts flooding through her head.

"Calm down Brigit, don't get ahead of yourself," she said quietly. "This is purely circumstantial; it could be just a coincidence. And if DeBoer was still in the habit of touching up girls, that might explain the high turnover of delivery drivers. He might have come on a bit too strong with Rula Merka, and he did say she was very attractive."

She sat back at her computer and opened a mapping program, typed in the home address that Rula had supplied and hit 'Enter', the program replied with 'No results found.'

"I need a drink," she said with an exasperated sigh, and grabbed a fresh bottle of brandy. "He didn't do a background check on someone that would be delivering drugs." She slapped her forehead. "Employing staff based on whether or not you are going to get a feel of their tits is unprofessional, Mr DeBoer."

Rula Merka. "Is that her name?" she muttered. "Of course it isn't." She wrote, 'drug delivery—accomplice?' on a sticky note.

"Circumstantial or not, she had enough time to deliver the medicines to someone to either adulterate or replace the drugs," she said as she stuck the note on the wall next to Allman.

Too Many Women

It was a Saturday; Malaya had the day off and decided to go shopping. It was the beginning of summer; the sun had burned off the early morning mist and the weather was glorious, not too hot, not too humid, and with enough sun to get a bit of a tan without being burned. It had been a good couple of weeks, she had cleared a load of outstanding paperwork and fancied a bit of a lazy day as a reward. She took a dress from her wardrobe, the one she had bought the previous year but had never worn. One good thing had come from her debacle with Anna at Don-Bahlia, and that was that she had resolved to dress in a more feminine manner on her days off.

The dress had a light blue floral print, with narrow straps over the shoulders, a much lower front than she was used to and with the back open down to her waist; and today would be a no-bra day as she didn't want to have any straps showing. The bottom half of the dress flared out slightly and came down just below her knees.

She fixed her hair, put on perfume, painted her fingernails and toenails dark red and put on lipstick of the same colour. She put on some stylish dark blue shoes, put on a pair of silver earrings, placed a large pair of sunglasses on her head, and picked up a designer clutch bag. She checked herself in a mirror, and satisfied with her appearance, left her quarters and walked purposefully to her car. This was a powerful drop-head two seat sports car that she had recently purchased; she pressed a button on the key fob and watched proudly as the roof opened and folded down behind the seats.

She got in and pressed the 'Start' button. The engine roared into life and settled to a pleasant throb as she put on her sunglasses, selected drive and headed towards the base main gate, aware that she was turning heads as she drove. Today was going to be a good day.

"Travel permit please ma'am," said the guard on gate duty.

"I don't need a travel permit, Sergeant," she said softly, then smiled sweetly and held up her ID card.

He suddenly realised who she was and quickly saluted. "My apologies General Malaya, I didn't recognise you in your clothes… err, you are free to go… I'll open the gate." Flustered, he reached into the guard house and hit the button to open the gate. "Have a good day ma'am." He saluted again and stood back, clearly embarrassed. She nodded respectfully then drove away smiling to herself. Having cleared the gate, she floored the accelerator and thundered off down the road, hitting eighty in seconds.

The sergeant watched in astonishment as she disappeared from view. "*That* was General Malaya?" he said. "Holy fuck!"

The planned day of shopping very quickly turned into a day of sitting outside a café, drinking coffee, eating pastries, reading newspapers and watching the people pass by. Women would walk past her, each in their own summer dress, they would acknowledge her and say, 'good day', as was the polite custom. Sometimes they would do a double take, and she heard a couple of women commenting on her as they walked away, speculating as to what film they had seen her in.

"This is very nice," she said to herself. She had expected to get a few corny chat-up lines from men and wasn't looking forward to it as it would certainly spoil the day for her. But there seemed to be very few men around, and because of this, she relaxed even more as the day went on. She watched groups of women as they went into shops and came out with bulging bags of clothes that they almost certainly didn't need or would only ever wear once before they were relegated to the back of a wardrobe, only to be thrown out next year when the new seasons' fashion hit the shops. And there were lots of pretty women out shopping. Suddenly she realised, there were just too many women.

She called a waiter over. "Is it normal for there to be so many women and no men on a Saturday?"

"Yes madam, it's quite normal, there aren't that many men in this town, they're all either in the military forces or are away working in arms factories."

She smiled knowingly. "Well, that's good news for a handsome young man like you. It looks like you're spoiled for choice with so many pretty girls to choose from," she teased.

The young man blushed. "It does have its advantages madam," he said and quickly walked away.

She reminded herself that she had spent so much of her life in the army, staying on the base or away on active duty or on manoeuvres, she didn't really have a clue of what civilian life was actually like. Part of this had been of her own making though. From an early age she had been attracted to females and refused to even try to change the way she felt or conform to norms imposed by others. Being gay was who she was, and she was proud of it, but she also had always known that this could cause her problems, so once she had accepted the inequity of her situation, she had deliberately avoided social events, and once in the military, she had little contact with civilians.

But being a lesbian was still a serious criminal offence in Correla, particularly so in the military, where even a suggestion of homosexuality would be enough to destroy a career. Her time with Karl Davat and his subsequent death had quashed any rumours but hadn't stopped her desires, and she was determined not to give in to temptation; staying away was the simplest way to achieve that. As she had got older, she had learned to keep her wants in check, but she was only human and even with her supreme self-control, she couldn't help but look at some of the women and fantasise.

"Every town and city in the country will have a disproportionate number of women," she said to herself quietly. Then it dawned on her. "A female assassin would be able to move through the country and not arouse any suspicion, they would hide in plain sight."

Now she viewed every woman on the street, not as a potential partner to take to bed, but each one as a possible killer. She got up, paid and went back to the base to put her thoughts down on paper as soon as possible.

She sat at her desk, still wearing her summer dress, and took a pen and notepad from the drawer. She lit a cigarette and thought back to the two heart attack victims: Van Loewen and Rickard. She wrote quickly as ideas flooded her head.

Both lived off-base, and all officers that live off-base use maid services, a perk for their wives who often have jobs. And maids are frequently left alone in the house.

A woman in her mid-twenties delivered Allman's medication. A fact already established from conversation with DeBoer.

She pulled Berg's police report, scanned through it quickly and noted that the last place anyone saw him alive was near the Silk River restaurant. A woman had been seen getting in his car and that woman looked like a waitresses from the restaurant. One of the waitresses left the day after Berg disappeared and had not been seen or heard of since. She made more notes.

Berg was seen with a woman in her mid-twenties getting into his car on the day before he was listed as absent without leave.

On the day he died, Zappan was seen leaving a bar in Mill Street, Balssen, he was with a woman in her mid-twenties

A strange woman, possibly in her mid-twenties was at Nillzen's residence.

She read the report again and established that the girl who should have been a waitress at Nillzen's party works at the mid-town grill.

"A woman to take out three guards at the Nillzen residence? Even I would find that difficult," she said aloud, as doubt flickered in her thoughts. She remembered Aster's words when she questioned his idea of a single assassin.

"... or one very good one."

He had said it with conviction. So maybe he was right about that as well.

She wrote: *Visit the Silk River, Mill Street Bar and The Mid-Town Grill.*

A flood of adrenaline shot through her, then she checked her diary and felt deflated as she realised that she would be on the other side of the country for the next few months.

Interviewing The SOG

Lance Corporal Galen and Privates Rez, Balazar, and Stoke stood to attention in Malaya's office. She paced silently in front of them for a few moments then sat at her desk. "You were all at Dantu with Private Dodi Zappan. Captain Berg commanded you and got promoted to Major after the Dantu operation. Both Berg and Zappan are now dead, and I want to know why." She spoke with a deliberate harsh edge to her voice and could see the men were intimidated. She handed a file to Galen. "Look at these pictures."

They were the police photographs of a decomposed body tied in a chair. Most of the flesh on the arms and face had fallen away; gasses in the body had built up and burst the stomach open. "This is a man, and he is—was—Major Berg. Nobody outside of the police has seen these."

Balazar gagged, all were visibly shocked as they handed the pictures along the line.

"Yes, ghastly aren't they. There were a couple of pornographic magazines laying near him with images of men being dominated by women. Do you think Berg was a man who enjoyed asphyxia?"

Galen stiffened. "Permission to speak for everyone ma'am."

"Permission granted."

"Most definitely not ma'am. We all knew Major Berg, that can't be him."

Malaya frowned, further intimidating the man. "Obviously his face is unrecognisable, his dog tags are missing and there are no fingers left to take prints from, but dental records say that it is Berg."

Galen shuffled nervously, and Malaya noticed. "If you have anything to say, say it now. Because if I find out you have withheld anything, your life will suddenly get very unpleasant and probably very short." She pointed to each man in turn. "And that goes for all of you."

Galen cleared his throat. "We all talk about the things we like to do ma'am."

"The sexual things you like to do to women, you mean." She frowned, understanding as she did, what a lot of Correlan men like to do to women.

"Yes ma'am," he said, sheepishly.

"Out with it then," she demanded.

"Ma'am, Major Berg was strictly Vanilla."

Malaya scowled at him. "Vanilla! What does that mean?"

"It means that he liked straight sex, ma'am, nothing kinky. He wasn't getting any sex at home and he had a lot of affairs," said Baz, rescuing Galen.

"Do you know if he used prostitutes?"

"No ma'am, I am certain that he didn't," said Galen.

"How can you be so sure?"

"He considered prostitutes to be filthy ma'am; he called them the rags of society, and anyway, he always said that he would never pay for sex. He had this saying: 'Why have rags when silk is so easy to get'."

Feeling the need to support Galen, Stoke interrupted.

"He didn't need to use prostitutes' ma'am. According to Zappan, Berg had a certain way with the ladies." He fidgeted awkwardly as he spoke and felt embarrassed. "He didn't seem to have to try very hard," he said, sheepishly.

"I see." This confirmed to her what she had already guessed. She had made her point and intimidated them enough, and now needed them to relax if she was to get anything meaningful about Zappan. She softened the tone of her voice. "Look at these pictures." She handed out pictures of Zappan's body. "Stand at ease."

The four relaxed and seemed relieved, until they saw Zappan's corpse. There were pictures of him lying on the ground, the patches of blood on the steps, and a picture of his body in full rigor mortis positioned awkwardly on a stretcher as he was being carried up the steps to a mortician's van.

"That is how he was found at six in the morning, it's been estimated that he'd been dead for around eight hours. The police report says that he was very drunk and probably slipped and fell down the steps. Cause of death was massive blunt force trauma to the skull during the fall and on impact with the concrete at the bottom."

She got up, moved around to the front of her desk and sat casually on the edge to put them at ease. "I have some questions about Zappan. You may speak freely."

"Thank you, ma'am," muttered the men.

"When was the last time you saw Zappan?"

"Must have been a couple of days before he died, ma'am, he bumped into us in the bar," said Rezza.

“The bar is your regular dinking hole?”

“Yes ma’am, when we’re in the area,” said Galen.

“You four are in a different unit now since the break-up of the SOG. Am I correct”?

“Yes ma’am, that is correct ma’am. Zap was reassigned ma’am,” Galen babbled, suddenly feeling nervous.

“How much could he drink in one session?”

Stoke laughed. “Loads. He could out drink us all ma’am.”

“Okay, was there anyone else in the bar that he spoke to?”

The guys looked at each other. “There was that girl.” Balazar reminded them.

“What girl?”

“There was this girl ma’am, she was sitting at the bar on her own and she beckoned Zap over ma’am. She chatted to him for a while, then suddenly buggered off. Zap seemed a bit pissed off, he thought he was up for a shag,” said Galen, trying to assert a bit of authority over the other men.

“Do you know her name."

“No, Zap didn’t mention it ma’am, I don’t think he knew.”

“What was she like”?

“Oh, she was definitely Zap’s type ma’am,” laughed Stoke. “A slapper, a bit whore like, you know.”

“No I don’t know, please enlighten me.”

Stoke shuffled a bit at being put on the spot. “Short skirt, probably no panties, high heels, crop top, no bra. That sort of thing ma’am.”

“Why do you say, ‘probably no panties’?”

“Girls like her often don’t wear any ma’am, it makes them feel daring.” He felt himself blush. “And it can save time, you know, later.”

Galen rescued Stoke. “Zap may have seen, you know, ‘it’. That might explain why he was pissed off ma’am.”

“By ‘it’ I presume you mean her vagina?”

Galen blushed. “Yes ma’am.”

“What did she look like.”

“Average height, short blonde hair, bottle blonde though ma’am, the roots were showing through. She had a good figure, and great tits.” Stoke smiled, “I remember them because she got them out just before she ran. Struck me as a bit odd ma’am.” He paused. “Nice though,” he muttered under his breath.

“What colour were the roots?”

"Brunette ma'am," Stoke replied.

"Anything else significant about her?"

"She had a cracking arse," said Galen, quietly.

Malaya let out an amused sigh. "Gentlemen. There are plenty of women in Balssen with 'great tits and a cracking arse' as you put it. I do need something a bit more useful."

"Well ma'am, Zap said that she was worried about being beaten up by some guy she was supposed to meet. He said that she was worried that she might get killed and that was why she looked so frightened and suddenly left. Maybe it was something to do with whoever that was ma'am."

"So she could have been a prostitute then," said Malaya, even though she didn't really believe it.

"Do you think that she's somehow involved in his death?" said Stoke, then quickly added "Ma'am," as he suddenly realised he was talking to a senior officer and had not addressed her correctly.

"The police report states that he was drunk, slipped and fell, hitting his head several times, they have concluded that his death was an accident, and who am I to question the wisdom of the civilian police."

Balazar raised his hand. "Ma'am, why were the civilian police investigating? Surely it should have been our own police."

"Ordinarily it would have been, but Zappan was not in uniform, had chosen not to live on a base and was not on active duty at the time of his death. As such, it is a rare case that falls under the auspices of the civilian police."

"Are you investigating his death, ma'am?"

"I am simply gathering information for my own use. I do not have the authority to carry out an investigation or to challenge the findings of the civilian police. So you will not disclose anything that has been said in this room, do not even discuss it amongst yourselves. That is an order. Dismissed."

The men stood to attention, saluted, and left.

"I do not have the authority to carry out an investigation or to challenge the findings of the civilian police…yet" she said to herself. She was now certain that Private Dodi Zappan's death was no accident, any more than Major Berg's death was a perverted sex game gone wrong. She opened the police file on Zappan's death and read through some of the relevant passages again.

'The deceased was seen drinking heavily in the company of a woman who was also drinking heavily. The couple left, and bar staff reported that they were very drunk. Witnesses reported the pair as inebriated, staggering along the pavement and being typically loud and obnoxious. A witness has stated that later, the woman told her that she had left the deceased sleeping on a park bench. The obvious conclusion is that at some point he awoke, made his way back to his residence where he slipped and fell, resulting in his death.'

"The obvious conclusion!" Malaya snapped contemptuously. "Did the witness see her leave him asleep on the park bench? Was that question even asked?" Malaya said out loud. "There is only the woman's word. Was the drunk woman really drunk, or a very good actor?"

The Mill Street Bar

Malaya felt irritable as she entered the Mill Street Bar. She had been outside for over an hour waiting for it to open. The past couple of months had been a hard grind of constant travelling and report writing. And she was frustrated that this had forced her to put a hold on her investigations. She called the barmaid over.

"What are you having love," said the barmaid with a cheery smile.

"I'm not having anything, I am General Malaya of the Correlan army and I'm on official business," Malaya said firmly, while showing her warrant badge. The barmaid looked uneasy, and subconsciously took a small step backwards. Malaya took a picture out of her pocket; it was of Dodi Zappan. "Do you recognise this man?"

The barmaid took the picture and studied it. "Yeah, he was a regular. He's the guy that died, isn't he?"

"Yes, he is. Were you here the day he died?"

"Yes."

"Was he with anyone?"

"I've told the police everyth—"

"Was he with anyone?" interrupted Malaya, raising her voice slightly. The bar manager frowned and came over.

"What's the problem?" he said, looking suspiciously at Malaya.

"Your barmaid needs to answer some questions."

The manager turned to the barmaid. "I'll handle this, you can go." She turned to leave.

"Stay right where you are," Malaya shouted at the barmaid. "You will answer my questions, then you can go."

"Now look here," said the manager puffing out his chest. "We don't have to answer your questions, we've already answered all the questions from the police, so leave my staff alone."

"No, you are right, and no, you don't have to answer any of my questions." Malaya relaxed and looked around. "This is a nice place you've got. Not like the rough, spit-and-sawdust places near the base. It seems that none of the more obnoxious elements in the Army come out this far." She leant casually on the bar. "You know, they do like to get very drunk and start fights." She moved forward, close to the manager's face. "And it would be a shame if some turned up here and trashed everything… wouldn't it?"

The manager looked alarmed but said nothing.

"Now, I could tell them about this place, or I could keep quiet about it. It's all up to you."

"What do you want to know?" said the manager gruffly.

Malaya turned to the barmaid. "Who was he with?"

"A girl," said the barmaid.

"Name?" snapped Malaya

"I don't know her name, she wasn't a regular."

"Describe her." Malaya demanded.

Timidly, the barmaid replied. "Short bleach blond hair, I think it's called a pixie cut, but it wasn't very good, and her roots were starting to show. She was about average height, brownish eyes, good figure."

"What colour were her roots?"

"Dark, brunette."

"How was she dressed?"

"A bit slutty, short skirt, high heels and a low-cut top. I remember her because she got her boobs out once. Thinking about it, she was with that guy then, it was a few days before he died."

"Do you think she was a prostitute?"

The manger protested "We don't allow prost—"

"Shut up, I'm not talking to you," snapped Malaya, not taking her eyes off the barmaid. "I asked you if she was a prostitute!"

"No, I don't think so."

"Were they drinking heavily?"

"Oh yeah, they were hammered, rolling drunk when they left. He had three litres of six-point-eight lager, and she had three double vodkas. They were so far gone that I was thinking about refusing to serve them anymore. The thing is though, he'd drunk more than that before and not got so wasted, but it must have been that he had it over a very short period."

"How short?"

"Less than an hour."

"Has she been in since the death?"

"No she ain't."

"You can go." Malaya turned to the manager.

"You have surveillance cameras; how long do you keep the tapes for?"

"We don't have tapes," he sneered. "The cameras are high definition, and they record to hard drives. You see, we are a bit more sophisticated around here." He was deliberately condescending, refusing to be intimidated by her.

"How long do you keep the recordings for?" she demanded.

"A year."

"Give them to me, you can keep all the once since the death."

"No." He crossed his arms across his chest in defiance. "I'm not going to give you my hard drives. You come back tomorrow with a five-terabyte backup drive and you can copy the files yourself."

Malaya knew that this was a reasonable demand and decided not to push it any further. "I'll be back tomorrow, just make sure you don't 'accidentally' erase any data."

"What do you want the recordings for? The police saw them and weren't interested in them."

"But I am," she snarled as she turned and left.

"What file format are they?" demanded Malaya as she plugged in the portable hard drive.

"MP4" snapped the manager. "And you don't seem like a person with a lot of patience, which is a shame, because this is going to take hours," he gloated.

"Then you can get me a coffee," she said, as she clicked 'Yes' on the file transfer dialogue.

"Are you going to pay for it?"

"No," she replied, not bothering to look at him.

"Then you can go fuck yourself, can't you."

Malaya turned and glowered at him. "I fight for you," she shouted.

"Oh really?" He moved close to her. "Is that why you made your little threat to send some of your 'as you put it' more obnoxious soldiers down? You may frighten my bar girls, but you don't scare me."

"You'd better watch what you say," she hissed.

He cocked he head to one side. "Or what? Will you stop fighting for me?"

She jabbed her finger at him. “You have a nice place here; do you want to keep it that way?”

The barmaid entered the office and interrupted the brewing argument. “There’s a man here who needs to talk to you.”

“Tell him to come back later.”

“He really does need to talk to you, he’s someone you used to work with.”

The manager noticed the look on her face and left Malaya alone in the office. He returned after a few minutes. “Yes, my bar is a nice place, and I will keep it that way, because for your information, the cameras at the bar record sound as well as images and got your thinly veiled threat; that file is locked and is off site.” It was his turn to point.

“I was a cop for twenty-five years in this town, and I’ve still got friends in the force. The man I used to work with, the man I’ve just spoken to, is a senior police officer, detective Chief Inspector Ellet to be precise. He now has the file, and he’s looked at it and says that there’s enough to bring charges against you; but I’ve told him not to do that—not yet.”

“What charges,” she snapped derisively.

“He’ll think of something.”

Malaya felt anger rising in her and found herself making fists with her hands, there was nothing she could do, but it was hard for her to resist the urge to attack him. He knew this and pressed his point. “The police are sick and tired of having to deal with the trouble your soldiers cause and would like nothing better than to prosecute an army officer. Now, if there is any trouble, he will start an investigation and that will affect your career, won’t it?”

He was right, any involvement with civilian police would put a stain on her record and could be enough to stop her from ever having a seat on the army council. As furious as she was, it was not worth the risk. There was a great deal of animosity between the military and the civilian police, and she knew that they would revel at the chance of bringing charges against an army officer.

“I’m still going to take the files,” she said. “It’s a soldier’s death that I am investigating, and I am not satisfied with the civilian police’s conclusion.”

“Take them, then leave.”

She sat down and carried on copying the files, anger seething inside her. The manager stood behind her all the time while the files were downloading. He said nothing, just scowled at her. After about an hour, she pulled ten Dhat from her wallet and tossed it onto the desktop.

"Get me a coffee," she demanded.

"You mean, please may I have a coffee."

"Please may I have a coffee," she sarcastically replied. "Oh, and you can keep the change."

The files finished downloading. She disconnected the drive and put it in her bag, then stood, glared at the manager then left. "Don't ever come back here," he said as she got to the door. "And remember what I said about your soldiers." He shouted as she walked out of the building.

She shrugged her shoulders as she walked to her car, it was a shame he had been a civilian policeman; she was actually impressed with his level of aggression towards her. He would have made a good soldier. Her investigation into Zappan's death would no doubt filter back to the police, but such was the antipathy between the police and the military, it was likely to be ignored. They had done their investigation and were satisfied with the conclusion and would consider her efforts irrelevant.

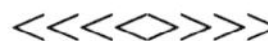

Off duty and back in her quarters, Malaya plugged the portable drive into her computer and opened only the security camera files that covered the bar. She poured herself a brandy and lit a cigarette, then settled down to what would be a long and tedious few hours viewing the video images. Eventually, she came across an image of a woman who was on her own. After a about twenty minutes, she recognised Dodi Zappan approach and start talking to the woman, but the ambient noise in the bar masked their conversation. After a few minutes, the woman seemed to get anxious, lifted up her top, said something to Zappan then left in a hurry.

"You showed him your tits, then left. You were priming him," Malaya said quietly as she poured another brandy. "You got your hook in then reeled him in a couple of days later. Very clever." She stubbed out her cigarette and immediately lit another while she studied the video intently.

She fast-forwarded the video until she reached the point a few days later where the two of them appeared at the bar. She saw the barmaid produce the drinks, and then saw what Zappan had not seen. While he had his eyes shut downing his beer in one, she poured her vodka into a plant pot.

She watched as they both had another drink and saw Astrid disappear for a couple of minutes, then return to order another round of drinks. She watched as

Zappan left and Astrid tipped her vodka into his beer. The video ended and there was a pause while the next video automatically loaded. She watched until the couple got up and walked out of shot of the bar camera.

She selected a file from the outside cameras and watched as Astrid and Dodi staggered away. Malaya leant back in her chair and lit another cigarette, she realised exactly what had gone on.

"You didn't need a piss, did you sweetheart?" she said. "You went and threw up that second drink, didn't you? You weren't drunk at all, but he was, and he thought he was going to fuck you, but you got him so drunk that he couldn't fight back when you shoved him down the steps."

She blew smoke up into the air. "Very clever, I think I would have done exactly the same thing." She poured another brandy and loaded the first file from the bar. "Let's see your face then darling," she muttered as she fast-forwarded the video.

Four cigarettes, two more brandies and an hour and a half later, she realised that there were no good images that showed the face on any of the videos. There were oblique shots of the side of Astrid's head, but nothing that could be used to identify her.

"Who's a clever girl then," she said, aware that her words were slightly slurred. "You checked out the positions of all the cameras, didn't you."

She rubbed her eyes and shut down the computer. It was gone midnight; frustrated, she went to bed. She laid for a few moments thinking; there were no facial images, only images of a woman wearing the generic clothes of a barfly. Audio was too saturated with background noise to distinguish any of the voices in the bar. She had nothing; though the barmaid would certainly be able to identify her if she was ever caught, but that was looking unlikely. Malaya wondered if she would ever find out who the woman was. Minutes later, the alcohol eased her into a dreamless sleep.

Malaya At the Mid-Town Grill

Malaya was in a good mood as she walked into the Mid-Town Grill, she felt confident that she would get some relevant information today.

"Is the owner here?" she said to a waitress.

"No, he's not due in until this afternoon, can I help you?" she replied slightly nervously and in a tone that suggested she didn't really want to help. A couple of the other waitresses noticed and came over for moral support.

"Captain Malaya, ministry of employment police force."

Malaya smiled as she flashed her old army Captain's ID card, keeping her finger over the 'army'. The ministry of employment police force didn't exist, but there were so many obscure government departments that such an arm of law enforcement was entirely plausible, and no-one would bother to check.

She would keep this conversation casual, intimidating these girls would get her nowhere and might get back to the real police. Besides, she didn't feel like being mean today, particularly as she thought that these girls were all quite cute.

"We're looking for a girl." She relaxed her shoulders and leant casually against the wall and laughed. "Don't worry it none of you."

The girls laughed. "Who are you looking for?"

"We have some names, but they're no use, we think she keeps changing them as she moves around the country, but we do have a description and are pretty sure she is getting jobs in restaurants. She has a bit of an obsession with restaurants."

The girls looked puzzled.

"She shouldn't be working at all; she has a mental problem."

"Oh that explains it."

"Explains what?"

"We had a girl like that working here for a bit."

Malaya felt her heart skip a beat but didn't let it show. "Can you describe her?"

"Well, sort of average height, mousey hair, with no real style to it. Bad glasses, you know, cheap frame, thick lenses with a tint to them, and that made her eyes look a bit strange. Walked with a bit of a limp. Not very strong, she even complained about the weight of the plates; she had a whiney little voice that was really annoying. Oh, and she had really bad skin, spots on her face that she tried to cover with make-up."

Another girl nudged her and pointed to her armpits and held her nose.

"Oh yeah, and she was a bit wiffy, didn't use any underarm. Altogether, not really what you want in a restaurant."

"Oh, you mean that simple girl," said one of the other waitresses, butting in on the conversation. "Eva Munck, you now, the one that walked with a limp."

"Oh yeah her. Bit of a weirdo, she was."

"In what way?" said Malaya.

"She could remember orders and that, but she was just a bit odd, kept herself to herself and didn't really mix, well, didn't mix at all. She hardly spoke, and when she did, it was this feeble little girl voice."

"That's because she was a fucking retard," said Dana, who had overheard the conversation and came over to join in and quickly dominated the conversation. She pointed to her head. "Nut job. The boss only employed her because he could pay her half what he pays us. And that's bugger all."

Dana turned to her friend. "Remember when those arseholes started a fight, and she hid in a corner."

Her friend frowned and nodded. "Yeah, she was fucking tragic, that's what she was."

"Yeah." Dana turned to Malaya. "There's an unwritten rule, when it gets physical, we all muck in to help the boss, but she just sat there, crying."

"That certainly sounds like her. Do you know where did she lives?"

"Dunno, none of us cared enough about her to ask. I mean, why would we?"

"How long did she work here?"

"Only a few weeks."

"Where is she now?"

"Dunno that either. She just didn't come in to work one day."

"Was there any reason, did she call in or anything?"

"No, not a peep. Can't say anyone here was bothered though. It was nice to have her gone so we could get someone normal."

"When did she stop coming to work?"

Another waitress, overhearing the conversation butted in.

"It was after that job at that stately home, you know, the one that was cut short when the old man was found unconscious."

"Yeah, that's right. I heard that she turned up there expecting to work. She wasn't supposed to be there in the first place. A woman got attacked. So it must have freaked her out." Dana frowned. "It was one of General Nillzen's parties. I was supposed to be there that day, but I didn't get booked."

"How are you normally booked?" Malaya sensed that this might be significant.

"I usually get a letter about a week beforehand. I'm the only one here that they book on account of my looks, they like a certain look."

One of the other waitresses piped up. "You don't think she nicked your letter then tried to take your place at the party, do you?"

Dana laughed incredulously. "What her, impersonate me? Does she look like me? I mean, look at me then think of what she looked like." Dana turned to Malaya. "We have to show the agency letter to the guards at the gatehouse, I've been at lots of Nillzen's parties, the guards all know me. Maybe you could ask them."

"I'm sorry to say that they are all dead."

The waitresses gasped. "What, all of them?" said Dana.

"I'm afraid so."

"When, how?"

"On the same night as Nillzen had his accident. The police think that some people had a grudge against one of the guards and a fight broke out." Malaya lied. This was all too much of a coincidence.

"I don't suppose you've got any pictures of her."

"We ain't got no pictures, but there might be something on the security tapes, there's one old video cassette that hasn't been taped over yet."

"Can I have it?"

"Sure, but it's not very good quality, the boss keeps saying he'll get a new digital system, but never does, he's so tight-fisted."

The waitress handed over a shabby old VHS cassette. "What do you want it for anyway, is she in trouble?"

"She's working in the country illegally, no work permit from the doctors. So, we do need to find her if only for her own safety."

She wrote her phone number on a card and gave it to the waitress. "If by any chance she does come back, just call this number," she said, even though she knew that the woman calling herself Eva Munck would never be returning. She took the tape, thanked the girls and left.

Malaya got in her car and drove away, certain that she was now on to something. Her mind drifted as she drove. "Pretty girls," she said softly. "They were all such pretty girls." Then she scowled and banged her fist on the steering wheel in frustration. "Stop it Brigit," she angrily said to herself. "Just don't go there. You're a general, you can command armies, you can kill people, but you just can't have the one thing that you really want, can you." She calmed down and refocussed her mind on the conversation with the girls instead of just thinking about the girls.

Back in her quarters, Malaya got her old VHS video player out of a cupboard, hooked it up to her TV and inserted the tape. The video cassette was old and had been reused many times, the casing was worn and the tape inside creased; and even with her own high-quality playback machine, the images were poor.

The owner of the Mid-Town Grill had rigged up his own CCTV and there was only one camera in the restaurant; this just covered the eating area. Fuzzy lines cut across the bottom third of the recording and the top two thirds jerked from side to side. Malaya could make out staff moving between tables and noticed that there was one girl who limped a little, but even when turned towards the camera, her face was unrecognisable.

It was possible that the police forensics lab could clean up the image a fraction, but she was doubtful that they would get any useable images. And asking them would mean admitting that she was conducting an investigation outside of her jurisdiction, and she wasn't ready to do that yet.

Zita And the Silk River

"No, no idea where she is." Zita sat opposite Malaya chatting casually as they sat at the restaurant bar drinking coffee. "She just called up one Saturday, saying she had to go back home."

"Did she say why?"

"Sort of, she was in floods of tears, she said something about her father being seriously ill, and some problem with the hotel he used to own. I told her not to worry, but that we couldn't guarantee to keep her job open."

"Has she been back?"

"No, and I've not heard anything from her either. I hope she's alright, we got on really well."

"What was her name?"

"Janie Fischer, though she said she was divorced, and I never found out if that was her married name or her maiden name. Why do you want to know?"

"I am conducting an investigation into the death of Major Berg. I just need some background information."

"Oh, he's the guy that they found in that warehouse. He'd been dead for two weeks, hadn't he. I read about it in the paper, it was horrible. Oh, the way they found him, naked and tied to a chair and all decomposed and rotting away." Zita shuddered as she recalled the graphic description in the paper.

"What can you tell me about him?"

"He was a regular, he'd been coming here since we opened. He used to come in with his missus on Friday nights when he wasn't away on an operation; table for two. His wife, well she was always miserable, and he seemed to try to compensate for that by being extra friendly."

Malaya paused for effect, then looked curiously at Zita.

"What was he like with the waitresses?"

Zita laughed. "Well he was a bit touchy-feely, in fact, that's why the last girl left, she said he put his hand up her skirt. She didn't want to take it any further though. Mind you, he did have warm hands."

"Did he touch you up?" said Malaya, genuinely shocked.

"Just a little feel of my bum once, nothing that bothered me though." Zita frowned slightly, then smiled. "But you know what, there was something about him, he was a handsome man, and he would give you this look that made you feel funny inside."

"What sort of look?"

Zita blushed, clearly embarrassed. "Well it was the kind of look that got you going, you know, it made you think about sex." She frowned and huffed. "I wish my boyfriend would look at me like that instead of just shoving his hand up my skirt," she muttered. "It's not a switch."

"Did he show any interest in Janie?"

"Oh yeah, plenty of interest, she was new and very pretty. I saw him giving her the eye, and I saw the effect it had on her."

"Berg was last seen getting into a car with a young-ish woman, and given what some witnesses have said, it could have been Janie, do you think she'd have got in a car with him?"

"I doubt it. She knew he was married, but then again, he'd obviously given her the look and some women like that."

"I don't suppose you have any pictures of her?"

"There's some surveillance tapes that haven't been wiped yet, well, I say tapes, they record to a computer hard drive." Zita looked worried. "Is Janie in trouble?"

"No." Malaya lied. "But other than the killer, she may well be the last person to see Berg alive and could have vital information. Can you show me the video and point her out please?"

Zita led Malaya through to the office and opened a folder on the computer desktop marked 'Hidden'. "We have some concealed cameras. The boss was robbed at gunpoint once, the first thing the scumbags did was to shoot out the cameras, so the ones you can see are dummies and the real ones are concealed. Neat, huh?"

"Very clever."

"They're high definition, but don't record sound, there's always too much noise so the sound is turned off. They are set in the walls, just above head height. Look around, you'll never see them."

The recordings were high quality with clear, pin sharp images, and Malaya hid her excitement that she may finally see the face of the assassin. She scrolled through the recordings back to Berg's last visit, pressing 'Play' when the time stamp hit eight pm. Both women watched as they saw Astrid interact with customers, and in particular, her constant glances at Berg, but somehow, the only shots of Astrid were oblique, with no good frontal images.

Malaya fast-forwarded and came to a shot of the corridor that led to the toilets and was puzzled to see Astrid apparently waiting. Moments later they saw Berg appear and the two embrace and kiss. They watched, riveted, as Berg fondled Astrid's breasts then put his hand between her legs; but the fascination was for different reasons. Malaya was desperate to see Astrid's face, but for Zita, it was pure voyeurism.

"Wow," said Zita, quietly. "Perhaps it was her getting in the car then. Maybe they were going somewhere to have sex."

"Quite possibly," said Malaya, though she now knew that the woman called Janie Fischer had got in the car for an altogether different reason.

A minute or so after he started, they saw Astrid say something, and saw him pull away. She said something else, and he turned and left her, but he had a lustful smile on his face. Astrid straightened her clothes, walked out of the corridor and without realising it, walked straight towards the hidden camera and looked up. Malaya instantly hit pause, capturing an image of Astrid's upper body. The image of her face could not have been clearer. With barely concealed excitement, she plugged in a hard drive.

"I need to make a copy of this. Can I take it?"

"Sure."

"Look, I know that the police, both military and civilian have already done their investigation and closed the files, but I have new evidence that warrants re-examination. Berg was under my command for a while, and I owe it to him." Malaya got a bit serious. "I would appreciate it if you didn't talk about this to anyone. I will be perfectly honest with you, I'm not supposed to be doing this, and there could be negative repercussions for you if the police ever find out. Don't worry though, I'm not going to say anything."

"Sure, I won't tell anyone."

Back in her office, Malaya plugged the portable hard drive into her computer and hit play, stopping the video as soon as the image of Astrid's face appeared. There were only two frames; she selected these and saved them as individual files, then opened them both in a photo editing programme and selected the

‘Merge’ tool. The two files combined, and the resulting image had even more detail and a bigger file size.

“So who are you?” she said, triumphantly.

Sticky Tape

Malaya entered one of the vehicle maintenance hangars in a small Army base that she had been inspecting for the past week. She was just passing, and as she had not been in this particular workshop, she decided to look in and was shocked by what she saw. Tools were strewn on the floor, as were dirty cloths, nuts and bolts, old parts being replaced and new parts waiting to be fitted. Oil and hydraulic fluid seeped from vehicles and sat in small pools on the floor.

"Sergeant!" she yelled. The sergeant in charge ran up to her. "Yes ma'am."

"Is this workshop always this filthy?" she demanded.

"We always clean up after the jobs ma'am," he said, nervously.

"That is not what I asked," she snapped. "Why don't you clean as you go?"

The man stood, unable to speak for a few moments. "The workshop is often dirty Ma'am, our priority is always to get the vehicles repaired as soon as possible, then we clear up. We have always worked this way ma'am."

"Not anymore," she said, menacingly. She pointed to a vehicle in a particularly dirty part of the workshop.

"Where is the technician who is working on that?"

"He is having a meal break ma'am."

"Get him and tell him to bring his meal with him."

The sergeant went and got the technician. The nervous young man put his meal on a worktable, stood to attention and saluted. Malaya looked at the meal, it was meat with some vegetables and some sort of gravy. She picked up the plate and calmly tipped the meal onto a pool of liquid on the floor, then placed the plate back on the table and pointed to the mess.

"Eat it," she hissed.

The technician hesitated. Malaya turned to the sergeant and frowned quizzically. "Why is your technician hesitating? Did he not hear my instruction?"

Suddenly very aware that he could be in a lot of trouble, the Sergeant yelled at the technician. "Get down and eat it."

The technician dropped down and started to pick up the food with his hands, eating as quickly as he could. Malaya watched in silence as he finished the solid parts of the meal and stood back up, even though he was not sure if this was the right thing to do.

Malaya looked him in the eye. “There are families in Correla who cannot afford a decent meal, yet you have not finished the meal that you have been given free of charge.” She pointed to the gravy on the floor. “Is it not good enough for you? Or are you going to insult those families by leaving that part of your meal?”

“No ma’am,” he said fearfully, as he dropped onto his hands and knees and started to lap up the liquid, grimacing as he took in dirt and machine oil. He finished, stood up and she dismissed him, then turned her attention to the sergeant.

“The state of this place is totally unacceptable. I will call in from time to time and if I find the workshop is anything less than spotless, you will be eating your meals off the floor. Do you understand me sergeant?”

He stiffened his back and stared straight ahead. “Yes ma’am, understood ma’am.”

She turned and left, and as she walked, she found that she was walking slightly awkwardly. She checked the heel of her right shoe and found that there was a small wad of insulating tape stuck to it. Not much, but enough to impart a change to her gait. She took a few more steps and realised that it was very easy to exaggerate her walk into a limp.

“That’s how she did it, that’s how she was able to maintain a limp without having to consciously think about it—uneven shoes,” she said to herself.

As she left the hanger, she heard the sergeant yelling, and saw the technician bending over a bin, throwing up.

General Tyke

General Tyke's body had been found by his estranged wife a few days after his dishonourable discharge from the army. They had separated a few weeks before, and he hadn't shown up for a divorce hearing.

Malaya read the printout: *Cause of death: Suicide*

The pathologist's report was stark. A clinical description of the end of a human life. An outline drawing of a naked man had a single line across both wrists.

Both wrists had the radial arteries severed with a single pass from a sharp blade.

Malaya scanned down to the toxicology, all tests for drugs and intoxicants read zero except one. Alcohol.

Blood alcohol content: 3.2

"What does blood alcohol content 3.2 even mean?" she said aloud as she grabbed a medical textbook and looked up the section of alcohol intoxication. A chart showed expected symptoms of blood alcohol content in a typical adult male, with overlapping concentrations to account for different levels of alcohol tolerance in the general population.

0.3 to 1.2, individual will experience euphoria and may become verbose. Inhibitions are reduced leading to risk taking. Sexual inhibitions are significantly reduced in both male and female drinkers leading to a desire for sexual intercourse, and more often than not, without adequate protection against sexually transmitted infections. For some males, the ability to achieve and maintain an erection is greatly reduced, this often leads to a feeling of inadequacy and humiliation which can manifest itself as violence towards the partner.

0.9 to 2.5, individual will display symptoms of excitement or agitation; movement becomes erratic and unpredictable, and some may become argumentative and display a propensity for violence. Some individuals may experience the opposite and become lethargic, morose or maudlin.

1.8 to 3.0, individual will experience confusion, speech becomes slurred. Balance is affected even when sitting. Mobility is severely affected.

2.5 to 4.0, individual will experience stupor, speech becomes incoherent. Vision severely impaired. Loss of control of limbs and/or bladder.

3.5 to 4.5, individual will lapse into coma.

Above 4.5. Alcohol poisoning. Areas of the brain that control heart rate, blood pressure and breathing become sedated causing loss of consciousness. Without prompt medical attention, death will occur.

A quick internet search showed that one whole bottle of 43% proof Whiskey drank within an hour would result in a blood alcohol content of 3.5 in a male with a body mass index of twenty. The pathologist's report stated Tyke's BMI as twenty-one-point two. She went to pour herself another brandy, stopped, looked at the bottle, put the cap back on and put the bottle away.

"Two's enough for tonight," she said quietly. She lit a cigarette instead.

She read the extensive military police report which showed that on the day that he died, Tyke had bought two bottles of whiskey and that the store manager had stated that he looked depressed. A photograph of the death scene showed Tyke slumped in a chair with his arms outstretched and surrounded by a massive pool of blood. There were close-up pictures showing the cuts to his wrists and a single sided razor blade on the floor. There was one empty whiskey bottle beside the chair and another half-empty on a table beside him.

"No suicide note," mused Malaya. "And with a blood alcohol of 3.5 he would have surely been too drunk cut his wrists so precisely, he wouldn't have had enough control."

She thought for a moment. "He was depressed, got very drunk and fell asleep. The assassin cut his arteries; the razor was sharp and coupled with the numbness caused by the amount of alcohol in his blood stream, he didn't feel a thing and bled out in his sleep."

She got up, lit another cigarette and paced the room. "Why kill him if he had been dishonourably discharged? Unless the assassin didn't know about that."

She sat back at her computer, tried to think, and regretted the two large brandies that she had drunk. “What links them?” She stared at the notes stuck on the wall, then took a note pad and started to write her ideas down.

General Nillzen: Founder of the SOG. Not dead but as good as. Wrote to the Army council suggesting improvements. Accident? (unlikely).

Major Berg: Member of the SOG. Not very bright. Died as a result of a perverted sex game? (no!)

Private Dodi Zappan: Member of the SOG. Died after falling down a flight of stairs while drunk? (pushed!)

Colonel Allman: Died in a car crash, accused of being a drug addict (falsely). Wrote to the Army council suggesting improvements.

General Lashay: Died of carbon monoxide poisoning (murdered). Wrote to the Army council suggesting improvements.

General Tyke: Suicide (apparently) the day after a dishonourable discharge.

She added one more name; *Major Pell: Slipped and drowned in a bath (but I don’t believe it).*

She thought about Pell’s death for a while, then opened his personnel file and skipped to the summary:

A gifted officer, very loyal, but known to be an advocate of the Arralan Army structure. Hubristic and arrogant, bordering on conceit. Has been known to criticise the army council’s use of mass attack strategy as out-of-date model in need of change.

“Pell strikes me as the kind of person who would write to the army council, but not Berg or Zappan. So maybe Zappan’s death was an accident after all, and maybe Berg was a deviant,” she said aloud but without really believing it.

“If Tyke had written to the Army council, then that could be the link.”

“Ah Aleska,” said Malaya as she sat down on the park bench. “It is so good to see you again,” she said, sarcastically.

Aleska flinched. “What do you want? I said I have given you everything, now leave me alone.”

"Yes, you did give me vital information, and thank you for that, but now I need some more information."

"You are never going to stop coming to me now, are you?" said Aleska bitterly.

"Probably not," said Malaya, relishing the power she had over the terrified woman.

"I'll ask for a transfer then," she said defiantly.

"Hmm. It's probably best that you never do that, it would look bad when I tell them your dirty little secret. It will look like you are running away, and thereby confirming what I tell them to be true."

"You're enjoying this aren't you?" said Aleska, angrily.

"Yes, actually, I am. You're my little puppet now, I pull the strings and you dance. You are paying the price for your stupidity. You were given a position of trust and you abused that trust, that was a big mistake, and the trouble with big mistakes is that they always come around and bite you on the arse. It's called karma."

Aleska went to stand up.

"Stay right where you are," said Malaya through clenched teeth.

"If I am arrested, I'll tell them all about you and what you made me do." Aleska tried to be brave but knew that Malaya had complete control over her now.

"Oh, that would be very unwise. Quite apart from thereby admitting that you had given away secrets, you are a civilian and I am a general; you will be arrested by military police and I will simply deny all knowledge of you. You see, there is a long-standing rule in circumstances like these where a civilian makes an accusation against a member of the military. And that is that the civilian is never believed, at which point your interrogation will become even more unpleasant, though I can't see how it could possibly get any worse."

Aleska put her head in her hands and resigned herself. "What do you want?" she asked, wearily.

"Just three things… for now. I want to know if General Tyke ever wrote to the army council, and I want to see his dishonourable discharge notification. And I also want to know if Major Pell had ever written to the army council." Malaya handed her the USB stick, "Usual method, and I want the information by next week. Don't disappoint me."

Malaya stood and went to leave, Aleska took the data stick and glared at her.

"I know what you are thinking," said Malaya with an expression of smug satisfaction. "Yes, I am a bitch."

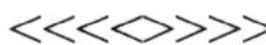

Honourable members of the army Council. Sirs, I feel the time has come to move away from the mass attack theory of war. War is changing, and it is clear to me that smaller units with the authority to make decisions without having to wait for instruction from headquarters, would make the army more efficient and ultimately save lives—on both sides.

Malaya read through several pages on how this could be achieved and found herself nodding in approval. "These are good ideas, it's just a shame that no-one would listen to them," she said to herself, then came to the last passage which seemed to have been written almost as an afterthought.

Furthermore, there is little doubt that there are both male and female homosexuals within all of the armed forces that are having to hide their true selves, and the constant fear of exposure must surely affect their performance. I propose a policy of 'Don't ask, don't tell'. This will remove anxiety from these individuals without the need to change the law and will certainly enable them to achieve their full potential and make the Army even stronger.

Your loyal servant, General Lukas Tyke.

"What the hell was he thinking?" Malaya said aloud as she finished reading Tyke's letter to the Army Council.

She closed the file and opened the scan of the discharge paperwork; it was a level two dishonourable discharge, this meant that no reason was to be given to the discharged soldier; that information would be classified.

Reason for discharge:
1. Attempting to negatively influence the army council.
2. Holding views and thoughts incompatible with the ethos of the army.
3. Suspected homosexual tendencies / sympathies.
Type of discharge: Dishonourable, level two, effective immediately.

Number three was the reason for the level two classification; it was inconceivable that the army Council would let it be known that a general could be a suspected homosexual or that he proposed tolerance towards homosexuality. The date stamp was the day before Tyke was found dead. She re-read his letter and in particular his reference to male and female homosexuals having to hide their true selves and living in constant fear of exposure.

"Tyke, you have no idea how accurate that statement is," she muttered, shaking her head in frustration and dwelling on her own situation. Realising the futility of this train of thought, she cleared her head and concentrated on Tyke.

"The assassin could not have known about his discharge," she mused as she poured herself a brandy. She lit a cigarette and lolled back in her chair. She swirled the glass and stared at the amber liquid as it condensed. She read the note that Aleska had included:

There is no record of any letter from Major Pell ever being received at Army headquarters.

This was not true, it was just Aleska's way of maintaining a small degree of control over the situation.

"So why did she kill Pell?" she said aloud, "Perhaps it was due to his knowledge of the Arralan tactics, maybe it was pre-emptive," she mused. "Kill him before he gets promoted."

She swirled the glass and downed the brandy. "What else connects all these men?" she muttered as she stared at the wall of names, pondering the parallels and differences. "All from different social backgrounds, all from different units. All lived off-base. Okay, that's something." She added the names of Van Loewen and Rickard who had died of heart attacks and had lived off-base.

"And all except Berg and Zappan were well educated. That's it, that's the connection. These men were intelligent and had written to the army council with ideas to improve the army and defeat the Arralans and I'm guessing that that two heart attack victims did as well. So the Arralans assassinated them, and just how did the Arralans know about the letters… Aleska?" she said aloud. "You have level one access and see every document. No-one checks what you look at. So, who else have you given information to, hmm? It's not just Aster that you talk to, is it? Oh Aleska, you're not a very good spy, are you; you're just a stupid little girl, aren't you?"

She thought quickly, Aleska had to be stopped, that was obvious, and the correct way would be to inform the military police, but when she was interrogated she would tell them about the arrangement with her and that would destroy her career and might even end up with a dishonourable discharge.

Her statement to Aleska that military personnel would always be believed when accused by a civilian, was a lie. The opposite was true; conscription was compulsory for everyone upon their sixteenth birthday, but voluntary enlistment was allowed from the age of fifteen and once trained, would have a fixed four-year term with the option of staying on. These recruits were easier to train and made better soldiers, and the army council was keen to not allow anything that might jeopardise the recruitment of volunteers. This desire often outweighed justice, and many army personnel were treated unfairly by the military courts.

Waiting in a hired car at the end of the road, Malaya saw Aleska leave her house and run to a waiting car. She got in and embraced the driver, hugging him passionately. Through her field glasses, she saw the man to be Colonel Aster. "Oh, you just can't keep your hands off his dick, can you Aleska," she said quietly. "So, what else have you told him? Probably nothing, but can I take the risk?" She closed her eyes and shook her head as she realised that there was only one course of action open to her.

Aster and Aleska

Malaya approached the armoury, knowing that it was run by a Sergeant who had been under her command when she was a Lieutenant. What she was going to ask would be highly unusual; what she is going to do will be extremely illegal and would challenge her morals. A careful charm offensive should work here.

The Sergeant stood up as she entered his office. “General Malaya,” he said respectfully, as he stood to attention and saluted.

“At ease Sergeant.” She smiled, then put her hand out and took his, shaking it warmly, a decidedly unusual action for a general to a subordinate. “It’s good to see you, Heinemann.”

“Good to see you too ma’am. I can’t tell you how pleased I was when I heard you had been promoted to general. I always knew you had it in you. I could tell from the first moment we were in combat together.”

“Thank you, Sergeant, and I’m glad that you decided to stay in the army after your accident.”

“Couldn’t bear the thought of leaving, ma’am, the army has always been life, and with only having sight in one eye, I couldn’t go into combat again. So after my accident I decided to transfer to the armoury, so I could make sure weapons are properly prepared and don’t blow up in anyone else’s face.”

“Good for you, and it’s good for the army as well. Personally, I can’t imagine life as a civilian, it must be so dull. Your injuries have healed well, but how are you emotionally?” she said feigning concerned sincerity.

“Good, ma’am. I don’t get the flashbacks anymore. Oh, that was poor choice of words wasn’t it, ma’am.”

Malaya faked a little laugh. “And how is your wife and family? If I recall correctly, you have a son and daughter.”

“Yes ma’am, they’re all good, ma’am. My son has just started senior school and my daughter moves up next year. Because of you, she has said she wants to join the army,” he said proudly. The conversation paused. “Erm, what can I do for you, ma’am?”

“The arms cache from the raid on the Northern Alliance compound, have all the weapons been checked and counted yet?”

“Not yet, ma’am, the shipment only came in last night.”

“Well, that’s not too important, the main thing is that we have them. I would like to inspect them, may I?”

Sergeant Heinemann paused for a second, this was an odd request, then he smiled. “Of course, ma’am, this way.” He led her down a long corridor and into to a room in one of the bunkers. Wooden crates were stacked at one end, all stamped ‘Nagler small arms’. A couple of crates were open, one had ten .38 sub machine guns, another smaller unmarked box had five Nagler .22 Precis pistols with silencers and boxes of ammunition all packed in loose straw.

“Do you need any help, ma’am?”

“No thank you sergeant, I just need to satisfy my curiosity. A batch of Precis pistols were stolen from Nagler before they were serial numbered.”

Heinemann gestured to the door. “I have some paperwork to do ma’am.”

“Okay sergeant. I’ll be fine here.”

“I’ll send someone down ma’am.”

“No need, I won’t be very long,” she said, trying hard not to sound dismissive.

“Even so ma’am, there are rules,” he said, as firmly as he dared.

She turned and smiled at him. “Yes, there are rules, you are quite right, and they do apply to everyone.”

Having corrected a general, Sergeant Heinemann was reluctant to make Malaya wait outside as protocol dictated. He saluted and left. Malaya quickly picked up one of the Precis pistols, these were powerful and accurate and although the calibre was quite small, they packed a huge punch due the ammunition they used—a full metal jacket round with an explosive charge designed to explode within the body causing devastating wounds that were always fatal.

This particular gauge of ammunition had been banned worldwide, but in a political fudge every country kept stocks of them as the ban was only on new manufacture and didn’t require old stocks to be verifiably destroyed. She picked up an empty magazine and quickly loaded ten rounds then slid the magazine into the pistol and put it in her bag, she picked up a silencer and put that in her pocket. She rearranged the straw to conceal the fact that a pistol and silencer were now missing.

She stepped outside the room, shut the door and waited in the corridor. After a couple of minutes, a Corporal arrived and saluted. They both entered, and she spent twenty minutes looking carefully at the pistols.

She turned and gave the Corporal a worried look. “Hmm, it looks like that there should have been five pistols and silencers in this box, there’s only four. One set was obviously taken before this cache was seized; ten rounds of ammunition are also missing, that’s one magazine full. Make sure that this information is included when they are counted.”

“Yes ma’am.”

She sighed and frowned with faked concern. “It looks like we might see some activity from the Northern Alliance now. These are the tools of a hit man. There’ll probably be an assassination; everyone will need to be extra vigilant for the next few months,” she said as she left the corporal.

She saluted Heinemann as she left the armoury. “Give my regards to you wife,” she said as she exited the building.

The sergeant stood and saluted. “I will ma’am. Have a good day, ma’am.”

The Nagler Precis 22 was the best weapon the company made; manufactured to a much higher standard than every other product from the company, and much more expensive as a result, and because of this, the army didn’t have any. Production runs were quite small and those that were in circulation were favourites with Northern Alliance hit men due to their killing power. The rounds did so much damage that a hit anywhere on the body was a guaranteed kill.

Malaya watched the Wednesday night routine, Aleska running to Aster’s car, getting in, embracing him, and hoping that no-one had seen her. The two of them then driving to the hotel on the other side of town, parking in the usual place in a deserted side road so the hotel security cameras would not record his car number plate.

She sighed and leant forward, putting her forehead against the steering wheel, breathing deeply for a few moments. “I have to do this,” she said as a tingle of anguish made her heart flutter. “There is no other way, I have no option.” She put on gloves, took the pistol from her bag, screwed on the silencer, cocked the weapon and placed it in her bag. She would take them as they walked to the hotel.

She had already parked and was out of the car as they drew up and got out and walked arm in arm, both happy and smiling in anticipation of a night of passion. She walked towards them; Aleska spotted her first and froze.

"Colonel Aster, how good it is to see you again. And who is this lovely lady?" said Malaya cheerily, as she looked directly into Aleska's eyes.

"Good evening General Malaya. This is err, Daniella, she is an old friend," he replied unconvincingly. Colour drained from Aleska's face.

Malaya looked up and down at Aleska, then turned to Aster and smiled knowingly. "A very good friend by the looks of things, but don't worry, your secret is safe with me." She laughed. "We all have secrets. Remember when I said that plenty of people have secrets that they hope no-one will ever discover? Things that would destroy them if they ever got out? Well my secret is…" She leant forward and whispered in his ear. "…that I am a lesbian."

She smiled and slapped him on the arm, Aster's jaw dropped open in shock. "You two have a good night," she said as she left them.

The pair started walking away. "I want to get out of here, hurry up, I'm frightened," said Aleska, her voice trembling. Aster was suddenly filled with a sense of foreboding; why had she told him that, when it was a crime that he was duty bound to report. The two quickened their pace; behind them Malaya raised the pistol and fired twice.

Aleska was hit first, the round striking the back of her head, the exploding charge blowing her skull open. Aster had turned slightly, and the second shot hit his shoulder near his neck, blasting a huge chunk of flesh away. Both crashed to the ground, Aleska was lying face down, she had been dead before she started to fall, but Aster was still alive, and had rolled onto his back. Malaya moved quickly to them; a bullet to his face blew the side of his head off. And in keeping with the tactics of Northern Alliance hit men, she then fired three times into his chest, then three times into Aleska's back; the detonating rounds doing horrific damage to both bodies.

There had been surprisingly little sound, and she had been far enough away to not get any high velocity blood splatter on her. Even if she was swabbed for gunpowder residue, she had been at the gun range all day and made sure she was seen. She walked quickly to her car and drove away, waiting until she had covered fifteen kilometres before throwing the pistol into a deep river as she crossed a bridge.

She felt no remorse for Aleska; her death was essential for many reasons, but she felt a heavy burden of guilt over Aster. He was a fellow officer and a good man, but she had no way of knowing what, if anything, Aleska had told him, and could not take the risk of him talking and destroying her investigation into the deaths, or her career.

"Northern Alliance hitman?" said a military police trooper to an officer.

"Yes, no real doubt about that. One to the head and three to the body, that's their usual modus operandi. And from the position of the spent cartridge cases, the shooter was about five or six metres behind them." He picked up a cartridge case, looked at the bottom and saw the words 'Nagler Precis' stamped into the metal. "Yep, Northern Alliance hitman, this pretty much confirms it. They're the only people who use these weapons."

The trooper bopped down to inspect the injuries to Aster. "He's got five wounds. Looks like he took a hit to the shoulder, maybe she got hit first and he instinctively ducked. Then the shooter finished him off." He picked up Aster's wallet and took out the ID card. He handed it to the officer.

"Colonel Aster. We were warned that there might be a retaliation for the raid on one of their compounds the other day. The shooter was probably going to hit someone at random and just got lucky, Correlan army officers are easy to spot, even when in civilian clothes, like this poor guy."

The trooper rummaged through Aleska's bag until he found her ID. "Aleska Mireille. Do you think she was a whore?"

The officer shook his head. "No, I met her once, she was a civilian working at army headquarters. But no guesses as to why the two of them were here."

"Yeah, men and women don't exactly come to this hotel for the view, do they?" the trooper replied.

"No, and it's ideal for when you have a bit on the side." The officer shook his head. "We're not going to find the shooter. Nobody around to see or hear anything, and the CCTV doesn't reach this far, but we'll send the Northern Alliance a message, something that might make them think next time."

He got in his car, leaving the crime scene technicians to continue their perfunctory evidence gathering while the trooper dealt with the hotel manager who was ignoring the bodies and the blood and complaining about his loss of earnings for the night while gesticulating wildly to the technicians.

Two days later, ten Northern Alliance sympathisers were taken from their homes, had their hands and feet bound and were put in a helicopter. They were then flown deep into the tribal areas. The helicopter hovered one hundred metres above a junction of two main roads.

"Lower," yelled a Sergeant. "I don't what it to be too quick, they've got to suffer, so that the tribes will see it then maybe they'll think next time."

The helicopter dropped and settled, hovering twenty metres above the ground, and the men were thrown out. The last of the sympathisers was an educated man in his late seventies. He glared at the soldiers but was stoic and held his head high and proud as they dragged him to the door.

"You can kill us, but you can't kill an idea," he said defiantly, in the refined, high form of Correlan.

"Shut up you old fool," shouted the sergeant as he kicked him in the back, tipping him out of the helicopter. The man fell in silence to his death.

"We've lost our asset at The Correlan Army headquarters," said DeSalva.

"Has she been arrested, sir?" said Astrid, concerned about the brutality the woman would face.

"No, she was killed in an apparent assassination. She was with an army officer, Colonel Aster, it's assumed that he was the target and she was eliminated to so as not to leave any witnesses."

"Was it by the Northern Alliance sir?"

"From what we can gather, that is what the Correlans think. It has all the signatures of one of their hit men. Though it's rare for them to send an assassin so far into the country, and there's been very little activity from the NA recently."

"I saw a report of a recent raid on a Northern Alliance arms dump, sir. Some tribal elders in the village were shot for assisting the rebels. Do you think that this assassination was in retaliation for that?"

"Probably, though the target was relatively low-ranking and seems to have been selected at random."

"Have the Correlans retaliated sir?"

"Oh yes, they've sent a message. We intercepted a radio transmission from a helicopter mission." DeSalva described the fate of the ten men.

Astrid shook her head and frowned. "They wouldn't have died straight away from that height, but it won't make any difference though, will it sir."

"No, the Correlans wanted the tribes to see what happened to the men, but those poor bastards are martyrs to the Northern Alliance now. If anything, they'll fight even harder."

Major Schally

Major Schally laid on the floor of the cell, hogtied; his hands and feet tied behind his back. He had been captured by a Correlan snatch squad organised by Malaya and was now in the basement of a remote building in the Talena army base.

His face already cut and bleeding from the guard's warm-up beatings. General Malaya entered along with some guards, she kicked Schally in the ribs, then bent down and whispered in his ear. "You are going to answer some questions now."

"You won't get anything from me," he gasped, trying to move to ease the pain in his side.

"Well we'll see about that."

She beckoned the guards over. "Strip him and string him up."

She stood back and watched while four burley guards tore off Schally's clothes and put manacles on his wrists and ankles. She found that she liked watching his efforts to resist. She remembered the fear she had felt during the tests as she had been man-handled, and she felt no sympathy.

She lit a cigarette and leant against the wall, relishing his futile struggle as he attempted to fight off the guards. She saw that he was not able to hide the fear in his eyes; she found this pleasurable. Chains were attached to the shackles on his wrists and ankles, and he was hauled up, spread eagled in an 'X' position, with his feet just off the floor.

"This is illegal," he said, mustering all the defiance he could, and grimacing from the pain that was already building in his arms. The guards stood back, and she walked over to him.

"Well, oh fucking dear," she said as she took her cigarette and slowly stubbed it out on his chest. He gritted his teeth and tried not to cry out. "I know that you have had training to resist interrogation, but I will break you, and the longer it takes, the worse it will get. Now, you can save me a lot of time and yourself an awful lot of pain by answering one simple question."

She took a picture of Astrid from her pocket and held it in front of his face. "Who is this?" she demanded. "Tell me, and all that will happen is that you go to a prisoner of war camp. If you don't tell me, I will torture you until you do."

"I don't know. And it doesn't matter what you do to me, I can't tell you if I don't know."

"Okay," she said and turned to walk away then turned back and viciously kicked him between the legs. He screamed as the pain exploded in his testicles. She grabbed his hair and yanked his head back.

"LIAR," she shouted in his ear. "You do know her name; I saw the look of recognition on your face when I showed you the picture of her, and you *will* tell me who she is."

She snapped her fingers at the guards and pointed to the door. One went out and wheeled in trolley with a small box on it. It was the box that had so terrified her during the tests; she knew exactly what it was capable of.

"I want you to meet an old friend of mine, I won't say he's a good friend, just an acquaintance really, but he is going to help you to help me," she said calmly as she held some cables up to his face. "Say hello to doctor sparky, you could say that he's an expert in electro-convulsive therapy."

Schally froze, and she could see his fear.

"Last chance," she said as she bopped down and wound one cable around his ankle. "This is your last chance to tell me her name." She stood up and started to wind a cable around his wrist, then noticed an indentation on his finger where the guards had taken a wedding ring off. She looked him in the eye, glanced back to the mark on his finger, then looked at him and smiled but with a questioning look on her face.

He looked at her defiantly, then turned his face away.

"So be it," she snapped. "You'll be no use to your wife after this," she said as she removed the cable from his wrist, bopped down and wound it around the base of his penis and testicles. She stood back, cranked doctor sparky's handle, then placed her finger over the button and waited. He looked at her finger hovering over the button, then looked in her eyes. He knew she was giving him a chance to answer, but he just closed his eyes and braced himself. She pressed the button.

His body jerked rigid, his eyes opened wide, his scream tearing at his throat as the current surged through him. The electricity stopped and he slumped in the chains. Malaya stood emotionless as she cranked the handle again, unmoved by his suffering. She pressed the button before he had a chance to recover. Again, his body tensed, his scream louder than before. Again he slumped in the chains, beads of perspiration covering his body.

"Now, is there anything you want to tell me?" she said calmly.

"Fuck you, fuck all of you," he gasped.

She ran her finger across his chest. "Oh, good, you're sweating, sweat conducts electricity better. Let's see now, should we make the shocks longer or stronger, what do you think?"

He gritted his teeth and said nothing.

"Oh well, the strength seems to be about right, let's make it last twice as long then." She turned the duration knob up one click. She took off her jacket and handed it to a guard, then loosened her tie and undid the top button of her shirt. She smiled at Schally. "It looks like this is going to take a while."

One of the guards looked away, unwilling to witness the man's agony as Malaya shocked him over and over again, but there was nothing the guard could do to prevent him from hearing Schally's shrieks of pain. The guards all noticed that she had a smile on her face every time she pressed the button. While the guards' brutality was part of their job, she didn't have to do this, and she was obviously enjoying causing his agony; eventually, Schally collapsed unconscious.

"Leave him there, start again when he comes around, and turn up the intensity."

She left the cell and stood in the corridor, smoking, lost in her thoughts. She was on the third cigarette when the screaming started again. After a couple of cries, Schally was unable to scream as the guards had turned up the intensity to the point where the current put his diaphragm into spasm. All she heard was the buzz of the machine then Schally's gasping when it stopped; she knew exactly what this felt like. She finished her fourth cigarette, then stepped back into the cell.

"I'm going to my office." She pulled the picture of Astrid from her pocket and handed it to the guards. "Find out her name and who she works for; don't come to me until you have it." She turned to leave and as she got to the door, she turned and pointed angrily at the guards one by one. "Do not let me down."

Three hours later, a guard knocked on the door of Malaya's office. "She is Captain Astrid Peterman, ma'am, she is from a specialist unit in the Arralan army run by Lieutenant Colonel DeSalva. She is an assassin, ma'am."

"Find out what else he knows."

"Not possible, ma'am. He is dead, ma'am. He had a heart attack and died just after he gave us that information and we were unable to—"

"Shut up," snapped Malaya, she thought for a moment. She didn't care that he had died, at least she had the name, but she knew that her superiors strongly disapproved of prisoners of war being tortured, and particularly so if it resulted in their death; at best they would want her demoted, but what was more likely was that she would be prosecuted and imprisoned for this. She considered them all to be old-school and weak, not willing to do what was necessary, and this was something she would change once she took her seat on the army council.

"Take his body to the crematorium, burn it straight away, burn his clothes and destroy all the documentation relating to him being here. Give me his rings and his dog-tags, I want absolutely no evidence that he was ever here. You and the other guards will not speak about this to anyone, or even to each other. That is an order."

She pointed her finger at him and scowled. "And if I find out that you have, I will make you all disappear. Is that understood?"

Despite his physical size and obvious strength, she intimidated him. "Yes ma'am," he said, taken aback by the harshness of her words and the blatant threat.

He saluted and left, and she thought back to her part in Schally's interrogation; she had been present during harsh interrogations before and had witnessed people suffering, but this was the first time she had personally tortured a prisoner. Her experience of the tests had changed her and humiliating herself with Anna had taken her to the edge; killing Aster was the final push that enabled her to suspend her empathy. She found that she had actually enjoyed causing Schally's pain and the power she had over him. She decided that she would visit the interrogation rooms more often and be much more 'hands-on'.

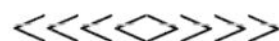

"You again," snapped the bar manager. "I told you never to come back."

Malaya kept her voice soft and calm, not aggressive as she had been before. "Please, just give me ten seconds, then you'll never see me again."

The manager eyed her suspiciously. "Okay but make it quick."

Malaya gave the picture of Astrid to the barmaid. "Is this the woman that Zappan was with?"

She barely glanced at it. “Yes,” she replied firmly, as she handed the picture back.

“You didn’t look at it for very long. So how sure are you?”

“One hundred percent. That’s her, she’s changed her hair, but that’s the girl he was with. I’m certain of it.”

“Thank you.” Malaya nodded respectfully to the manager and the barmaid and left, hiding the triumphant feeling as she went.

Malaya and Kedara

Eighteen months after receiving her first star, Brigit Malaya stood in front of Major General Kedara as he pinned two new epaulettes on her. A ripple of applause ran through the assembled generals. Later that evening, as they celebrated in the Talena officer's club, Kedara took her to one side.

"Congratulations Brigit, I knew it wouldn't take long before you became a two-star general."

"Thank you, sir."

"And no test this time."

"I don't know if I could have done the tests again sir."

"Nonsense, you breezed through them last time," he said, laughing.

"If that test was a breeze, I don't know what a gale would be, sir," she laughed.

Kedara noticed a look on her face. "I sense that there is something you want to tell me."

"Yes sir, there is something, but now is not the time."

"Is it sensitive?"

"Yes sir, very sensitive."

Kedara frowned and thought for a moment. "I'm going down to Kandalan tomorrow, come with me, it's a long drive south. We'll talk in the car."

"Yes General."

"I leave at nine-thirty sharp."

The glass partition slid up behind Kedara's chauffeur creating a soundproof compartment.

"Well?" said Kedara.

She knew he would only accept a rapid and truthful answer and took a deep breath. "Sir, I have been conducting an investigation into the accidental deaths of officers over the past few years. It has been done in my own time and has not had any impact on the reports I have been compiling for you. The only army resources I have used have been my staff car and my level one access to the mainframe."

"I see," said Kedara, his face betraying no emotion.

There was silence for a couple of minutes. Malaya was nervous, if she had misjudged Kedara, it could end very badly for her. She didn't know whether she should speak or not, an unwelcome feeling of anxiety flooded through her. The silence felt like hours.

Kedara spoke without looking at her. "Does anyone in the military police know about this?"

"No sir."

"Does anyone else know about it?"

"No sir, just you."

"Good, keep it that way. The military police are imbeciles, I doubt they could even spell 'investigation' let alone carry one out. And the civilian police hate us, so they'll never do a proper investigation of one of ours."

Encouraged by his comments, she opened her briefcase and took out a hefty sheaf of paper. "Sir, these deaths were not accidents."

"Do you have evidence to that effect?"

"My evidence is circumstantial, but overwhelming sir."

"Go on." Kedara's tone of voice was flat, and she found it difficult to read him. Despite being emboldened, she felt distinctly uncomfortable and forced confidence into her voice.

"Two of the victims, Major Berg, and Private Zappan were seen with this woman prior to their deaths sir." She handed him the picture of Astrid.

"She has been positively identified as Captain Astrid Peterman of the Arralan army under DeSalva, their head of counter-intelligence. I believe she is an assassin."

Kedara studied the image, then handed it back to her.

"You said you were investigating the deaths of officers, why is Private Zappan included?"

"His could be an accident, sir," she said nervously. "He apparently fell down a flight of stairs while drunk but was seen with this woman on the day he died. He is directly linked to Berg and Nillzen, so I don't think that it's a coincidence sir."

"And that link is?"

"The Special Operations Group sir."

"Ah, the Special Operations Group. The saviour of the army," said Kedara with a hint of sarcasm.

"Nillzen was a good man, but his plan was never going to be fully accepted by the army council, and we all know why they let him create it." He frowned slightly. "I knew Nillzen quite well and tried to dissuade him from forming the SOG, but he went ahead anyway." He shook his head. "I've spoken to the doctors, and they say he's never going to come out of the coma."

"I understand that the doctors want to turn off life support, but the family are saying no, sir."

"Yes, that's right, they're a loyal family, but they're only prolonging the inevitable; it would be kinder to all if they just let him die. Then they could get on with the rest of their lives instead of sitting by his bedside day after day, admirable though that is."

He looked at the stack of documents. "Are they all for me to read?" Again, his tone was flat, and Malaya found it hard to read his intention.

"Yes sir, they contain details behind all the deaths and my reasoning as to why I don't believe them to be accidents." She paused, worried that she had given him too much information and was risking him dismissing her theories, rather than spending a couple of hours reading her reports. She hurriedly produced another document.

"This is a one-page summary, sir."

He waved his hand dismissively. "I don't want that, I shall read these," he said as he placed his hand on the papers on the seat between them and picked up the first report. It was Lashay's.

For the next two-and-a-half hours, Malaya sat in silence, trying to hide her anxiety as Kedara worked methodically through her reports, taking a pen and annotating every page, underlining sentences, making notes in margins and all the time showing no reaction. Eventually he put the last file down and sat silently digesting her evidence.

After several minutes he spoke. "These reports are, as you freely admit, purely circumstantial."

She felt her throat going dry and coughed nervously. "Yes sir."

"And you have no direct evidence, no proof. In fact you have nothing concrete whatsoever," he said, nonchalantly looking out of the window.

“That is correct sir.” She swallowed hard. This was not going how she had planned. He looked at her and raised his eyebrows. “And do you really think that this woman was responsible for putting Nillzen in a coma and for the deaths of Lashay, Allman, Tyke, Berg, Pell, Zappan, Van Loewen, and Rickard, and was able to make Tyke’s death look like a suicide, the others look like accidents, *and* single-handedly kill the three fully armed guards at Nillzen’s residence?” He said with more than a hint of incredulity which disturbed her.

“Y…yes sir, I… I do,” she stammered nervously, then stiffened and held her head high. “Yes sir, I do,” she said confidently. “And I believe that she had some involvement with the deaths of Colonel Aster and a civilian named Aleska Mireille.”

She swallowed hard again, and a knot formed in her stomach as she thought about what she had just said. She hadn’t lied, but at best had been disingenuous; she could hardly admit to killing them both. Despite the bravado she was now displaying, her hands were clammy, and she could feel herself sweating as she remembered that she had murdered an army colleague, something that she would have to live with for the rest of her life. If Kedara noticed, he wasn’t showing it and she hoped that if he had, he may put it down to her obvious nervousness at his blunt questioning.

“And you also believe that the army council also knows these deaths to be non-accidental and are covering them up so as to not appear weak.”

“Yes, sir, but I wouldn’t put it in such a way. I would never dream of calling the army council weak.”

“Well they are weak, they’re old and they’re stupid,” snapped Kedara.

“Sir!” gasped Malaya, shocked at Kedara’s language.

“They are holding the army back; fighting the Northern Alliance rabble and their rag-tag army is one thing, but if we’re to take on and beat the Arralans we must modernise. The grand field marshal’s wonder weapon—whatever that is—can’t be deployed until we are deep into Arralan territory, and they’ll cut us to pieces as soon as we cross the border. All the time we are concentrating on the peasants in the north, the Arralans grow stronger.”

“But you will change this when you are on the army council, won’t you sir.”

“Yes, most definitely, provided I’m not assassinated.”

“Their policy of assassination seems to have halted sir. I believe that the Arralans may have lost a source of information. I think that Captain Peterman is now fighting with regular forces.”

She cringed inside as she spoke, knowing full well that she removed the source of information when she shot Aleska. 'I'm not lying' she told herself.

"Well, I sincerely hope their policy of assassination has changed, because I am determined to be on the council, and I want you to take my position as Major General Malaya, commander of the Kandalan base, and then I want you on the army council, sitting next to me. And together we can make some real changes." He put his hand on the stack of reports and smiled broadly. "This is excellent work Brigit, I believe you."

"Thank you, sir." She found it hard to hide her relief, or the pride she felt in Kedara's confidence in her. Kedara became serious again. "Do you have any these documents stored electronically?"

"Yes sir, all are on a password protected memory stick in a locked drawer in my office."

"Good. Destroy these paper documents, we can't risk them being seen. We'll keep your theories strictly secret until we've taken our rightful places and can act on them." He pulled Astrid's picture from the file. "In the meantime, I'll have this picture copied then circulated and shown to every member of the armed forces with the order that when caught, she is to be summarily executed, no interrogation, just a bullet in the head. It will undermine moral if what she has done becomes common knowledge."

They pulled in through the main gate of the Kandalan base, Kedara turned to Malaya and smiled. "Come to dinner tonight Brigit, I've told my wife all about you and she is simply dying to meet you."

"I will sir, thank you sir."

Major General Brigit Malaya

It was four years since her conversation in the car with Kedara, and six months since she was promoted to Major general and took over the command of base number one. Though it was not how she wanted, she was a three-star general for only six months before Kedara was killed in a car crash. She had been devastated; Kedara had become a close friend and confidant. At first, she wondered if the crash was really an accident or the work of Astrid Peterman, but the military police investigation and her own inquiries convinced her that it was genuine accident and the tragedy of it hit her hard.

She was certain he had known her secret. Why else would he have mentioned that *A lot of women are there on their own* at Don-Bahlia? Why would he have said that *you can do anything you want there, absolutely anything! You can have whatever liaison or assignation you desire—with anyone.* Why would he say that if he hadn't known? Why would he have said that the staff would not mention anything they saw.

He must have guessed, but in all the time she had known him, and with the regular contact she had with him, both through work and socially, he had never alluded to it again. If he did know, then he had been just the sort of forward-thinking man that was needed to modernise the army. It was not only a loss to her, but a loss to the army and a loss to all of Corella.

For the first time in her life she had cried over the death of someone. "It wasn't supposed to happen this way," she had said over and over as she sat on her bed on the night she was told. "He was supposed to take his place on the army council, then I would follow him and together we were going to change the army."

She had been put forward for promotion to Major general and amongst the other names was the brutish General Lothar Valerian. Eventually the list reduced to just two names, hers and Valerian's. Records were scoured, and all aspects of their service were rigorously examined. He had won more battles than her, but his victories had cost the lives of far too many men under his command.

She had known Valerian for all of her military life and considered that his lack of sophistication and crude, blunt-force strategies symbolised everything that needed to change in the Correlan army. If he won the promotion, the army would never change and could even get worse. She needed him out of the way and had achieved that on the day of her promotion.

She quickly recovered from the shock of Kedara's death and got used to her promotion, and her position as the commander of the army was useful to lay the groundwork for changes that she would make once on the army council. She only had to wait for one of the council members to die before she could take her place. One life was all that stood in her way now.

As a Major General, she now had authority over all branches of the Correlan military, including the military police, and could issue pardons and order annulments without an explanation as to these actions. She opened Allman's file, if she pardoned him, it would still show that he had been a drug addict, so instead, she issued an annulment notice, declaring all the evidence against him invalid, all references to drug use to be deleted and the file to be sealed. This was unusual, but no-one was going to question her. She then sent an order to the Army administration instructing them to start paying Sara Allman her husband's wages as per army regulations, and to include back pay for all the years since his death. She would pay Sara and Yasmine a visit and inform them herself.

She could do nothing directly to end Tillman's incarceration though. He was in a civilian prison, but she would lean heavily on the parole board and use her impressive powers of persuasion to pressure them to move him to a low security prison and then have him released on parole early.

Over time, Malaya started to lose her anger at Astrid. She began to recognise the logic of the assassinations; there had been a few more questionable deaths, but this was war, and these things happen in war. Her anger was slowly replaced by respect for Astrid's skill, then admiration, then fascination and eventually obsession.

She had picked Captain Krall to be her personal aide; Krall was efficient, worked hard and was organised; she also bore a striking resemblance to Astrid. Deep down, Malaya often wondered if this was why she had chosen Krall when there were plenty other candidates equally suited to the job.

A few months after she started working for Malaya, Krall had suffered a vicious assault, the beating she had received had been intended to kill her and had nearly succeeded. She had been off-duty, and a group of guards had mistaken her for Astrid, and without any weapons to hand had decided to beat her to death. The assault had only stopped when one of the men rummaged through her bag and found her identity card.

Five days in a coma, three weeks in intensive care, five weeks as an in-patient, and three months of twice weekly trips to the hospital physiotherapy unit had changed her. She was quiet and sullen now, distrustful of all except for General Malaya. She had a warrant card issued by Malaya that she would shove in the faces of anyone new that she met and was particularly intolerant of the guards.

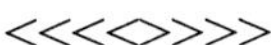

It was late on a Friday evening when Malaya poured herself a larger than normal glass of Brandy and slumped in a chair in front her computer, she took off her tie and undid the top three buttons of her blouse, pulling it wide open as if this would somehow let some of her tension flow out. She sighed and rubbed her forehead as she lit the third Cavana cigarette in a row; it had been a hard week and she was at an emotional low point.

Her role as commander of the huge Kandalan base brought with it a workload far greater than she had expected. She was lonely, and desperately wanted a long-term partner, someone to come home to, somebody to love, somebody to talk to. Someone else to take charge every once in a while, so she wouldn't always be the one making decisions. Someone who would just sit and listen while she unburdened her frustrations. She wanted a woman that she could surrender herself to, a woman she could give pleasure to rather than taking it, but there was nobody and nothing she could do about it.

Her time with Karl Davat, as humiliating as she had found it, had at least provided her with a cover story and stopped any awkward questions being asked, but didn't help her in any other way. She finished her brandy then poured herself another, downed it in one and thought back to her time with him; she shuddered with revulsion as she recalled the things that she had done, things that she had to do; all the disgusting things that were necessary to protect herself.

She opened another packet of Cavana cigarettes, took one out and lit it with an ornate lighter that had been given to her by a male colleague. It had been a crude preamble to a sexual advance, she had immediately recognised this and successfully deflected his attention. She kept the lighter as a memento of the episode; it reminded her of how pathetic some men can be.

She took a memory stick from her desk drawer and inserted it in her computer, then typed the password that unlocked the 'Assassin' file. A folder opened with all the details and notes she had acquired. She had bullet point summaries of all the murders, she opened them one by one and read them again. She remembered the glorious summer day when she suddenly realised that the assassin was female.

"You are resourceful, cunning, skilful, intelligent, and you are an utterly, utterly ruthless woman. You kill without a second thought." She thought of the scene with Zappan at the bar where Astrid had exposed her breasts. "And you even use you your body as a weapon. There's nothing you won't do when you are on a mission, is there?"

She drew deeply on the cigarette and blew smoke directly at the screen. "You sound just like me," she said quietly.

She opened a word processor program on computer and drafted an order rescinding Kedara's instruction for Astrid to be summarily executed and replaced it with an order for Astrid to be taken alive and unharmed and presented to her at Kandalan. "You will spend some time with me before your torture begins."

Far away in her quarters deep inside Arralan, Astrid opened her knife drawer. She had decided not to replace the Falchion, effective as it was, its size meant that it was no longer suited to the style of close combat that she was now engaging in. She took a combat dagger from the drawer and examined it, running the tips of her fingers along the edge, feeling for rough spots.

Her last fight with it had been tough; she had taken on a Correlan sergeant who had been much stronger and skilful than she had expected. It had been a knife fight; she had won, but while fending off a strike from him, the blade had been chipped. The chip wasn't bad, but the blade was now less than perfect; a few hours with an oilstone would easily grind the damage out.

She fixed herself a drink, then placed an oilstone on a tray on a table, squirted some lubricant on the stone and sat easing the blade in a figure of eight motion, gently grinding the edge and slowly eliminating the chip.

She liked sharpening blades; it required little concentration other than the maintenance of a constant angle and she was able to think through issues that had arisen over the past few days. One thing that had occupied her mind was a summary on the recent promotion of the three-star General Malaya to the rank of Major general in the Correlan army, this made her the most powerful officer in the army, answerable only to Hallenberg and the army Council.

She stopped momentarily and reached over to open a file, it was short, containing only a brief description of Malaya's career and a grainy picture of the woman taken at a great distance. Astrid went back to sharpening the blade as she read, and suddenly became aware that she was applying too much pressure. She checked herself and made a mental note to not let her emotions cloud her judgement. She also made a mental note to get a copy of the full report on Major General Brigit Malaya.

After an hour and a half, she was satisfied that the chip was gone, and the curve of the edge was correct. She turned the stone over and honed the edge on the ultra-fine surface. After twenty minutes, she wiped oil from the blade, then threw a cotton cloth up into the air, slashing it as it fell, cutting the light fabric in two.

She placed the dagger back in its sheath and put it back in her knife drawer then sat at the table with the report open. She looked at Malaya's picture. "I will kill you if it's the last thing I do."

She took a pen and wrote 'Sniper?' then crossed it out. She wrote 'Gun, close range?' then crossed that out. She went to her knife drawer and took out the blade she had just sharpened and studied it for a while; she wrote 'Knife, up close?'. She crossed that out as well.

"No." Astrid said aloud. "No, when I take you, when I kill you, when I make you pay for what you did, it will be so, so much more personal."

Against army regulations, and along with a text file of her thoughts and speculations about Astrid's sexuality that she had saved on her computer, Malaya had a master copy of the only confirmed photograph of Astrid Peterman. She opened the image, enlarged, enhanced and cropped the picture to show Astrid's upper body and face. She saved the file as a new image, along with all the other photo manipulations of her. She poured herself another brandy then opened a large picture of Astrid's face. Malaya studied it while she slowly drank, staring longingly at the image.

"And you are so pretty. Why do you have to be my enemy when you could be my lover?" She sighed as she closed the image.